Book One of the Zombie Honky Goofball

(or How I Single-Handedly Won the Cold War with Half My Liver Tied Behind My Back)

COLD WAR SERIES

Henry Edmund

Copyright © 2024 Henry Edmund
All rights reserved
First Edition

NEWMAN SPRINGS PUBLISHING
320 Broad Street
Red Bank, NJ 07701

First originally published by Newman Springs Publishing 2024

Warning!

This work is entirely fictional. All people or events described resembling anything that has ever happened in human events is pure coincidence. This is *all fiction*. Obviously, there was no such thing as foreign countries, history, men, women, cars, music, world leaders, or a "Cold War." So calm your tits. Hakuna your tatas. Soothe your boobs. Stop being a little pansy, and just enjoy the book. If you are getting upset about this for whatever reason, put down the book, and go back to your ignorant, unhappy life. Seriously, piss off.

ISBN 979-8-89061-600-5 (Paperback)
ISBN 979-8-89061-602-9 (Hardcover)
ISBN 979-8-89061-601-2 (Digital)

Printed in the United States of America

Dedicated to my father and my son, the best Americans I have ever known.

"Liberty is not cheap; real men pick up the check…"

PREFACE

Welcome to the mid-to-late 1980s and the Cold War. A time when the world made sense and all life on Earth stood on a knife's edge of total nuclear annihilation. Cigarettes were still good for you. Everyone except a few used-up hippies, or worse, like most of today's news industry, loved their country. Ronald Reagan was president, and America was great again after decades of losers from all political stripes had been sitting in the Oval Office. National Republicans were becoming as conservative as Democrats in local Southern political offices, whereas Democrats in national office were slowly becoming more liberal and statist…and increasingly rare, further proving God loved the world He created. Communism was the enemy to all good people, and our best were willing to serve God and country music in uniform to keep those bastards from taking over the world. Let's face it; at least the previous generation stopped them at Berkeley, California. Were they real Americans, there would have been no insidious invasion…were they French, they would have surrendered to a sneeze. Being Californians, almost Americans, they did what they could, I guess.

As you probably remember, signs of the decline of the West were everywhere after WWII. There were strong communist parties in parts of Europe—even the parts not in the Warsaw Pact. Disco. Movies about the Vietnam War made the conflict itself and our warfighters appear pathetic and wrong when instead, the truth was some bad motherfuckers kicked ass fighting that war. The designated hitter rule. Parachute pants. Emasculating fashion for men from the 1960s through the 1970s and beyond. Women wanted to be equal to men instead of remaining better. Abortion. The loss of melody in popular music and manners in popular discourse. And the decline of

Americans remembering what being an American was; yes, we were slowly losing our knowledge of our history, but there was a quiet reawakening, thank the Lord.

By the 1980s, none of those ills mattered. "President" Jimmy Carter was returned postage—due to Fat Chance, Arkansas, or wherever that goober-jawed maggot was from. The counterculture was in the dustbin of history where it belonged. Blues-based rock and roll had returned, albeit through long-haired, makeup-wearing freaks with great guitar chops and ridiculous outfits. The babes were bathing and shaving their legs again. No one had facial hair. Physical violence, not ever really vanishing, had made a welcome comeback. There is nothing like the threat of getting your ass beat to remind you to mind your manners, huh?!? Movies glorified American themes like violence, dead commies, and teen angst—causing real Americans like me, the ultimate Cold War warrior, to decide he might be wrong in thinking Hollywood should shoot fewer movies and more actors. (I got over it.) Other movies were funny and libertarian, like *Ghostbusters*. Computers were being used, and there seemed to be a future in the damn things. America's pastime, baseball, was built on speed, pitching, and defense—the way God intended. Blacks were accepted and happy (thank you, Dr. Heathcliff "Cliff" Huxstable!), and Rubik's Cubes were being solved. Men wore suits, or at least button-down shirts, instead of dirt and bell-bottoms that, like the hippies, recently had gone extinct.

And what a gift President Reagan was to us all! The economy was freed from constraint, and taxes were lowered. Military spending was up, recognizing the Soviet threat. Yes, there were lingering bits of flotsam and jetsam from the previous decades of rot in the form of the Kennedy family and new viruses like AIDS, the gay cancer. Space exploration was back in business, and everyone had a Walkman and/or boom box to play the new, great music that was all around us, not counting the obviously faddish and quaint styles like rap, thrash metal, and hip-hop that couldn't go away fast enough. Even people with no life at all could do things like play video games instead of make money, get drunk, and have sex like the rest of us. But Reagan did something no one else did: roll back Soviet gains. Doing so made the world more dangerous since those evil, wide-jawed Slavic bastards would likely not go down with a whimper instead of a bang, but who gave a good goddamn? It was long past time to put up with losing. Losing is for morons wearing jelly shoes or thinking breakdancing is an art. Or wearing shoulder pads in everyday clothes. Or acid-washed jeans. What the hell is acid-washed? And what the hell was up with all of the neon too many useless bitches wore? They thought we only wanted to get in their pants, but we also wanted to get those damn retina-thrashers out of our sight. Thank God for Ray-Bans or we'd all be blind from all the chicks we didn't disrobe and put to good use getting our ashes hauled. Luckily, that fashion died along with pastel-colored Chevrolet Camaros, leg warmers, Swatches, and Members Only jackets. As to the latter, how do you make the Ike jacket look gay? Leave it to fashion designers. Good for them that we were off to kill commies or those fuckers would have been goners. Sheesh…

Anyway, enjoy the tale, or go away. I hear most of you people in the future are worthless, ignorant losers. Maybe *you*, dear reader, are one of the few who isn't.

—Hjalmar "Hal" Haroldsson
Location unknown

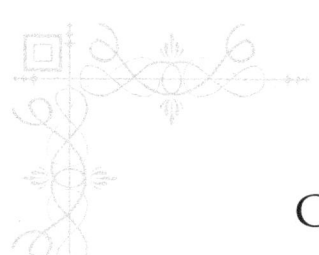

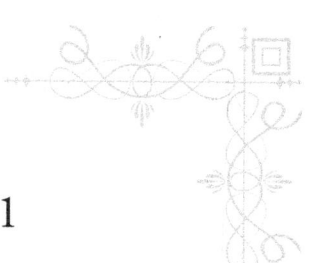

CHAPTER 1

Not Really a Day Off: The Evening After the Last Overnight Shift

"It's not the end of the world, Hal," said the righteous piece of ass from Wisconsin, Christina Crosse. Seriously. A hottie from the north country fair, as Bob Dylan once said. Go figure. Not beautiful, but damnation if she wasn't easy enough on the eyes with the most righteous, big round ass on a white girl as if she were a hotter version of Cindy Crawford from the waist down. Not that I am going to pursue her. She is dating the other token Yankee around here, some kid-faced lanky goof from New Jersey who loves Frank Zappa and Kiss. IKR? What the hell is his name again? Albert Amish or something.

Welcome to Misawa Air Base, Japan. I am sitting in a soul-depriving common room with phlegm-colored walls, bad furniture, and worse aesthetics. It is nearing the end of another cold winter, and the snow drifts are no longer all the way up to the third or fourth floor of the barracks. Winter leaves and rainy season follows. This means weeks and weeks of very cold rain and sleet, which is worse than winter. This section of planet Earth goes from "winter wonderland" to mud, ass, and ice. And one asshole is inviting us to play in it.

"Bullshit," I say with a small amount of aggravation. "Manning still sucks, and we are needed at work despite the weather. The commies are used to bad weather. And," I say, realizing I had better not say too much, not being in a secure location, "there is a lot going on." Like I said, the unsecure location was the barracks dayroom. You remember, almost every floor of each four-story barracks has one. Good place to watch TV, read a book, or have a conversation if your roommate needs some rack time, especially if they work a different shift. Of course, your roommate may need some privacy to get superimposed and horizontal with someone. Let's face it; instead of attending college, we are saving the world, but we have the same wants and needs of our more delicate fellow citizens. If only at this remote site, the locations were not so distant and we so few.

The damnyankee rises to the occasion. "This may be all your fault. The Chief hates you all and for good damn reason," she says woundingly as she shifts her position in her skintight jeans on the day room couch. That she is right on many levels—the top enlisted NCO of our enormous intelligence organization hates us because we are not ideal, bright, and shiny Airmen, and he is petty enough to pull some shit like this—hits home. I can't believe that big Jersey geek brings her to orgasm. I can't believe I will be playing softball in the sleet for weeks because of Chief Master Sergeant Frenchy von Holstein instead of sleeping in-between rotating shifts. I can't believe I forgot to bring a bottle of Jack Daniel's from my barracks room. I should readjust my focus to the chief who hates us. It's a struggle.

A door opens down the hallway from the direction of my second-floor room. The Alan Parsons Project's "I Wouldn't Want to Be Like You" plays for a second before the door shuts. Wow. Gay called, and it is for them, huh? Crosse and I share a rueful look for a moment or three when delicate fingers come from behind the couch to my neck, and a sweet voice says, "You forgot this." She places a half-empty bottle of JD between my legs, and her fingers linger on my groin for a moment. I was not expecting this and surprised myself by not jumping out of my skin. Probably fatigue. That I was sprawled all over the couch and not exactly in a launching position might have helped, too.

"Thanks," I say as she walks slowly away. "You're welcome," she says as she leaves, wearing a very long T-shirt, and I would not bet on whether or not she has a stitch on underneath. Nice legs and damn if that isn't a nice thigh gap. I have trouble placing her. I never saw her face. I need coffee. Alan Parsons is wrong; I'd like all of that or whatever. I think I gasp. I think she giggles in response. Her hearing is as good as mine. Nice.

"Who is that?" asks the Badger a bit jealously. Seriously, I never saw her face. I am at a loss and shrug. "Miss Misery" by Nazareth plays somewhere else, and I think that is poor volume and judgment. Poor noise management since we all work different shifts in this barracks—someone is always sleeping. And that 7–10 split piece of ass walking away has not disappointed me yet. Miss Misery indeed. Of course, she may have just spent time fucking my roommate, the male whore. Where else would she get my JD? Then again, maybe I am getting someone else's cooties from their bottle of Tennessee's Finest. Fuck it. JD cures all. Yes, I drink a wee bit or so.

"I bet you fuckers are dead because of Grace Jones!" the increasingly less hot damnyankee concludes. Maybe. Damn, that was a night. All of us, after fourteen days on, ready for our nearly three days off. Remember? What you do is have breakfast at the chow hall after your last night shift, hopefully not get food poisoning, imbibe a drink or three, and then sleep the sleep of the righteous. When you wake up, you shower, dress, and get ready for a couple of days of snatch and whiskey! Woohoo! Well, that is not what happened that night. Oh well. Not happening right now either.

"Could be," I reply with less-than-perfect conviction. "I am sure it'll all blow over." Actually, I don't know what is going to happen to all of us involved with the Great Grace Jones Incident. Maybe we'll be called to testify against the crazy bitch. Who knows? Of course, it is not the real Grace Jones, just a psycho who looks like her. It occurs to me that the Badger is shifting irritatingly in her bewitchingly tight jeans on her full thighs and divine fulcrum. She may be saying something. "What? I am sorry. My mind was far afield," I say. Who *was* that hot bitch in the T-shirt?

"I was saying the Chief will drag this out. We matter, and he doesn't despite his rank. No one respects him," she replies while playing with her thick brown hair. It appears good, old-fashioned grammar turns her on. She sees me staring and blushes politely. Damn, a polite Yankee. More correctly, I am guessing she should be called a Northerner; it isn't like she is from Bahstun or Noo Yawk. An animated conversation from the other side of the day room is getting louder. That larger crowd should be on the couches the Badger and I are on instead of the few rickety chairs and floor on the other side of the room. Of course, I don't know how the damnyankee hottie could fit on the same couch as me with her voluminous ass and my erection if we tried to make room for the ruckus makers.

"What you need," she continued "is some top cover, but too few people with real rank have the balls to help a kickass troublemaker like you." Damn she is perceptive. Maybe she has had some coffee. Coffee is hard to find in the barracks, unlike at work where we make it blacker and thicker than an Alabama porch monkey, as Eddie Murphy the comedian said. Funny guy. Went from nothing to SNL[1] to arena stand-up shows, best-selling albums to movies. Lucky. Still, I'd rather be me. God is watching us all, and I am certain He prefers those fighting the atheistic commies to some freak in red leather outfits making dick jokes or whatever it is comedians talk about. I take another polite pull of the Jack Daniel's. And by polite, I mean the perfect liquid is disappearing like polite discourse in political discussion.

Miss Crosse is waiting for me to respond. I think she thinks, by my lack of answering quickly, that I think what she said was profound. It certainly sounds correct. I am not awake enough for this conversation. I try something else to turn her on. "Perhaps the Chief is simply after us *pour encourager les autres*," I say with a better accent than I normally possess. You should see the effect; I think she is going to slide off the couch.

"You know French?" she asks with incredible and unexpected excitement.

"Famous quotes mostly. You?" I ask with some trepidation. I don't want to get into an intellectual conversation that I am not awake enough to withstand without coffee and several months of sleep.

---

[1] Saturday Night Live.

"A bit. It is part of being from Wisconsin since the French set up a lot of the early towns, like Eau Claire and Fond du Lac," she replies with becoming shyness. "Do you remember where that quote comes from?" she asks slyly. It appears she thinks she has stumped me. She has no idea with whom she is dealing.

"I do. Voltaire said it about the execution of Admiral John Byng in 1757. You probably remember that Byng was sent to relieve Minorca in 1756, but he and his fleet had their asses handed to them by the French. He thought discretion was the better part of valor and withdrew from a fight that was unwinnable. The British public freaked, and their ministers jailed Byng for court-martial. Of course, public opinion changed after finding out it was the ministers who sent him into battle with insufficient forces. He was shot anyway *pour encourager les autres*. The ministers saved themselves by their actions, or so they thought." I was pretty pleased with this response. There was a time during it that I thought Christina was going to rip off my pants with her teeth, but something got in the way. It turns out it was a thought. Brains and perception in a woman can be either a blessing or a curse. I am not certain which it is right now.

"You sure know your history. Damn. I didn't know all that. But you got me to thinking," she countered. "This is like what the Chief is doing to you pricks. You *are* right in that. But what if he goes beyond simply making an example of you miscreants?" she asks this with genuine concern. I wish she was more concerned with my incredible need to have my ashes hauled, but she is dating that damnyankee after all. If she is, where in the hell is he? Maybe Crosse just needs an intelligent conversation. He makes her smile, but I very much doubt he makes her think. Or orgasm. She should leave him. I'd tell her to do so, but I don't cheat, and I don't break up couples.

I was about to respond when the other crowd, which had gotten even larger without my noticing, came over to the larger area where only Crosse and I were.

"You assholes done fucking yet?" asks some redneck bastard who attempts to sit on my head. From my reclined position, I grab him by the hip and ass and fling him sideways from left to right to where he slams his right jaw on the coffee table on his way to the floor. That stops the emigration for just a moment.

"Guess the po' buckra gotta learn manners somehow," says a wonderful comrade, Jewface. That he is speaking like he is from the Delta is hilarious. He may be smarter than all of us combined and is the color of good strong sweet tea. A fine Southron. My temper is slowly subsiding and does so increasingly after seeing him smiling at me. "Poor lil' fella just got heah, too," he says with an impish smile and an accent quite unlike his normal intelligent, reasoned speech. Normally my temper does not recede like the tides; it remains. This instance is a rarity…or I have good Southern manners.

I sit up and gesture for the rest to sit down and for Jewface to leave that JEEP[2] on the floor. I am a Virginian after all: well-mannered until provoked. Someone has a boombox playing tapes at a polite volume. Another soul who doesn't trust the Far East Network, aka the Forced Entertainment Network, to play good music. Sammy Hagar's "There's Only One Way to Rock" is on. Not my style, but not bad. Mindless chitchat is engaged. Normally this irritates me to no end, but now it is nice. I realize I am among similar creatures. We come from everywhere. Well, usually from the South, but still. The mixture of backgrounds is immense. The Tarheels and those from the Secession State are constantly at each other's throats about everything, despite nearly sharing a BBQ style and many other idiosyncrasies. We Virginians are given more respect than we probably deserve based on geography and history. The stories one hears from the Deep South are usually from country boys and are often not safe for green plants and small children. Texas is not only a different Republic, it is a different planet. There are very few damnyankees and those from the crazy left coast. However, all of us agree that Atlanta is proof of what more than a quarter million or more Southern boys died trying to prevent.

"I met those guys!" I say with some politely quiet enthusiasm when the boom box plays "Blood and Roses" by the Smithereens.

---

[2] Just Enough Education to Pass. The Army calls their new losers NUGs, New Ugly Grunts.

say too much, not being in a secure location, "there is a lot going on." Like I said, the unsecure location was the barracks dayroom. You remember, almost every floor of each four-story barracks has one. Good place to watch TV, read a book, or have a conversation if your roommate needs some rack time, especially if they work a different shift. Of course, your roommate may need some privacy to get superimposed and horizontal with someone. Let's face it; instead of attending college, we are saving the world, but we have the same wants and needs of our more delicate fellow citizens. If only at this remote site, the locations were not so distant and we so few.

The damnyankee rises to the occasion. "This may be all your fault. The Chief hates you all and for good damn reason," she says woundingly as she shifts her position in her skintight jeans on the day room couch. That she is right on many levels—the top enlisted NCO of our enormous intelligence organization hates us because we are not ideal, bright, and shiny Airmen, and he is petty enough to pull some shit like this—hits home. I can't believe that big Jersey geek brings her to orgasm. I can't believe I will be playing softball in the sleet for weeks because of Chief Master Sergeant Frenchy von Holstein instead of sleeping in-between rotating shifts. I can't believe I forgot to bring a bottle of Jack Daniel's from my barracks room. I should readjust my focus to the chief who hates us. It's a struggle.

A door opens down the hallway from the direction of my second-floor room. The Alan Parsons Project's "I Wouldn't Want to Be Like You" plays for a second before the door shuts. Wow. Gay called, and it is for them, huh? Crosse and I share a rueful look for a moment or three when delicate fingers come from behind the couch to my neck, and a sweet voice says, "You forgot this." She places a half-empty bottle of JD between my legs, and her fingers linger on my groin for a moment. I was not expecting this and surprised myself by not jumping out of my skin. Probably fatigue. That I was sprawled all over the couch and not exactly in a launching position might have helped, too.

"Thanks," I say as she walks slowly away. "You're welcome," she says as she leaves, wearing a very long T-shirt, and I would not bet on whether or not she has a stitch on underneath. Nice legs and damn

CHAPTER 1

Not Really a Day Off: The Evening After the Last Overnight Shift

"It's not the end of the world, Hal," said the righteous piece of ass from Wisconsin, Christina Crosse. Seriously. A hottie from the north country fair, as Bob Dylan once said. Go figure. Not beautiful, but damnation if she wasn't easy enough on the eyes with the most righteous, big round ass on a white girl as if she were a hotter version of Cindy Crawford from the waist down. Not that I am going to pursue her. She is dating the other token Yankee around here, some kid-faced lanky goof from New Jersey who loves Frank Zappa and Kiss. IKR? What the hell is his name again? Albert Amish or something.

Welcome to Misawa Air Base, Japan. I am sitting in a soul-depriving common room with phlegm-colored walls, bad furniture, and worse aesthetics. It is nearing the end of another cold winter, and the snow drifts are no longer all the way up to the third or fourth floor of the barracks. Winter leaves and rainy season follows. This means weeks and weeks of very cold rain and sleet, which is worse than winter. This section of planet Earth goes from "winter wonderland" to mud, ass, and ice. And one asshole is inviting us to play in it.

"Bullshit," I say with a small amount of aggravation. "Manning still sucks, and we are needed at work despite the weather. The commies are used to bad weather. And," I say, realizing I had better not

Welcome to the Cold War!

Everyone looks at me. No one is paying attention to the music except me. I pay attention to everything. I fear I am surrounded by simpletons, or I am an obsessed human being. Probably the latter. Foreigner played before, but who cares? By this time, "Sledgehammer" by Peter Gabriel is on. I must have been dozing or off in thought before. Maybe I was lost in thought before I recognized "Blood and Roses" by the Smithereens was on. Everyone is still staring at me and my outburst. "No, seriously, I was in Boston at a record store and had just bought some cassette tapes. When I got out to the sidewalk, everything was crowded so bad that I was stuck. Some damnyankees asked me what I bought, and I showed them tapes of the Smithereens and Fahrenheit, two regionally popular bands. These guys told me they were the Smithereens. I was not convinced. One fellow was a big son of a bitch,[3] and the rest looked like yuppies. They told me to compare the tape with their countenance. They were right." Everyone in the middle of nowhere Japan seems stunned. "It's alright. They were poor musicians, and the checks had not yet started pouring in. Besides, it is not a profitable profession; look at what Tom Petty had to do." None of them are convinced. Don't get me wrong; they were convinced I met the Smithereens, especially after I mentioned the singer is going to go as bald as I will one day. These people are all intelligent but often from simple circumstances, thinking fame equals money.[4] Nope. Oh well.

Francis looks like he wants to ask me something but is too shy. Poor lil' fella. He is painfully pale, plain, and looks like he is ten years old. Weak-chinned, muscle-free, skinny, and short. I don't think he has ever spoken to a girl who wasn't his mother. As a Christian and Virginia gentleman, I try to help him.

"So where are your furry little faggot friends, Francis?" I say, breaking the ice. He blushes politely, and a few people giggle while Camel guffaws, spitting out a bit of cigarette he was chewing. Yes, you read that right. Camel got his name because he only buys unfiltered Camel cigarettes, but only to eat.

---

[3] Pronounced sumbetch, of course.
[4] Probably like novelists. Hmmm…

"We were talking about English over there," he replies. I don't know if I am surprised or not. Being in the signals intelligence business, we are the best of the best. Then again, it is sort of our Friday night, and we should be discussing important things like sports, music, and the opposite sex. Then I remember that little Francis is not likely to have those pursuits. The man is wearing corduroy pants, for God's sake.

"Cool. Wait, the English or our common language?" I reply, trying to be polite.

"Man, he a Virginian—he don't know," states Smitty. Smitty is as black as the last banana and much more intelligent than he sounds. Great memory for enemy frequencies, too.

"The language, Hal. I was explaining that it was far from being evolved from Anglo-Saxon tongues," Francis continues. "Being Scandinavian, I thought you might know more."

I put a hand up to stop Smitty before he jumps in again. "You are correct, sir. English is a mixture of Anglo-Saxon and French by people who knew little of either. I don't know if Fran here explained it, but the Normans were Vikings who conquered the part of France that ended up being called Normandy and tried to assimilate. They did…poorly. Then they got a wild hair and invaded England. Now you know why there is so much bad French and Norse Viking talk in English," I explain.

Some people are riveted with this conversation. Others are bewildered. Crosse seems miffed. Oh, the girl beside me seems overly interested. I think she is new to this duty station, like the damn piece of white trash I knocked cold. I forget her name. Brigid or some damn thing. Talks like a bright hillbilly but has all of her teeth. I have no idea if it is a good idea to make Crosse cross. We'll see.

"Okay, how do you know all of that?" Jewface asks as if I am setting everyone up for a joke or something.

"Yes, Smitty, I am a Virginian. However, I was adopted by Norwegian-Americans from Minnesota and learned a bit about Norse mythology in addition to my being a typical Virginian with a love of history," I reply with certainty.

"Wh-what are some of the words you said are from that Viking talk?" asks the new hillbilly girl shyly.

"Good question. How about the days of the week? I might not remember them all after so little sleep and coffee, but Tuesday, Wednesday, Thursday, and Friday are named after the AEsir while common words like *north, south, east,* and *west* come from Norse mythology," I educate.

"No kidding. I know about Wednesday and Thursday, but the rest is new to me," says Jewface with astonished praise. "Pray tell, elaborate."

"Mandag is Monday—the day of the moon. Then it is Tyr's Day, Woden's Day, Thor's Day, and Freya's Day are common knowledge," I continue. "Saturday is named after the planet Saturn while Sondag ends the week and is literally named for the sun. Nordri, Sudri, Austri, and Westri were the strong dwarfs in Norse creation myth that were placed at the four corners of the Earth to sustain the world on their shoulders. Yup, the directions of the compass," I explain.

"Dude! Okay, what is the ass here?" asks Smitty with some enthusiasm.

It takes me a moment. "Oh, sorry. AEsir is the name of the collection of Norse gods. I should have said that. That's probably all I have on that for now. I'm hungry but feel too lazy to go get anything. What time is it, anyway?" I ask the group.

"Too late for the chow hall and too early to get in trouble downtown—even for you," says poor little Francis. Is the little dude flirting with me, or is he just happy someone is speaking to him with respect? I really don't want to know, I guess. I don't like feeling sorry for people. Nothing colder than charity, and pity is the worst kind.

Everyone seems to be as lazy as me. No one is going out, and various conversations spring up all over the room. I look around and notice Crosse is looking at me with disappointment on her face. I am betting it is because I stopped spending all of my attention on her. Bitches are crazy. She should be with her damnyankee goof instead of checking me out.

"*Ca va?*" I ask her.

"*Ca va*," she replies with little enthusiasm.
"*Ou est ton amant?*" I follow.
Her eyes get a bit bigger. "*C'est une mauviette?*" she counters.
"I already knew that, he is a damnyankee after all!" I laugh. "Does he know you are speaking and hanging out with other men?" She just stares. "Maybe you should check on him," I softly suggest. Like I said, I don't cheat or break up relationships.
"Maybe you are right. Thanks for the history lesson. His name really was Bing?" she asks as she gets up.
"Yes, with a *y*. B-y-n-g. A poor old fool shot to teach others a lesson." I explain. She looks at me, and I can read her mind. *Don't follow his example.* I nod and she turns to leave. I stare at her hips and ass as she goes. Every other real man does as well. Wow. She is built like a 1972 Chevrolet Chevelle and ready to ride. Wow.
When I come back to my senses, it appears every man is still getting over Crosse's buttocks, and every woman is mildly uncomfortable. As if they wouldn't stare if Tom Selleck or whoever strolled by. I look around. Amazing how an open room with ugly furniture, one TV no one is watching, and a couple of vending machines can do for us on the other side of the world from home. Conversations continue. Someone mentions Steele, and I ask them to repeat what they said.
"He has finally been transferred from the Japanese hospital to one of ours—Kadena,[5] I think," interrupts Jack McInnes as he pulls invariably on a cigarette and crosses his legs like a bitch with legs fully crossed like a skirt-wearing hussy. I had to gain weight to get in the Air Force, but Jack is taller and skinnier than me. I guess that is how he can sit like he has little bone structure. His back is a bit curved, but that may be from years of bending over a keyboard and listening to faint enemy signals on those old Racal radios we use. He is older, nearly as homely as Honest Abe, with a terrible complexion, and is as good a friend and man anyone can know. Apparently, he had pulled a chair over from the other corner of the room.

---

[5] An Air Force Base in Japan. Get on your Googles, and look it up.

"Good to see you, Jack," I say sotto voce and a smile. Everything is better when Jack is around—a calming presence. He is a bit more mature than the rest of us, past military marrying age. He is also less excitable and more stoic than our generation, what country folks would wrongly call philosophical. "How are his chances?" I add.

"He was treated by the Japs instead a' our docs, so I figure he is better now than when he drove on whiskey and ice," Jack says slyly. I smile. I get it. I don't know if anyone else does. Steele was driving while imbibing hours away from base and lost control on the winter roads. We heard he needed to be repaired from head to toe. Worrying about the legal ramifications can come later. Jack is from the middle of fuck all nowhere Tennessee from terrible circumstances, but his acquired intelligence and manners shine through all that. Then again, so does his slicked-back hair. I need to remember to tease him in reference to the Laker's coach, what's-his-name…Pat Riley, the fucker that looks like a Jersey wop. I think his hair has more chance of surviving a nuclear war than all of the world's cockroaches and Tom Landry's hat. The boom box just started playing "Come On, Come On" by Cheap Trick from the Budokan concert. Niiice. I hope it's not just the one song. My lethargy is leaving. I pray whoever just changed tapes is playing the whole concert—epic. If so, there is no hope of me being calm like Jack.

"Thanks. What are your plans for the evening?" I ask with no intention of leading him astray. Honest.

"I'm hungry, but at a loss. Where should we go?" Jack replies.

"I heard someone over yonder"—pointing vaguely across the room—"talk about raiding 007s," I reply.

A universal response was had in favor of the idea. Some remind us all that Companions has the best food on planet Earth, and they are right. Cobra walked in wearing what must be his jammies at that moment and reminded the detractors that Companions is likely to be rather busy, considering the hour and it being all of Charlie Flight's first night off—our Friday night. Someone, I think that dumbass Texian who is waiting for his Mexican wife to show up so he could move out of the barracks, said Companions would likely be "busier than a brothel on nickel night." I hope that bastard never breeds.

How did that ASVAB-waivered fucktard get into the intelligence business? Sheesh…

"007s it is," I conclude. "Are we all going together?" The answer is a universal yes. Makes sense with so many new folks not knowing anything about their new base. "Alright, get your coats and wallets, and meet out front in ten." I notice the new-to-Misawa redneck piece of trash is starting to stir.

"Cobra, are you coming with us?" I ask. He shakes his head and is about to leave the dayroom. "Can you help me pick up the stupid bastard?"

"Let me help," says Jewface.

"Thanks." We got his dumb ass propped up on the couch.

"Should someone stay with him?" Cobra, despite his size, is such a worrying little bitch sometimes.

"I'll stay," replies the bitter ginger who is Justin's roommate. I can't place his name at the moment. Staff Sergeant something stupid. Dirk, I think. "I pulled something at the gym—bring me some grub whenever you get back? I'm going to watch some television and make sure none of the kids get in too much trouble." The joys of being a dutiful NCO. That and he is as ugly as homemade lye soap with a personality to boot. Fair softball player, though.

"Nopraw—any favorites?"

"Surprise me—and thanks." He sounds like he means it. I smile in return and go to my room.

I arrive at my room, and I am in a hurry. My roommate is awake and reclining in his futon while shaking his head. "Dude." Wow. So enthusiastic. If it weren't for cigarettes, I am unsure he would ever move. Yes, my roommate is lying on his futon, smoking. He is the laziest, horniest white man I have ever met. He is the cause of me oftentimes falling asleep or reading in the dayroom since he is so frequently shacked up with some broad. Allegedly he is good-looking. Being a man, I have no idea. His eyes are barely open. Also, he is a true democrat—small *d*. He will fuck anything with a snatch. Hard to dislike him despite all that. At least he isn't one to abscond with my booze; gnats have a greater tolerance for whiskey than this pansy.

"Duuude…" He shakes his head with a tired grin and narrowed eyes as he draws on his Marlboro Light and looks at me with admiration. "Who was *that*?" Forrest Graham Hobarth gestures vaguely.

"Who was what?" I am hurrying to get a coat and such.

He looks at me like I am an idiot. He could be right. "The hot bitch, that's who," he retorts with genuine wonder. "I ain't never seen anything like that. Said her name was Candy."

So *that* is who gave me the Jack Daniel's. Damn it, that is the second fucking time I did not have a fucking time with Candy. I have never seen her, uh, dressed like that. Son of a…

I try to play it cool. "Oh, some young lady I met a couple of weeks ago. Nice girl. Good sense of humor. Healthy appetite. Doesn't complain. I need to ask her out on a proper date one of these days."

"For a piece o' ass like that, even I would marry it." Graham is so lazy, he would probably ask someone else to go get the ring for him.

He could be right though. It is no wonder so many in the military get married so young. The Air Force promotes alcoholism, tobacco addiction, and marriage. All three are an easy sell. Living in the barracks sucks ass. Eat at the chow hall every day. Living in a tiny little room with another guy and sharing a bathroom with the next room over. And in Misawa, only 10 percent of the Airmen are females. Thus, there are a lot of ugly bitches who think they are queens. Marrying a Japanese girl is often out of the question. The language and the culture divide are a big problem. And this is akin to living in Appalachia Japan; not a lot of Nip supermodels out this way. Besides, if you aren't Japanese, you are *gaijin*. That is politely translated to "foreigner." It really means "barbarian." The Japs are as racist as anyone in the world. The more I see of their culture and of ours, I can only reply with "good for them." They'd have to be awfully desperate to lower themselves to marry an American.

"You could be right. Thanks for letting her know where I was. Gotta go."

"Where are you taking her?" he asks lecherously.

"Nowhere. Candy saw I was already entertaining other females and dropped off the JD."

"Other bitches? What the…?"

"I keep 'em waiting in line while treating them right. You should try it sometime. Gotta go," I say for the umpteenth time.

I can hear the crowd on my way down the stairs. They should be outside, despite the cold. There are barracks rooms near the front door as well, and all shift workers need their sleep. I get there just when the acting dorm chief shows up. Since we are the Air Force, our barracks are called dorms. They aren't, but we are supposed to call them that. Like calling a janitor a sanitation engineer. Yeah. The stupid bastard is thinking about the first-floor fellows trying to get some rack time. Or he is a dick. My comrades are not too loud yet, but they will soon be there.

"God damn it!" he bellows. "What the fuck is wrong with…" He goes down as easily as the dumb redneck bastard upstairs. Someone pokes their head out of their room wearing a bathrobe with a question on their face. I point to the maggot lying unconscious on the floor. A sly grin and a thumbs-up are my reply as they shut their door. Dumbass the Acting Dorm Chief needs to learn to be quiet for our shift workers—I was just doing the Lord's business.

"Damn, Hal, you have got to stop doing that," Jewface says both quietly, emphatically as well as unconvincingly with a big grin. His enunciation was so overdone, he sounded like a British scientist observing an experiment.

"I cain't stands white folk," I reply with dramatic, quiet drama. His grin nearly separates his head entirely. I gesture for some to take the loud maggot to his office. Then I start walking, and all follow me out into the interesting weather of Misawa Air Base, Japan. A song that is apparently called "The Best of All Possible Worlds" plays down the hallway from the first-floor dayroom. I see Jewface smiling in recognition as well; I am not the only one with great hearing. It's even funnier considering him. Dark but with a strange New York Jewish grocer's face. The nose itself could serve you a kosher sandwich. He could be eighteen or fifty-five. I keep meaning to remind myself to ask Jewface where he is from. Clearly the South like most of us. Funny. However, it is past time to enjoy the less-than-welcoming weather. No wonder these kids were waiting inside.

Hats are of no fucking use, but I am still wearing a Richmond Braves ball cap. I wore the one with the lower case *r*. Other fully brimmed hats would be blown off the head. I need to get one of the new versions similar to the parent team with the capital *A* and the new darker colors, like the real Atlanta hats that I hope the Richmond Braves should try to emulate. It rains, sleets, and snows sideways more often than anything. Being a nerd who wears glasses, this is a wonderful situation. I am wearing a light-brown suede winter jacket over a white button-down shirt, blue jeans, and black cowboy boots bought during a visit to family in Minneapolis before my enlistment started, which completes the outfit.[6] I should probably ask for a Twins hat for Christmas, too. We all bend our heads into the weather like good Southern soldiers into withering Yankee fire. You do what you have to do. The weather quiets a lot of the conversations while we trudge our way across base to the front gate and the promise of happiness and food. I bet we look like a pack of disabled retards as we walk through the slush of near spring; some ice forgives, and some does not. Niiice. Arms fly up for balance. Feet slide. No, there are no buses to take people to the front gate, but everyone is allowed to own a car. I know, right? Permission is big in the military. I hear there are bases where you cannot own a car. But why take a car to the front gate when circumstances may get you drunk and you can't drive drunk on base? Driving drunk off-base? Encouraged. No, I am not kidding.

Jack sees me checking out some marginal chicks on their way back from off-base to their barracks. "So how is that girl of yours back home?" He couldn't have asked a worse question. Maybe the bar has coffee. Doubt it. I am now cold from the breeze in my soul thinking about her.

"She is in college and is pissed off at me…for good reason. I think we are done," I say regretfully. Cheryl Elizabeth Baughman is a peach. Lovely. Shapely. Intelligent, but not so clever as to not fall in love with me. "I have never admitted that to anyone…even myself,

---

[6] Cowboy boots on ice and snow are clearly ways I am trying to impress you, dear reader, with my genius.

until just now." I feel numb now, and it has nothing to do with the cold. I pull on my bottle of Jack Daniel's that I forgot to leave at the barracks. It has little taste.

"Well, you have lived enough to know that people fall in and out of love before they find the right one. It's just the first one that is hard to give up. Look at that Block 8 fellow whose wife wants to rip your pants off with her teeth," Jack responds. He is right. That hot-assed bitch gets crazy every time she drinks. What the hell is wrong with that woman? She is married to a man who looks somewhat similar to me and has two kids with him. He needs to put her in her place and fuck the hell out of her. God knows I want to rip the pants off of that bitch. Maybe they married too young. Happens in the military. Oh well. I answer with, "Uh huh."

We zigzag on the ice and snow on our way to the front gate, and Jack asks, "What do you think of the new kids that showed up?"

I hesitate to answer. I am not impressed, but what did I look and act like when I first got here? Luckily, I am saved by the people behind us.

"Yo, Hal! Did you hear that song from the first-floor day room before we left? I mean, while you were striking a superior officer and all?" I wonder who is asking this. The wind is loud, and there are other conversations going on. That and we are still walking like idiots even though the closer we get to the front gate, the clearer the walkways are. I look around, and I get a lot of nods of recognition from Camel, Casper, that skank Flo, Gnat, some dumbass, and Toad… why are they in alphabetical order? Anyway, Jewface looks animated.

"We gots a bet!" Why he is talking like an idiot, I have no idea. Then I see him, and he seems to be toying with some sack of white trash standing beside him. Jewface might not be a Christian. Yes, there must be money involved. That is just mean.

"Yes, I heard the song. Sounded good to me, but I have no idea who does it. What do you want to know?" I remain suspicious as to where this is headed.

"It was Kris Kristofferson," Jack interrupts. Jack is not normally a musical guru. Interesting.

"The communist sympathizer? What the hell, man?" The stares that I get are not kind. Hmmm…

"He was no such thing. He was a Ranger in the Army back in the day. Then he was a country singer and actor. Yes, he is a free spirit and free thinker and all, but he is no communist," Jack informs.

"Oh," I answer quite contrite, "my dad is a bit of a narrow-minded conservative monarchist who thought Kristofferson was a communist for appearing in a show called *Amerika*. No offense intended." I also don't want to be hit. I am hungry and need coffee, and no one will let me alone to do that.

"Damn it, Hal—answer the question!" Jewface is smiling when the white trash asks this. I start to do the same.

"Sir, perhaps you will ask the question I am supposed to answer," I reply with utmost courtesy. When my courtesy is up, it means I am grabbing my manners with both hands. When I let go, it is time to throw hands.

"Oh, was that song we wuz a-talkin' about based upon a philosophical?"[7] Oh my—what erudition is on display by the new guy. Public schools have gone to hell in a handcart, huh? I think it was Sobran who said we have gone from teaching Greek and Latin in common schools to teaching remedial English in college. At least our schools can't possibly get worse. No wonder the Japanese are ruling the world, and the Cold War is not over; we are nearly as dumb as the Slavs. Jewface looks at me expectantly. Prick. I have an awful streak of honesty, and he knows it.

"Ah, the phrase 'the best of all possible worlds' comes from a Kraut named Leibniz when he tried to solve the problem of evil. He created a theory to attempt to solve said problem. Now you know," I answer benevolently. Jewface is not happy. Not enough. I am sighing, knowing that I have to further discredit a perfectly fine hillbilly and his diet mullet just trying to serve his country. Damn it. Honesty wins out.

"Leibniz took on the question of theodicy: if God is in charge of everything, how can we account for the suffering and injustice

---

[7] This is pronounced "philOsofical" by said redneck.

that exists here? The conclusion that Leibniz came to is that He is in charge of thinking about multiple universes and that God cannot do wrong, so he only allows for one. Thus, God can do no wrong and is experimenting. Enjoy your situation, you are living in the best of all possible worlds." I hope my addition adds solace.

"By theodicy, you mean like theological?" the Bubba asks with great interest.

"Yes, sir—very good. Of course, Leibniz's idea assumes that God is good in the way we understand good," I add and watch the Bubba start to redden in anger. "Remember, the ways of the Lord are mysterious." This seems to calm the Skeeter down.

"How do you know so much about all this?" the jibber-jawed fellow asks as he practically chews the words as they come out of his face. I am just glad we aren't slipping and sliding so much since we are nearing the front gate of the base as this part has been shoveled and plowed a bit. Appropriate, since most people go off-base to get plowed in one way or another.

"Each cat has his own rat. I read too much. I bet you are an expert in the things I know nothing about." Notice how politic I am with this rube. Just trying to keep peace in the Middle East.

"You are too kind. My friends call me Bubba—I am going to be in Block 1." Wow. I guess stereotypes really do save time. We shake hands.

"Hal in Block 2," I answer.

He looks at me like he knows something I don't. "Everyone knows who you are, Hal." Go figure.

Toad makes the turn to the right up Green Pole Road and Forever's Bar. I miss Karu, Forever's owner. I realize that some village is missing their idiot. Or worse, some Army platoon is missing their Second Lieutenant. That boy couldn't find his own ass with a map and compass. Always in a state of rectal defilade. If that boy was any dumber, we would have to water him.

"Toad!" This comes from nearly everyone. He looks astonished and nearly hits the deck on the semi-icy sidewalk when he spins around.

"C'mon," I say sternly and keep walking toward 007s. Everyone follows—even Toad who returns from his wrong turn. Jack is beside me, smiling broadly. He doesn't do that very often, so it keeps me wondering what he is thinking. The conversations seem to have largely quieted down. Maybe it's the weather. "Skinny Jim" by Eddie Cochran comes out of one of the dives. I haven't heard that since I was in the house I grew up in back home in Richmond. I instantly remember everything; the ugly green carpet, thousands of LPs, Dad and his cheap beer, the wall full of Mom's books, the up-against-the-wall piano, the smell of Lutheran food, and loud 1940s–1950s music. My old Virginia home. The vision fades from that living room when Cheryl comes to mind. Ouch.

We turn on the road, almost more like an alley, to 007s. I hear a familiar voice. Oh goody.

"But I ain't done drinkin', niggas!" Damn it. Eamons. Nearly everyone in the intelligence business here is crazy in one way or another, but Eamons is truly out of line with the other ducks. As black as asphalt, and he hates black folks. No, he does not recognize he is black. He is the most racist person I have ever witnessed. Watching him is like watching performance art, but worse.

"Yo, Eamons!" I call with great enthusiasm.

He looks around with eyes ready to kill a motherfucker. He sees me and smiles like the monster he is. "*Haaaaaaall!*" To him, despite my being adopted and taste in old blues music, I am "surprisingly" not black.

"I got you, sir," handing him my half-finished bottle of JD. Well, maybe just a little bit emptier. I realized, too late, that no bar would let someone bring in their own whiskey. I also wonder how I got off-base carrying a bottle of Jack. Base security is an oxymoron, I guess.

"You done saved my lifes!" he answers enthusiastically as he looks excoriatingly at his companions. They do not wither under his visage. All three are walking out of 007s.

"Try any of the snake sake?" I ask with a smile, and a large number of new folks are wondering about the answer, having no fucking idea what snake sake is. Well, we need the bodies. I pray the new kids are worth the price of admission.

"Da ownuh wuz just about ta step-ladduh on me when dese niggas done dragged me out!" Eamons is astonished at the un-American actions of comrades trying to keep him out of jail. Wonders will never cease. The wind is swirling the snow and ice from the ground a bit. Looks like Justin and Uncle Tom are with him.

I realize they are less than pleased with my gift to Eamons and his demons. I am less than concerned. "It's a pacifier," I explain. By the look of their narrowing eyes, they are not convinced. I hope they are not just taking care of him for racial reasons. I hate people who think minorities are inferiors who need extra coddling.

We walk into 007s. I am surprised; they are playing "Wrote a Song for Everyone" by Creedence Clearwater Revival instead of hair band music. The place remains enormous for its purpose. Like seemingly every Japanese bar, the bar is to the right where the huge glass tubs of snake sake rest. No kidding, real snakes are encased within the sake, and smaller containers have lizards and other strange critters. I don't see Eamon's stepladder though.

As we work our way down the steps to the couches and chairs and tables, the music changes to Kingdom Come's "The Shuffle," which makes a helluva lot more sense in this place than CCR. The owner is no longer trying to drive away Negroes (if that was what he had been doing) but welcomes us newcomers, a representative crowd of racially mixed Americans. A thought: are Negroes allergic to CCR? Hmmm...I need coffee. The Japanese are willing to take advantage of white Americans, but blacks are usually verboten when not leavened with white friends. Not only verboten but gaijin. Knowing violent crime statistics back home and more, I don't know what to think. I want to think God made us all in His image. Of course, regular Japanese think all Americans are gaijin. They are probably right.

Everyone settles onto the couches. I order a ton of food. Yes, I still eat like a runner. Yes, the running may be one reason I am so damn skinny. I had to gain weight to get into the Air Force in the first place. That and I want to help out the worthless NCO watching the moron back in our barracks. Yes, remember him? I never forgot. Going to get my grub and fuck off. Try to be a nice boy. I know, right? Well, despite my temper issues, I was properly beaten as a child.

Jack is saying something to me, but my mind had been wandering through the cigarette smoke, and my eyes were moving about the crowd. I don't like crowds. "Sorry, I wasn't listening."

"I was saying that you should check out all of the hot bitches checking you out and move on from that former lovely flame of yours from back home."

I look about and see a surprising number of American females in the place considering the base demographics—ten guys to every girl. Maybe Jack is onto something. Then again, every single girl is attracting guys like undernourished kids in Africa attract flies in a UNICEF commercial. A lot of the new Airmen are women, I guess. I make a decision.

"I'll let them come to me or meet them in a better place."

"Better place?"

"Church. Work. Not a meat market."

"Oh. Maybe that is why you have women checking you out... smart."

I don't have the heart to tell him he is older, has a complexion akin to the surface of the moon, and is not the most handsome of men. Don't let Hollywood fool you; bitches are as shallow as most presidential candidates. What a damn shame. Books would have you believe women and politicians, back in the day, were once good. Then again, men these days leave something to be desired. I realize I should answer Jack. Perhaps my pause will make him think I gave proper thought to his observation rather than not telling him that girls are not all that interested in someone on a short list of people I actually like.

"The trick is manifold. If you act like you don't care whether they like you, they are more apt to come after you, and the long game is also a good idea." I raise a hand to stop his question before he asks. "By that, I mean a quiet interest in her, her background and family, an occasional clever remark in a social situation, etc. Later remembering what she said like remembering a family struggle and asking if it all worked out. After a while, even someone as ugly as Cretin can get a girl." I nod above where we are to the bar where Cretin is talking to a girl. No, I am not certain where Cretin is from; I just know to keep him from alcohol as it turns him into a beast. Good thing he is at the bar, huh? "Women love being listened to—especially when it appears that you care about what they are saying. Sadly, they rarely talk about something that matters to men."

"I bet they think the same of us," Jack wisely retorts.

"It's worse than that. Guys are so desperate to get their dicks wet, they won't shut the hell up," I say, grinning.

Jack is smiling all the way through, taking a small pull on a beer I didn't know he had. I think I am the only person not drinking, quite the anomaly. Black Sabbath's "Into the Void" comes on the radio. At least it isn't too loud, but damn if the Japanese don't think old classic hard rock is modern Top 40 radio. Probably because they toured Japan so much when real rockers like Chuck Berry and such did not. Oh well. At least they play baseball…sort of.

I catch his eye to get Jack's attention to ask, "How much mission will be missed short-term while incorporating all of these kids? Even with all of them, there still are not enough…does anyone have a plan?" I say this sotto voce for OPSEC reasons. The loud music helps.

"Scuttlebutt has it that people like you and Justin will be free to pursue the most important bits while we sort the kids out." He raises a hand to prevent my outburst. "I know. We need more coverage."

"So the KGB is running our signals intelligence mission. Niiice. I can't think of a better way for us to miss essential intelligence short-term." Personally, I wouldn't piss on our leadership if they were on fire, dear reader in the future.

"If you think of a better plan, let me know, and I will press it forward. They hate you, but they respect you. They want the kids into the mission ASAP for the long-term while knowing they will sacrifice some near-term coverage. No matter what is decided, I don't see a path where we don't sacrifice something."

He has a point. I am too tired to come up with something immediately. I tell Jack I will ponder the dilemma. Bennie at the bar is waving me over to grab my food. I bet everyone's order is fucked. Bennie is the only imprecise Jap in all Nippon. I think he just likes fucking with Americans or wants us to feel at home. Funny.

I give Jack and as many of my crowd as I can get eye contact the high sign and point to the bar. Jewface is talking to Bubba; apparently, there are no hard feelings. Jewface sees me and points at Cretin. Oh goody, he has a triple-shot glass full of snake sake. He is trying to impress a future ejaculate receptacle. Must be a new girl; she looks too young to drive. I nod to Jewface and head over to Cretin. Cretin is facing left, and I come up behind him as Jewface arrives right in between the couple *just* before the glass gets all the way to his lips. From behind, I grab the glass with my right hand and knock his right arm down off it with my left.

"Hey!" He is surprised and a little pissed. I slam the drink. Bleagh…

I look into his date's eyes. She is confused entirely. "He is a good man. Great softball player. Good operator. Someone who will make a good husband and friend. In a bar fight or in the military, you want him on your side. But do *not* let him drink alcohol. None of us are perfect, and we all have our Achilles' heel. Do *not* let him drink. He is allergic to alcohol." I look into his eyes and smilingly say, "He breaks out in handcuffs." Turning back to his hoped-for ejaculate receptacle, I end softly, "But he would make a better husband and Airman than anyone else here except for that."

Prick will probably order another drink after I am gone. I tried. I go to Bennie to unfuck the food order. Some idiots are just trusting Bennie and are trying to walk out. Mostly new kids. I call them back. They need to learn something: the only perfect trust is in the Lord.

I run into something. Shit, it's that new girl from the Ozarks… what's-her-name. What a hick. The Rolling Stones' "Factory Girl" comes on. How appropriate. "Excuse me," I say. She just looks up at me. I forgot how short she is. I suddenly realize the bar is now crowded, and I need her to adjust. "Excuse me." Not working. "Make a hole!" I announce to the crowd. Yelling is nearly as good as violence. Maybe that is how Moses parted the waves. Now I get through Ozarks and everyone else. Niiice.

"Hi, Bennie." He is not pleased. He is used to being accepted and not messed with. I am now behind his bar with him and my hand on his collar. "How bad did you fuck all this up, you silly twat?" I let him go, roughly, and he nearly falls. He straightens up and starts to walk away, and I grab the bastard and pick him up slightly off the floor. "You *will* help, motherfucker." I drop him to Earth. He does not look happy. "We aren't niggers, Bennie. Fuck you. Fix this." He stares daggers into my eyes. I am gaijin. Fuck him.

All orders are opened and examined. Nothing is right. I order everyone in a line and start handing out food to fill each order one at a time with the help of Jewface, Jack, Toad, and others. Toad is not much help. Bennie cannot keep up and is ashamed at being called out by Americans, of all people. To a Jap like him, it's like being called an idiot by your pet hamster and the rodent is right. As we near the end of the boxes of food, some people will not get what they want since too much of some stuff was made and not enough of others. I try to keep peace in the Middle East.

"There are thirteen boxes and twelve orders, which means there is one extra order. I am ordering for multiple people and should have four boxes of food. How about this—y'all here pick out whichever you want, and leave me with the final five boxes of duck vomit or stewed cat or whatever, deal?" They are amenable to the compromise. It is a quick process, and we leave without a backward glance. After we are a few blocks away, I realize that we probably didn't pay for the food. That bothers me a bit; I do have a horrible streak of honesty, after all. However, I am not going back through the sleet and snow to give Bennie money he didn't earn. This must be God punishing the bastard. Fuck him. It is a quiet walk through the main gate and back to the barracks when I remember that we prepaid. The taxi drivers must be busy or on leave. Jerks. A quiet but long cold walk to the barracks. Oh well. At least it clears the mind. Well, a bit—my conversation with Jack is still on my mind. I don't want to lose the war. Hell, I don't want WWIII at all. My purpose is to prevent it. Is that enough to have left my girl back home who has probably left me? My mind says yes, and my heart disagrees.

Jack turns to make a shortcut through the married folks' neighborhood on this side of the base. There appears to be a fracas, perhaps a car wreck, blocking our previous route. Married folks. The lucky ones, I guess. Most of them earned it—the right to live in these houses, I mean. I think you have to be a senior NCO or an officer to live over here. Still, there are other ones in new high rises on the other side of the base away from the bars and all happiness. Apartment living—another reason to never get married. Luckily some of my friends live off base. I need to visit them again. They work in the Post Office. I met them at tech school at Fort Devens, Massachusetts. Damn that was a time. Cold there, too. In the sticks surrounded by damnyankees. I can't decide which was a more remote, un-American assignment. The good citizens of Boston were just as racist in their own way as the Japs. Of course, the Japanese hate everyone while the damnyankees just hated…everyone not them. Still, I prefer the Japanese. Oh well. Postal work looks tough, but at least the non-Christmas hours aren't too bad. They didn't make it to graduation at Signals Intelligence Collection school. No shame in that; most don't. I sure as hell had a hard time with copying Morse code, for instance. Just copying it for no reason was not engaging. Much different now. And Rhonda's friend isn't too bad on the eyes. I think she likes me. I think her name is…

"Know any of the people living out this way?" Jack asks, interrupting my thoughts. "This Is Radio Clash" sounds out by the Clash from a nearby home, which means these people might be a little groovier than I had thought. Funny how I use the language of what these older folks in base housing would use. Groovier indeed.

"No." I wonder what life must be like for these people. These houses are older than the brand-new high rises, but I don't know what they look like on the inside. They look nice enough, I guess.

"Lots of our best guys live here." Jack could be right. I have no idea why, but the weather is helping me not care. No Jack Daniel's, huge sacks of grub—some of which is not for me—and increasingly slippery conditions that are getting windier, snowier, and colder are not my cup of tea or shot of tequila. "Ever heard of Sammy Watkins?" Jack knows a lot more about the entire organization than I do. "He lives right there." I see him gesture toward some house that looks like every other house.

"No. Is he one of us?" I am unsure. Of course, the question is instantly understood. You are either a warfighter or someone filled with garrison thinking, aka a POG.[8] Worthless. I figure after a certain age and turning your balls over to a wife, one loses one's edge. Then again, I am not sure Jack has ever had an edge, and he is okay. Ever hear the Walker Brothers sing "The Sun Ain't Gonna Shine (Anymore)"? He's like that. Yeah, good man. Cools off a tense situation. Not a warrior. He might be like that song. I hope he finds his own ejaculate receptacle, but I don't want him with me in a bar fight. Good operator though. Really good at the mission.

"He isn't just one of us, he is one of you." Color me intrigued. I ask for more.

"There is talk that he will switch flights.[9] It turns out that our shift needs help in areas you are not involved in." Hmmm...

Looking around, I say, "That means everything but Block 2...what the hell? The operators are fine, just ship away the other NCOs." I have no idea why Jack is both happy and upset.

"Block 3 is a mess. There is talk of him sorting that out. They are also considering moving you over there to sort things out operationally and otherwise." He sees my gorge rising. "Now don't freak out. Yes, I know you are needed at the Soviet Rocket Forces mission...just letting you know."

"Great. Moving me away from the strategic to the tactical. Have anything to do with my 'welcome' for the lovely visitors?" I am referring to my actions with some assholes from some unnamed alphabet

---

[8] People other than grunts—a nonwarrior.
[9] Each USAF shift is called a flight. Go figure. The only flying we SIGINT ops did was on alcohol. Well...mostly. God, Jesus, Buddha, Allah, and L. Ron Hubbard only know what the grunts, leathernecks, and the squids call their shifts. Well, I guess it doesn't matter what those ASVAB-waivered fucktards and faggots think or do, right?

agency in dark suits who were not exactly successful in browbeating me. With friends like these…

Jack seems conflicted. "I see their point. They came to me to see what I thought. You are the best at figuring out what the bastards are doing, and I don't think they will try something like what you discovered before again any time soon." He looks around. We aren't exactly in a secure location, and we are talking shop—highly classified shop. "The code where you are now is easy to copy, and we have a bunch of kids who can handle that. The higher-ups are afraid the next flashpoint will be 'stupid human tricks.' You know, sending a MiG over one of our bases again or doing something stupid to another of our surveillance flights. Also, they are worried there might be a lot going on that is not being tracked or figured out. They think you, and you alone might be able to do that."

"I see." I look at him in complete understanding. We work well together, but he agrees that maybe my talents would be best used over in Block 3. It isn't far away, but once at work, one is so involved, it is akin to being on a different planet if you are in a separate block. Jack and I normally do not see each other socially. He sees it as the end of a friendship similar to when one is PCSed to a new duty station, leaving friends behind. Jack is a good soul.

Jack has his head down, and it isn't from the weather. I understand. I had no idea he felt so close to me. Who knows…maybe he has no other friends. Dear reader from the future, please pray for him if this is the case. Despite everything, I pick up that a house nearby is playing Steely Dan's "Black Cow."

"It may take a minute for this to happen. Besides, it may help Block 3 and Block 2 work together better than ever," I say with a hopeful grin. He replies with a sad smile. Damn. I was just internally dealing with a breakup with a girl; never thought I'd have to deal with one with a guy. Where is the Navy when you need them? Yes, I am kidding, dear reader in the future.

I realize we have gone to and come back in nearly a group. Good. I tell them all to mind their manners for their fellow shift workers as we enter the barracks (sorry, a "dorm"). The stupid bastard who nearly woke up the entire first floor is walking and wandering around in a circle. Others are standing there, worried.

"It's okay, let's get him back to his post," says someone in the crowd. The other idiots help. Nice. I nod for them to do whatever they were about to do. Dumbass, at the sight of us, starts to become lucid and mean. I give him an uplifting speech, "Shush!" and knock him out again. Schlemiel. They always put the losers in this type of role (e.g., someone who cannot get a security clearance, etc.). Morons. Some kids take him back to his office. At least he is now back at his desk where he belongs.

I go upstairs. No, there are no elevators. I arrive and walk to the NCO and the kid I knocked out in the second-floor dayroom. I tell them about the cluster that was 007s. I give the NCO the prime choice (I hear his night was *very* interesting). We have a contrite Airman. I tell the ugly NCO, "Pick something." He grabs the top meal without looking and a nod of thanks. While Dirk picks up chopsticks and soy sauce, I motion for the JEEP to pick a meal.

His response was, "I don't know what any of this is…"

The NCO beats me to the punch. "Goddammit, you piece of shit! *Why* do you hate *America*? Why do you exist?"

Wow. Basic training part 2. I think I should follow up with the silly bastard. I pass him a box, not knowing what it was along with sauces, napkins, and chopsticks. No, not gracefully.

"No harm, no foul. Enjoy your dinner. Fuck with me again, and I will put a boot knife in your neck. Watch it, dumbass." Teacher. Delicate flower petal. I rock.

"Yes, sir," says the dumbass, properly chastened. Time to give my useless roommate food, eat my own food, and pass out. I still need coffee. Oh well. Rotating shifts are a bitch.

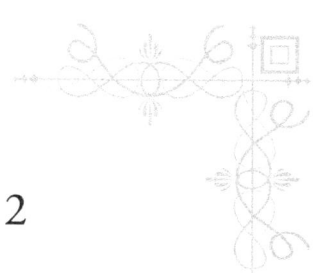

CHAPTER 2

The First Full Day Off

Oh God. There is nothing like waking up with a takeout food and no-coffee headache. I throw on some basic clothes, yes, the same as last night, and stumble to the chow hall. No clue as to where the male whore of a roommate could be. I hope that cause of misery is open—the chow hall, not my roommate. He is probably shacked up with some broad. What time is it? I have no idea. It is gray and dark outside, but it looks like it might be trying to become daytime. The chow hall is open. This realization is both good and awful. Yes, I might get fed, but who knows if I will get food poisoning?

I head toward a table with my tray, having received my grub from the surly bastard behind the counter. The table has Preacher, Justin, Christina Crosse, some really cute girl I have never seen, Gunny, and Hesse. I take the last chair, and everyone starts commenting on the contents on my tray: hard-boiled eggs, hash browns, biscuits and gravy, grits, bacon, sausage, and four cups of very weak coffee and some orange juice. I have friends that don't know you can get OJ without vodka. The usual "how can a skinny bastard like you eat so much and stay skinny" talk goes on and on and on. Pricks. I decide to fuck with them. Messing with me before my fifteenth cup of coffee? Fools.

I keep my face impassive with a tinge of feigned sorrow. I answer Preacher with, "Unlike you, lazy bastards, I burn this off." Preacher is a nice guy. Round face and belly. No muscle tone. Anyone could pass the annual Air Force PT test asleep, but I bet it is a strain for him.

He only drinks wine instead of real alcohol and wants to go to a seminary to be a preacher or priest or some damn thing after his enlistment. He does not chase skirts and knows nothing about sports. He is not as unmasculine as Francis, but this man is not exactly a warrior. Good analyst though.

The coffee is gone, and I am attacking the food with gusto. Christina thanks me for the talk last night. The cute girl beside her starts appraising me; they must know each other or something. The new cutie points at me and says, "Akula." I laugh, which surprises her. Akula is the classified Russian name for some new damn Russian submarine or some such "shark." I stare at Crosse across the table as she explains, looking into my eyes, that I am smarter than I look. I cannot answer with a mouth full of food. Remembering how hot Crosse looked in jeans last night gives me a raging hard-on. Not a welcome development. I think of the song "C. C. Rider" and nearly giggle. "C. C. Rider, see what you have done…" How appropriate. I'd love for this "CC" to take me for a ride. No. No, she has a boyfriend, Mr. Happy.

My food is nearly gone, but I am purposely uncommunicative. I keep feigning sadness. I hear nearly human noises from Hesse. His Christian name is Herman. It may be years before he can communicate in a viable language. He is the most baboonish human I have ever seen. Shy. Nice. Seems to function okay as a Morse code copier. I have enjoyed the company of some serious white trash in basic training, but how this biped from the forest ended up in signals intelligence is a mystery. "Wh-wh-what wrong, Hal?"

Wow, it came out. Words. Fascinating. I have a mouth full of food. I lower my eyes and shake my head slowly. When I am done chewing, I say, "I just found out something, but I don't think I can talk about it." Usually I have only two moods: humor or anger. Horny is a constant, so I am leaving that one out. Apparently, sadness does not become me.

Now everyone is captivated. We SIGINT operators live in a world of secrets here at Misawa Air Base, Japan, but this promises to be both interesting and unclassified. I have the cute JEEP mesmerized. Shit, she has a wedding ring. Oh well. Gunny is genuinely fascinated and tells me I am among friends. Gunny is funny and not just because he is wearing a T-shirt in public and not in a gymnasium, for cripes sake. Another damnyankee from nowhere Pennsylvania. Says words like "yinz" instead of "y'all" like normal Americans. Preacher assures me they are here to help. Preacher looks like a blow-up doll for priests. Only Justin is sitting back, smug. He knows me too well. This asshole might be my best friend. He is from upstate New York. Most Airmen in our business are Southrons, but they tend toward marriage and such. These godless Yankees are different. What does that say about me? Hmmm...

"I think...no, I know...(sigh)...that my roommate is gay." I know, right?

You cannot imagine the silence after I said this. Then the hue and cry started. I, once again, feign sadness, as if I carry an emotional burden and more. Still, they cannot believe the apparently handsome male whore roommate of mine could possibly be gay. Seriously, who could possibly be gay in the first place? The idea of the gay sex act is absolutely disgusting. Rooting around in feces is for swine. I remain in false despair. They begin to wonder if I am telling the truth since I never act like this. Usually, the most unbelievable lies are the ones more easily believed. Then again, the Nazis did well repeating lies over and over again. The crowd starts to ask for evidence.

I remain heartbroken in appearance. I slowly shake my head with my eyes closed. When I open them, Justin is looking me dead in the eyes, and I almost lose it. I stare down at my breakfast tray and say, "Graham is gay. I know this because...his dick tastes like shit."

I am met with initial silence, followed by very loud groans from most and laughter from Justin. I look up with a sly grin. Not everyone is happy with my subterfuge. They had been had. I wouldn't mind if I had the two chicks at the table. One is taken, and the other is married. Bitches. Justin seems to want to have a talk. The girls stand up, so we all do, and the girls tell us they have to go. Christina adds that she and Corrina must take care of some in-processing for the hot JEEP with the wedding ring. We wish them well and check them out as they leave. Corrina is a bit short, blonde, and a wee bit too fit, but has cute staked out. That is one girl who should not wear jeans near traffic. Wow. "Corrina, Corrina" by Bob Dylan comes to mind. "Gal, where you been so long?" Oh well.

"I'm out. Want to go to the Class VI?" Justin read my mind. Good on him.

"Hell yes. Now?" He nods. "Cool. Let's check the weather before we go. Should we check on the usual suspects to see if they want to tag along?" Another nod confirms. Hesse looks confused. Gunny asks if he can tag along. I don't think Gunny has many friends. A goodhearted damnyankee who is losing his hair and is as old as Jack... and no wife. That ship may have left for him. Too bad. I welcome him on our hunt for booze and beer. Preacher asks if we can look for some damn wine. Freak. I tell him to write it down since I cannot remember all of his frog talk. He tells me he will meet me at the front door of the barracks with everyone else with the list of "if they have this great but if not this and if not that and..." Pretty picky for an Airman in Japan. The soft bastard will drink it all in one night so he should come with us and haul a case of whatever he wants. Oh well.

Hesse seems confused as to what went on in the chow hall. I thank him for helping me fool the others. He is not reading me, but he nods as if he does. Poor kid. I try to rethink my assessment of him. Communication is not his forte. However, like that kid Bubba last night, he is willing to leave home for the other side of the planet to serve God and country music to save the free world. That accounts for a lot in my book.

It's a short walk from the chow hall to the barracks. The weather is dreadful but not as horrible as it normally is at this time of year. Terribly cloudy, a wee bit cold but okay. I don't mind the cold, but the long walk to the liquor store might prove me wrong. Also, there is always the promise of icy rain during rainy season. Sucks being in between cars. I go to my vacant room to tally my booze needs. I am first to the first-floor lobby when a visibly troubled junior NCO comes out of the dorm chief's office.

"You work with Smitty, right?" Uh oh. I nod.

"He got a phone call from back home, and he isn't in his room." My Class VI comrades show up at the same time from various directions.

"We'll find him," I assure him. As some of you may remember, an international phone call was a big deal back in the day. Hard to do. Expensive as all get out. It's never good news. The whole barracks building shares the one phone in the office. There is talk of putting one on each floor, but that will probably never happen. Phones are overrated anyway. I prefer getting a letter or telegram to getting a phone call. Less ephemeral. Besides, getting the news sooner doesn't change anything.

I turn to Justin and Gunny. "Smitty got a phone call from the world. I say we find him before we hit the Class VI, okay?" After they readily agree, I ask for suggestions on a search plan.

"Does he have a girlfriend?" Justin is pretty smart. Snatch first. I shake my head.

"Then we should go to the usual stops, the closest first, like the Shoppette, and work our way farther out," Gunny says.

"Good idea," I say as Justin nods. "To the Shoppette." We leave as White Lion's "Tell Me" plays on the small radio in the dorm chief office. All I can think is they sound like an experiment for male tampons. Then again, I may be surly for lack of real coffee.

We "Three Horsemen of the Apocalypse" head into a cold and uncaring world under cadet gray skies. Someone is yelling at us from the barracks we just left. Another gay sound, I guess. I want to ask him if he has any tampons on him and decide it just isn't the time. It's the Preacher and his damn wine list. I tell him we are on a mission from God and explain. I ask if he can check Smitty's room every half hour in case we miss him. The Preacher straightens up like he, too, is on a mission from God as I facetiously thought seconds before. "Will do. And thanks." I don't know if he means the mission or me fetching his frog juice. I guess it doesn't matter to a tree.

We finally get on our way. There is not too much talking. It really is a big deal getting a call from America. News from home by phone is about as welcome as the cold and misty weather we are walking through. Justin is characteristically smoking. He has a weak mustache; his dirty blonde hair is parted in the middle for no apparent reason, and he is an inch or three shorter than me. He tends to drink Michelob instead of whiskey. I think every time he drinks a beer, he doubles in weight. "Two Tribes" by Frankie Goes to Hollywood is playing somewhere nearby, and Gunny is the only one who does not physically embrace the song in a silly dance.

The wet-smelling air is hitting us sideways at about twenty miles per hour. We all lean into the wind as we weave our way toward the convenience store through the leftover wintery muck. At least Justin is wearing a coat. Gunny has on a flannel shirt and a trucker mesh baseball hat and seems entirely unaffected by the weather. Maybe they breed tougher men in western Pennsylvania. He is slim and farmer-fit with broader shoulders on a taller frame than the rest of us. Good man. Always eager to please even though he is a little older. It just occurred to me that we forgot to ask around as to who would want to join us. I guess Smitty is more important at the moment.

As we make our way through the wind and remaining patches of ice and snow, Gunny speaks, "What do you think of old splotch-top's nuclear concessions, Hal?"

"Gorbachev's nuclear disarmament?" He nods. "Let me give you an old quote:

> War to the hilt between communism and capitalism is inevitable. Today, of course, we are not strong enough to attack. Our time will come in twenty or thirty years. To win we shall need the element of surprise. The bourgeoisie will have to be put to sleep. So we shall begin by launching the most spectacular peace movement on record. There will be electrifying overtures and unheard-of concessions. The capitalist countries, stupid and decadent, will rejoice to cooperate in their own destruction. They will leap at another chance to be friends. As soon as their guard is down, we shall smash them with our clenched fist."

"Manuilsky, the Comintern nerd. When did he say this, Hal?" asks Justin.

"1931, I think. Guess they are running a little late," I say with a grin.

"But the Sovs can't even beat those goat-fucking wogs in Afghanistan," Gunny observes.

"I see it as a long war exercise in the worst terrain on the planet. Practicing mobility, sustainment, logistics, and so on. I bet they will withdraw to rest and refit, and then will attack the West. Their withdrawal will be one of their concessions. Meanwhile, our president is spending us into oblivion trying to bankrupt the Soviet economy. If the commies are smart, they will not try to keep up and will instead beat us with a rapid conventional attack in Europe with their overwhelming numbers before we can bring up follow-on forces to aid our weak allies," I conclude.

"So we're fucked?" asks Gunny. Steely Dan's "Deacon Blues" plays on a passing car.

"Nah. *We* are only fucked if a conflict goes nuclear…or if there is an accident leading to a nuclear exchange. Of course, NATO may be fucked in Western Europe."

"What about the issues we hear about on the other side of the Soviet Union?" Justin asks.

"I don't know. It could really be the beginning of the end, or it could be more of the concessions and perceived freedoms we just talked about." We are nearing the Shoppette. "Isn't that Eamons?"

"Shit!" Apparently, Justin is not pleased. "You know he finished that bottle you gave him before we even got back to the barracks last night." The memory makes him more displeased.

It *is* Eamons. I think he is trying to leave the Shoppette. I also think he is talking to the door, the outside wall, his imaginary childhood friends, and the sidewalk at the same time. Wow.

"Hey, Eamons, have you seen Smitty?" I ask this as he figures out his issues. Note how polite and gentle my voice is despite the weather and dealing with pissy damnyankees.

"Hal! Who?" Eamons went from excitement to bewilderment to the realization that he did indeed know Smitty. Eamons's skin is much darker than his Baltimore Colts hoodie, but now his eyes look like as white as a ghost and about to explode out of his head. "Dat nigga?" He starts to rave and stomp around. No, I am not kidding. Charm City indeed. "Useless, smelly-assed, nappy-headed, banjo-lipped motherfucking niggas! Damn them all to hell! What did that remote control do?" he asks as he comes face to face, nose to nose with me. "I gets him fo' you, Hal. Whar he at?"

The others are a little taken aback, Gunny more than Justin. I keep my cool.

"Eamons, Smitty got a phone call from back in the world. We are trying to find him to let him know. Do you know where he is?" This seems to calm him down. Thankfully, he takes a half step back as well since his breath smells like JP-8[10] and ass.

"No, but I heps ya. First, we gotta look for sign." Eamons starts bending over and looking over the small parking lot. I look to my comrades inquisitively.

"He means like scat or deer tracks," Gunny says helpfully. Oh my.

"Look! Looka heah!" Eamons is a wee bit excited. "Lookie dar, a chicken bone!"

Oh God. What was I thinking?

"And over thar, a pack of Kools!" Eamons is practically jumping up and down like a little kid after hearing the ice cream man. "What off dat way?" Eamons is using the DF from the detritus in the convenience store parking lot, the chicken bone, and crushed pack of Kools.

I am still not perfectly awake, I guess. I was about to say something like shit weather only slightly better than the likely future of a nuclear winter and ugly phlegm-colored military base buildings when Justin says, "The NCO Club, I guess."

"Dey have white women thar?" Eamons's eyes are expanding again. Sheesh…

"Uh, yeah." Gunny still can't believe all of this. I understand. What was God thinking when He made Eamons? Then again, what was God thinking when he allowed communism and the Soviet Union? Best of all possible worlds, my ass.

---

[10] Jet fuel.

Eamons adjusts his Walkman headphones up his neck a bit and hits play on the tape player. "Eine kleine Nachtmusik" of all fucking things is being played loud enough for us all to hear as he practically skips toward the NCO Club. As crazy as this all is, I once read that Mozart was a little out of line with the other ducks, too. Maybe not like this though. We have to run/walk to keep up with Eamons who decides green and red lights do not apply to him as we get nearer and nearer to the club. Honking and screaming from drivers *just* missing Eamons does not mix well with Wolfgang's most popular tune.

"Eamons!" He looks back at me. "It's not a race, Hoss. Besides, we should all go in together."

"You be right, Hal. We put up a better diplomatic front together. Niggas be 'fraida me." They aren't alone, Eamons. Trust me.

We find the club open and nearly as empty as a campaign promise. In fact, the only customers are Smitty and the stereotypical two white girls with him. That Eamons was so absurdly right strikes me as funny. I ask Eamons to turn his music down, which he does. This brings everything to its proper solemnity as I begin to speak.

"Smitty, we came here for you." He looked like he thought we were there to drink and might want to abscond with his white girls—or at least cockblock him a bit. Now he is looking at me. "You got a phone call from home. It wouldn't do to keep your family waiting." I look at his hoochies—not too bad on the eyes. "Sorry, ladies."

Smitty looks like he got hit by a brick. "I, uh, I got to settle the bill." As he walks to the bar, I ask the girls to go with him. I tell them if there really is bad news, that we know Preacher can pray with him, and I tell them wine boy's room number. I don't think he is friends yet with Preacher. I also ask what Smitty likes to drink since we are, after all, going to the Class VI. They agree to the plan and tell me what I need to know. Nice to be surrounded by good Americans.

Smitty comes back and apologizes to the girls. They insist on going with him, which brightens up his mood just a hair. You can see the foreboding in his eyes. He turns to me. "Hey, uh…" He looks, at first, as if he wanted to shake my hand in thanks and instead gives me a ferocious bear hug. I hug back. We're all Christians, our brother's keeper. He leaves quickly, perhaps embarrassed about hugging a man. I think I see a tear in his eye. That's okay. The girls race to catch up to him.

Eamons looks at me in disgust. "I bet you got nigga all over you now." Thanks, Eamons.

"Hey, do want to come with us to the Class VI?" I ask. Eamons is amenable, so we all slowly make our way. The crazy bastard turns his tape player on again, and "Moonlight Sonata" by Beethoven plays. Compilation. Nice. Apropos as well. To the weather. To the circumstances. Poor Smitty. We pass a few moments in silence.

"Nice tune. Is that some French fag or something? It's pretty, and I ain't never heard music like that," an enquiring Pennsylvanian wants to know.

"It's Beethoven, hillbilly. So is this," Eamons says in a professorial tone as the music switches to "Fur Elise." I wonder how many people there are in Eamons's psyche. Wow.

"I know, right?" I say to Gunny to calm the situation. No one likes to be belittled—especially by the insane.

"It makes the two world wars and Naziism even harder to understand," I add. Clearly Gunny agrees. How did the same people who could create this music try to eradicate an entire race of people from the Earth?

We enter the store, and I ask the clerk for a mop. He looks at me like I am crazy. I explain that I know he is the only one here, and there is a puddle forming around the rug at the door. No doubt from snowmelt from the roof. He doesn't have time to attend to it, and I do not want an aging SNCO, a useless officer, or a retiree slipping. He smiles and gets me the mop. Good kid.

The others are trying to figure out what is available and what they actually want. There is some back and forth about things one has not tried and another has and if it is any good. Personally, like Gatorade should only be green, there is only one whiskey; Jack Daniel's. I was just about done mopping when I nearly got knocked back by the door. I should have drank more of that awful, weak chow hall coffee. Funny that this happened just as the good part of "Claire de Lune" by Debussy starts playing on Eamons's Walkman.

"Damn, you needed extra work?" It's that hillbilly girl with all of her teeth who wanted to know about that Viking talk. Cute enough, I guess. Eyes as black as her hair. She has a sly smile when she asks this. I try to smile back, but it doesn't quite work. "What's wrong?" she asks with becoming concern.

I tell her about Smitty, and she understands completely. I ask, "Have a hard time finding the Class VI?"

"I shouldn't since I was born here. Dad PCSed when I was a baby. A pain in the ass to learn to drive on the wrong side of the road though."

"You drove?" I ask this with quite some hope.

"Oh sure. Some desperate bastard PCSing wanted to unload a junker, and I picked it up for nothing." She looks me up and down. "Need a ride, big fella?" All of a sudden, everyone who had come here with me went silent. She smiles and wonders, looking like she is going to find out I have a harem filled with officer's wives with me or if I am here alone.

I smile back. "No, just some comrades who helped me find Smitty. Do you mind taking us and our purchases to the barracks? What are you driving, anyway?" Japanese cars hereabouts tend to be small enough to have to be put on like a jacket.

She beckons with a single finger, opens the door, and points. It is an ugly red station wagon, something that is as rare as fur on a fish in these parts. "I'll be happy to help, Viking Talker." Quite the flirt, this girl.

"Thanks. Welcome to our Class VI." I ask the clerk for a box, and he is only too happy to oblige. He is staring at my new friend. Maybe she is better-looking than I thought. Hmm…

"Guys, we have a Mother Mary. She is giving us a ride." They look up like prairie dogs in other aisles. Funny. I go look for Preacher's frog juice. I have no idea where the wine aisle is. I doubt one exists on a military base, but I am wrong; no doubt for officers' wives.

I buy two bottles for the Preacher, hoping he can earn it for Smitty. Beer and lots of JD for me. I have given up Heineken beer. After several thousand, it sours on the tongue. For the longest time, it was the only thing the Class VI sold other than Budweiser and Miller

Lite. I get Smitty's booze. My comrades finally figure out what they want. Justin, after giving Gunny and Eamons lots of hilarious bits of disinformation, comes forward with a case of Michelob.

I look at the other two. "Will you two maggots put that shit back and just get what you want!" I look at Justin with a mean eye. He is about to laugh. I smirk. "You prick." My eyes narrow, and he smiles wider. Hard to hate this man.

"Move your ass, maggots, before Bridget the Midget leaves us!" I hope my enthusiasm moves them. She isn't very tall. I guess she needs little in the way of booze. She only has one bottle. Chick juice of some kind. My box is more than full. I make sure to buy hers, mine, Smitty, and the Preacher's alcohol. The poor kid behind the counter has trouble doing his job.

"Thank you," she says with a genuine smile.

"Thank you for helping the war effort," I reply with an equal smile. "Sorry about the amateurs."

"Amateurs?"

"Amateur drunks. What the…c'mon, guys, the hottie with the car is about to leave us!"

She grins. The dorks finally show up. Michelob, bad bourbon, and worse show up at the counter. Wow. Time was lost for this. Do the Soviets have this problem? Probably not; it's likely they have fewer choices.

We eventually pile into the junker and head back to the barracks. After we park, I thank her again. She says that she has been invited to watch movies somewhere the next day; would I like to join her? I agree and tell her my room number. Meanwhile, we all split up. I drop off my beer and JD from my box into my room, but my roommate still seems to be shacked up elsewhere with some broad. I go back to the first floor with some of the rest of my purchases to the Dorm Chief's office to check in on what happened to Smitty.

"Hal, his grandparents, the ones that were raising his nephew and niece, died in a crash!" The young NCO is trying not to cry when he says this. I heard Smitty lost his brother and sister-in-law recently not too long ago as well. I thank the kid and hand him a cold six-pack. He looked like he needed it and seemed grateful.

Then I go to Preacher's room. He answers very soon after my knocking.

"Hal, I took care of Smitty. No one should hear that over the phone. I hope I helped."

I give him one bottle. "This is what you asked for." I hand him a second. "This one is on me, thanks for helping Smitty."

"Bu-but, how did you know?"

"I had faith in you." He practically glows. I am glad and keep my male tampon questions on hold.

"I gave the local chaplain's office the news. The Air Force may send him home on a hardship discharge." Good heart on the round religious POG. I thank him again. On my way back to my room, I see one of Smitty's chicks. Says she needed something from her room and was going back. I give her Smitty's bottle of Hennessy and tell her to tell him it is from all of us. I also ask her to reach out if there is more that I can do. Poor Smitty.

It's later and my roommate is still not back. Guess he is too lazy to stop fucking his latest broad. After writing an apologetic letter to Cheryl back home, I was in the dayroom reading a book with a bottle when I was joined by some comrades. They seem rather eager to go to the NCO club and then downtown. Guess it is getting close to being nighttime. I am at the left end of a couch in the dayroom with a book sitting beside me so no one is sitting with me. The hillbilly with the red station wagon asks to take the last empty spot. I lift my book and join one of the conversations. They appear to be talking about the Late Ruction, aka the American Civil War.

"What are you nerds talking about now? Sounds like y'all are getting a wee bit animated," I say playfully. Some just stare in annoyance and others all start talking at once. "Damn...calm your tits. One at a time. What the fuck?" I say the last bit gently. What an old smoothie I am becoming now that I am over twenty years old.

"Gunny was yacking about how brave the Yankee troops were at their epic failures at Fredericksburg and at Sharpsburg..."

"Antietam!" Gunny interjects.

"Whatever, damnyankee. Meanwhile, the cognoscenti were discussing the beginning of the war and the moral rightness of the

South seceding. What do you think, Hal?" I forget this redneck's name since he works on the other side of our building on Security Hill, but I think he is O'Phelan's roommate. He has a Red Man chew expanding his cheek like Lenny Dykstra.

"It is one of the gaps in my knowledge." I raise a hand. "Yes, I grew up in Richmond, VA, but my parents were from Minnesota and were uninterested in the topic, and the schools simply said that wonderful Yankees fought and died to free slaves from evil Southrons." This is not met well. They don't want the truth?

"Damn, you were indoctrinated. How can you be so damn smart and so damn stupid?" Jewface is shocked.

"Can't know everything. Should I care?" Nearly universal evil staring. Nothing like winning over a crowd, huh?

There is a rush to talk, but Jewface wins. "What caused the war, Hal?"

"Sumter, I guess."

"No, dumbass…why?" Jewface looks like he is going to win this.

"In school, they said the South fired upon the flag," I say uncertainly. "I'd love it if you would tell me and stop asking, like a child asking why the sky is blue, and enlighten me." Freak.

"South Carolina 'fired on the flag' because the new Northern administration kept telling the Confederate peace commissioners that they would evacuate CSA territory. That damn racist tyrant Lincoln violated the armistice by sending aid to Fort Pickens at Pensacola and Fort Sumter in Charleston after telling the local governors he would not do so. Violating an armistice is an act of war. He could have called the Senate to order but purposely kept them out of office so he could have his war." Damn, Jewface is obsessed. Or maybe he is right.

"Oh well. It was never a big deal in our household. I did check out the Revolution a bit," I say hopefully.

"But what was the war about?" asks Bubba with a large, mixed contingent behind him.

"No idea. They taught us in grade school that wonderful freedom-loving Yankees invaded the South to save poor Negroes from slavery." I put up my hand from the coming vitriol. "I had my doubts, but had other interests—music, sports, girls, and other points in history…" I am not sure I calmed the madding crowds down.

"The Civil War decided what America became. It is the pivotal point in our history. As a result, our country has become what it has become—good and bad things," Bubba explains.

"I heard that the South fought well despite being outnumbered in military size and industrial capacity," I say hopefully. "So why did the Southern states secede? I remember the Northern states wanting to secede during the war of 1812 and in 1848, the latter because of the war with Mexico." Yes, I am trying to recover. When did I stop being the smartest person in the room? And damn it, why is the hillbilly so interested in me on my right?

"Really?" The hillbilly is interested in the topic and not just me. "I never heard that."

"Wait a minute, I was thinking secession caused the war, but Norway seceded from Sweden, and there was no war. Wasn't it Portugal that needed four wars to earn their independence from Spain?" Just trying to flank these self-righteous geeks.

"Correct," says O'Phelan's roommate. "The southern states seceded, and in the Deep South, it was mostly over slavery. They feared the Black Republicans would somehow end slavery despite Lincoln saying they wouldn't. Many 'Pubs were abolitionists. Then again, Lincoln hated slavery, and he hated blacks and wanted to free them and deport them all to Liberia," he says with a grin. Wow, Lincoln *was* a jerk.

"Okay, but why did the Confederate forces fire on Fort Sumter, even if the USA was on CSA soil? Wasn't that the act that galvanized the North?" Yes, I ask the best questions.

"Good question, Hal. They had every right to shoot the Yankee bastards for having cannons and such pointed at the CSA on their own land. I guess you could say it was the most 'get off my lawn' moment in American history," Jewface says with a wide grin. "But what was the other reason for secession aside from decades of acrimony between the two sections? Lincoln wasn't even on the ballot in the Southern states, and Abe ran on a platform of raising the Tariff of Abominations from around 20 percent to over 40 percent."

"Ah, taxation without representation. That's right—fledgling Northern industries wanted a tariff wall, and the free-market South wanted free trade since our tariffs were reciprocated by our trading partners. Damn. And it was South Carolina that was forced by Andrew Jackson years before to stay in the Union decades before over a ruckus over that issue?" This is getting interesting. Decades of acrimony indeed. The little hillbilly seems fixated on me. Maybe there is something hanging from my nose. O'Phelan's roommate looks like he wants to answer me.

"Exactly. I guess you aren't a total loss, Hal," O'Phelan's roommate says with a grin.

"But we are missing the answer: why did the CSA fire at the few troops in the harbor right then?"

Jewface looks like he is about to administer the coup de grace. "The Yankees were manning the most important tariff collection site in the South right there in Charleston harbor. *The Confederates' first target was against tax collectors.*"

Wow. This is astonishing. "Son of a…" I can't continue and wonder if this is true.

"It's too damn bad you were raised by Yankees, Hal," observes Bubba.

"Yeah, like being raised by wolves or something, like Tarzan," Toad adds. I hope he never breeds. There is, however, some laughter at his hopelessly foolish observation.

"Hey, thanks for the educational moment," I say, meaning it. A bunch of variations of "no problem" are a universal reply.

The little hillbilly picks up the book I had been holding as I notice "You Shook Me" by the first Jeff Beck Group plays on someone's tape deck. Too bad Led Zeppelin went on to destroy this version since this isn't half bad. Then again, there was one Led Zeppelin, and then God broke the mold.

"*Thus Spoke Zarathustra: A Book for All and None* by Friedrich Nietzsche," she observes, butchering the Kraut's name horrifically. She is looking over the front and back cover. I let her gaze at the book and the writeups for a moment. "A New Day Yesterday," Jethro Tull's second-best song, comes on. Good taste. I look around to see who is playing the music but can't figure it out. I finally notice the dayroom is rather crowded with people, smoke, and their beverages of choice. That reminds me to take a medicinal pull off of my bottle. Most everyone else seems to be drinking beer. Freaks.

She looks up at me. I am guessing she is too embarrassed to ask about the book. "Nietzsche was a Kraut philosopher who was very influential. This book is in four parts. Ideas within include the eternal recurrence of the same, a parable about the death of God, and a prophecy about the idea of a superman. In this poor translation, superman is 'overman.' His mustache is more impressive than his philosophy, but he is clever at times. His views on Christianity are interesting and wrong, for instance." During this exchange, a lot of other interesting talk is about.

Fleetwood Mac's "Oh Well" with Peter Green comes on next. Who is playing this great music?

"How did you know my name was Bridget?" the hillbilly asks. I start to laugh.

"I didn't. My father used to play humorous songs when I was growing up, and 'Bridget the Midget' (The Queen of the Blues) by Ray Stevens was one of the more modern. He also adored Spike Jones. Sorry, you were a wee bit shorter than the rest of us in the Class VI today," I respond, genuinely hoping she is not angry. "More often father played big band and swing tunes."

"It's okay. It's been great meeting you. I have some people to meet that I was stationed with before. Have a good time tonight," says good old Bridget the Hillbilly Midget.

"Thanks. You, too." Nice girl. Not totally hot but not bad.

I thank the world for a moment of peace and quiet. Well, me being alone in a crowd while tuning them out to read good old Fred. I am nearly done with this book. Nietzsche is so smart and misses the point so often. Quite disconcerting. Ahh…I get through a whole page or two when I have to stop.

"Son of a bitch!" She is not too bad on the eyes. A little top-heavy for my taste. There is something familiar about her. What the...?

"Hal!" Oh shit. This is the crazy bitch who was dating an acquaintance of mine at tech school at Fort Devens, Massachusetts. Not bad on the eyes. A little too happy to see me. Then again, it is PCS season; it isn't just new kids, it is people coming from other stations. I am guessing Bridget is one of those. This one is definitely no kid. Bridget has the air of someone who is on their second or third assignment. I am still on my first proper duty station after extending my tour in place.

"Hey!" she says as she grabs my bottle and drains a bit of it. "Let's catch up!"

I am amenable. Someone asks why the girl from *Cheers* is in the Air Force. That's right; the Cajun is a dead ringer for Kirstie Alley. I'm not one for television, but it was a topic of conversation in signals intelligence collection school. I think she is from Louisiana. Then again, people confuse me with Balki Bartokomous from that hit show...whatever it is called. I think the actor's name is Bronson Pinchot.

"Did you want to go out on the town and have a quiet drink?" What a gentleman I am.

"Sure! Let me get a coat and stuff in my room." She sees my questioning eye and says, "First floor."

"Perfect." I follow her after I set down my stuff in my room nearby. She isn't so bad on the eyes from this direction either. If memory serves, her name is Stacy Breaux. At least that is what her uniform nametag in Western Mass said, I think. Makes sense that she is from Cajun country with a last name like that. The view gets better as she bounces down the stairs. Damn. I wonder if she is still with what's-his-name the boyfriend. I didn't see a ring, and it has been quite a while. Hmmm... She gets to the bottom of the stairs and turns left toward Justin's part of the first floor, but not too far down the hallway.

"Come on in." I do. She gets busy doing something or other, and I check out her room. Typical chick room. She and her roommate have proper beds instead of space-saving futons, but they have maximized space as best as possible. Her roommate must be at work or out on the town. I continue to look about, not wanting to see whatever private female stuff she may be digging into. All of a sudden as I was looking askance, she is right in front of me. I can feel her breath. "I missed you so much," she says softly as she puts her lips to mine. Being a gentleman, I assist. It appears we are not going out right now. In fact, without words, it appears there is mutual consent to stay in. We do not go to sleep until nearly dawn. Come on in, indeed.

CHAPTER 3

The Second Day Off

The sun is up, and I am trying to wake up. Stacy tried waking me up a few minutes before by giving me a shot of bourbon. Interesting choice of beverage. I hope it has a lot of electrolytes. Cajuns are crazy. My head fell back onto the pillows. I still feel drained and close my eyes. She has a small radio on, and it is playing "Never in My Life" by Mountain. How fitting. "Mississippi Queen" might have been even better. Now I hear talking. Who cares? I am utterly exhausted.

I open my eyes and notice there is some woman who is less than perfectly pretty but with a lovely figure staring at me. It takes a minute for me to realize I am uncovered and naked on Stacy's bed. Too late now; this stranger can have a free show. Nice jeans on this girl. Must be a roommate or something. Small-breasted and wide-hipped the way God intended. Hmmm…

"I am *so* sorry," Stacy says to whomever this is as the Cajun dashes from the bathroom bare-ass naked toward me, tits flying everywhere. "I need you to wash my back!" She grabs my hand, and we go to the shower. "Mississippi Queen" starts to play. Funny. Must be their greatest hits. We end up very clean, and it only took us about an hour. I might need another medicinal shot of that rotgut. I bet that swill has all the vitamins I need. Right…

After putting on our clothes from the night before and I find out what time it is, we decide to dash to the chow hall to get some grub before they close. Despite my exertions, I feel pretty damn good. Food will be great since I am still a growing boy. I am not in an impecunious state, but not having to pay for food is a nice benefit in the military. Of course, it's free and worth every penny. Food poisoning is quite prevalent. I think it is like airline and hospital food, a lack of motivation. It's as if they are saying "let's face it, not everyone is going to make it, so why make an extra effort?"

Stacy and I make our way through the line, and she is also astonished by the metric ton of food I order. "I Got You" by Split Enz is playing somewhere nearby. Then she is impressed at how I put the maggots behind the counter in their place who do not want to give me what I want. The Jap at the register acts like he has a problem with Stacy's order to be paid by typing up something off of her orders until I light him up with wonderfully loud profanity. Don't want the slant-eyed bastard to do the same to all the new kids in town who also don't have their meal cards yet. Prick. I have heard this works with the French as well. Light the bastards up, and they quail.

We sit down, and I ask Stacy about her old boyfriend, home, family, etc. I use this time to try to listen and devour my alleged food. It turns out her situation is rather out where the buses don't run. She is legally separated from her first husband, but he and the Catholic church are making divorce difficult. She is no longer dating her tall ex-boyfriend, my acquaintance from Fort Devens, Massachusetts. Apparently talking about her family is verboten, or whatever word is appropriate in Cajun. She also, as she talks with her mouth full sometimes, tells of a time when she was in high school and went to spring break with her college-age sister. Apparently, they were the type to use recreational drugs. Well, it was the early 1980s, and not all of America's vice was in Miami. They were in a hotel and invited everyone to do a line of cocaine, with little Stacy going first. She had never done such a thing and did her best...and then sneezed all of the rest of the lines into the shag carpets. Now *that* is funny. Allegedly she met the band Zebra the same weekend. This reminds me that I already know what is behind Stacy's door.

I notice Bridget is at the next table with some guy on my shift. Mike Greenbaum on the electronics side of the house, if memory serves. Bridget catches me grinning and says, "Mike is an old chum." I say that Stacy is as well. Bridget says she will take a rain check on the movie date I had forgotten about, and I graciously say that I understand. Imagine what would come out of a mating of that Jew and the hillbilly. I wonder if he is related to the gentleman who performed "Spirit in the Sky." I wish them well and return my attention to Stacy.

"I know I am acting like a shift worker, but I have no idea what day of the week it is. Is there someplace you need to be?" The perfect gentleman.

The crazy bitch decides to use the moment to devour the last of her breakfast. I wait. "I am supposed to be in-processing, but that can wait." She has a decidedly indifferent attitude to the mission.

"As much as I'd like to entertain you all day, the mission needs everyone. Even with the addition of you and the kids, we are at 30 percent of mission readiness. Do you have a driver's license here yet?"

"No, what's the big deal?" She has no idea.

"They drive on the other side of the road. The steering wheel is on the wrong side, too."

"Sneaky motherfuckers!" She is not embracing change. "Don't they know that they aren't English?"

I am amused and decide to mess with her. "Well, they are tea drinkers, they drink a clear alcohol named sake instead of gin, and they are quite fastidious like the English. Think about them being an island people with few resources wanting to be an empire. Too bad for them it fell out of favor, huh?" The recently righteously fucked Cajun is not amused. "And like the English, they think themselves quite superior to everyone else. It's only their language that is as guttural as the Germans."

She contemplates her situation. "This in-processing thing is bullshit!" says my recent paramour. I know, right? How disappointing that the fate of the world is interrupting her social life. How terrible. "Papa's Got a Brand-New Bag" by James Brown ends, and "I Can Help" by Billy Swann comes lightly out of the chow hall speakers. Quite the course change in music.

Bridget is about to part from her gentleman and tells Stacy that she is in-processing as well starting today as it is Monday. Since Bridget the Midget has a car, it can be done much quicker than by bus. I nod. The Cajun acquiesces. Thank God; my penis and I need a break. Well, for a little bit at least.

Wow. A day off and no plans. After stopping at my room, I realize something has been bothering me, so I decide to visit Justin. After politely knocking and the inevitable "come in," I am surprised by what I see. Gatherings like this usually don't happen on a day off in the morning. Justin and a few other familiar faces are with a gaggle of the new kids. As they are all young men, I am certain this is not a completely social gathering. I don't even see an open adult beverage. My interest is piqued.

"Ah, perfect timing," Justin says with a grin. "I was just about to send someone to find you." "Sign of the Gypsy Queen" by April Wine is playing in the background. Justin's taste in music sometimes goes off the reservation.

"Not to sound like we are in the Navy, but I guess you and I have some sort of radar love," I respond. Some are looking at me in an odd way, so I add, "Thank God my date from last night has to in-process. She knocked my balls out of the park all night and this morning. So what's up?"

"Date with who?" asks Justin.

"Stacy from Fort Devens has arrived. Remember her?" I answer.

Justin thinks for a moment. "The one with the epic tits that looks like Kirstie Alley?" he exclaims.

"Yeah, well those tits are worse for wear after last night. What's up?"

"We are having an unclassified talk about how important our mission is. The JEEPs ended up here in a group when their in-briefing was cancelled last minute. Well, I accidentally waylaid them."

"Okay." This might be hard for me, not having prepared for this. I gather my thoughts for just a second, inhale, and begin. "The fate of the world depends on you, and no one will ever know. I doubt the Cold War will end anytime soon, but if we win, there will be no protests and no parades. In that way, your return to the world will be even more disappointing than the previous generation of Vietnam veterans." I pause. I am not selling this very well so far.

"You are here because you are the best, the brightest, and the bravest. The threat is real and dwarfs anything the United States has ever faced. The Soviet Union itself covers about one-sixth of the land surface, about 8.6 million square miles or so, with 300 million citizens. Our enemy has encompassed half the globe and is twice the threat to the world that WWII's Axis powers poised with tens of thousands of nuclear weapons, the Warsaw Pact, and more. The Soviet Union's military machine is more powerful than all other powers combined—we rely on technology and skill. As inefficient as their economy sometimes is, their military attracts their best and brightest and is no joke. Only their lack of original thinking and adaptability gives us a chance to win the next shooting war. That is a war that, if we do our job, we will either prevent or at least give our side the best chance at victory."

"It's really that bad?" asks some kid who doesn't look old enough to shave.

"It's worse. I am not done." I pause to take a sip of the inevitable pint I was carrying in my back pocket. Honestly, I not only needed the drink when thinking about the threat, but I needed another second to collect my thoughts.

I go on. "Our best option to deter the Soviet menace is our SIGINT operations—us. Essentially, we work for the NSA. The NSA has other operations that are ridiculously expensive and ineffective. The CIA is a joke. The Soviets have pretty fair SIGINT ability, but their HUMINT operations are special, easily the best in the world. Every country in the world is riddled with intelligence and counterintelligence operatives. Yes, including our own country." The kids seem shocked.

"Americans don't betray America!" exclaims some other kid. Naive, and he sounds like he grew up off the paved road.

"I wish you were correct, young man," says Justin. "Go on, Hal."

"Remember the 'greatest generation'?" Nods all around. "Here are just a few examples of Americans back then working for the Soviets. Alger Hiss was the assistant to SecState for FDR and helped set up the UN while also working for the Soviets. Harry Dexter White was assistant to SecTreas for FDR. He killed aid for Nationalist China, which sent a significant portion of the planet into communist slavery. FDR was told about White, and that crippled bastard still put him atop the IMF. Lauchlin Curie was the administrative assistant for FDR and a Soviet spy. Likewise, Duncan Lee was the chief of staff for the OSS—the precursor to the CIA. FDR's vice president, Henry Wallace, may or may not have been a Soviet spy…but he sure as hell acted like one and associated with quite a few. I'll let you look that one up. Owen Lattimore helped us lose China at State. Joseph Davies also shilled for the Soviets as FDR's ambassador to the USSR. Harold Ickes was the Secretary of the Interior for President Franklin Delano fucking Roosevelt who ran the League for Peace and Democracy, a group run for Stalin. That's just during WWII and shortly after. Nothing has improved since then." The kids are stunned.

"Is it always Democrats?" asks one. "Is it always Yankees?" asks another. One of them looks like an Injun. The lighting here could be better. Justin prefers dim lighting. Speaking of dim, Queen's "Don't Stop Me Now" follows the Canucks.

"There is an argument to be made both ways. It appears being a Yankee Democrat is the main subset, aside from having three names and attending an Ivy League university or is as discriminating a factor as far as I can tell," I respond with a smile. "Doesn't mean there aren't others."

"What can we do? I mean not just us, but America?" Naive speaks and asks a good question.

"A lot of this is above our pay grade. Worrying about things we cannot control will drive you crazy. Focus not only on each day one at a time but each task one at a time. The baseball catcher, Rick Dempsey, once said something that applies:

> You have to play this game right. You have to think right. You're not trying to pull the ball all the time. You're not thinking, hey, we're going to kill them tomorrow—because that may not happen. You're not looking to do something all on your own. You've got to take it one game at a time, one hitter at a time. You've got to go on

doing the things you've talked about and agreed about beforehand. You can't get three outs at a time or five runs at a time. You've got to concentrate on each play, each hitter, each pitch. All this makes the game much slower and much clearer. It breaks it down to its smallest part. If you take the game like that—one pitch, one hitter, one inning at a time, and then one game at a time—the next thing you know, you look up, and you've won."

I look each JEEP in the eye one at a time to make sure they each got it. "That is how we will win on our end. Whatever your mission is, find your targets. Report what needs reporting through your analysts. Don't let the enemy surprise you. As boring as they usually are, they will surprise you in astonishing fashion on occasion. I'll tell you more about that once we are in the SCIF on Security Hill. Now that we have a near sufficiency of manning, start keeping logs of frequencies used by target and by date. We need to have reference libraries instead of a scant few older folks with information in our heads. Learn what your enemy is trying to accomplish. As you get acclimated, start thinking of other ways to improve the mission." It seems I have calmed them down. "When and what is the next step in your in-processing?"

"Dunno. They didn't seem to know what to do or why," said some young handsome black kid in well-spoken disappointment.

"If they were worthwhile, they wouldn't be clerks. Give me a minute," I tell the promising kid. "Be right back. Have anything other than Michelob to drink?" I ask Justin.

"Not for you," he responds slyly. He looks at the masses and says, "In a few minutes, all of you need to hit the Class VI and get your own beer and more." In response to the questions in their eyes (I don't think any of them are twenty-one years of age), he says, "Welcome to an overseas assignment."

Jack McInnes's room is on the first floor on the other end of the barracks. I tell him of the situation with the kids, and he brightens up from his solitude and says he will get right on it. I make sure he knows he has me at his beck and call to be his designated asshole. He smiles and responds, "I am going to enlighten the new group commander—he seems okay. Oh, and watch your ass. I hear he is going to visit us."

Wow. That is news. The last guy, the most useless man ever created, was the worst commander possible. Once, we had a war exercise and, because he was uncomfortable wearing chem gear, said five minutes into the exercise, "Exercise over." I am betting he was on the horrible side of affirmative action. Elevated before he was ready. Promoted when no one thought they could fire him for fear of calls of racism. He came to the intelligence gathering building only once… and was humiliated. Gave a speech in the Fish Bowl, and everyone draped him surreptitiously with taped paper with messages on them like "I killed Rock Hudson." His crowd started laughing, and this bastard thought he was funny. Sad. When he retired, no one accepted the invite to his going away party. He ordered everyone in the unit, with a threat of an Article 15 to all ranking from senior NCO on up, to attend. No one did. And no, it was not racism. White, black, yellow, red, plaid, polka-dotted, or striped, if you are capable, you are fine with all of us. Useless in this mission, and you will be lucky to leave upright. The mission is that important. Thank you, Air Force and that new term—political correctness. You are racist in setting up people to fail. A fad that will soon end, God willing.

Of course, the true prize winner was our last flight commander. Got her commission in college majoring in the flute. A Charlie Flight commander who did not reflect her troops with her vacant eyes and flaccid body. She stuck out like a Jew with an ant farm except that both of those are usually capable and efficient, in my experience. During our last war exercise, she didn't know what to do…so she sat down and cried. I hear we are getting another woman to replace her. Oh goody. Whomever is pending has to be an improvement, right? Flute, the dumb blonde bitch we had before, is long gone, thank God. Everything has improved with no one in the flight commander chair. Addition by subtraction.

I walk back into Justin's room. "We are on hold, but your situation should be unfucked shortly," I inform our new comrades.

"When?" I ask Justin. He shrugs his shoulders. "You are cutting into my cocktail and tail hour, damn it," I respond. He shrugs. Maybe Yankees have few polite responses. After all, he is a friend.

Justin follows up with, "Come back here, BYOB, and we will answer your questions and more. Tell your friends. I hear the weather is going to get raw tonight, so you should stay in. Besides, you will have appointments first thing in the morning. Miss them due to too much drink and you are fucked." Good man. I volunteer to attend and help while the kids all agree it is a good plan. Justin gives directions to the Class VI as they start leaving. "If you do not find us here, look in the dayrooms."

I wink at Justin and blow him a kiss, and once again, all the kids are probably now questioning my sexuality. Funny. Back to my room to check on my lazy, needy, and perpetually horny roommate. No joy. I remember to check on Smitty. I visit the main desk first. Only four of the six beers from yesterday are gone, but he seems to have calmed down. It appears he has only recently gotten back on shift. Once he sees me, he brightens up. "Smitty is in as good a place as possible. The bitches and some friends are with him, and the Preacher keeps checking on him. I bet he wouldn't mind seeing you though," he finishes.

I assure him that was already my planned next step and thank him. I trudge up to the third floor to his room. After a polite knock and a welcoming word, I walk in. He was right; it isn't just the bitches, but other people are there, mostly black. I disregard this unintentional racism and ask Smitty what I can do.

"*You* bought the bottle, didn't you, Hal?" Yeesh.

"Well, yeah, but I was too shy to ask for everyone to buy in. What's the SITREP?"

"Early word is that I am going home. Honorable discharge due to emergency. Yes, going home now is a shock. How do I provide for the kids? Jobs are scarce and low-paying back home," he admits. Damn, I had not thought about that. I think he told me once that he was from the toolies way down South. I assure him that I will put that issue to the test. He brightens.

"I will let you know what I find out. Do you have an address back home? You may be leaving in a Yankee second to take care of those kids." He responds by writing an address on a nearby piece of foolscap and stands to hand it to me.

"Thanks," he says this with real meaning and then gives me a more meaningful hug. I return the hug, and I am happy to see the tear has left his eye. It's all going to work out. Thank God.

I go back to Jack's room and tell him about Smitty. He hadn't heard but thanks me for taking the lead. I tell him what Smitty is facing at home, and Jack says that there may be a path to a Veterans Administration job or something else. He assures me he will pursue this as well. I raise an eyebrow, and he responds with, "I got this and will update you." I assure him I am depending on it. Then again, if there is someone more dependable than Jack, I want to meet them.

The roommate had crawled back to the room while I was out and promptly asked me, the nanosecond I entered the room, to buy him cigarettes from the machine down the hall. He was on his floor futon lying about in a completely invertebrate manner, smoking what must be his last fag. I respond with something along the lines that the lazy bastard in my room can get them himself. He grins in response. Damn if he isn't a sloth.

"Anyone I know?" He shakes his head, but answers with, "She'd get me the cigarettes though."

I am guessing this one is not a supermodel. Graham does not discriminate based on looks despite being handsome, if some women are to be believed. Like I said, my roommate is a true democrat. Whomever this one is sounds grateful. Poor girl. I spend a bit of time sorting out my gear and uniforms for work and such. Then I decide I gotta go, so I saddle up with a bottle of Tennessee's finest and a beer in each back pocket of my jeans. No shoes and jeans cuffed up like a degenerate Huck Finn complete the look.

Once I get down to the first floor from the second, I turn left toward Justin's room and nearly run into that tech sergeant who nodded and smiled at me after I knocked out the bellowing acting dorm chief. He is still wearing a bathrobe. Maybe he thinks he is Hugh Hefner. I cannot remember his name. He seems nice enough. We live in a transitory world. Probably can't wait to put on one more stripe so he can upgrade his digs. Unmarried senior NCOs live in better barracks...er, dorms.

"First, thanks. However, you cannot keep solving everything with your fists. That rat bastard needed a ride to the hospital...he might have a concussion, Hal." Hugh seems genuinely concerned. Getting in trouble for doing the Lord's work would be irritating. It's a little sad that he knows my name, and I have no idea who this guy is. Seems nice enough.

"Alright. Hey, it must be a cast iron bitch living on the first floor. Any ideas on how to get everyone to shut the fuck up? Signs or something?" I am clearly a caring, delicate flower petal.

"Dunno. I have to be somewhere, but let's follow up on this."

"Roger that. Have fun," I say ironically. Going somewhere with hardly any clothes on, I see. Hmmm...well, there are missions, and there are missions. All of it essential, of course. No doubt with some young bitch who wants to upgrade her station in life or some such by marrying above her pay grade.

After noticing we were standing and conversing on the exact spot where I delivered the concussion, I smile and proceed down the hall. I politely knocked before entering. Justin is packing up. He anticipates a large crowd. He may be right; there is quite the throng in his room already. I can't even enter. He and his six-pack of beer lead the way to the second-floor dayroom as there isn't a proper one on the first floor. I wait until all the kids are out of his room and shut the door. None of these kids look old enough to drive. God have mercy; we are going to win the Cold War with infants?

I finally arrive at the second-floor day room, and it is a bit more crowded than I anticipated. After all, it is much bigger than Justin's room. There is no place to sit, and I do not want to sit, but many of these children are standing and asking me to sit in their place. What the hell is wrong with these people? I must look elderly or something. Justin is sitting in the back, quiet and grinning at the scene. Smoking, but he is always smoking. Intelligent and quiet is my friend Justin. Not what one would expect from a damnyankee—normally they are more brash than Texans. Well, I think he is from upstate Noo Yawk. The only things he is lifting are Michelob beers and cigarettes. Prick.

I tell everyone to sit and calm down. "Operation: Mindcrime" by Queensryche is ending. I settle in and ask whomever the nerd with the boombox is to turn the music down. I like "Whole Lotta Rosie" by AC/DC as much as anyone, but this is the first lesson. "The first lesson is polite noise. We are all intermixed. Different flights and different missions. We have SIGINT folks, maintenance jockeys, electronics nerds, and more all in this barracks. All on different shifts. When you come to this building, shut the fuck up. It's just good manners." They all act like I have given them the word from God. Damn.

Whoever has the boom box was clearly not listening. Slayer is on, and the volume has been increased. A friend described Slayer as "Cream with a death wish." He was wrong. I ask for physical help to turn the noise down. Violence is administered, and the music is soon softer. Someone is now a new friend.

"My name is Hal." This is followed by various "we know who you are" stuff. What the hell?

"However, this is just us all getting to know life in Misawa and a wee bit of the mission without breaking any security rules. Don't hesitate, we are all colleagues. Any questions?" I am so nice.

"Why do you keep hitting everyone?" asks some kid from the teeming crowd. Quiet chuckling ensues.

"Not everyone was properly beaten as a child. The Bible teaches us to be each other's brother's keeper. Some people need a bat to the head to learn what they should have learned in their infancy," I answer delicately. "Some people need to be sorted out to help the rest. I don't advise it, being in constant trouble is not a great way to make a career." I pause. "Some people need a knock on the head to remember that they are not alone here." What a little jerk. Shrewd though.

"How bad is the outlook of our situation? I mean, are we going to lose the Cold War, and are we all going to die?" asks an exasperated young female. Wow, tits. Nah, gigantic tits. Imagine what she will look like when she is older. Yuck. There is hardly a more honest truism than breasts do not age well.

"It depends," I reply. "Our fate stands on a knife's edge. The work you do may decide the fate of the world."

I look about. "Seriously." The young lady has brought up a very good question…and has really serious tits. I don't even like tits, but damn; it's like looking at a car wreck. "Your work will decide the future of the Cold War and the world. Do we have a nuclear holocaust? Do we end up subjected to a bunch of Soviet puppet masters? Or do we win? What you do will decide this. No, I am not making this up." No one is pleased, it seems. Or I may be wrong. "Remember that this conflict has gone on for some time. It may be that we will be dead of old age before it is resolved." You can feel the tension lower after I say that last. Good.

"What's with the weather here?" asks someone with great trepidation and a Florida accent. Why is this day room so dim? I think I am going to blame Justin. Well, some trepidation-filled bitch needs an answer.

"Imagine living in Buffalo, Japan. We have one lake, Lake Ogawara, on our west and the Pacific on our east. In the lake, you will find Mitsubishi Zero fighter planes as they thought that lake would be a great place to practice attacking Pearl Harbor and more. However, you were asking about the weather. If you know Buffalo, Lake Erie is on its south, and Lake Ontario is to its north. So in the city, they have tons of snow during storms whereas a wee bit farther inland only gets an inch or two. Before you ask, yes, we should have put this base somewhere else. I hear it is far worse across the Sea of Japan in enemy territory. It is always wet enough to precipitate and cold enough to snow—well, for much of the year. What else?"

Bingo, an old salt around here like me, says he has to bingo. Needs to visit the ER. I wish him well. Some little cutie-pie seems awfully interested in these last proceedings. "Is he going to be alright?" the little chick asks desperately. I nod.

"Usually. And you are…?" I ask.

"Tanger. My friends call me Tango." She puts a hand up. "I know who you are." Had no idea I was so famous. Am I required reading back at Fort Devens? Imagine the outbrief. "Like in regular society, you will meet unsavory characters. Just because they are pretty fair intelligence operators and are well-read like Hal in Misawa, do *not* fall into their traps of intelligence success, drunkenness, and disrespect for authority..."

The end of "Born to Run" is on the chastened radio...damnyankee freak. Emmylou Harris follows. Niiice. Discussion ensues, thankfully without my assistance. I only interrupt the worst of it all. The nerd running the music needs some equilibrium. Really? God will send you to hell going from Emmylou Harris to The Human League. That is nearly as wrong as alcohol-free beer. No wonder the Soviets remain such a threat.

I scan the room. It is intermingled with us veterans and the new folks. What the...the next song is "Rock Rock (Till You Drop)" by Def Leppard. Def Leppard is not bad, but this music selection is like taking Imodium and laxatives and watching them fight it out. The world is going to hell in a handcart. I take a pull from my bottle of Tennessee's Finest. I hope to God, Jesus, Buddha, Allah, and L. Ron Hubbard that the National League is not being summoned Ouija-board-esque to ruin our game by gaining the DH. Amazing that the NFL is becoming so popular. I can understand the "Yea Team" from graduates rooting with their alumni in college, but the NFL? It's okay to watch during a storm with nothing to do, but still.

"Into the Fire" by Dokken is next. The world seems to be regulating itself. I am not saying I am a big fan—well, the guitarist is pretty good—but I was fearful of some Betty Boop thing after what was played. I realize I have been talked to, and I have not been listening.

"What are the Soviets like?" repeats some skinny dweeb. It occurs to me that I have no idea which ones will be on my shift and which ones I will be working with I have not met yet. Oh goody.

"Wait one," I say to the dweeb. "Do any of you know what flight you will be on after in-processing?" Empty looks respond. Great. Maybe we don't have a sufficiency of manning. I had not thought about the new bunch being spread out through four shifts. Shit. I leave just as Joe Satriani's epic "Satch Boogie" starts. Son of a...the things I do for the mission. Damn it all.

I ask them to enjoy their booze and conversation for a minute. Then I go to see Jack to make sure the kids are not only going to be served but situated into their shifts.

"I told you I got this. They were already argued over, but there was already a list to set them where they should be. Yes, a training plan in every block on each shift is already set up. And yes, we may be losing you to Block 3. Soon. A month or two at most. However, it could be any time. Sorry." The lines on Jack's face grow hard as he says this. I wonder if I am one of his only friends. Damn, if I am, he is truly close to friendless. Wow. I didn't know I'd feel like this with a male comrade—thought relationships were just a man/woman love thing and not a colleague. Guess I have always been popular. I had a million acquaintances and few close friends growing up.

"I know you got this. And maybe after I get situated in Block 3, you and I can improve both areas with better comms between the sections," I say again. I step back to start leaving when I am reminded of something. "Lots of the newbies are young women of military marrying age. We need to get you hitched and laid," I add with a smile. "I'll introduce you."

Jack gives a jagged grin and grabs my hand to shake it. "Done... and thanks." Nothing like putting the best face on disappointment.

"Seriously, at some point soon, come up to the second-floor dayroom. I am giving the kids the ins and outs of living here. You could come follow up to say that you are on top of taking care of the kids so they can see a real human is all over it. Also, after your brief entrance, I can praise you to the skies to the kids." He looks skeptical. "You are as dependable as gravity, Jack. And maybe some young female will take a look at you and be lured. Not every young lady is turned on by young roustabouts. Many like calm, reliable stability along with being married to a higher pay grade," I allow to his increased pleasure.

"Well, you are constantly putting burdens on me, but I will happily help the war effort," he responds. We both laugh. After mutual well wishes, I tell him I have to go, and I do. Besides, I forgot my JD up there. Must be the music that screwed me up. You, dear reader from the future, can imagine what a sacrifice it was to leave a Joe Satriani song.

I race up the stairs and turn right toward the dayroom. It's too close to my room in my opinion. When Baker Flight is on break, their bumpity hippity-hop bass-filled music shakes the building from the dayrooms. For some reason, many of our black, African-American, Negroes of color end up on Baker Flight. Black Flight. Other races are there as well. Maybe all the colors of the rainbow get stuck together. Oh well.

Looking through the haze of smoke and bodies, I find my bottle. Thank God.

"I saved it for you," says a familiar voice to my immediate right while a familiar hand is now in my left back pocket.

"Missed you, Stacy," I say and I did. Mr. Happy is instantly about to burst my jeans. Thank God Justin found a way to dim the lights to keep that unnoticed. The kids seem envious. First, I appear to be world famous. Second, I am seemingly dating Kirstie Alley.

"JEEPs, this is an old chum, Stacy Breaux. She just got here too, after an assignment on the other side of the planet. Stacy, JEEPs," I say with a sweeping gesture.

I was about to kiss, and possibly mount, Stacy when I hear something.

"Sir, you were going to tell me about the Soviets," says the dweeb. Shit. Figuratively fuck the Russians because I literally want to invade Stacy. With great difficulty, I maintain my outward calm until the radio geek starts playing that godawful song by Chris de Burgh, "Don't Pay the Ferryman."

"Who is the useless piece of shit playing the goddamn music!" I ask in a raspy stage whisper.

Someone with pimples answers. He explains that he is simply playing the Far East Network, aka Forced Entertainment Network. Looks like he is about to cry, and I am not sure he has not wet himself. I apologize a bit, and promptly ignore him.

I meet the other one's eye, and answering the dweeb, I say, "It depends on what you mean. The culture? The military? Their aims? Their lives? Their economy?"

"Perhaps you could give us an introductory overview. I mean, we want to go out and drink as well," the dweebs observe.

"Warriors drink together, Hoss," I answer a bit meanly. "The weather is a bit raw to go out in. It wouldn't do to end up in the brig or the hospital since you just got here. And you have in-processing to do in the morning. However, I'll do my best on the fly. Russia has always been fucked. They have always been behind in regard to civilization and scientific progress in every way despite the fact they have always had all the resources they needed to be great." I am about to go on when the little shit interrupts. Stacy seems fascinated, but I am not interested in her brain at the moment. Little shit.

"Yeah, but we need to learn about the Soviet Union and not ancient Russia," says the dweeb.

"Great," I answer sarcastically. "Do you really think the Russian character ended at communism and a name change?" He looks stunned. Apparently, he had not considered that. "Every change in Russia comes from the top, find a biography of Peter the Great. Robert Massie wrote a great book on that and more. Note how great change in Western democracies, usually America, comes from the bottom. You'll find statists who want to plan societies, and economies get upset at such innovations. America embraces change, even when unpleasant. A strict economy and state like the Soviet Union? Not so much." I take a good swallow and continue.

"The issue with the Soviets is manifold. They are more devious and patient than us, usually. Their HUMINT resources are the best, so they are able to steal our innovations. Our society is free, so they can infiltrate us whereas we would stick out like fur on a fish over there." Grand Funk Railroad comes on, "The Loco-Motion." I jump up from where I was leaning and do the dance. Stacy declines. I grab Tango and start a line. Everyone starts to smile. We are probably too loud, but it might be worth it. The kid with the radio is about to turn the sound up when I put my eyes on his and my fingers to my lips. Besides, "Magical Mystery Tour" was the next song. The Beatles are overrated. "Rock and Roll" by the mighty Led Zeppelin follows, but I again put my finger to my mouth. I then return to the topic at hand to the disappointment of Mr. Happy and delight to the little prick who asked about the Slavs.

"There are intricacies I will not cover here. How some Soviets are referred to as radish communists and so on." No one understands. "You should have gotten all of this in your training at Fort Devens. How many of you went through SERE[11] training?" I ask. Wow. No hands. No nods.

"What about the required Cold War training about the history and the SITREP of the Cold War?" I get vacant responses. What the...?

"Then what did you people do at Fort Devens?" I ask less impolitely.

The overall answer is something like they learned Morse code, but little else.

Maybe, we will lose this war...what the fuck are the tech schools doing? Son of a...

I am about to leave the room, go out of the building, and scream in disgust at the situation when Jack shows up. His presence brings me back into the world we live in and assures me that Smitty, the kids, and everything else has been taken care of. I tell him the rest, and he is shocked. *Shocked.* Then he tells me that the nerds behind the lines at the alphabet agencies think we are at the final battle or near the end of the Cold War. My reaction is not kind.

"What the fuck are these useless motherfuckers thinking? A bunch of kids not knowing anything and not reporting what they see because they don't know what they are looking at." Yes, an ongoing trend.

Jack interrupts. "Hey! Calm down. They think we have won." I look with derision. "Seriously, they think it is all over. They are even

---

[11] Air Force Survival, Evasion, Resistance, Escape (SERE) Specialists are the only DoD specialty specifically trained, equipped, organized, and employed to conduct SERE operations for the duration of their career.

thinking of reenacting the old idea of the Watchers program that never happened."

It takes all of us old salts a while to stop laughing. Then he looks at me. "Seriously." Now that is stupid. What the hell. Of course, my generation of operators knows what the Watchers program is because we received some education and training.

"Who would go?" I ask incredulously.

"I guess we will find out at work, huh?" Jack says, knowing he probably shouldn't have brought it up here. I catch him staring at Stacy.

"Oh, Stacy, this is Jack—a fine American. Jack, Stacy." As I say this, Stacy, on my right, puts her left hand back in my left back pocket, picks up my bottle from my right hand with her right hand, takes a swig, wipes her lips on my right shoulder, and says, "Hi, Jack." She hands the bottle back with imprecision, knocking my nuts a bit with the bottom of the bottle. "I have to debrief Hal." She has her face very close to mine. I can feel her breath on my right cheek.

I look at Jack. "Yeah, uh, we have to debrief each other…gotta go." Y&T's "Summertime Girls" is on the box.

"Oh, good luck," he responds with some envy.

We start to walk out of the dayroom, and Stacy calls back with, "Oh, he is totally getting lucky!"

Yes. Yes, I did. Stacy and sleep do not mix.

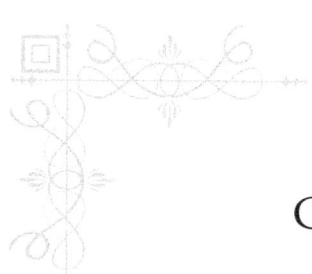

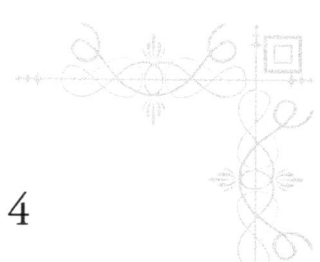

CHAPTER 4

Last Day Off

I awake with reluctance. It takes me a minute to place where I am. Stacy's room. Cool. The ceiling is not very interesting. Neither is the wall to my right. I look left and see plain generic panties on the nicest ass on the planet. The buttocks are attached to a female facing the other way, looking through a closet. Well, it sounds like closet rustling; my bleary eyes are transfixed.

She doesn't even turn around before she says, "You have a cute snore, Hal." She could feel my eyes. Yup, that ass has superpowers. She turns around with an impish smile. "I guess being a nudist in this room is becoming something of a tradition, huh?" Oh. Once again, I am completely nude on Stacy's bed looking like I am all ready for batting practice. She has a plain, generic face that has hints of intelligence and a gentle smile. I wonder if her personality is as epic as her butt.

"My apologies," I respond with a small amount of shame. "Of course, we Virginians are all about good manners and tradition."

"Shitshitshitshit…I am so sorry, er, again," adds someone from the powder room. Stacy is also nude.

"No, it was *my* pleasure," the roommate says with a bow. When she bows, her face gets way too close to the, uh, baseball bat. Don't women curtsy anymore? Damn…

"He needs to wash my back again," Stacy interrupts. Once again, she grabs my left hand and drags me up awkwardly. I am unsteadily walking toward the bathroom and the shower.

The roommate has walked to the far corner and adds, "Hey, Stace, someone came by and said your first day is the third shift tonight."

"Fuck! I have to work one night before the whole shift gets a few days off? They couldn't wait a day or three? Idiots!" Cajun ladies are delicate flower petals, huh? She turns to me and asks what I am doing tomorrow and is unhappy to discover that, apparently, my shift is relieving hers—maybe. I need coffee.

The roommate comes up behind me and slaps my ass with authority, which nearly causes me to jump through the ceiling. I land facing Ms. Perfect Ass. No, she is not entirely pretty but has friendly eyes that I can see just over the shot glass full of cheap bourbon she is handing me. "Here, you need some nutrients before…bathing Stacy. Find a way to clean out her fucking uncouth language while you're at it, okay?" she says this with quite the sly smile.

I drain the shot and do not fall into a coughing fit somehow. With a husky voice, I say, "Roger that, anything for God and country. Once more into the breach!" I declare this as I turn toward Stacy. I hear a wee giggle behind me. "Let's clean and cheer you up, pretty girl," I say to Stacy and her bountiful tits, which makes her smile a bit through the frown she had on.

"Pricks!" she adds as we make our way into a clean time.

"Nope, I only have one left, dear," I reply, which gives Stacy the soft laughs.

We enter the shower with a great lack of grace. "If I can walk after this, you are fired," she dares while looking directly into my eyes. Being an all-American boy, I do not disappoint. I even cleaned her mouth out. However, she is a wee bit heavier than she looks—or I need to bulk up. I just got her to her bed, and she started snoring the second her head hit the pillow. I barely remember to dress and leave quietly after leaving a note explaining that Able Flight is on swing shift, not mids, and to call for clarification. Perhaps Stacy could remind her shift she is still in-processing.

Wow. Charlie Flight's last day off and I do not feel like I have had time off yet. I have to hit the sack early to get to work tomorrow at NLT 0600 hours Lima.[12] As I slowly make my way down the first-floor hallway, I see Jack leaving his room on the other end of the building. I don't want to do anything except eat and take a nap. I am drained all the way though. Jack gives me the high sign and walks to me hurriedly. Shit. Maybe he just wants to ask me to join him at the chow hall. No.

"Hal! We have something we have to do," he says. Prick.

"I know. Eat. Recover. Get ready for fourteen days of work," I dutifully respond.

"No, your country needs you." He has this earnest expression as if we are going to waste commies right now. Scrawny Jack would lose a fight with a caterpillar. "Hey, do you still have that race car?"

"Nah, wrecked it driving on ice. Why, where are we going?"

He responds by leaving me for the dorm chief office. He grabs the phlegm-colored government phone and dials fewer buttons than are normally needed. Clearly military phones don't require the coloring of Air Force One. Jackie Kennedy blue is lovely. Maybe it was selected for camouflage reasons. Elegant camo job or whatever for the unfriendly skies. Who knows? Guess at some point, such an elegant color on Air Force One will be changed, probably by some other damnyankee. I am betting all military phones will remain fucked. Phlegm, like the buildings. Not, of course, morale building. I guess it is better than French pantalon rouge, but WWI horizon blue was gorgeous. Yes, I am worn out and sleepy.

"There will be a car in a minute," he assures me. He does not look at me but seems certain. Shit. I need a gut grenade,[13] ten cups of coffee, and a nap.

He starts walking through the front doors, and a nondescript car pulls up. We pile in, and the car moves before the door is shut or the seatbelts are on. What the...

The car travels off-base and into the surrounding countryside. Blue Oyster Cult's "(Don't Fear) The Reaper" plays softly. Soon, I have no idea where we are. Yes, I keep dozing off. Then the car stops,

---

[12] Zulu is zulu. Lima is local. Grow up—everyone knows this.
[13] An obnoxious hamburger.

and I am jolted to my senses. I look at Jack, but he is already headed out of his side of the back of the car. Yippee. I start to open my door on the right when a car nearly hits it. You keep forgetting how narrow these roads are. I get out. Very nice countryside. Terrible parking job. Rice fields among hills and mountains in the distance. Of course, I am wondering if I am being set up for a joke. How could the war mission be out here?

The car races off as I walk after Jack into what looks like a big shed or barn or whatever. Instead, it is a really cool dive. Some American who needs a haircut gestures for me to sit on the floor on the other side of a Japanese table where I would have to get a dirty ass on a floor that needs sweeping and sit cross-legged. I couldn't do the position in the first grade or even during my high school years running marathons. Flexibility is not essential to long-distance running. I bypass that and go to a fine table by a couch. He gets up and sits down facing me.

"I have heard a lot about you," he says with an intensely peculiar glare through light-brown hair and light sunglasses that are definitely not Ray-Bans. Aviators. He looks very 1973. A 'Nam vet? He also looks too young, slightly, to have been in that unfortunate conflict.

I just return his glance calmly. I have no idea why I am here. I am hungry. I am thirsty for coffee and, if I am ever fed, Jack Daniel's for dessert. I sit and wait. If this prick makes me wait long enough, I may doze off. Fucking Stacy will take it out of you. Then again, this prick might need an ass-whuppin'.

"You think you can take me, don't you?" he asks.

"I don't care. Get to the fucking point, asshole," I respond less than respectfully.

He laughs. "Sangfroid. Good. Did anyone tell you who I am?"

I answer with a shake of the head, but before I can follow up, Jack adds, "Hal, this is the Sage."

Jack came up behind me to say that. Otherwise, he has been on watch duty, I guess. Hmmm...perhaps Jack is more than I thought.

"Hi, Serge. What do you want from me?" I am nothing but polite and direct when some hippie asshole is keeping me from food and coffee and JD and happiness.

"In a bit. First, what do you need from me right now?" asks the semi-hippie.

"Three cups of strong coffee, breakfast or lunch, and a bottle of Jack Daniel's."

The hippie snaps his fingers, and I have it all in no time flat. Wow. I am impressed. Hot little Japanese girls all bearing stuff. If not for the Stacy Olympics, I could fuck all of them. He begs me to eat while he talks. Tough, but I do so. I tend to avoid being so impolite as to eat while someone is talking to me.

"You found it. The Sovs fucking up the INF Treaty. Good man," he says with a grand smile on his face.

"Yup." I am tearing up the coffee and Jap food. Hippie could have done better with the victuals, but I'd eat the ass out of a dead rhinoceros right now.

"I know the guys you met in the black suits," he follows... Hmmm...

"Did you like any of them?" I enjoy waiting for a response. The food and coffee are cheering me up.

"Well, I never liked the one you pissed on," he replies which gets a snort/laugh out of me.

The guys in the black suits...
Wow. Now *that* was a morning. Months ago, I showed up to work slightly hungover, burnt out from too much work, JD, and sex and was heading toward the head, as the Squids call it. Pugly, the short senior master sergeant, tells me I have to go ASAP to the ugly conference room. I reply with a "copy" and inform him of my biological requirements. He tells me the conference room comes first. Apparently, he isn't understanding how things work around here. Then again, I could use some manners when it comes to rank. I accede and head toward Ugly. Little Walter's "Roller Coaster" is playing on a nearby radio. Great tune.

I walk in to see two assholes in black suits. The door hit a third asshole when I flung the door in too hard. "Make this quick," I order. "I have to piss." Number 3 shuts the door and locks it. Now I am getting pissed in two ways.

"The fuck do you want?" I am asking this like I am Gunny with Western Pennsylvania syntax.

"Sit down," the short black-suited prick on the right side of the room orders while gesturing to a chair.

"Fuck you," I respond. Both of my hands are slipping off of my grasp on my manners.

I had not realized the second prick had made his way behind me. He grabbed my upper arms and tried to force me into one of the conference chairs—black to match their lovely funereal suits. After a short second of surprise, I get down on my haunches quickly as if I am playing catcher, which breaks his grasp, and leap up headbutting him in the chin with the top of my head. While he heads toward the floor, I punch and break Shorty's nose. Doorman (remember #3?) pulls some sort of chick gun while I spin toward him. Stupid bastard did not flick the safety off. I break his leg below the knee with my booted right foot while taking away his firearm. Before he starts shrieking like the bitch he is, I shove the gun in his mouth and punch his lights out.

Then I make my way around the long table toward where Mr. Lullaby League has dragged himself, leaving a trail of blood on the carpet. I kick him in the chin, knocking him out, and proceed to have the happiest piss I have ever had. Yes, on Mr. LL. It wouldn't do to have the poor lil' fella's face covered in blood, would it? The eons pass, and I still piss. My bladder was backed up all the way, man. Being a gentleman, I clean off the midget's suit a bit, too. When it is over, I feel rather good about God and the world he created. Ever know the feeling when you start pissing and it hurts because you waited too long? Yeah, but the removal of pain and discomfort of it is wonderful. Then I pick up the firearm, unload it, and slide it down the length of the table.

Practically tee-heeing at what I had just done, I walked quickly to the door before my workplace reported me as being AWOL. Just as I was reaching for the doorknob, a thought came to mind. I hit the door with the side of my fist and reported in an official-sounding voice, "The interrogation is over, open the door." A fourth black-suited prick opened the door and was quite surprised at the scene.

He had been about to say something to his buddies, but the vision shocked him. I threw him into a slide across the table like I did the pistol and locked the door from the outside. Funny how far he slid, too. Maybe he landed on piss boy. Turnabout is fair play, right?

As I was about to head to the Fish Bowl, I caught the eye of my roommate, the lazy and horny mediocre analyst, and motioned for him to alert my block that I was at work but needed a minute. Not normally the most efficient of mammals, I was pleased that he appeared to get right on it. I proceeded to Pugly's desk and start chewing him a new ass. Not exactly proper military bearing since everyone there outranked me, but I am not in the Navy; I don't like getting fucked in the ass.

"What did they want?" asked the Senior.

"I still don't know—who were they?" I screamed. I am looking down at him very close to his face. Eamons taught me well.

"You killed them?" the little fella shrieks. How are we going to win the Cold War with this? Damn.

"Not yet. Have someone you despise clean them and the room up, interrogate them to find out who the fuck they are, and charge them for assaulting an Airman," I retort. "You sent one of your people to meet strangers in a locked room?" I accuse the little motherfucker with a glare.

"I, uh, I didn't know!" What a pathetic excuse for a SNCO.

"Exactly," I say dismissively. I gesture vaguely and order, "Do as you're told."

Another SNCO, Fatty, walks up to me in anger and states, "You need to respect rank, mister."

"If I ever hear your voice again, I am going to put my boot knife in your throat, you fat sack of shit." I gesture toward the Fish Bowl and order, "Go to work or something." I leave the bastards in my dust, as it were. Then I finally get to my duty station. A day in the life...

Back to the conversation with the Sage...

My mind returns back to the Sage, his little Jap hotties, the end of my coffee, and victuals. It's nice out here. Quiet. I wonder who the

Sage works for and his specific mission. I am only inferring that he is okay based on what he has said in Jack's presence. Hmmm…

"Healthy appetite. Where do you put it?" The Sage is as big a prick as everyone else, I guess.

"My dick," I say, and he smiles.

"Stacy seems to think so. What do you think of her?" He seems to know everything.

"An old chum and good ER. Now who the fuck are you, and who do you work for?" His distractions did not work.

"ER?" He seems genuinely puzzled.

"Ejaculate receptacle. New generation lingo. Not losing wars anymore," I respond cruelly.

"Mmmm…how would you like to win or lose this one?" he asks while keeping his temper down.

"Depends on how this asset would be used. Right now, I think I am where I should be. Even the flight assholes think so. Now who are you, and who do you work for?" He thought I forgot.

He looks at Jack who responds with a nod. "A lot of our war effort is asymmetrical. I was in military service in the Army, and I am now an essential contractor for multiple alphabet agencies. Yes, I heard about your work on Charlie Flight. I know about how you found out about the INF Treaty[14] being broken. However, there is a genuine need to find out if the Cold War is really over. The Watchers idea is one way to confirm. Are we going to end with a bang or a whimper? We don't know. We want to proceed as soon as possible." He seems certain about this.

"Ever heard of a weather report? History? Want to wait a few weeks? If you people are this fucking stupid about these basic things, maybe I should stay where I am." He looks at me with newfound appreciation.

"You could be right. We had our blinders on. Worrying about political and other events instead of other things. I want you to be at the 'closed' nuke base to find out what is really going on." He holds a hand up. "Why? Because I will get the truth from you. Others will

---

[14] Intermediate-Range Nuclear Forces Treaty.

be pressured into stating what the brass wants." The hippie seems authentic. That damn base is a wee bit off the beaten path though.

I just now notice the music. "Minute by Minute" by the Doobie Brothers is on. How appropriate. I wonder if it is from FEN. "Who else is going?" I ask when I realize I have just given the impression that I will volunteer.

"No one you know. I also know the answer to your next question. Four, maybe five. I talked some silly twits out of sending a few score to the minimum necessary," he says with no small amount of self-satisfaction.

"Yeah, the Air Force wanted the CIA to send hundreds back in the day. It was when…about the end of the Berlin Airlift, wasn't it?" My question is received with slightly raised eyebrows.

"Thereabouts. We do have a problem or three." He raises a thumb as the first of fingers as he counts them out. "No one can know about this. You will be missed at your workplace in terms of collections lost. You have not received the training I think you need to get this done on the ops[15] side. The same with the others on the intel[16] side. Sending men to their deaths is always disappointing. Also, I want this over with as soon as possible. Your trip will be among the longest there and back," he concludes, fingers in the air. Sounds silly to me.

"The Sovs don't have many bases of that kind any further west in the Far East District," I observe. He grins.

"Smart boy. You are the only one going in from this side of the world. The others are going in from the European side where there are actual roads and methods of transport. Of course, you are also the only one who isn't fluent in Russian and so on. Yes, I agree that this is the more important side in terms of the Soviet Rocket Forces, but the higher-ups still look over the Atlantic Ocean before the Pacific for threats or land masses ripe for another war," the Sage says with certainty.

---

[15] Operations.
[16] Intelligence. Of course it is, you damn idiot.

"No wonder we keep fucking up wars on this side of the globe," I say as I shake my head. "Is there anything else? I have to get some things done and get sorted for work tomorrow. Oh, and how will we keep in touch as we prepare?" I am a bit done with this conversation and need to mentally digest what is to come with this mission.

Jack intercedes, "There is going to be a 'mandofun' softball tourney starting very soon as well. If Hal is missing, everyone will notice. If everyone sees him play, they will think nothing of him being gone for a wee bit afterward."

"Good. That gives us all time to set this up. Here, a going away present." The Sage snaps his fingers as he says this. He hands me a box with a case of a Japanese beer I had never heard of and a bottle of Jack Daniel's.

"The beer any good?" I ask skeptically.

"The best. It's so good, it'll give you a bigger hard-on than my girls here," he assures me.

We shake hands. He follows with, "It was a pleasure meeting you. I hadn't anticipated that."

"Likewise. My initial thoughts were wrong. Don't bother getting a haircut, hippie," I quip with a grin. "Oh, how do you maintain a cover and fund all of this?"

"I own a few of the bars that you have thrown up in. Much of the profit goes back into the mission and things 'off the books' that I do for God and country." Niiice.

I grunt in happiness at this state of affairs. "Get your ass back here alive after your little journey, and I will host the best party you have ever even dreamed of," the Sage says after tossing a carton of smokes at Jack.

"Deal." I nod and turn with my box of goodies toward where Jack was at the door only to find him pulling open the rear door of the same car that had taken off after our arrival. What an efficient operation.

I sit and contemplate what I have learned and with what I have been tasked. Jack is looking forward, all business, discreetly looking about as we meander back toward base on a different route than how we got here. I am lost amongst the different back roads and my future paths in terms of mission. As we get closer to base, I recognize vaguely familiar places. I ask Jack, "How long have you known the hippie?" Note my OPSEC. I am so damn awesome.

Jack doesn't even turn toward me. "Long enough. He may be a contributing factor in getting Smitty on his feet back in the world though."

Wow, the Sage has some influence. I wonder if that was held in reserve for my benefit had I been reticent in my agreeing on the mission. Then again, maybe I am reading into this too much in my natural arrogance. What if I am simply both capable enough and very expendable? The latter almost more so since I am certainly not, as Crosse put it, a "shiny little Airman." Independent thought and actions, even in the intelligence world, are about as welcome as a whore in church within the military. Of course, "soiled doves" should, but don't always seem to, belong in church. I have gotten laid more with good Christian girls I met in church than chicks at the bar. I guess my thoughts are wandering, huh?

We get to the barracks (dorms!) and get just enough time to get out of the car before it hauls ass. Jack looks like he wants to say something and stops. He turns toward the building with a brisk step when I talk to him.

"Jack." He turns back with many emotions playing around in his expression. "Thanks. For everything. It will all turn out okay," I say with the supreme confidence of one who has no idea what he is getting into.

He replies with a forced, crooked grin. "You bet."

I get back to my sorry excuse for a room and, after getting the alcohol stowed away, start getting ready for tomorrow. Stupidly, we are still wearing blues on day shift. I guess the new colonel is still getting settled in…that is, if he really is a good officer and will cut out the bullshit we have been dealing with since I got here. I wonder what the new flight commander will be like as well. She can't be worse than the last one. How did the last one even get into military service? Maybe sexism has achieved affirmative action's terrible racist aims, allow in the useless, and promote people before they are ready. All it does is add to the resentment of fools who don't think either should be in service. I hope the Slavs have equally limiting issues. I turn on my room radio. "Skating Away on the Thin Ice of the New Day" by Jethro Tull comes on. It gives me pause.

My work shirt and slacks now have enough starch to beat a person to death. The iron is on high, and I put them both to rights. I follow up with the rest of day shift's shirts and slacks. Ribbons on all the shirts. My boots are already shiny, but I improve them. Yes, I am one of those rare people who wears boots with blues—an old Achilles tendon injury acts up in low quarters. The Yardbirds' version of "I'm a Man" comes on the box. Wilson Pickett's "New Orleans" follows. Someone has their groove on. My washing was already done. I am distracting myself from my soon-to-be tasks for the Sage. Then I get the brainy idea to write down what I think I will need for my new trip, knowing it is a huge OPSEC violation. Yes, I will keep it hidden until I can get it all to the Sage:

- Accurate map(s) of routes to my destination(s) with waypoints.
- What am I bringing? How will I be dressed? Am I supposed to mingle through or avoid society? Will I have a fake ID and papers?
- Information about local cultures, industries, habits, etc. ad infinitum.
- Excuses for authorities—memorized lies or whatever.
- Contacts—how many, where, and who are they? What help can they provide?
- How do I meet the contacts safely?
- How do I leave the contacts safely (for their long-term safety)?
- Method(s) of transport.
- Equipment and rations.
- Options for dealing with Soviet authorities
- Once at the destination, what to note and how? (English language notes might be a disappointment if captured.) And how long should I stay? Why can't satellites do this

if they are sending in someone who does not speak the language?
- What to do when things go wrong? (Everyone knows that no OPLAN survives the first contact with the enemy.)
- How am I getting back?

A knock breaks my thoughts. "A moment." I stash my notes. "Come in."

It's Justin. "Haven't seen you about. You left with Kirstie Alley and never came back."

"That's because I came so many times with her," I say cruelly to a man who has not had a lot of female luck.

"There are kids in your dayroom that seem nervous. You are informative and funny…sometimes," he says with a grin. Before I can decline, he says, "They really need to know that all will be well. Barring that, they need to smile." That makes some sense.

"Alright. I think I am done here. Let me shake hands with the Devil, and I will be right there." Justin bows his head and leaves. Damn it. I just wanted to think, smoke, and drink. Little pricks. I take mine to the restroom as I said I would do.

I walk into the dayroom, and "You're All I've Got Tonight" by the Cars is on. Yeah, I bet a lot of these kids will be fucking each other due to being thousands of miles away from home and the fear of the uncertain. They all look up to me with such hope. Idiots.

"Well, you have already had some interesting times in the military. Does anyone want to share?"

"You first, Hal," says someone in the madding crowd. Sigh. The music comically is followed by the Quik's "Bert's Apple Crumble." Nice to hear a proper organ from time to time. Jon Lord can't do every damn thing, for Pete's sake.

"Okay. Remember that I was like you not too long ago. It doesn't take long to become this cynical, oversexed, and live a drunken, malnourished lifestyle that makes one question the existence of a benevolent, pro-American God." My words are greeted with bewilderment. Oh goody. It's like discussing metaphysics with fungi.

"Okay, like many of you recently, I was learning the craft at Fort Devens, Massachusetts. A group of us went by bus to Boston. And yes, by 'group of us,' I mean a bunch of naive young Southerners. We were wandering around in the late afternoon to early evening in some raw spring weather when one of us suggested we try to go to a bar, despite our youth. After the 'wow, reallys?' we walk into the nearest bar—O'Dowell's, if memory serves. I know right, an Irish bar in Bah-stun?" The crowd giggles at the memory of those damnyankee freaks and their hideously funny accents.

"We go in, and it is surprisingly busy considering the early hour. Now I had never been in a bar, but my comrades encouraged me to order a beer since I looked the oldest. Okay. Cream's 'I Feel Free' is playing on the bar stereo. I know, right? Makes one of the greatest bands sound like a stoned lounge band managed by Mr. Rogers. So I asked the barkeep for a beer. Immediately, I am confronted by a toothless drunken illiterate mick at the bar spouting nonsense."

"Yoo fahkin Suddenners...ya racshshist bahstids!"

"Wow. This damnyankee prick does not hold his punches, huh? All of this makes us Southerners look like guppies, all of us with our mouths open. Said damnyankee turned out to be the Energizer Bunny of insulters," I elaborate and some of my audience starts to recoil. I try to continue before I am interrupted.

"Weren't you part of the SpecOps team?" asks someone else from the crowd. Shit.

"No. I jumped once and went through SERE training like I am sure you did. Back to Boston. So this toothless, illiterate, drunken mick went on and on until he noticed nearly half of us were black. 'Who let the fahkin Niggas in heah?' he asked. Yeah, *we're* the racists. Freaks."

"Dude, you jumped?" asks some kid.

"Yeah, I was voluntold to jump with the Green Berets. All of my training sessions were canceled one by one. I was told what to do *on the plane*. I just figured I would do what the grunts did and it would all work out. One soldier showed me what to do with the parachute after takeoff. Some grizzled and scarred-up old NCO picked me up and said, 'Yew are about to jump outa perfectly good airplane wit a parachute made by the lowest possible bidder. What do you think about that, smurf?' I told him, 'I think it fucking sucks, Sergeant!' He told me I was a good boy and threw me out of the plane. After tumbling forever, I pulled the thing and proceeded to miss the landing zone and the post entirely. Some nice Yankee hick in an old pickup truck took me to the front gate. Good times."

An absurdly young-looking female (Tango?) looks irritated, small, and uncomfortable.

"Yes?" I ask.

"I hate when I go up North and go to restaurants, and the waiter comes to take my order, and I'm like 'do y'all have sweet tea?' And they're like 'no, sweetheart, but we have unsweetened iced tea, and we can give you some sugar packets!' I'm like no you fucking damnyankee because the tea is already cold so the sugar won't dissolve in it, and it'll all just sink to the bottom and be nasty! Learn basic solubility. This is ninth grade chemistry! That is why sweet tea exists in the first place, freak!" She got in such a tither, she was practically spitting like the Bahstun bar mick halfway through that diatribe.

There is a plethora of reactions, mostly laughing. I am laughing with a thumbs-up to said female. Someone observed as the radio is playing Billy Joel. "Anyone ever really listen to the "Piano Man"? For a song with that title, the harmonica player just won't shut the fuck up." Laughter ensues, less than before, thank God. Good though; I do not want this all to be about me. The Eurythmics' "Would I Lie To You?" starts to play, and I nearly start to dance. What a great pop song.

Some kid says, "It's like how the word *bed* looks like a bed. And *no* one is saying anything about this." Some laugh. They seem to be relaxing as Justin intended. He is smiling in the back and takes a pull on his Michelob. All that does is remind me I do not have my JD. Damn it. And that he is of no assistance on this goodwill mission.

Another says, "That's like how, in Florida, the further geographically north you go, the further culturally south you are." Now that is an apt observation.

"Hal, did you notice that some Airmen had better spit for shining boots when you were at tech school?" asks that Injun kid I noticed earlier.

"Oh, hell yes. I don't know how or why, but I bet it has to do with body chemistry and diet leading to a level of acidity or something in their spit." I see and hear there are some scoffers. "Hey there is a reason certain horses in parts of the country with the best water and grass are the best racehorses and why the best whiskey comes from a certain spring in Tennessee. Just the right amount of lime in the soil et cetera." Most come to reason. Some do not. Fuck 'em.

"Yeah, and grandma spit can clean any stain," says another kid with a rural Southern accent.

After some laughter, there are some rude observations about what little old ladies may have been like in their youth. "Yeah, I wonder if the queen from England ever sucked dick," wonders one. The Injun replies, "Dunno if it was all of them, but I bet Freddie Mercury did." Hilarity ensued. Good.

I put a finger to my lips and say, "I have some things to take care of before getting some rack time for work. Make sure you get enough rest before you start your first day. And keep a clear eye so you can sponge up the knowledge you need to save the world, okay?" They all thank me for coming by. Good, because I didn't want to be there in the first place. I wonder how many of these children will be on my flight. Guess I will find out.

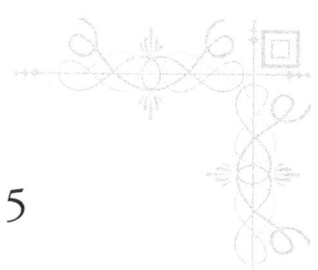

CHAPTER 5

First Day of Day Shift... Not Really Back at Work

After getting up at 0300 hours to go to the gym to work out, hitting the steam room, returning to the room to shower, and getting dolled up, I arrived at the chow hall just as it opened at 0500 hours. Of course, I had to bang on the doors to get the bastards to open the hell up. Aside from the dealers of death and food poisoning behind the food counters, there is just about no one there. It is usually a bit sparse this early, but still. I eat the swill while thinking of what the Sage and I discussed. Before I was confident. Now I am wondering how far I am in over my head.

I just barely catch the early bus, being currently carless, and arrive before nearly everyone on my shift. I like to get there early so I can catch the Soviet weather transmission. That is a fast-moving bitch of a Morse code message to copy at the end of the midnight shift. After making the long walk from the parking lot, through the security gate, past the half-assed takeout restaurant, and through a mile plus of hallways, I make it to Block 2 and the weather section. The handsome Baker Flight Negress at the weather desk raises a hand and then points a thumb at the Block 2 leader. I nod and go past the other mission desks, including my Soviet Rocket Forces section, and go to Sergeant Shmuck, or whatever his name is.

Of course, you'll note the hand gestures. This is not rudeness. Nearly everyone has headphones on trying to find enemy signals and record them. Rudeness would be excessive noise getting in the way of good Airmen trying to hear the godless communists through the static.

"You've been reassigned, Hal," Schmuck says, never even looking up but points a thumb toward Block 3. These people are all thumbs, I guess. "Oh, and here is a note," he says as I walk toward Block 3. I reach back for it, and it is from Stacy. I read it while on my way to the head of my new workplace. Apparently, she has more mission in-processing, but they understand they got her shift time wrong. Getting confused as to day/month/year is part of the shift work life. Somehow, I avoid tripping over the detritus of a long shift. I wonder if the previous Block 3 shift nerds are slobs or if it was an exciting night. It wouldn't do to throw away perfectly good intelligence data while assuming it was trash. "She Sells Sanctuary" by the Cult comes on as I continue toward the front of the block. Some kids have questions.

"Hal! Who is…"

"The Cult," I answer.

"Yeah, but who…"

"Billy Duffy."

"Yeah, but…"

"White Falcon," I tell the kid with an evil grin.

Before he begins again, I say, "Gretsch…because I am better than you," as I leave him in my dust. A senior master sergeant is at the front of Block 3 poring over some paperwork as I come up behind him.

"If one more useless motherfucker asks me a stupid question, I am going to snap his fucking neck." Whomever this is, I already like him. He must have seen my silhouetted shadow from the ceiling lights block the paperwork he is fussing with.

"Senior Airman Hjalmar Haroldsson at your service," I respond with amusement.

He turned around slowly on his wheeled office chair with a rueful look on his face. "Hal. I have heard about you. We have a *lot* to talk about. Sammy Watkins Jr. Sorry about the outburst." He doesn't look that sorry, but who cares? No wonder Jack likes him. Sammy and I are the only ones in the building in blues at the moment, which is how I figured he was in charge of Charlie Flight's Block 3.

At the same time, we both say, "I have bad news," which makes us both laugh. "Sir, you are now my boss, would you please be so kind as to go first," I allow.

"That damn fool Holstein of the 6920 Electronic Security Group HQ wants to have a mandofun softball tourney, starting today." He sees my expression. "No one got any notice. Early word is no one even knows if every shift and others can put out a team in time. If you don't mind, I'd like you to get Charlie Flight G2G[17] on this and show this bastard up. Okay with you?" He can tell I will hate this.

"Copy, sir. Will the HQ administrative pukes put out a team?" I ask through bared teeth in a regrettable tone of voice.

"Oh, it's better than that. They will have a team, and the chief is the head umpire for all games. No bias there, huh?" Sammy shakes his head.

I am, however, starting to like the idea. "That bastard has to be out in the sleet with us, with *all* of us?" I ask with increasing interest.

"Uh, yeah. So?"

"And he will get to watch us pound his obedient puppies into the freezing mud? This could be great!" My grin is obscene considering the early hour.

"Oh. Damn, you do have a hard streak. Makes sense though. Two things, you and I need to talk mission. Second, you had something you needed to tell me," he notes, showing a good memory and a skill for comprehensive listening too rare among us all.

"I don't mean to sound impertinent, but may I ask if you are cleared for it?" I ask with regret. Not the way to start out a work partnership, but it has to be done. "I will advocate for you to be included."

"Okay. If it is like that, make sure you go elsewhere, too…like picking up grub for us both. I like mine with butter," he says with a smile. Smart man. If I go to see Jack, I should make it seem like I am

---

[17] Good to go.

simply asking if he wants something from the Walkaway Diner up front. Very smart.

"Copy, and thanks," I reply, meaning it.

I see the Block 3 mid-shift leader leaving and I stop him. "Did you give a brief to Sammy?" A nod. Uh-huh. I drag the bastard to Sammy.

"Did you see the clusterfuck they left us with no brief at each station?" I tell my new boss. Sammy gets livid.

"You pricks!" I just keep him from punting this asshole into another universe. Damn.

"You, and I mean you personally, will clean up this clusterfuck. Then every fucking day, I will attend each brief from every station. Do *not* disappoint me, maggot." Sammy seems happy after this outburst.

I head over through Block 2 and catch Jack's eye. I nod toward the hallway that leads to the snack dive. He agrees not only to the idea but accompanies me to the loud, antiquated Japanese kitchen with the little old ladies. What the cackling little hens lack in Southern manners, they more than make up in Yankee efficiency…if stereotypes are to be believed. I tell Jack I will need to work the "vacation planning" through both Sammy and him and he agrees. Then we enter and stand in line. Like most things run by the Japanese, the little diner is strange and efficient as all get out. I should kidnap Bennie from downtown and have these little old ladies teach the bastard how Americans who are saving his country's ass from Soviet domination deserve to be treated.

You, dear reader from the future, might remember the takeout place. Enter on the right when arriving at the enormous building and snake to the left first in the bank-like twisting waiting line. We are about a half dozen people back in line, having just made one of the turns when the leftmost little old lady yells at me. Jack says, "butter," to me sotto voce. I grin and answer the LOL with eight walkaways, six with butter, two with mayonnaise. As you probably remember, a walkaway is a righteous, hangover-curing gift from God Almighty himself. An English muffin with fried ham, cheese, and eggs topped with either butter or mayonnaise. When asked if these are meals with tater tots and coffee, I respond the six with butter are but all need coffee. I don't know who needs what, but might as well impress with abundance. By the time we reach the register, everything is ready, and there is no need to see if it is correct. I ask for stirring straws, salt, pepper, hot sauce packets, cream, sugars, and lots of napkins. They are produced in the time it took me to hand over the money needed to pay the bill. Jack protests but is ignored. "I need you to join me at breakfast to work out regular mission and 'other' mission issues," I explain. Jack nods in resignation and helps carry the feast. I guess he thinks that, because he outranks me and is in on the whole other mission thing, he should pay. Nonsense.

We get back to the SIGINT area, and after nodding to Sammy, we enter the token admin room.

"No offense, but we need you to take your chair and redeploy until you are just outside this room," I tell the kid at the small desk with the secure phone. He is used to such treatment and leaves to sit in the Fish Bowl, not having a book, a newspaper, or anything…just moping. What does he expect? He is a receptionist for a phone that never rings.

Fatty makes his way to the room while we divvy up the food after seeing his kid got kicked out without his permission. He slams open the door and begins a tirade until he sees me. Then his face changes from rage to horror. I pull a boot knife and "race" toward him. He shrieks like a little girl and runs away. As he continues to run into the Fish Bowl, people sway and fall to get out of his way. No, I am not really running very fast, and I allow my comrades to catch me while still in the room. As I turn back around to them, who have the most fearful of faces, I greet them with an outlandish grin and a bit of giggling. Pursed lips and unconvincing hard looks greet my having had them both. Well, a bit. Fatty needs to die. One of the only things preventing that is my genuine fear of hell. I wonder if something might happen to supersede that. Wow, what a thought before a second breakfast. If I keep eating like this, I will either be a properly fueled athlete or a Hobbit.

"Bringing on the Heartbreak" by Def Leppard plays on the Forced Entertainment Network on a small radio in the corner by the kid's desk near the door—a rare, good song. I bet we will be listening to some outlandish chick music next. I divide the food on the generic table. Sammy is impressed at the variety and thoroughness of the whole operation. Jack is impressed with my generosity. I am thankful we are all together finally.

Sammy looks at my two sandwiches and says, "Goddamn Almighty, Hal! Where do you put it all? I bet you ate at the chow hall before work, after all." He means well, I guess.

"I burn it off dick first. Jack, the fucking tourney is starting today, and no one has a schedule." Might as well dive into it instead of sticking a toe in. "I'll follow up and recruit the usual suspects. Please get that to all supervisors, or let me kill the chief. Having every section know about the turn of events will help me when I get to every section—less explaining. Also, Sammy needs to be read in on my excursion so he knows how to set up his section accounting for my absence," I say to poor old Jack.

After getting the broad strokes on my improvised mission, Sammy replies, "Shit. I have heard good things about Hal, but this?" Nice to have a new supervisor concerned. "Then how am I supposed to set up my section and then adjust when he comes back?" That he asks as if I am guaranteed to come back is welcome. I am becoming less confident by the minute.

"Fire Woman" by the Cult comes on, and it reminds me of something. "Hey, can y'all keep an eye out for my ER while I am gone?" Jack nods, and that is good enough for me. We chow down. I can barely swallow the fact that FEN played two decent songs in a row. We continue eating, me more manic than my companions as I am playing catch-up since they ate while I described my imminent TDY. I wonder when I am going to meet the Sage while working *and* playing softball in inclement weather. I am sure Stacy will want to take some time away from sleep and mission as well. It will be too bad to give her the best fucking available on the planet and then leave her alone for a bit.

"Lady in Red" by Chris de Burgh comes on the box next. What is it about this asshole that drives heterosexual people with IQs approaching double digits or more to like this prick? I doubt he is

American. That's right; the other song he has is about a ferryman, I think. Most of that nonsense exists with those freaks in Europe with their high prices, lukewarm beer, weak defense forces, and bisexuality. Morons. FEN did finally strike back at us, though. Will the next be back to a good tune? The room is silent for a minute while we devour the grub. Oh, God no. I think the next song is called "Walk the Dinosaur" by some assholes who must be hell-bound for this travesty. Seriously? Dance music at this hour?

We are all near the end of breakfast, even the tater tots for the other two and most of the coffee. Sammy puts hot sauce on his tots. Obviously, we are barely able to handle the music when the next song comes up; "I'll Tumble 4 Ya" by Culture Club comes up. We all laugh, and I nearly lose walkaway number 2 that I was inhaling. After a coughing fit, I add, "They'll probably be playing 'Papa Don't Preach' next by that damn slut…er, what's-her-name."

"Hey, I think she is hot," retorts Jack.

"You'll be hot too after you fuck her, and she gives you multiple organisms," I add. There is generic and mostly universal laughter at this. It took Jack a second.

"Be fun while it lasted though," he responds.

"Fucking a snatch bigger than the Alaska Pipeline? No thanks, Hoss," I retort with a grin.

We all laugh. I am glad we all get along. Also, I am glad that rank is no issue with us. It usually isn't in the intelligence field, but it can be. That leads to douchebags like Fatty.

It's also nice we are able to let the moment relax as we think about next steps. Like watching a baseball game. When it appears to some that nothing is going on, real baseball fans know there are a thousand possibilities and adjustments available, and few will happen. Reflection is underrated. So is patience. For instance, you don't know a damn thing about how a baseball season is going during the first week or so. It's like watching an ocean tide; it takes a while to know whether it is coming in or out.

Sammy clears his throat and opens with, "I don't like losing my number 1 mission guy before I can even start with my new block.

That's one. I also get the impression that Hal's mission is just winging it. This is one mission that the Air Force should not wing." Nice pun.

Jack adds, "After thinking about it overnight, I agree on the latter. I have some ideas on the former…" and Jack floats a trial balloon or three.

I add, "It might be good for the kids to learn how to use the equipment and the basics while I am gone. When I get back, I can learn the new-to-me mission along with them and show them advanced ways to attack the mission." Nods show agreement to my idea. Of course, this assumes my absence will be short.

I add that I want a pipeline to the Sage so he can address my concerns and get me information. Jack starts looking like he is swimming poorly under a rising tide. "Delegate it somehow. Have the Sage arrange a drop-off or something. It'll all work out," I assure Jack. I add the same about the tourney. "Just get runners to advance the word." Jack looks relieved.

"I've Got a Tiger by the Tail" by Buck Owens comes on. How appropriate. How rare for FEN to play a country classic tune, too.

"Be better if you had a car again, Hal," Jack adds.

"I have the solution!" Sammy looks manic. He shocked the hell out of us both. "Shit! I have to get rid of an old car *right fucking now* and replace it with something fun that just arrived. Remember, only two cars for families and so on. So, Hal…want an old car?"

I grin. "Sure. How much JCI[18] has it got left on it?" It turns out it has as much JCI as my time in service before I can get out of the military or change duty stations. Kismet. We negotiate. The price is good, an allegedly great car on condition that I can fuck his wife if

---

[18] Japanese Compulsory Insurance—like our annual inspection back home, but the Nips are awesome about this. Every two years, all cars get inspected. Every bulb is replaced. Every wear part is replaced etc. The cars on Japan's roads were designed and built well. With this law, you never see a broken-down car in Japan. However, after a car is ten years old, it has to go through this every year. Which means a car bought for a case of beer and a blowjob needs $600 American every damn year to pay the JCI. Not a lot of old Nip cars are on the road because of this. Of course, the oldest cars are owned by Americans since we only stay temporarily. It all works out.

it breaks down, for $20 and a case of this supposed "great beer" recommended by the Sage. Sammy had neither drank it nor even heard of it. Perfect. We promise to take care of the transaction over lunch. I am off to recruit an ad hoc softball team instead of winning the Cold War. What the...as I walk out, "Godzilla" by Blue Oyster Cult comes on. Funny. Old Japanese cars tend to look like Matchbox toys. Godzilla likes to throw buildings and cars and whatnot.

First, I go back toward Block 8 to those geeks since my number 1 fellow softball coach, Happy, works back there. On the way, I see a couple of the usual suspects and ask if they are up for a softball tourney to beat up the other shifts but especially the HQ admin geeks. They give the thumbs-up, and I tell them I will pass out the schedule when I find out about it. As I circle around that part of the building, I pick my way through all the Buck Rogers equipment and wonder about the tiles I am on. Electricians are always using huge suction cups to get to the thousands of wires underneath us. I am glad the tiles are so strong.

I get to Happy's section, and Happy is not happy. Maybe it is because The Human League's "Fascination" is on a small FEN radio nearby. I tell him that I nominate him to lead the mandofun team, and I will be his number 2, like always. The wishy-washy geek starts to hem and haw and mumble. I hear him say something about his wife, and I let him have it. "Damn it! Just fuck that hot assed wife of yours into submission and put her in her damn place. Besides, you can sell it in many ways. First, you are the coach, the leader. Second, she can look like the dutiful wife and mother with her and the kids in the stands. Third, if you don't stop being her slave, she will leave you out of a lack of respect. Now are you in or not?" The truth does not always arrive with flowers and candy. It's not like I am arriving with smallpox blankets. He assents and his posture improves.

As I leave, he says, "Yeah, I'm in. And, Hal...thanks." I turn while still walking, smile at him, and continue on.

"Hmmm...you don't look bad in uniform either, Viking Talker," says Bridget. "Fuck her into submission?" I smile and give a light laugh in response. Then I tilt my head away from Block 8 toward where I am going. She follows.

"Glad you are on Charlie Flight, Bridget," I say when we are out of earshot. "Happy's wife is a housewife who treats him like shit—I think through a lack of self-esteem. Guess she needs a hobby or therapy. Which section are you working in?" I ask her. She is standing a little closer than is perfectly polite.

"Block 8 with Happy. Got to go. Good to see you, though," she says, looking up at me with a smile. I return her smile and go to continue my rounds until I am interrupted. "Oh, where is the in-processing paperwork drop-off?" she asks. Better to ask someone you know, I guess.

I turn and ask, "Do you know where Block 1 is?" She nods. "You will see what looks like a mail slot just past them as if you are on your way to get a walkaway immediately afterward in the wall on the right." I am so helpful. She gives me another smile and a thumbs-up. Now I really get back to my rounds when I see another jerk. We are near a radio that is playing Vivaldi's "Four Seasons, Autumn," if memory serves. Then I go forth to other sections, but I do make an observation.

"Milt! Goddamnit! Why don't your people know about the tourney?" Bad enough that I already don't like the man. No one over on this side knew about the softball games. The yelling is somewhat acceptable since there are no headphones, and it is all Buck Rogers crap that is, in the end, of no use since neither the NSA nor the CIA can figure out what they are recording. "Chief von Holstein ain't going to put his dick on your molars again if you keep fucking up his pet projects." By his look, he didn't know it was the top SNCO of the whole group who dreamed this nonsense up. I also see he doesn't really have a response. Then I am sickened by a sadly familiar odor. "And clean up your spic!" Lots of laughter erupts over that observation. I feel bad over those who have to work near that asshole. Clearly bathing and deodorant are foreign to the man. I forget his name. One big-bellied Mexican who is a surprisingly great runner. We need to dump a gallon of Lysol on his desk and him. And his Third World–sized family. Imagine what his house smells like. Yeesh…

I turn back past all of the black and gray racks of equipment with their black and gray areas with black and gray wiring over light gray and white tiles. If it weren't for the blinking lights on some of the equipment, this would be the most soulless place on earth—outside of a karaoke bar in the Dallas-Fort Worth airport, I guess. No wonder The Human League was playing earlier. This place must attract lifeless music. My announcement to DF[19] about the softball tourney is met with derision. Dirk haughtily tells me he only plays fast-pitch softball. "And I only fuck women. Thanks for your help the other night though," I respond. "Where did that POS end up?" He shrugs. I grin and leave.

I circle back toward my side of the building. I see that new squirrel, Corrina, nearing the female head. I ask if she is finding everything okay. "I have a husband," is her hasty response. I help her out.

"Didn't ask you to get on your knees. Besides, you'd have to get in line," I tell her. Through her semi-shocked expression, I wish her well and that I hope to meet her husband. She looked like she was about to say something, but I move on. Dumb cunt.

Just when I turned toward my new work area, I hear and see a commotion. It appears to be in the main hall passing the remaining blocks. There is a crowd in that hallway past block three in between the entrance to blocks one and two. As I get nearer, people get out of my way. Their expressions do not bode well. I get to an NCO I actually respect, and he fills me in. We call him "King!" and he hates it. More on that later.

"One of the new people fell through the tiles. She is between ten to fifteen feet down. Hit the edge with the back of her head and neck on the way down, so she may have a broken neck. She broke through some of the wiring, and she looks like she is stirring a bit. We are trying to get a rescue team here but getting them through security might take hours. If we wait, she might roll into an open wire and be electrocuted. Also, we may be shorted out, and the Soviets could do anything, and we wouldn't know it," the man on the spot says. He

---

[19] Direction finding. It's how we can confirm from where a signal is coming. They triangulate the signal direction from multiple bases. What this really means is that this is where guys who aren't very good at my mission go. Like a football defensive back really means "crappy wide receiver."

looked increasingly at wit's end as he spoke. "Does anyone recognize her?" he asks the crowd. Apparently not. I look and I do. Her face is covered in black hair, and her body position is almost ghastly, but I know who it is—Bridget. Shit.

I look at the man in charge, King, dead in the eye and ask, "Is there a way to lower me down to get her out?" Everyone expresses doubts, but I add, "I am the strongest skinny bastard here. That and I am willing to do it. So how do we get this done?" Ideas come forth, some of them better than others. A call goes out to our biggest and strongest to get over here. I ask if we can get the guys who work down in through the floor for ideas and equipment. Someone runs to get them. I take off my shirt[20] so as not to snag on a wire. I was about to take off my undershirt when Cobra says behind me, "You should keep that on, Hal." My expression shows I do not like the suggestion. He says that lifting a human might cause me to sweat and the undershirt may catch that sweat and not go into the exposed wires. Smart man. Big man as well. Not strong. Not so bad as to be called a bigger version of the Preacher, but, er, close.

I look to the HMFIC[21] and give him a preliminary plan. I look at some kid on my right and ask, "Do you know where DF is?" He looks confused, but a female voice behind him says she will help. I tell him, "Get Bam over here. Tell him we need the strongest, baddest motherfucker on Charlie Flight to save a life." The kid nods and goes the wrong way but is swiftly corrected. Bam is five foot six and was the top wrestler in the state of Wyoming. He is also the meanest bastard in this conflict. Doesn't play softball like other Americans. How he got married, I do not know. If he married Godzilla, that bitch would be barefoot and in the kitchen, doing as she was told.

I look back at the HMFIC and say that we need a medical team expedited into this secure area—none of the usual bullshit. And they need all the broken neck/spine shit with them. He is about to leave when I say he has to follow up with a plane on the deck at the flight

---

[20] This is the era of the utility uniform being those old green tuck-in shirts into green slacks. Of course, it being day shift under old rules from the previous commander, we are in our blues—in case you forgot.
[21] Head motherfucker in charge. Please tell me you knew that. Sheesh…

line ready to go or have a Japanese hospital on alert with an ambulance. The light goes on in his eyes; he grins and attacks. Advanced care does not exist on this base.

Bam and the electronics weenies show up at the same time. I explain to both what is needed. Bam says, "Let me do it, Hal...I can do this!" Good man. He might be five foot nothing, but I pity the fool who fights him. He is not thinking the situation through but already has his mad on. The strongest guys show up next. Good.

"I am not as strong as you, Bam. Besides, I have longer, skinnier arms. Would you trust me to lift both you and Bridget, or should I trust you to do so to me with the help of these other gentlemen?"

He thinks over the situation and nods. "You're right."

The equipment shows up, and we get it set up. The worst music of all time shows up, "Situation" by Yaz. Where is God when you need Him? The device we are going to use is a thing that has two spinning wheels, one above and one below the lip of the edge to act as a sort of pulley. The crowd gets excited, and I calm them down. "If you wake her up, she gets electrocuted, and the Sovs win the Cold War. Shut the fuck up!" I say this intensely and quietly with teeth bared, and it results in relative quiet. Almost immediately, the quiet becomes intense. You can feel it. There is a small piece of wood with wheels at the ends, like a car repair thing, that is lowered down from the winch. There is also a very thick length of thick rope that is attached around the bench to the bottom but lying on top. I confer with Bam.

"I go first. I will get on this damn thing, grab the rope, and get beneath it. If, for any reason, you feel electricity, let go. Don't follow me to hell if I get electrocuted. Remember, you have a wife."

"Yeah, but she is a bitch," says Bam. I grin.

"But she is *your* bitch. And she'll want to know how her husband was the most important man in a team saving someone." He seems to like my thinking. "Every hero deserves extra blow jobs, Hoss," I add with a smile.

I am about to go in. Some nerd tells me to cradle her head and neck. I nod. You know, because I have a third and fourth hand to handle the rest of her. Idiot.

I lower myself on the temporary deck, grab the rope, go below, and tell Bam to get on the top side.

I call above that I do not see any broken wires cut near where she lies, but that there are wires fucked en route. This makes everything easy for me. I tell the large mammals through Bam to get me down to the bottom. Quietly. Don't want to wake and stir her. Of course, the enormous pile of thick cables is where Bridget lies. The rope did not burn and break because of the winch wheels. I get there, and she stirs. I stop. Her eyes half open, and I tell her everything will be alright. That she is tired and needs to sleep. She smiles softly and nods off. When she does so, her head moves, and I catch it.

I call up to Bam and say, "Wait a sec…getting her sorted out." He copies, and I end up cradling her like a sleepy toddler. I hold her head and neck, use some rope to secure us, and wrap my legs around her and the lowered device after warning my comrade what I was going to do; Bam was not taking up the entire topside. I quietly call up, "Bam, go ahead up." I can hear the assholes up above increasing their volume. "And tell those assholes to shut the fuck up!" I say sotto voce.

Bam merely puts a finger to his lips, and the wimps shut the hell up. Wow. Physical fear rocks. The whole operation starts to rock a bit, so I ask Bam to tell the male Amazons to calm down. I also ask them to let him off gently and to do the same with us. He responds with a thumbs-up. I could go into combat with this bastard. Then again, he may not think the same about me. Roxy Music's "More Than This" is on. Yes. Now. While we are saving a life through great physical effort. Whatever…judging by the music, someone hates us all. The best of all possible worlds my ass.

I tell Bam to tell his guys to slow down and let him off slowly. Another thumbs-up. We approach the top and wait a moment. Bam gets off the platform. The guys yank too hard, and I yell, "Hey!" Inadvertently, of course. I understand. Bam is off, and the weight is lighter. I hear Bam berating them. Being Bam, this is not a delicate diktat for the operation. Bridget stirs. I continue to hold her head to my shoulder to keep her from having a further neck issue. The electronics nerds have told the big bastards to let them hold us above the opening and then for them to give us some lead so they can lay us both to the side of the hole. Smart. My arms and hands are still around Bridget's head and neck. I am using my lap, thighs, and more to support the rest of her.

She wakes up, reluctantly. "Hi. I..." And she passes out. People call me away, but I affix them all with a harsh look. I have her neck and body secure as we are placed on the floor beside the hole. We wait...and wait...

The HMFIC finally delivers. They are too enthusiastic, and I correct the med techs. I look into Bridget's eyes and ask if she had any problems with her head before. She answers with misty eyes and a soft grin, "Never had a complaint yet." I only let go when they have her head and neck secure. Others are taking over. Not as gently as I wish. Some military EMTs can be morons. She gives a thumbs-up, and I grin. I just stand there watching as she is wheeled away. I didn't see him coming, but Sammy was behind me.

"Damn, Hal. You are in the midst of everything," he says with an astonished expression.

"Sammy, need a favor. This will get out. Have Public Affairs get a sanitized version of the events with Bam as the hero," I say tersely. I reply to his quizzical look, "It wouldn't do to have my name out there considering the 'vacation' I am about to take. Besides, without Bam, this could not have happened. Add the gorillas and the floor electricians who got us the equipment as well, if you want."

"You aren't such a bad guy, Hal. When are we doing lunch to get you my car?"

"Fifteen minutes. I'll meet you just outside the security gate. I was finishing my softball recruiting when I found out Bridget fell through the floor. Oh, do you have the tourney schedule?"

He shakes his head and suggests we get it at 6920 ESG/HQ on our way to his car. He gets a side fist bump from me, and we both head our respective ways. I finish my recruiting run while putting on my shirt and make my way out of the gate. Sammy is already there with his van, and we go out of the secured area parking lot a quarter mile to HQ.

I tell him to hang out in the loop for a second while I dash in to get a schedule. I break into a run and go in to see my roommate's sometime flame. I forget her name. Dark hair and lightly tanned skin. She stands when I enter. Even from the side…niiice. Pretty. Dumb as a bag of hammers. Friendly. Athletic figure and great softball player, but too dumb to make good decisions in the field (e.g., when playing center field, even if the play is at second base, she will hurl the ball to home plate or even over the backstop, just to show she can). Like I said…idiot.

"Hi, Hal, remember me?" she asks coyly. Shit. What's her name?

"Of course! The supermodel who plays softball," I respond, and she blushes to the clavicle. Yes, I really have forgotten the hot dumbass's name.

"Everyone, especially us, needs a softball tournament schedule. Harder for the shift workers to adjust without knowledge beforehand, you see."

She looks slightly embarrassed. "Yeah, the new commander is not happy about the mandofun event but does not want to mess with his chief on his first day on station. I think they went to lunch to finish the schedule, and we should have it in an hour."

I thank her and inform, "The new commander may very well be judged at how well he can unfuck HQ. Maybe you can pass that onto him as if it is general scuttlebutt you have heard." She beams at the idea of someone thinking her smart and useful. "Gotta go. Oh, thanks." She replies with a shy smile. "Ah, how would you like to be another promoter of the mission and OPSEC?" She nods eagerly. "Tell the new patient that the 'Viking Talker' says keep his name out of this for mission reasons. Did you hear what happened in the building?" She shakes her head. "Oh, then I will tell her myself." The hot-assed admin has no idea what I am talking about.

Sammy looks at me with mild derision. "Guess she was cute, huh?" I reply with a recounting of what was said inside. He remains quiet for a moment and then, "You know, even when you use people, you do it for their benefit." I had no reply. Guess I was raised right.

We head on toward wherever the car is. It turns out it is at his house, the one Jack pointed out when we were coming back from that bar food run. An older but pretty woman about Sammy's age with wonderful baby-making hips comes out of the house. "I need the keys!" he calls out to her, pointing to a tiny copper-colored car. He just stands there waiting for the woman instead of going with her as I would.

"Your wife?"

"Oh. Yeah. I should have introduced you two, I guess. Want to fuck her?" he asks with a leer.

I sigh. "Nah, I avoid married women—even the pretty ones. Besides, I bet the car won't break down," I answer with both serious and mock sadness.

"Thanks. Twice over. Oh, here she is." His missus makes her way to us, and she is only looking at me, sizing me up. Like I said, nice hips. "Bobby, this is Hal. We are working together now." I incline my head, and she puts out her hand like a female Brit from a bad WWII movie. I shake her hand bitch-style. It wasn't quite put toward me Southern belle "please kiss my hand" style anyway, thank God.

"Nice to meet you, Hal," she says with a bit of a British accent through a slight lady mustache.

"Thanks," I say with a crooked grin. I have to admit that I stare as she walks back to the house when we leave.

I try to draw my attention to what Sammy is saying while trying not to stare at his wife's jeans. Apparently, this ancient car is both awesome and needs help getting aroused enough to work. It is a 1978 Hondamatic—essentially a Civic that is an automatic. Good thing too; I still don't know how to drive a stick very well. I should have asked about that before we all got caught up in events. We go to the main base office to get it changed into my name, and I drive Sammy to work with the promise that I will drive him home after work. Starting the thing is a gas, no pun intended. You have to pull a choke[22] out of the dash with your left hand after pumping the gas a few times, and then turn the ignition key. Then you have to let it

---

[22] Apparently, the foot pedal for a manual transmission would be called a clutch. Wouldn't want to piss off the people who actually know how things work, right? The thing I pull out of Penny's dash is a choke, not a clutch, for instance.

warm up. Once warmed up, it is invincible if Sammy isn't completely full of shit.

We got back to work to find things only mildly screwed up. Sammy begs off to get back to work. I ask if we have a softball tournament schedule since I have a moment between missions and block workplaces. The answer is no. I see Pugly and bring him up to speed.

"Now? That bastard is having the tournament now?" The Fred Flintstone–looking midget is clearly not all that pleased.

"Right. No one cared about the mission. They keep forgetting they are in a support position. Instead, they think we work for them," I remind the SNCO. Senior is shaking his head. "And we don't even know the schedule—the tourney is supposed to start today," I say with an evil grin.

Pugly goes red. "Wait-wait-wait-wait…it isn't just happening during rainy season, it is happening *right fucking now*?" Wow. The little fella is furious. I lean my head toward the admin room, the scene of the crime that was my second breakfast.

The kid gets up, assuming he is getting kicked out again. I lash out a wee bit, "Sit *down*, bitch!" The Senior starts to grin.

"Dunno if you'll turn out to be a great or horrible NCO, Hal, but it'll never be boring." He turns his head to the kid and tells him to get the big chief on the line, pronto. The kid is shaking but does as he is bid.

The kid stutters something to the effect that the chief cannot be disturbed because he is finalizing something with the new commander. Senior loses his mind. "Put us through on the speaker!" Somehow this happens.

"Greetings," says the new commander over our speaker. Senior is having none of it.

"Have you undone the clusterfuck that is this stupid fucking mandofun softball tournament to be held in the worst weather of the year in the middle of the most important mission transition we have ever had?" Senior's neck muscles are bulging. I could grow to like this son of a bitch.[23]

---

[23] Pronounced sumbetch, of course.

"Thank you for the information and the passion, sir," says our new Commander what's-his-name. "We just finished the final schedule. You have the early version, of course?"

"No, sir, no, sir, no, sir—most of us just found out today that there would be a tournament." You can feel the look the new commander is giving the chief over the phone. "On top of that, we are taking in a whole raft load of new kids and transfers on top of a large reorganization," says Senior. "This event should be canceled."

"Thank you, but it is a little late for that. I will have schedules sent by runner immediately," the colonel says.

"When exactly does this cluster start, sir? We had an incident in the midst of all of the moving mission parts. We may or may not have lost one of our new incoming NCOs today because of faulty work from your people's contractors." I could really like Pugly. He mutters the start of a "do you want me to mention you" type of thing, and I wave off. He doesn't need to know why.

"No, sir, I have insisted that we wait until tomorrow to start. Sorry, I realize this is still impolite notice, but it is what it is. I trust you and the other shifts and so on will adjust," the full bird says with lovely politeness, a rarity. I am almost eager to meet him. Almost. Still, the colonel added a "sir" to a senior enlisted man. Hmmm...I have met officers who think the enlisted are "the help."

"Sir, thank you. I look forward to meeting you and teaching you the mission and the organizational issues we face. Best wishes," Pugly ends.

"Copy all. Thank you for your concern. Out."

"How did I do?" asks the senior. I was not expecting that.

"Fine, sir. What do you think of the JEEP?" No, one does not normally call one's new commander a JEEP.

"He doesn't know shit about the mission, doesn't know what he is walking into...but he may turn out okay. You?"

I smile. "The same, sir. I have to get at it. Please let us know what the schedule is when it arrives. We have a lot of arranging to do when we know about it. Thanks." He grins. I think he might be starting to think I am all mission instead of all asshole. I hope so.

On my way to other issues, I mention to Sammy that this is the one day we leave work on time. He nods and does not look all that happy. I think he understands the weight upon him, and I will not be able to help him shoulder it in a few weeks. I empathize and sympathize. What a bitch of a situation. I hadn't thought about my absence being a problem, I guess. The mission, before, had become somewhat routine. Well, crazy in its own way, but routine. Damn.

Among my other travels, I catch a runner with the tourney schedule. Hmmm…thankfully, it's very short. Oh, and a short playoff. Niiice. That means we can meet the admin kids at one point at the beginning and then probably in the playoffs. Like I said, niiice. I am not saying we are the most talented team, but I think we are going to roll. I write out two quick copies and hand the original back to the runner.

I take Sammy home on time, and he asked if he can be on the team. Shit yeah, he can be on the team. I hear he is a slugger and a mediocre fielder. We'll adjust. We have too few people as it is. I thank him for the car as he leaves. He thanks me for allowing him to get some adventure vehicle. Okay. Remember, they don't really make those in the northern end of Honshu, Japan. I look forward to seeing whatever he bought with no regard for his wife in the same way he called for the keys.

On my way to the barracks, I decide to go to the medical center to check on Bridget's status. I go into a building too small to properly serve Misawa Air Base, Japan, and as I approach the check-in desks, I hear an angry voice. Pat Benatar's "Little Too Little" is playing on a small radio.

"You stupid maggots! You aren't sending me out to another hospital, and you cannot keep me here, so send me back to the barracks!" Ah, Bridget is okay.

"But we can't release you until it is in someone's care, and we don't want you driving and…" some clerk says. Dumbass. Glad I showed up.

The little Airman behind the desk looks up at me with a questioning expression but no words.

"I am here to pick up the Tech Sergeant Select. Yes, I have a car. Bridget, do they have your medications and bed rest orders good to go?" This is me bluffing. Her expression changes from serial killer to friendly. No wonder she isn't married...yet.

"All they have is their heads up their ass so far," she replies with something like relief with acidic drops of malice. "Nothing broken as far as they can tell with X-rays. Probably a concussion. I really don't remember much after you gave me directions to the drop-off," she adds with a self-admonishing shake of the head. I smile a small crooked smile in response.

"Good to hear." The morons are just standing there. "Maggots! Have you got her meds and paperwork sorted out or what? Knees to chest, knees to chest goddammit!" They all scurry, two of them into each other. Thank God they don't work on the hill with us. I guess the grandchildren of the Keystone Cops are now in the USAF.

We are just standing there, rather comfortable with each other. I wonder if she thinks I have been flirting or pursuing her when I have just tried to be a good man. I tell her that I am not to be mentioned if she is asked about the event. She does not understand but nods.

She looks up at me and asks, "Anything exciting happen after I tested the tiles?"

"As a matter of fact, yes. We are having a mandofun event. A softball tournament. Starting tomorrow in the sleet. Instead of sleeping, drinking or...er, whatever, we will be playing softball instead of dealing with all of the new Airmen," I say gesturing to include her, "or the tactical transition of existing personnel to other internal assignments."

"Let me guess, a senior NCO with garrison thinking and too much time on his hands," she mutters in disgust. I could grow to like this woman. "I bet the fighter wing on this base doesn't have to go through this shit," she remarks with admirable venom. Good girl. Knows her way around an Air Force, huh?

"Yup." Notice my changing my tone to match Miss Appalachia. "It is Chief Master Sergeant von Holstein of the 6920 ESG/HQ himself. Clearly, a genius," I add with a devilish grin. I look back down the medical hall and add, "Goddammit, why in the hell are we still here? Civilizations have risen and fallen since we told you maggots to do your damn job!" They all jump, but it does not look to be helping effectiveness. "We will lose the Cold War because you useless motherfuckers can't do your easy jobs, dammit!"

There is a stir not far from the midget and me. "One Thing Leads to Another" by the Fixx comes on the box. A colonel, who looks like a complete duffel bag, comes out wondering what is interfering with his siesta. Trying to become worthy in bearing of his rank, belied by his pajama-uniformed appearance, he tries to make the noise stop.

"What seems to be the bother," the useless bucket-head doctor says disinterestedly as he puts his shirt into his blues pants.

I put the bastard up against the wall. Hard. "Nothing works here, you useless maggot!" I startle the bastard. "How is your unit's incompetence affecting the fighter wing's performance and Security Hill's ability to win the Cold War?" I ask with an incredibly evil Eamons-esque grin into his face.

"I, uh, uh..." Impressive retort.

"IG[24] will be here shortly, dumbass," I say this just as Bridget gets her waiver slips and meds. I look at her, and she nods that she has all she needs. We walk out like we own the place. No, I am not even an NCO. That "colonel" needed sorting out.

We get to my fine new-to-me car, and Bridget laughs. I had been giving her glowing reviews that were not entirely false, but they were certainly misleading. She giggles and asks, "Remote fuel door opener?"

"Yup!" I answer with all sincerity and reach out from the driver's side out the window and pull it open.

"How and why will you be upgrading the stereo? I bet fueling this thing up already doubles its value." That's just mean...and sadly accurate. She gets in. No, I did not get the door for her. Thankfully she had waived me off. Didn't want her to think I was trying to flirt anyway. I have enough pussy problems at the moment.

---

[24] The Inspector General's office.

I start the poor thing after pumping the gas and pulling the dash choke, which gets Bridget laughing again. "We have to let it warm up," I explain. "I am going to buy a spare boombox and put it in the back to play tapes. Radios are not too expensive, and I will keep these tiny rear seats down since no proper American human, even most American kids, can fit in them."

"You might need a flight checklist to start this hunk of junk when you are hungover," she observes.

"Maybe. I guess it's like having sex with a frigid woman. It may take a while to get her going, but once she is, she can go for a long, long time," I say with a smile. This gives her a small grin until I ask, "Speaking of that, how was your date with Greenbaum?" Her smile is exchanged with a reproving look in her eyes that is not mad.

"Like I said, he is an old chum. It didn't work out before either," she says with a sigh. "Oh, and how is Stacy?"

"The same, crazy as a rat in a tin shithouse, but she has fun moments. Thank God she is on Able Flight or I would go nuts," I respond.

"Oh, so you two are not about to get married?" the little hillbilly asks with a crooked grin. Marrying remains an ever-present part of living in the military, as I have said before. Of course, instantaneous marriages lead to infidelity, horrible long-term relationships, and sometimes an evil divorce. At least there is the Class VI, huh? I put the car in gear to finally get the tile victim back to the barracks.

"You can put your dick in crazy and have a great time, but marriage? No," I respond. "I am not against marriage, but I am not looking to get married anytime soon with anyone. This freethinker wants to enjoy life a little all over the world until he gets married and ends up with the inevitable children."

"Huh. Well, someone like me will fail you in that regard. I can't have kids," she says with an expression that I cannot tell is regret or something else.

I take a detour through housing to see if I can see Sammy's "adventure vehicle." I do. I cannot believe it. I know it is a brand-new vehicle, or close enough, but really? A Suzuki Samurai? The adventure will be keeping that thing running. Oh, and it is a convertible like a diet Jeep Wrangler. Sheesh. I glance at Bridget with quite the reproving look.

"Whut?" She thinks she has irritated me, maybe by not being able to have children or whatever.

"Sammy bought a Suzuki Samurai. That is why he had to get rid of Penny here. Swear. To. God."

"Oh," she replies, sounding relieved. Then she giggles. "What the hell can he do with *that*? I don't think those things can even clear speed bumps." We both have a small laugh at Sammy's expense.

"Exactly. I see his other car is one of those Japanese vans—smaller than VW hippie vans. Damn." Well, I guess he has his reasons. I wonder what his wife would want. I wonder if he cares what she wants. The way she looked at me says she wouldn't mind if I found out what was within those awesome jeans of hers.

I drive slowly and make certain I do not turn corners quickly as is my wont in order to not further injure her neck. We get to the barracks and park in the dorm chief's spot. He is gone for the day and does not deserve a spot anyway. I wonder what he will try to do to us next. I had a previous roommate, before he got married, who had a great top-of-the-line Gibson Les Paul guitar with a Bigsby for no apparent reason. Me? I have a Japanese Les Paul copy by Fernandes. No, I have no idea why the Nip company named their company something Mexican. Anyway, the dorm chief once told us if we'd sell my roommate's guitar to him for $100, he'd stop harassing us. Said his son might like one. First, our guitars are ours. You know how it is; you bond with your guitar. Also, giving away nearly $2,000 of guitar, in a time when that was real money, for $100, was theft and worse. We said no and came just below threatening him with violence. He remains an irritating presence.

Bridget looks worried. "Are you allowed to park here?"

"Nope. Fuck him. Let's get to your room safely," I reply honestly. I want to see her safe in her room to make certain I do my part. After that? She is an adult. I guess we'll play it by ear at that point. She assents and we go. It turns out she is on the fourth floor. She has no problem getting up there, thankfully. Remember, no elevators.

We get to her room, and she unlocks the door. "Thanks," she says meaning it. At first, I thought she was about to give me a hug but stops herself and puts out her hand instead. I take it with a small grin.

"Hungry?"

"Famished, but I am too tired to go to the chow hall," she says with regret.

"I was thinking about having a meeting with the softball team over a beer in town. I can pick you up whatever you want—chicken, rice, etc." She brightens.

"Even though it was Appalachia, my Japanese mother raised me on Asian food. Whatever will be fine." She pauses. "Thanks...for everything. Really," she says as she gives my hand a squeeze. She had held it for longer than was necessary.

"Happy to help the war effort. I better get at it, huh? It may be about two hours or so until we get back, is that okay?" She is acceptable to the hardship, and I leave.

First, I hit Smitty's room to no response. Then I start making my way to the dorm chief's office, knowing that the big black bastard dorm chief won't be there that time of day, and on the way, I see a softball teammate—one big son of a bitch.[25] I tell Zeus what I am thinking with the caveat that I will be happy to buy the first round for all to attend if only he will dig up a few others to discuss strategy for the tourney. I tell him to meet me at the front door in twenty minutes, and he races off. Nice kid. Despite his "Bull" Luzinski-esque size, he isn't much of a slugger. Good man, nonetheless. He is not as slow as me, but it is close. At least I am quick. If you don't understand the difference, dear reader of the future, an explanation will not work.

I go to Jack's room, hearing Canned Heat's "Poor Moon" on the way, and update him on Bridget and hope for updates regarding the interesting vacation and other things.

---

[25] Pronounced sumbetch. I am betting you will never learn, dear reader from the future.

"I saw that. Damn. What is it about you?" I shrug in response. "Anyway, someone called about what you did at the medical center. Between us, good job. Officially, the medics are a little pissed but will be more so when the IG[26] I called shows up," he says with a grin. "Oh, good leaving your name out of the papers—per Sage." "Devil With a Blue Dress" by Mitch Ryder and the Detroit Wheels comes on from another room. Softly, but I hear it.

"Also, Smitty is almost out of here. State and federal agencies are on the mission of getting him a job, especially with the addition of being grateful for the publicity of helping a warfighter. Of course, they can use it as another instance of them helping minorities while supporting defense services in the press, etcetera, etcetera." It seems Jack abhors racism as I do, but I am glad Smitty will not be left in the wilderness.

"If those motherfuckers give Smitty less than his due, I will use my next leave to put my cowboy boot heel on that damn governor's neck," I add. "Tell Sage that Smitty is *not* to be treated like a nigger, but also to not give him a job above his abilities, setting him up to fail."

Jack appraises me and says, "You really care, don't you? That's nice." A rare nice from anyone. To Jack's benefit, he sounded like he genuinely meant it, and now I am suddenly surprised by the sad rarity of good manners these days. Pretty sure manners will return to our country soon. The hippies killed our country's sartorial display, and our manners followed. With the hippie generation getting old, our manners should return, right?

We have a nice moment thinking about we just learned when I remember to fully update him on Bridget's condition. I include the car acquisition and all of the funny aspects regarding Penny. I ask if he wants something on the food run I am making with the softball kids.

"Companions?" he asks with a raised eyebrow. "Better than 007s," I answer. Jack responds with a yes, the usual. He is about to look for money when I raise my hand.

---

[26] Inspector general. I already told you once. Pay attention, damn it!

"Fix the comms between us, especially me and the Sage. Take this." I hand him a full list for the Sage to ponder. "Sammy's right."

Jack grins. "Okay." He gives a small nod of assent and thanks me.

I make a brief stop at my room. Graham must be still fucking that girl. Poor bitch. No food for him.

I go to the dorm chief's office to ask the resident drone about Smitty. He says Smitty is about as good as gone as he can be, as far as he knows. It's the same good kid who I gave the six-pack to before. I pull a sealed JD pint out of my back left pocket and hand it to him. I ask that I be apprised at every change in Smitty's status. He tries to deny the need for Tennessee's Finest, but I assure him it is a happy gift. He glows and assures me that he will do what he can.

I am outside the front door in the still raw, gray weather waiting on the softball kids when I see that big kid, Zeus, huffing and puffing past the front door hither and yon inside the barracks. Funny. The Jeff Beck Group's "I Ain't Superstitious" is playing somewhere. The winter has made many of us out of shape. I work out at the gym as a stress reliever more than for any appearance or sports reasons. The steam room calms the muscles and helps sweat out all of the whiskey I frequently take in polite, medicinal doses. Although the sky is cloudy, the wind has died down, and much of the snow seems to be melting. The sky and the government phlegm-colored barracks do not match an ideal picture of nature very well. My barracks building is 672, between others. Well, I guess the buildings and the meeting of sludge, salt, and worse somewhat match the buildings.

Some kid comes up beside me with a small radio playing something I have never heard. "Duncan and Brady" by the Johnson Mountain Boys, he says. Against my better judgment, I kinda like it. Damn. It's like listening to Jimmy Reed for the first time. If you can hear a song like "Honest I Do," you will always be happy. The rest of the hillbilly music is also good while we wait for the absent maggots. I feel ready to leave them in the dust until I remember another JD pint in my other back pocket. I take a medicinal swig and continue to wait impatiently.

I was thinking about pulling. No, not all of the JD but from these slow motherfuckers. Fuck these morons. Well, I say that in my head until I hear "Christine Le Roy" by the same band. Damn. Did she kill them both? Did they kill her? What the hell? The same kid is playing this on his small tape player. I explain how the music is hitting me, and he says it is still the Johnson Mountain Boys—then he asks me about Bridget. Yes, I got her out of the hospital. Well, apparently, the two have a similar background, being from the same woods or whatever. I was about to ask more about him when the rest started coming out the front door.

"C'mon," I say, and I make my way toward the gate from the front door of the barracks. More call out as they see us leave the barracks and jog to catch up. I take another pull from my convenient rear pant pocket beverage, and they all remark about their absence of bringing their own electrolytes against the cold. Their bad. There is a bit of yacking, and some are asking for a swig, which gets them a stare from me. Fuck them. They can have their own cootie bottles. We'll be off base soon. Well, not that soon. We trudge through slightly less detritus of ice and snow than a few days ago and pass through the front gate to Companions. I tell them to order takeout one by one after me and go a few doors down to Karu's bar, Forevers, for a free beer. I make an order for takeout food and then tell Karu next door to wait a second for a large order for beer. I celebrate this by having a swig from my back pocket Jack Daniel's. He looks at me oddly, and I raise a finger for him to wait and smile. He smiles back with the notion that he has no idea what is going on.

I ask the next nerd who shows up to count how many are at Companions. When he comes back, I tell Karu to bring out a certain number of beers for my folks and I pay for it all. Karu starts to put out Japanese glasses, and I thank him. He gives me one with a smile as I give him a generous tip, but I tell the nerd beside me to wait to drink until everyone arrives. This takes a minute. Since he has to wait to drink, he tells the next one to wait for the beer, and he gives the same instructions and so on. Since these beers, as you will recall, are enormous, I am buying one for every two teammates.[27] I see an error just in time and ask for an alcohol-free beverage for Cretin. Karu gives me an uncertain look over giving anyone an alcohol-free drink but does so. I assure him we still need the already paid-for beer. He does as he is told, and I am G2G. Luckily, Cretin is the last to arrive, and I raise my suds and say, "L'chaim!" and drain my beer glass. Cretin is not happy with his club soda on the rocks with a lime. At least it looks the part. Besides, I tell him sotto voce that, in similar fashion, diabetics don't eat cake at birthday parties. He isn't happy, but he understands that I am trying to have his six. Donovan's "Barabajagal" is playing on the stereo.

As I continue to give Cretin a stern look, I tell everyone what is going on and the probable lineup tomorrow, the married folks like Happy and Sammy not being in attendance. Everyone is less than pleased until I tell them the benefits; we can beat not only the other shifts in the sleet, but we can beat the hell out of the administration jerks in this weather. Yes, Frenchy will be the umpire for all the games, so making his life miserable might be nice, which brings a gleam to the eye of every real man who has been here at Misawa for a few minutes. I also stress the limitations caused by the weather and its probable effect on field conditions. Then I propose some ideas on how to make the most of that situation, leading to nods all around. Then I go on as the tall beers are attacked relentlessly. I gesture to Karu to keep Cretin's glass filled with club soda, and he does, even adding a fresh slice of lime.

"It's a short series with roughly two games per shift. We aren't the best, but we are the most consistent. It's double elimination— you lose two games and you are done. In that manner, we can quickly get rid of teams and not have to play a long playoff; it will just be the two remaining teams playing a championship. We can do this. Also, with such biased officiating, when we meet in the one-game playoff, we can physically beat the hell out of the day-shift admin rabbits!" I conclude. Everyone cheers. Well, Cretin less so. I remind him with

---

[27] Trust me, this is quite generous. Normally one tall Nip beer serves four.

a look that I have his six. He nods and heads toward Companions. Good player, though.

I tell the rest that the greatest food on the planet is waiting next door. They should pick it up, take it home, and then get ready for work. I make certain Zeus knows the extra beer is for him that had been mistakenly ordered for Cretin in exchange for the big man's help. My orders are ready when I get to Companions, but I wait until all who immediately want their orders get theirs to make sure there are no issues. Those who wish to stay out and drink can figure their own selves out. When I finally leave after chatting up the workers at Companions, I find myself alone. When I get through the gate, I see a lone taxi. I hire him to take my load of food and me to the barracks. The kid at the front desk is sipping on the JD I gave him when I leave him a dose of good food and remind him of his obligation. He is speechless.[28] Jack McInnes is equally thankful for his food.

I go up to the fourth floor and give Bridget her dose. She must have been dozing but is thankful at my generosity of Japanese fried chicken, fried cheese gyoza, and fried rice. I pay it no mind and head to my room to eat my medicinal two doses—more than I distributed to the others. I am, as I said, a growing boy. Johnny Bond's "Hot Rod Lincoln" is soon playing on the room stereo. Niiice. Good times. Then, to get set for another day, I set up my sartorial display and gear for work. No, there is no roommate in sight. What a pity. Poor girl. For a good story, I might have let him have a dose of great food.

---

[28] Always have the people doing something for you taken care of; have their six. No, not just a thanks. It's not just good manners; it's good karma.

CHAPTER 6

Second Day of Day Shift

Day 2 of fourteen days on and three days off. I go to work after my usual visits to the gym, the shower, and chow hall. Nice to be able to just get in a car and drive whenever you want to get somewhere. Public transportation lacks a certain something. One hears that Europe and Japan have good train systems, so maybe it's only the United States that can't figure it out. My mind is wandering as I am still waking up. Chuck Berry's "Maybelline" is on the car radio. Some asshole said South Korea has great trains and the best buses on the planet. Hmmm...hard to focus. The weak chow hall coffee is not exactly helping the war mission. That and I am avoiding thinking about my pending trip. Probably for the best; why ponder when one knows so little?

I go through the lengthy walk of getting from the car to my new work area. Sammy is already there. Prick. He sees me and grins. "It's my wife's fault. She gets up ungodly early for her job at the BX since she just got promoted again." I remember his wife. For her age, damn if she didn't have some sweet baby-making hips.

"No kids?" I ask politely. I may have asked this before. Yes, I need coffee.

"Nah, we are too adventurous for that. When you return from your vacation, you should grab some bitch and come camping with us. We go everywhere." I put on a little smile and nod in reply.

"What is Block 3's coffee situation?" I ask, knowing I am a little foggy despite only the usual medicinal evening dosage of alcohol the night before and plenty of rest. Maybe it is all the changes going on. Maybe I need to go to church for the first time in forever. Maybe I should go to Stacy and get my ashes hauled. I realize I never went to Block 2 to check on her this morning. She probably thinks I am a jerk. Oh well. I'll leave a note on her door telling her the work and softball situation and ask if I can do anything for her.

"It sucks. I have my wife on that, she will get us a better coffee pot or whatever. My only worry is that other shifts will fuck it all up. Is there a place to store our gear?" he asks, and that is one perceptive observation. We should have a little folding table, snacks, and a righteous coffee maker. "Oh, anything you need, Hal? From the wife, I mean...at the BX." Forgive me if all I could immediately think of was grabbing those hips sans clothing and putting her to rights.

"First, let me check with some electricians. They may know of a storage area for a coffee setup. My barracks neighbor is a genius at devious shit like that. Second, I need a tape-playing boom box for the new automobile. Thanks for the car, by the way. It is perfect," I say, meaning it. "I need to have the patience to wait for it to properly warm up though. I forgot this morning, and the damn thing almost petered out."

"I know we shouldn't be taking lunch breaks, but I need to run an errand...want to join up? I can call the missus from here and have the boom box waiting," Sammy explains. I agree on the condition I get him his case of beer for the car—he already has the cash. We shake hands and get to the mission since shift change is just about to take place.

"I am going to check on Jack and the, uh, situation and then help the kids here, okay?" Scottie lifts a chin in assent at me and turns to his pseudo desk. Tom Petty and the Heartbreakers' "Anything That's Rock N' Roll" is ending on the little radio, followed by the Police's "Regatta de Blanc."

I walk the short walk to Block 2 and introduce myself to the new Block 2 leader, a female Senior Master Sergeant. Her uniform was creased, starched, and G2G, but the nametag is askew from her boobs at the side; the nametag looked like Derringer. I find out later she came from Dawg Flight due to a divorce. She seems okay. I see

Jack, and he raises a finger, letting me know that he saw me but is sorting things out.

I don't idle well, so I pace around the Block 2 equipment while I wait for Jack. I was wondering if I should tell the new Senior[29] if she knew of Jack and my situation and thought that I'd leave that to Jack. I am about to turn a corner when some kid I did not see coming stops and comes just shy of saluting me. At that hour, I am not sure if she clicked her heels like a Prussian, but she sure acted like a perky Prussian on happy juice. It doesn't go well with the music.

"Airman Michelle Tatiana DuBois, reporting for duty!" Oh god. Yes, lowercase god. God would never create this, would He? Not the best of all possible Airmen.

I try not to grin, and I think I succeed. I see an underemployed kid near me and motion for him to take care of this…whatever it is. A Sergeant Benjamin moment. I wander in from afar to see what happens to this ridiculous bitch.

She is introduced to the Senior by the kid with a bow. "May I present M. T. Da Balls." He bows again with a grin and leaves. The JEEP is astonished. The new block leader isn't having it.

"Nice to meet you, Balls," she begins. "C'mere." I could grow to like this woman. No garrison thinking from this one.

"What's so funny?" Jack asks, not having been privy to the scene. I tilt my head to the side, and we walk out toward the hallway where Bridget fell through the rabbit hole.

"What do you think of the new Senior?" I ask.

Jack shakes his head. "Too soon. She seems a bit blunt. Don't know what she knows about the mission."

"Okay. So, anything new from our friend?" Right to the point.

"I told him you have a ball game today and that you should keep your cover. He likes your early thoughts on the TDY and was already thinking along the same lines and more. He wants to see you after work tomorrow and after the game the day after tomorrow. Says it'll be a great way to drink for free and talk," Jack says as if he was

---

[29] Senior Master Sergeant, aka new Block 2 block leader.

told to memorize the speech. Not like him to be this way. Good man. Naturally smart man. It's just that I have never seen him like this.

"Agreed. Are you coming?" He nods. "Okay, then I guess I am driving, and you will be the navigator. Am I supposed to bring anything?"

"Nah," he says with a shake of his head. "Between you and me, I think he is impressed with you. I thought he was going to sub out for you or cancel the whole thing due to your lack of operational experience, but when he met you..." he shrugs. Wow. Is this a good thing? Dunno.

"Oh my. This is good," I say as I see another young woman going into Jack's block, Block 2. What a piece of ass. I don't even like blondes, but I am thinking thoughts that, er, never mind. I can't place it since she isn't beautiful or entirely shapely. You just take one look at her and want to get on all fours, bark, and roll around with her for a few days. Damn. She is followed by a brunette that is shaped like an elongated, sad upside-down pear. Maybe she has a nice personality.

"Damn, Jack, enjoy your hoochies," I say with a sly look.

The day goes as well as can be expected but too busy for Sammy and my lunch run. We would be missing too much of the mission. I wonder what the other shifts are going through. A couple of the kids on the team forgot their softball clothes and gloves, so after shift change, I drive them back and check on Bridget. It's lonely here when you don't know anyone at a new duty station and one is stuck in their room. I knock, and she answers, not expecting company. I do not think she has showered or combed her hair.

"How are you feeling? Any concussion symptoms? Any other symptoms?" I ask. She seems touched.

"I'm good. I owe you, by the way," she responds earnestly.

"After the Class VI run, I figure we're even." She gives me a small smile in response.

"So, Hal, what are your plans?" I have no idea how she is asking this. I am just trying to be nice. Her expression all the way around is a wee bit suggestive of...I don't know what.

"I have a softball game to win. Are you able to drive, or should I drive you to the game?" I ask this, thinking she will decline given her unkempt appearance.

"Shit yeah, I'll go! Wait one second," she said as she stirs around.

"You'll be in the same small car with some male children," I inform. She gives a mock double thumbs-up. Okay.

She finishes in no time at all, wearing sweatpants, short socks and sneakers, some sort of sports hoodie, and a baseball cap that has her copious black hair through the back adjustment area. Good enough. Appropriate for the event, actually. When I get outside with Bridget, the others are waiting for us. The head Dorm Chief is there, too.

"Goddammit! You cain'ts park in muh place!" He seems a bit animated.

"The only place you deserve is in hell, maggot," I say like Eamons' millimeter away from his face. "Fuck off or lose some stripes." I leave him fuming like one of the volcanoes that might end Japan.

We start to pile in when I tell the kid wanting to sit shotgun to make way for the lady. Then I tell Bridget to move the seat up so they don't go all Navy on each other by accident. They "tee-hee-hee" like children. Not exactly their war faces. There is so little room in the back of Penny that the two teammates are sideways knee to knee and unhappy.

We drive up back near Security Hill to the softball field. It looks like shit. It is as wet as a Filipina whore. Dirty and muddy as one, too. I tell the guys to jog around their positions to check on hidden puddles, especially in the outfield. I bet the administrative kids have them zeroed like a sniper with nothing else to do all damn day. I stretch. I am getting pissed. Then I see Jack in the stands. I walk over and give him some instructions. He nods and leaves.

We all start warming up our arms and such when the Chief, who gave us this clusterfuck, comes over and tells us we do not need to warm up. I know we are cutting into his cocktail hour by a few hours. The silly alcoholic bastard did not think about that when he dreamed this up.

"Do you really want good Airmen laid up for lack of good practices, Chief?" I ask.

"Besides, we have a real job. No one would miss you," adds Cretin. I could kiss him if not for the obvious. Good man. He gets a sour look from Frenchy.

Just then, the Chief gets slugged in the ribs with a softball bat. "Dammit, Chief, we are trying to warm up!" Sammy just grins and cocks the bat again. I have a hard time keeping my composure. Let's face it; poor Sammy is just warming up. Then I see a late vehicle. Good.

I walk over, and his wife is really bitter. He and the kids pile out, too.

"Hey, kids! Damn, your face is so long, I could putt on it, Happy. You know you could eat the soul out of a rainbow, Missus," I say with a dark glare to his wife. "Pull your head out of your hot ass, or you might lose what should be a happy life with Happy," I finish. Happy looks at me with horror. His Missus is about to start bawling at me when I help out.

"Making the usual scene will ruin your divorce and any idea of future love. Shush!" She is about to respond when I help her out. "No American man wants a bitter beer or a bitter bitch. Shut *up*!"

I look at Happy. "You see? I fixed your problems. Now don't fuck up the game," I tell him in a jaunty voice. He doesn't look jaunty at first, but after wrapping my arm around his shoulder while walking to the dugout and my giggling, he starts to grin.

Back at the dugout, I look at the team. They do not want to be here. Me neither. I should be fucking some chick. Or drinking and reading. "Look. That is the enemy. *Those* people are the reason we are out here. They have cheated us by being out here instead of drinking, fucking, and relaxing. These motherfuckers deserve an early death. They are no better than us at softball, and we are better warriors than them. And they have the officiating on their side. However, they are aimless, useless, and *we are warfighters*. These people are not worth the sweat and lint off our taint. We need to beat these people…and I mean *beat*. Play smart softball. Most teams lose games instead of win them. Oh, and I may have a secret weapon," I say with a finger to the lips. The boys cheer lustily. Niiice.

"Play ball!" says the fat, alcoholic bastard. I lead off...just to piss the bastard off. I take my time getting ready. There is an enormous frozen puddle behind the plate. The Chief is so up the catcher's ass to avoid being in said puddle that I have worries about their work relationship. I keep swinging off to the side, warming up to get rid of the giggles.

Also, I look out into the stands and see what I want to see. Kickass. Jack done good. They must have been on the way anyway, seeing the cheap beer cooler they brought with them. I look out to how they are playing me in the field. Predictable. Then I stand in the batter's box at the plate.

The first pitch is too low to be a proper arching softball pitch, and I try to nail it in a line drive toward right-center field but instead come around too hard and lace it to the shortstop's left, who was playing me to pull. He leaps to his left side and knocks it toward the back of second base just on the grass. He slips in the mud trying to chase it. The second baseman does the same. I race as fast as I can go toward first base where the big fat first baseman waits for a throw before the ball is fielded. I run into him, knocking him down but damn near knocking the wind out of me due to the size difference, while rounding first and heading toward second base. The second baseman, late with the ball and not seeing me turn to second, throws the ball without looking to first. I understand why the second baseman did it. What moron would head toward second at that point?

I am that moron.

There was no one to catch the errant throw at first since their first baseman slipped in the mud trying to get up to catch the unexpected throw after I knocked him down. I went to third and stopped there, thinking I should not press my luck. The completely unbiased umpire who is in charge of the admin kids pronounced that I just fucked up and said I was out for running into the first baseman. Hmmm...

"The first baseman was blocking the path," said another Chief with a mildly Boston accent. I smile. Jack done good.

"What?" the ump screams.

"You can't just call out people you don't like, Frenchy. Hal was interfered with. Everyone saw it," said Chief Bender. I could grow to like him and his slightly stronger Bah-stun accent. Clearly Chief Scumbag von Holstein did not see the other chiefs arrive. Chief Bender is sitting with some other old guy I do not recognize with the nice, large Styrofoam cooler full of beer. He toasts the umpire and says, "Play ball, boys."

Someone else from the stands called out to the umpire, "Yeah, you are as useless as a knitted condom!" Frenchy was less than amused, but the game continued. Spaz, our shortstop, grounded out. Sammy launched a long fly ball that was caught in deep center, so I tag up and score. Turns out to be our only score of the inning. After the inning, the umpire came up to our stands and admonished, "You people need to keep your military bearing even out of uniform."

Chief Bender spoke before anyone could insult him. "Respect is earned, me boyo."

"You've Got Another Thing Comin'" by Judas Priest comes on a radio in the Charlie Flight stands.

The game proceeded, and it was rather routine except for some surprisingly good fielding on both sides. The admin pukes had bad luck hitting since they would drive the ball right toward our guys. The only bit of excitement was when our second baseman, Gunn, due to a bad hop to the seeds, went down in pain at the bottom of the sixth inning. He was in a fetal position being surprisingly quiet, suppressing his pain. After a while, he composed himself but decided he should leave the field.

I looked at Happy. "Zeus to first?" He nodded. "Zeus, you're at first." Zeus got up off the bench, nearly forgot his glove, and I went to play second base. I looked at Townie on third and his roommate, Spaz, at shortstop and said, "Accurate throws to first, okay?" They nodded in knowing agreement. Zeus does not have my catching ability or mobility.

Some of the chatter in the stands and with our team was rather amusing. Jack told me not to get hurt after the first-inning first-base collision. "Jack, there's no kill switch on awesome."

Bingo is rather tall and was sitting in the stands near Bridget. She asked, "Do you play basketball?"

He responded, "Do you work for Santa?"

After one bad call, there were a lot of noisy boos, and someone yelled at the umpire, "Jesus would slap the shit out of you!" No doubt this was one of the many Airmen sharing Chief Bender's cooler full of beer. It sounded like Tango.

Rodriguez was eating loaded nachos from a vendor staged in the parking lot and was offering some to Balls. She demurred, saying she didn't like hot sauce. He told her, "Hot sauce is just sexy ketchup." She tried one and immediately went rogue, waving her hands in front of her mouth and breathing hard. Someone handed her a fresh beer, and she drank half of it. "Oh my...I don't even drink," she observed when she realized what she had just consumed. Then she started the waving hand bit again and finished the beer. The shamed look on her face was priceless. You'd have thought she just raped the Pope or something.

The studio version of "Free Bird" by Lynyrd Skynyrd comes on the radio next. Given the nature of the servicemen present, the live version may have shut the game down for a bit, it being the unofficial national anthem and all.

Tango soon started yacking Bingo's ear off from the opposite side of Bridget. He saw me looking at him in amusement when our side was hitting. His eyes were haunted. "It's no mistake man's best friend can't talk." He nodded in agreement and said he had to go to the ER. Once again, Tango seemed shocked and clueless. Oh well.

At the top of the last inning, I brought the team together by the bench. "Look, we only have a one-run lead. No more 'angry outs.' Skip trying to hit home runs, and flatten out your swings. Some will be caught, but others will go in between their fielders. We need baserunners. The field conditions suck, so it is to our advantage to do this. Got it?" They did, starting with Zeus. He barely got to first despite hitting the ball into right field. Thank God these games were confined to seven innings...this weather sucks ass.

Townie called out some encouragement to Zeus, "One million sperm, and *you* were the fastest?"

Everyone on the bench groaned at the thought of him clogging up the bases, but I was glad. "Look, guys, the running conditions are ripe for us to get hurt trying to haul ass around the bases. Be smart, we have a lot more games after this one is over," I remind them.

Cretin slammed a line drive to the center-left field fence and ended up with a double since Zeus was so slow to third. Even Sammy got on base by accident; he swung for the fence and hit it off the end of the bat. We ended up scoring five runs. The admin guys got two guys on base in the bottom of the inning, but we stranded them. Yes, we won 6–0. Niiice. The stands were filled with very happy, slightly tipsy cheering fans. I caught Bridget staring at me in a way that worried me. Didn't think I had done anything to warrant such admiration. Guess she is easily snowed…or still concussed.

We cleared the field for the next game. As I go to the stands to give Bridget a ride to the barracks, I see Happy's hot wife and kids. "Hi, Hal," she says with far too friendly a smile. I wonder how many beers she had consumed.

"Hello back. Congratulations, your wonderful husband pitched a great game," I say. "You are a lucky lady. Oh, I must take the patient back to the barracks. Take care." Before she continues, Sammy calls to me.

"Hey, Hal, Bobby Jo says she has a boom box waiting for you at the BX." Sammy is walking toward his "adventure vehicle." I think I hear Bridget giggle slightly. We stop at my new-to-me car, and he asks, "What do you think?"

"It's perfect. Thanks," I reply with a grin.

I unlock the passenger side and let Bridget in and then get in to perform the requirements to get the heap started. While it warms up, Bridget opens up. "I had no idea Happy's wife had it so bad. She wants your pants off…you can just tell. What are you going to do?" I fire a fag and think on this.

"Be correct and polite whenever I see her, but avoid her at every opportunity."

"You don't think she is attractive?"

"She is smoking hot, and were we both single, I'd rail her every chance I had. But I don't cheat, and I don't break up relationships," I say with polite conviction.

She is quiet for a few moments, and I put the car in gear. "Landslide" by Fleetwood Mac ends, and "The Boys of Summer" by Don Henley comes on.

"Oh, uh, how is your Stacy?" She seems to be uncertain about things all of a sudden.

"I have no idea. I don't know if we are a proper couple or not. We, uh, we don't talk that much," I say with a grin. "Next time I see her, I will ask. Don't worry, it was something I was curious about as well."

It's quiet as I drive the speed limit on roads that sometimes still have black ice spots. Well, quiet except for the soft sounds of ZZ Top's "La Grange" coming on in the background. I break the silence.

"Are you hungry?" She nods, looking happier. "Good, then let's hit the chow hall and chat, okay?" Her grin is back. Damn, I am just trying to be nice.

We get our less-than-appealing-looking food and go to sit down. I see people I know and go to a nearby table. Bridget sits next to me as if we are a couple instead of the other chairs. Sheesh.

"Great game, Hal," one says, and others chime in with agreement. "I know you don't really know me. Tommy from the other side of the building. I used to work near your old roommate. I'll be in Block 3 soon. Yes, he has told me stories like the one when he woke you from a drunken stupor to sing on his recorded rendition of 'Down South Jukin'' by Lynyrd Skynyrd. Then he let you pass back out!" he says laughing.

"Thank you for your kind words, sir," I say with mildly mocking humor and grin.

"We have to get together sometime. We can share tunes…I *live* for music," Tommy insists. "In fact, I live and die for rock." He gets a thumbs-up from me.

"You sing, too?" Bridget asks. Yeah, and I can speak Chinese as long as it is in English lettering on a menu. What is it with this chick?

"A bit," I answer and take a huge bite of military slop. It's something and cabbage. I'd tell you what else it was, but I can't. Maybe it has calories. We'll see. "I Need a Lover" by John Cougar starts playing quietly somewhere nearby.

"Wow. Oh, what was wrong with that girl—Balls?—drinking beer?" she asks as if Balls is not an American. "I think she said she is from Peoria, Illinois." Figures.

"She could be stupid or a Southern Baptist. I have no idea," I admit.

"I'm a Buddhist, and I really don't know much about Christianity," she replies.

"Like I said, I have no idea. Maybe her family is a temperance family, but it really should never have anything to do with Christianity." Bridget looks a bit bewildered. "Seriously. You were probably surrounded by Baptists growing up. We, other Christians, tolerate them. Think about it; thousands of years ago, juice had to be fermented like vegetables for preservation purposes. There was no refrigeration. No one drank grape juice; it was wine. For instance, Jesus's first miracle was at a wedding at Cana where he turned water into wine," I inform.

"No way. Seriously?" Everyone in the surrounding tables is listening to us. Just call me E. F. Hutton.

"Yes. The Bible is rife with instances of righteous partying. And there is more. I once educated a Muslim gentleman about the differences in Western religions. I said, 'A Jew does not recognize Christ as the son of God. A Protestant doesn't recognize the Pope as the leader of the church, and Southern Baptists do not recognize each other at the liquor store.'" Universal laughter ensues. Then something erupts. Oh my.

"Alcohol is evil!" Ah, Balls is here. Nice shrieking.

"That is like saying candy or fire is evil. Their overuse is evil, but they are not evil in and of themselves." I say with a calm lack of emotion. "Besides, although a drunkard may temporarily forget God, a prohibitionist tries to be God."

"Demon rum. You should be ashamed of yourself," she replies with taut emotion.

"Perhaps you will one day deal with the issue dispassionately and with common sense. You will find your current views defy Christianity and reason and will get over your methyphobia. There is a good reason our Lord Jesus made wine the center feature of the covenant. Please excuse me, I need to eat and entertain my patient. Good evening, Miss." Tension remains, but no one responds. Good.

I look at Bridget and say, "Now you have a deeper understanding, thanks to Balls."

"Wow. She is so passionate about it," Bridget says sotto voce.

I shrug my shoulders while I chew down some slop. "Another witch-burning damnyankee. Oh well. So, what would you like to talk about?" I am such a gentleman.

"Okay, why did you join up?"

"Family tradition. That and the fate of the world is in the balance. I couldn't not do my small part."

"Really? I just wanted to get out of eastern Kentucky. There is nothing there unless you are a coal miner."

Tommy interrupts, "That's right, I heard you were from the hills. Where exactly?"

"Outside of Paintsville. You?" she asks with increasing interest.

"Outside of Salyersville. We were practically neighbors and never met. Hal, Bridget is right. It is beautiful, but there is nothing there," Tommy adds. Ah, the young man that was playing hillbilly music by the Johnson Mountain Boys.

"So, how close are these thriving metropolises?" I ask with some amusement.

"Well..." Bridget starts and is slightly flummoxed for some reason.

"Close on a map and far away due to the difficulty of getting from point A to point B because of the rocky hills," informs Tommy.

"Thanks. I was trying to figure out a way to put it like that, but my brain froze."

"Ah, a first complaint about your head," I observe. Tommy is at a loss. Bridget grins.

There is a pause in the discussion as we all finish our alleged food. Bridget wipes her mouth with a paper napkin and asks, "When do you think you will see her again?" I know exactly which her she is referring to.

"No idea. However, we should all get ready for work. Are you done?" She nods.

We walk around the parking lot between the chow hall and barracks and into the building. When we reach the second floor, she looks at me and says, "I can get to my own room by myself, Viking Talker. Maybe another time." I give a slight smile and go to my room to get ready for another day.

CHAPTER 7

Third Day of Day Shift

Oh goody. Fourteen days on and three days off isn't the best idea in the world, but it is one solution in maintaining constant SIGINT vigilance against the commies. Besides, I felt pretty good after the usual gym visit, shower, and breakfast. I nearly forget to warm up my copper-colored gem of a car before putting her in gear. I did remember to bring cigarettes this time. A nice relaxing Camel ensures I let the car warm up for the right number of minutes. I take out a little notebook from my pocket and remind myself of things I have to get done today (e.g., pick up the boombox for the car, visit the off-base club owner for vacation tips, etc.). No names. OPSEC always.

Driving to work is a breeze in the little beater despite the dreadful weather. The wind gusts are moving the sleet sideways at over 30 mph. I know, I know; I am in a part of the world where the metric system is used. Well, even if most of the world using it, they are wrong. How do I know? If God wanted us to use the metric system, there would only have been ten apostles, so there. I'm just glad we aren't scheduled to play softball today.

I remember to pass by my old block where Stacy works on her shift. She has not been relieved but looks like she is ready to be done with her shift. At least she has a tired smile for me when she sees me coming up. "I've missed you," she says quietly with a gleam in her eye.

"Same here. How have you been getting along? Hope your roommate isn't too upset over my absence," I observe with a sly grin.

"She thinks I am lucky. Oh! A bunch of us are going to see Jerry Reed and his USO band tomorrow night! I'd love for you to come with us, but it's probably going to be a hen night—roommate included."

"Thanks for the offer, but I have a job-related task I have to take care of after tomorrow evening's softball game." Seeing her questioning look, I say, "Can't talk about it, but it's something I have to do—no big deal." I added that last bit rather unconvincingly to keep her from getting worried. "Looks like y'all are getting changed out. Get home safe. Pleasant dreams," I say, giving her hand a soft squeeze. She looks a little sad as I turn to walk away toward Block 3.

Sammy is making the rounds at each rack to get the changeover brief. I stand back behind him listening. When it is over, I ask, "What are the targets you copy at this rack?" The Airman tells me the USAF designation. "Yeah, but what Soviet units are they? You know that they know we, the 6920 ESG, are listening to them. Wouldn't it be nice for you to know who they are, what they are trying to accomplish, and with whom they are doing it?" All of the Airmen listening look shocked and impressed, Sammy only the latter.

"That will be all. Everyone with a relief on Able Flight can leave." Sammy looks at me and then puts his hand out. We shake and he states, "Now I really wish you weren't going TDY." I grin in response. "Why don't you help out the kids at their stations instead of getting on a rack yourself? Oh, and the Missus still has that radio for you."

"I'll stop by to get it on my way to the off-base meeting after work." He gives me a sour expression that combines a grimace and a smirk and goes to his desk up front in our block near the Fish Bowl. I do as he bade.

It turns out Tommy the hillbilly really is now on Block 3. He is digging his mission and the FEN station playing "Blow My Fuse" by Kix. Great song by an underrated band. Thankfully, Hesse is now in Block 1. Nice enough, but something about him barely being human freaks me out. Then Tommy calls to me, breaking through my thoughts on Hesse.

"Hal, meet Rocker. He plays a mean heavy metal guitar." I shake Rocker's hand with a grin. Black men playing guitar is sadly not the most common thing one sees anymore.

"So, do you get compared to modern black shredders like Vernon Reid and Tony MacAlpine, or guys like Hendrix?" I inquire, getting wide-eyed amazement from Rocker.

"You know your guitarists. But hey, do you know which black guitarist I really dig?" he asks with enthusiasm.

"Hopefully it's the Minneapolis Midget," I respond as he immediately begins nodding excitedly.

"What do you know about him?"

"He went to the same high school as my parents. Are you two okay with your equipment and assignments?" They nod. "Good men. I have to help the kids. Let's catch up sometime."

I bypass Walker. Justin likes him since they have served together since basic training, but I find him to be lazy in every regard. Every female thinks it's cute he wanders around the barracks in gym shorts that say "Da Butt" on his big ass. We call Zeus by his name because it stands for "Zero Enthusiasm Unless Supervised." Walker is lazier, at least during war exercises. I continue on and see a clusterfuck.

There she is, the girl with the vapid expression and train wreck tits. Isn't she too big around the waist for her height to be in the military? She has headsets on, and I can hear the Morse code coming through them from several feet away. I go over and knock gently on the tiny tabletop beside her so as not to startle her. I motion for her to take off her headset and then instruct her to turn down the volume.

"What's wrong?" I ask softly. She looks like she is about to cry.

"I don't know what to do!" she responds just shy of bursting into sobs and leaking.

"It's okay. First things first, once you lose your hearing, it never comes back. Besides, it is easier to concentrate when the volume is much lower, okay?" She nods with a tiny smile while wiping a tear away and turning down the sound levels. "Now, how did you find this target?"

"The guy who left the last shift said we have to copy this target whenever he sends," she replies.

"Good. Remember, I am learning the Block 3 mission, too. The code sounds pretty easy. You passed tech school when so many did not, so you must be plenty good enough to do this, okay?" She begins to sit up a bit and nods. "Then you take care of this doing nothing more or less than what you have been taught. If you need any help, you just ask."

"Thank you, Hal," she says in her soft, tiny child's voice. Clearly this transition is going a little too fast and not managed well enough no matter what anyone says.

I walk the rest of the way to the front of the block to Sammy. "Mind if I put on some cans and dig around?" I ask him. He gives an expansive wave. I am about to walk away when I remember to ask, "Is there a continuity book of targets and mission SITREP around here?" He looks at me like I am asking, were he a lottery winner, if he wanted the annual payout or all of the money now. The best he can give me is a smirk, a shoulder shrug, and another expansive wave. Block 3 really is in deep kimchi, huh?

I check through some dusty cabinets and areas for a good while looking for search data when I decide I need a break. I go to my station at the top of the block across from Sammy and hook up my headsets. You remember what those were like. Not like the old "cans," but proper big headsets that you could wear around your shoulders and shrug up a shoulder if you heard something. My tennis wristbands around the earpieces are striped, unlike the usual plain black-colored ones most of my comrades used. Yes, there is a reason. I check my Racal radios and my new "computer." I miss the old teletypes despite the hard typing one had to do. I don't miss hearing the bitching about hand arthritis from the old-timers over the hard-punching one had to do on them. I still punch the keys too hard out of habit from the damn things.

"Hal!" Apparently, Walker is alive and actually working. Perhaps he is only lazy with manual labor. I tilt back my head to acknowledge him. "Got something weird, but can't dial it in." He gives me the frequencies,[30] and I dig in.

I follow up with a "got 'em" and ask him to direct DF on them. Just hearing them is very difficult. I wonder how far away the bastards are. Glad he got me on this as they are sending me *Z* codes. To refresh your memory, the commies send Morse code with the letter *Z* to be followed up with a two-letter/digit follow-up, like ZHG or something. It is usually *very* important. I start copying. It is slow code to ensure perfect receipt, like the Soviet Rocket Forces station in Block 2. I wave over Sammy, who is fascinated. I also start to wonder if the weakness of the code is so we evil capitalists won't hear it from a distance, despite our technology.

Haltingly, between code transmissions, I ask Sammy to find out how many are on the receiving end acknowledging this message. Then to get DF to place them as well. It will help us identify the bastard and what their intentions are. Sammy gives a thumbs-up like a good SIGINT man and goes to Walker. I keep at it.

The target seems to be winding down, and I am wondering if anything else is going right. The signals seem to be fading, and I am trying to squeeze copy out of every little bit out of the transmission. There is some outside noise, and I raise my hand for quiet. That does not work. I try to listen through the noise, and the signal becomes unintelligible because of those rat bastards. "Be quiet!" I admonish the maggots. I keep trying. No good.

"Godammit motherfuckers, shut the fuck *up!*" I shout. I get the last few bits of code and alert an analyst who looks like a dying frog. I turn around wanting to kill a motherfucker.

Then I see a gentleman. "Ah, *you* must be Haroldsson," he says with his hand out. What is he, British?

I stand, grab the short motherfucker, and start yelling at him to STFU when the real men are doing their job saving their ass. Frogface comes up behind me.

---

[30] Referred to more frequently (haha) as *freqs*—sounds like "freaks." Like many of you people, no doubt.

"What do you think?" I ask and tell him to keep alert and check with Soviet Rocket Forces, my old gig. I never let go of whoever this asshole is. Then I turn to the situation at hand.

"Who the fuck are you?" I ask the diet Brit with less than available politeness. There being little available, he gets what he gets.

"Your commanding officer. Please, accept my apologies. I have always been in operational units before. Why do you think you could not hear your, ah, target?"

"He was either far away or lowered his signal strength to keep it from our technology. It could be an exercise, or it could be an announcement to begin the next Pearl Harbor-esque attack. Might have been nice to hear all of the encrypted code that was sent," I respond with menace and no regard for rank with this colonel. At least this pilot-sized bastard seems to be interested in learning the mission.

"One should think we should be able to hear everything on the planet by now," he stupidly states.

"I'll brief you when I am sure this is over," I respond with slightly less temper. Then I let him go.

The frog-looking analyst responds that the Soviet Rocket Forces have sent a QBE, exercise ended.

I respond with a yell, "Get the Block 2 leader here!" She looks around the corner. "Get your best copiers on the Soviet Rocket Forces, in case they are in a full exercise!" She responds with a very calm thumbs-up that reassures me. I like people who don't get worried in a stressed environment.

"What is going on?" asks the new commander.

"Shut up and watch," I respond. He tries to interrupt, but I shut him down with a look.

Train Wreck Tits comes up with a piece of paper. It is an XXX message. Shit!

I give it to Frog Face and tell him to also send the Z messages up along with these new ones. Iron Mike, who used to rule this mission, but got reassigned, gave me a slip of paper with freqs. I am not as experienced here in Block 3. I say thanks and do not chide him, yet, for not making a continuity book. I find a signal calling for a strike on all sites in PACOM.[31]

I tell the Frog to get ready to send CRITIC messages to DC. Someone may have to wake the president and tell him how we lost WWIII. Then, everyone starts calling out.

First, the Block 2 leader yells out that I was right, those devious commie bastards are either sending nukes or are practicing the procedure. The code breaks that the Politburo is airborne. Then, all at once, Tommy, Rocker, Train Wreck Tits, Walker along with the linguists in Block 1 start calling out that all of the nearby Soviet air bases are launching their entire fleets at PACOM targets. I call Frogface.

"Just send a general CRITIC message stating both that the Politburo is airborne, and so is the entire USSR Air Force and headed our way. Add 'more to follow,' and we will then begin sending proper messages in the correct format, got it?" He gives me a thumbs-up and a wink, then runs toward the transmitter. The new commander is taking it all in but is shutting up and not interfering with questions. Pugly does, or tries to do so. Just before I answer, the new colonel raises a hand to stop me and gives Pugly the SITREP. I grin and get back at it. The new colonel might work out. "Get It On (Bang a Gong)" by Power Station is playing softly somewhere.

I call DF and ask what they got on the targets that sent the original Z messages so I can add it in my code copying on my computer screen. If we all die, at least Washington, DC, will know the source of all of this. They give me better than I hoped and less than I wanted. I thank them and ask them to wait a second. "Who is copying the positions of the planes heading toward us here at Misawa?" I ask. Rocker raises his hand. I then tell them that I know they must be overloaded but to give Rocker priority. It might be nice if we could tell the 432 Tactical Fighter Wing, Misawa Air Base's combat wing, target information. They get the idea of self-preservation immediately and ring off.

---

[31] The command for the Pacific region for all services.

Pugly runs back to the Fish Bowl. I tap the commander's arm and say thanks before I run to Block 2. I give Sammy an index finger, indicating I'd be back in a minute. The colonel follows me. I ask the Block 2 leader, whose name is Dillinger instead of Derringer, what the Soviet Rocket Forces SITREP is. She is ice-cold and calm. She has two Morse code operators copying the main message sender since the code is being sent really fast and duplication may improve future accuracy. I ask if there is someone else out looking for tertiary messages, and she nods. She also adds that the weather station has one ear out for their job and one for the more important mission. I look and see that it is Jack. Niiice.

"I just had an idea that I was never smart enough to have when I was here in Block 2. Get one of the printer geeks to record the CRITIC-level transmissions on reel-to-reel. Afterward, we can slow it down for a true transcription," I tell her. "By the way, great job, ma'am."

"Call me Dinger. And thanks. I'll be squeezing your brain for more ideas in the future. Git!" I done did that. Good girl.

I hustle back to Block 3 to find everyone is doing a pretty damn good job. Tommy and Rocker are very busy, so I proceed to Walker. I raise an eyebrow, and he nods while lowering his cans.

"My guys have shut up, Hal. Should I be doing something else?" he asks me, showing surprising initiative.

"What is your exact mission? Remember, I am new here," I explain. He tells me, and I reply that he should keep on his mission and help others if they ask. I say that last while pointing my chin behind him to Train Wreck Tits. He smiles, nods slightly, puts on his cans, and gets back at it. Huh, maybe I was wrong about Walker. "Of course, if you have a spare Racal that you want to search with..." I add with a smile, which is returned. He understands. Keep a lookout, er, sound out, I guess.

I go over to TWT. She looks like she is doing rather well, considering. I have great hearing, and her cans are still too loud, but she is copying accurately and with good formatting. I give her a bigger grin than she deserves after bending down so she can see my face. I also give her a happy slap on the arm at her two stripes and a thumbs-up. She gives a happy, determined smile and blushes a little. I point to her Racals and then to my ears so she knows to turn down the volume a bit. Then I proceed back to Sammy.

"How are you holding up, sir?" I ask the man who is as new to the Block 3 mission as I am.

He gives the commander a look, then says, "I can't believe you are going, uh, TDY when this stuff keeps happening unexpectedly."

"Ours is but to do and die, Senior. It'll all work out. Need anything more from me?" He shakes his head.

"May I speak?" Ah, the commander is alive.

"Certainly, sir. Sorry for my temper before."

"Your treatment of me was well-deserved…please don't do it again." I grin slightly and give a small nod. Steve Miller Band's "Take the Money and Run" is on the box.

"Do you think this is an exercise or war?" He is keeping an outward calm, but I can see and hear that he is concerned. He had no idea what he was getting into coming here and was happily ignorant of the world's possible imminent destruction while flying around like an idiot in an F-16 Fighting Falcon. Of course, we call it the F-16 Lawn Dart due to its reliability issues. Funny that these thoughts are going on during this song. Remember, war is often just theft on a grand scale.

I look at Sammy for his estimate, but he defers to me.

"I would bet 6–4 or more against war, sir," I answer. Sammy nods in agreement.

"You seem so sure—why?" The colonel is astonished.

"Sir, either the attack planes will be called off within three minutes, or we will meet our destruction. After three minutes—" I stop for a second, shrug, and then continue, "I say we finish up our reporting. Then Sammy and I can fill you in, okay?" He nods in a bit of bewilderment. "We will meet you in the admin room. If you need a minute, you can rest there. Or you can watch us and find out one way or the other." He decides he needs both and sits in a nearby chair, making me smile. Old people. Go figure. The Kinks' "Catch Me Now I'm Falling" is playing.

It turns out I was correct and the planes were called off. There are cheers all around. I give Sammy the same index finger and head to Block 2. I jot down some freqs and remind the Block 2 leader that we can always lose to commies without their planes via a nuclear attack. What if they continue on other frequencies? She gives me a nod and an evil grin. Always monitor and never trust the evil bastards. Recently, they have been sending QBE messages and then have started resuming transmissions after they think we are done listening, usually on new frequencies.

I quickly get back to Block 3 where Sammy lifts a chin toward the admin room. I ask the commander if he is ready for his brief, and he lifts himself up as if he has the weight of the world upon his shoulders. We enter the admin room, and I gently tell the kid he has to go…again. Poor kid.

"Please, sir, be comfortable. What would you like to find out first?" I ask in all kindness.

"Why did you think it was just a war exercise?"

"The timing. Day shift. It's in cold weather, so we have a good read on their signals whereas the sun in the summertime burns our ability to hear them then. It's also probably a weekday. I think they simply decided to test us by surprise, especially knowing all the new kids arriving and the reorganization within this building," I answer baldly.

He looks at me in disbelief. "Bullshit. There is no way they know that."

"Sir, there is no way they do not." I give him the same rundown I gave the kids in my "greatest generation filled with traitors" speech. "There are people in this building providing a pipeline to the enemy. There is likely at least one, as well, on your staff. Sorry. Welcome to the Cold War, sir," I say with an improper, but small grin.

"Okay, how is it that someone who has not even reached the rank of Sergeant is the one indispensable person in this kind of situation?" asks our new colonel.

"Shit! Shitshitshit…give me a minute." Sammy leaps from his chair and tells the kid outside the door to get Jack from Block 2. The kid has no idea where Block 2 is. Sammy profanely tells him and comes back to the table where walkaways once thrived.

"Wait," is all Sammy will say, but I know what is coming. I also know the answer will be no. "Bad Motor Scooter" by Montrose plays on the itty-bitty radio behind the kid's desk. FEN must have a rogue DJ. I think Sammy wants to jump around and sing with the song. Appropriate since there is a Sammy singing it. Then Jack comes in. Good.

Sammy asks, "Jack, is the new commander cleared to talk about what you and Hal told me?"

"Definitely not," answers Jack decisively.

"Damn it. I understand, but please relate to your people that Hal was instrumental in what happened today," Sammy adds. I am touched but acknowledge the summation and sentiment in silence. I had not really given much thought about how big my part was the mission here was. Just doing the job.

"What do you mean 'I have no need to know,'" asks the new commander.

Sammy takes this one. "Sir, we send things even the president does not want to know about nor has a need to know. Welcome to the intelligence world."

"Plausible deniability. Okay." The colonel does not look well. Then he perks up and asks a question.

"Hal, you mentioned that we can't just up and hear whatever we want to…and then you said something about the sun. What gives?"

"The reason we can listen to anything is the AN/FLR-9, the large and circular 'Wullenweber' antenna array at eight locations. We call each an 'elephant cage.' The antenna array is composed of three concentric rings of antenna elements. I believe Germany, England, the PI, AK, Turkey, the Thailand, us here in Japan, and Italy have one each. They're just really good radio antennas, sir. Lots of things interfere with that, like line of sight, distance, atmospherics like the sun, etcetera. There are also physical limitations. Personally, the more we rely on technology worries me, one example is turning from the old teletypes to computers and so on."

"Sounds like a win for us. What do you mean?" the commander asks directly. He is reasserting himself. Not a big man, but he has a presence and intelligence. His black hair mirrors the Japs.

"Our technology can always be circumvented. Look at the Korean War, the way the Chinese attacked at night and used whistles and trumpets to communicate while attacking in the dark. All of our superior artillery and air power and technology became null and void. What if the Soviets send an EMP to shut down some or all of us? It could end the functionality of our military or the entire Western world."

"EMP?" he asks.

"Electromagnetic Pulse. A by-product of a nuke. You should look it up, sir. Along with the mission brief that you clearly have not received. Please include your Chief in that brief. He is the most garrison-thinking bastard I have ever met."

"Duly noted, Haroldsson," he says with a smile. He pauses. "And good luck with your trip. I look forward to your return," he says, meaning it, having no idea what mischief I will be into.

"Yes, sir," I say with a grin. We might be able to work with this guy. Jack caught me on my way out and said he had to cancel. Stevie Ray Vaughan's "Couldn't Stand the Weather" begins playing as we leave.

After work, I make certain to dress in a generic fashion. A bit like an American peasant, that is, button-down shirt and jeans. Common shoes. A plain baseball cap displaying no allegiance of any kind. Plain black cowboy boots and matching belt. Since the car was just in use coming back from work, I do not have to warm it up so much. Yes, I remembered to bring some tapes from the barracks room. Once I get across base, I go to the BX's customer service desk to pick up my boom box. Bobby Jo is there and is in heavy flirting mode.

"I have everything you need, Hal," she says. She is wearing tight slacks that make me want to rip them off.

"Where is the boom box?" I ask with a less-than-certain voice.

She turns away, and I about lose my breath. Niiice ass. What the fuck is up with Sammy? Then again, if you wake up every day with the pyramids, they seem routine. Damn. No matter, I do not cheat, and I do not break up couples. My raging problem is another issue. Makes me wish I carried Stacy in my back pocket for just such a need. I try to think that maybe it all looks old naked underneath those tight slacks. I reach back to my back jeans pocket and find only JD there. Oh well; can't pull it out here...in more ways than one. "Love Removal Machine" by the Cult comes on a nearby radio. Hmmm...

Bobby Jo comes back with a smile, batteries, and a radio. I thank her. The smile is nice. Her demeanor remains flirty. Being distracted by her slacks and demeanor, I am having a hard time checking out the radio, so I thank her again with a grin of my own, mention how lucky Sammy is, and go to the counter to pay for the radio. Some cute dependent is manning the cash register. I realize that I have little cash and have no idea how much the radio costs or what functions it has. Ah, it does have a tape player along with the usual other aspects, a CD player, and enough power to shake my car windows. Perfect. Of course, CDs are so new that I have no idea if they are a fad or what. Would a bumpy road screw up a CD? Guess I should stick to tapes.

I see all of this because the little teenage cutie is checking it out before she rings it up. "This thing is boss!" she says, which causes me to grin.

"I hope so. I never did see a price tag—how much is it?"

Bobby Jo hands the girl a slip of paper, telling her it's discontinued and discounted. I hope BJ is talking about the radio instead of me. She gives me a wink, and I get to stare at her ass again as she leaves. Damn.

"You lucky duck!" She looks at me with envy and rings it up. Just shy of $50.

I dig out my checkbook and fill out the date last. Shift worker. We never know the day and worse. "What day is it, please?" She tells me. "The month?" She tells me that with a smirk.

"Work on the Hill, huh?" She nailed it. I nod, smile, pay, take my receipt, and leave. I see Bobby Jo checking me out as I go. I give her a wave and a smile. Just being polite. "Finish What Ya Started" by Van Halen, aka Van Hagar, comes on the store radio, which is probably turned onto FEN as I leave the store. I keep walking. Too bad Jack canceled.

Once outside, I pop up the hatch in the back, inject the batteries and a tape, and set the radio in between two empty beer boxes and rags to keep it from sliding around hither and yon. I close the hatch and sit down, starting up the car. After Cheap Trick's "Need Your Love" (live) ends, Aldo Nova's "Fantasy" comes blasting. Great sound quality is heard, which I improve by adjusting the EQ settings. I could grow to like this. Then I head off base for the meeting with the windows down and God by my side.

It might be nice to learn how to properly drive a stick shift. This old car is a little sporty due to its light weight. More power than you would think, but not too much to get you in trouble on the narrow, curving roads off base. "Free Will" by Rush comes on next. Kickass. The drummer, Neil Peart, wrote the lyrics, if memory serves. Heavily influenced by the atheist, Ayn Rand, possibly the smartest human of this century. Atheist, a woman, and Russian-born. Despite all that, her works rock. I find the guitar solo to be good but themeless, like atheism. It is nice to have time alone to reflect. Of course, I am trying to remember how to get to the Sage's shack as well. I should have brought Jack against his will. "Bad Moon Rising" by CCR comes on next. What a mixtape.

If you remember, all of us buy blank tapes, recording assorted hits for each other and so on. We make copies and share. Many of my tapes have no labels or notes on them; I just know they will usually be good. Contrarily, I think I am on the wrong road. I stop at a beer machine in the middle of nowhere and buy a beer. No Pocari Sweat for these good rice farmers. I turn around and go by instinct on the roads since my memory is failing me. "American Girl" by Tom Petty and the Heartbreakers is next. I seem to date girls that match this description. Not just American, but country girls in one way or another. Strange. Ah, now I am on the right road…and there is the shack. Niiice.

I park the car and proceed toward the door. I knock, and a very cute Japanese girl answers the door with a seductive smile and a gun pointed right at my chest. One would hope for something else.

"Oh, coming in, Hal-san. Sage no here. Coming in," she keeps chattering as she opens the door. "What you need, kind sir," another one asks.

"A cold beer, a bottle of Jack Daniel's, and a blow job. Oh, and a notebook and pen, if you please," I answer. I heard back home that successful traveling salesmen would ask for special services as a joke for a hotel reservation like a cute redhead, a bucket of good iced beer, etc. Thus, I was just being silly.

"Roger, Hal-san. Come over here," she says as I think she is leading me to where the Sage and I will speak. Instead, I get my pants dropped and a great blow job. I could grow to like this gig. Soon, I gave the cutie some fireworks. It didn't take long. Afterward, she motions me to a restroom so I can pee. The door doesn't shut completely, and I see the BJ master talking to someone else in Japanese while I am clearing out my barrel after shooting. I have no idea what she is talking about.

I walk out of the restroom and back toward the large open area where the Sage and I spoke the first time. Another cutie rushes to guide me to the bar. A notebook, pen, a cold beer, and a fifth of JD are on the bar.

"Are you hungry, Hal-san?" I can't tell them perfectly apart. I mean, they look a little bit different, but I am terrible with names, and we have never been properly introduced.

"Food?" They start freaking out, and I tell them to calm down. Just an order of California rolls. A big hairy steak will put me to sleep at the time when I should be plotting the saving of my life on my excursion. They bring me the food, some soy sauce, and a fork. I ask for chopsticks, and they happily comply. Funny. It appears they are very interested in serving my every need, despite where I probably am in the pecking order. I cannot decide if I like it. I ask what Thing 1 was saying to Thing 2. Apparently, I am too tall, too skinny, too long, and too much. I respond with that was just the first time, and the poor girl blushed to the clavicle.

Just now I realize there is music. "Wasting My Time" by Jimmy Page is on. It sounds like Jimmy Barnes on vocals, but someone once said it was John Miles. Whatever. Great rock, but not apropos, considering recent events. I ask how long it will be. I am pacing. No, I don't idle well. Shrugs. I ask for tea, and I get polite bows to get some. The tea arrives just when the bastard finally arrives at his own house. I go to the bar area.

He walks in like he owns the world and wishes he had kept the receipt. I get a chin raise of acknowledgment, then he motions to the girls. He is quickly set up with very good beer and hot sake. Good for him.

"You have become a problem, Hal," he starts. He pours a sake, shoots it, and does the same twice more. Wow. He has tired eyes. He looks to the girls and tells them with only hand motions to kill the *Outrider* album and replace it with something else. A calming Asian music comes on. I wonder if this music can be easily bought by Americans. It's wonderful. Not that usual Jap crap that is supposed to be traditional. The Japanese are awesome, but the old crap they play for Americans is *very* boring.

He looks at me with a disapproving glance and shoots another shot of sake.

"You may have *fucked* all of this up today, Hal," he says. Shit. What?

I say nothing. I wait with what I hope is a neutral expression.

He takes a pull of his beer, looks at it, holds it up, and says, "To life."

"L'chaim!" I respond with a clink of my beer.

"You are still a complete bastard. Want me to explain?" he asks.

"In a second, may I ask the cutie pies to get me a shot glass for the JD and a Japanese beer glass for the beer?" He looks at me with an odd expression, to which I respond, "Wouldn't want to put my cooties on the bottle of JD, and I have gotten used to drinking the local beer that way. Thanks."

"Okay. Whatever. Girls, you heard him." He gestures to them to fill my requests.

He looks at me dead in the eye, and I cannot tell if he wants to congratulate me or slug me. Maybe both. I am getting curious. Is he pissed about me getting a free blow job? And how would he know?

"I heard about today," he says with an odd tone of voice. He gently shakes his head again. "Do you realize what you have done?"

"My job. It was routine. You know they have these exercises from time to time. Today was only tense because of what we are going through with all the new kids, others PCSed in, transfers, and the organizational changes. Otherwise, what's the big deal?" I am glad that this is all this is. The Sage knew I was good at my job. This isn't *Movietone News*.

"It wasn't routine. I am betting they knew of our difficulties, and they cannot imagine how we were able to detect exactly what they were doing, where they were doing it, and how they were doing it. We had a response in the air exactly where it needed to be as if we had zero problems on our end. It was terrible," he concludes.

"Now I am not following you. Like I said, we did our job. They know we can adjust and improvise better than they can. Can't they think we just got lucky? And are they coming to this conclusion by what we did or from leaks?"

"Yes. And don't ask how I know all of this," he says with steel in his voice.

"You'll note I was already there, Hoss," I say with a grin. "Silver Springs" by Fleetwood Mac comes on the box. I might not have been paying attention to the music. Strange.

"Yeah," he says with another pour from the sake bottle and slams the little Jap ceramic shot glass. One of the cuties brings him a freshly baked bottle of sake after pouring the rest of the first one into his little cup. He grunts a thanks and takes a long pull from his beer.

"It's worse than that, Hal. Much worse." He stares into the distance through the window behind me. "Now no one wants you gone for one minute to anywhere, and no one wants to risk you on a mission of this kind," he says, informing me of his conundrum.

I nearly laugh. "How nice of them. Unless you have a HUMINT spook handy, then it probably has to be me. Since the 'Cold War is over,' and I am so allegedly important, maybe now we can get the assets we need to make this work. Also, after a week or two, things will fall back into routine, and the call for my being indispensable will quiet down. Meanwhile, we can set everything up. If we get the waive off at the last minute, oh well. I say we make the best of things. You?"

"I never thought of it that way…maybe this does help us! Hey, need a blow job?"

"Sage, you are *not* my type," I reply as he was slamming a cup of sake. He seems to nearly die of a coughing fit, but that does not dim his enthusiasm.

"No, one of these party girls! After you left the last time, they all went on and on and on about how handsome they thought you were. Just pick one," he offers.

I look up. They are all standing in a line side by side behind him. I start to grin, and they all reply at the same time, "Too late!" Their lovely laughter fills up the room.

"Damn it! You are good at *everything*!" We laugh even more.

"Maybe. You still have my list?" He nods. "Then let's you and I start just talking through how and where I am doing what, okay?" He is in full agreement.

I leave three hours later. The drive home rocks. "Fat Bottomed Girls," "Panama," and "Next to You," the latter by the Police, if you have forgotten, are played at about a quarter ton of decibels through the darkening countryside. The first is from the immortal Queen and the second, of course, by Van Halen. I turn it all down as I approach the front gate. I put a spare Virginia Commonwealth University hoodie over the bottle of Jack I was given as a token parting gift by the Sage, show my ID card to the gate guard, and drive to the barracks. I hope I can sleep. The future looks to be…exciting.

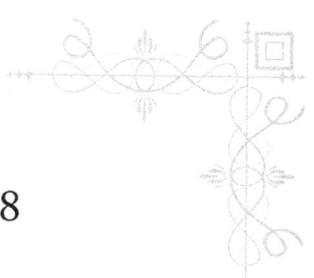

CHAPTER 8

Last Day of Day Shifts

Tomorrow's day of work will be swings. Honestly, I am working less now than I ever have in my adult life. Before, I was working like the Japanese due to the manning shortages. Then again, I was obsessed with defeating the commies despite us having too few to do the work. The disruptions and changes have done wonders for my health. Sleep is underrated—go figure. As a younger man, I thought sleep was for the dead.

Surprisingly, last night, I slept well and a little longer than I should have, did the usual gym and chow hall thing upon waking, and took Penny the Civic to work. What happened at the chow hall was the interesting thing. I saw the Post Office girl there, Rachel. Comely in her own way. A little broad in the hips without the benefit of other improvements. I wonder if she is an Injun. She does have lovely, slightly wavy black hair and tanned skin. Oh well, I am too polite to ask about her heritage. Anyway, I was bringing my heavy tray of food out, and she waved me over to her table. It would have been impolite to refuse the invitation. "Wasted Time" by the Eagles is on a radio somewhere.

We go through the usual "what have you been doings" and so on while I wolf down my megaton of food. Knowing our lives in the 1980s overseas Air Force, you can imagine what happens next.

"Damn, where do you put all that food, Hal?" she asks in wonderment.

"I burn it off, dick first.[32] What is going on with you and your comrades at the Post Office?" I ask politely. Babes think I am good at listening. I think it gives me a minute or three to eat.

"They are all getting pregnant, wanted or otherwise. Now, Hal," she says this leaning toward me with an earnest look, "I need you to knock me up and marry me."

Somehow, I manage not to choke to death on the big hunk of breakfast in my mouth.

"Really? Trying to keep up with your comrades, I see," I say with a husky voice caused by nearly choking and the subject matter. "Don't you have other choices?"

"Not better ones, Hal. You know I have always liked you. C'mon, after work, let's fuck like banshees and then plan on our wedding while we recover afterward," she says with all seriousness.

"I am not ready to be married or be a father, Rachel. Sorry. I'd be a lucky man to be your husband, but I have some things to do before I acquire a missus," I reply as politely as possible.

"I hear that after you have a kid, you have better control of your hoo-hah. Just think, you'd have great fucking on tap every day for the rest of your life. Please? I really want to be Mrs. Haroldsson. Besides, my biological clock is ticking." Her booted foot starts tapping after saying this.

"May I think about it?"

She nods with a grin. "Thanks." I did not know how to get out of this conversation any other way. "Besides, I am late for work. I am usually there by now." I quickly slam down my two remaining weak coffees and pick up my remaining bacon. "Have a great day, Rachel."

"You bet! I can't wait to tell Rhonda!" Sheesh…

As you can imagine, being back at work was a relief by comparison, although I missed seeing Stacy before the shift change. It turns out there are more kids filtering onto our shift as they continue to in-process. The hick chick from the Ozarks, the short one who was blocking my way for a second at 007s, is happy that the

---

[32] Obviously, this is my standard answer—I should try using it on the clergy and see what they think.

Injun-looking lad is with her in Block 1. Some of the others have sometimes taken to calling her Fern after the kids' book and movie. I learned this from someone who had the giggles while telling me the Injun is named Dusty Rabbit. Whatever.

There is also some chick who really could give Private Benjamin a run for her money. Leanda De Loughrey. I bet she drinks tea out of a little itty-bitty demitasse with her pinky sticking out. She sounds like old Southern money. Probably spent a few years studying Southern peasants before getting a graduate degree in tea drinking and knowing what fork to use to eat escargot. She has joined us in Block 3 on a temporary transfer. You can tell everything surrounding her is beneath her standards, but she is adjusting without complaint. This is her "walked fifteen miles uphill, both ways, every day to school" moment, I guess.

Sammy has been listening to the shift change briefings as best as he can to learn more about the mission. He sees me and asks, right in front of the other kids, "How did it go?"

I have a wonderfully truthful and devious reply, "With the meeting or the marriage proposal?"

He is quite flabbergasted. "Whut?"

I laugh. "We'll talk offline, okay?" He nods.

I go over to Walker and thank him for his work during the Soviet exercise while Ozzy Osbourne's "You Can't Kill Rock and Roll" plays. I also remind him that he is the most experienced Airman in Block 3 on Charlie Flight. We may need to lean on him like a butter bar leans on a Chief Master Sergeant. I stop by Train Wreck Tits afterward and ask her how she is. She looks better than yesterday. After yesterday, I think she realizes she can adjust to meet the mission standards. I tell her that at some point, we will have to teach her how to search for targets instead of just waiting for a few to transmit, while assuring her it will be a while till that happens and that she will rock. She smiles and blushes. Good girl. Nothing like giving these infants some confidence.

I was going to go back up to the front of Block 3 when Tommy and Rocker call out to me.

"Hey, Hal, when is the game tonight when we beat those Able Flight pussies?" This sounded like Tommy, but my head was turned. I tell them both the details of where and when to be at the game. They said they might be bringing a friend who just arrived, some guy named Mattison whom I will get a kick out of. They seem very convinced. I thank them and move on. Maybe I can get Mattison to marry Rachel from the post office. Then I will be impressed.

I am finally rounding the top corner toward the right past Block 1 when some of my comrades call out to me. "Hal!" is yelled from many. I turn with a small grin. What is with these people? Clearly, I need more coffee. "Gonna pound those Able Flight pussies after work or what?" This was asked by the mob, but even Crosse and Schmidt are in on this. Crosse is really glaring.

I ask, "*Et votre amant?*" She shrugs. "It'll be good to see all of you there," I tell the crowd, not wanting to publicly flirt with Crosse. "Bring beer and noise, okay?" The cheers rise, then wane, and thankfully, they get back to work.

I decide to visit Block 2 before heading out to the electronics section and more. Jack is standing there at the weather rack where he can cover that mission and assist some of the new kids. He was smoking a cigarette and was about to speak when Zeus yells, "We is gonna beat them Able Flight pussies! Woohoo!" Jack and I start to quietly giggle when Balls shrieks. Robert Plant's "Burning Down One Side" has been playing somewhere. Not too bad. We both slowly turn our heads in surprise and see Balls leave her station and run to Senior Master Sergeant Dillinger, Block 2 leader.

Dinger looks up from her paperwork slowly with a poker face. She seems to take her mewling Airman in slowly before asking, "Yes?" The sobs now include choking. Dinger adds, "What is it, Balls?"

"Senior, please, you have to…please, do something about the language," Balls pleads.

Dinger doesn't seem impressed. "What language?" No change in expression or raising of her voice.

"They keep calling people…a female body part!" she exclaims with a shocked expression and an open hand over her mouth. I give out a little snort. FEN is on a small radio nearby, and the final stanza of "Crying" by Roy Orbison is on.

"Ain't nobody calling nobody a female body part, yew stupid twat!" Ah, O'Phelan's roommate has joined the conversation. His accent just gets past the big chaw in his right cheek.

"He's right," Jack adds, only to have me interrupt what he was about to say next as we approach.

"Pussy is short for pusillanimous, which means weak or lacking in determination," I educate.

"Marked by contemptible timidity," adds Jack. It occurs to me that we are talking like Scrooge McDuck's nephews or some such. Balls is thunderstruck. "Seek and Destroy" by Metallica follows Roy Orbison on FEN as delicately as someone loudly shitting themselves in church after reciting the Lord's Prayer.

O'Phelan's roommate decides to calm the situation. "This," he says pointing to Balls and looking at Senior, "is why traditionally women could not drive, could not vote, were not allowed to do real work, and were definitely not allowed to be in the military!" His voice got a wee bit louder as he went on. He was about to go on when Dinger put up a hand to make it stop. Thank God, because that shit needed to end.

It appears the Block 2 leader is at a loss. I catch her eye and raise my eyebrows, asking nonverbally to speak. She raises her chin, and I say in a quiet voice directly to Balls, "This is a warfighting organization. Let's pretend these warriors really were doing what you thought they were doing. Warriors are not only intelligent, but they are not here to eat crumpets. They curse and break things. The military did not join you; you joined the military. It is you who must adjust to the warrior culture." Tears well up in her eyes. "It'll all be okay. Everyone here is a forgive-and-forget Christian. Just pull your head out, okay?" She nods.

Dinger follows with, "Gentlemen, thank you. Will you please excuse us?"

We all nod or say "yes, ma'am." Jack looks at me and proposes, "Let's absquatulate!" As I leave, I hear Dinger tell Balls, "You're fucking this up for all women. Grow a pair, or join the Salvation Army, okay?"

Jack and I return to his rack. He throws his cans back upon his neck and smiles. "Hmmm...gonna pound those Able Flight pussies, huh? You've been doing a lot of that lately," he finishes, and we both laugh. I ask if he wants to tag along to the game and then to the Sage's afterward. He agrees, and I leave him to his work.

My travels around the building are met the same way. I encourage all to come to the game and bring beer. It is a shift change day, after all. Nothing like going from day shift to swings. A good day to drink. The workday goes in normal fashion.

Afterward, time to go to the barracks and then the game. Cleats. Stirrups. Knickers. Shirt and hat. No, no two outfits on our team are alike. The Able Flight pussies are similarly uniformed to each other, instead of the great variety on our team. I hear gay couples like to dress alike, too. But we have to wait; the previous game is going into extra innings.

I look out over the field. It is a quagmire. The frozen puddle behind the CMSGT umpire is waxing. I see my guys and get them over to me. "Hey, the field sucks. Nobody gets hurt, okay?" Nods abound. "The team that wins this game is the team that does not lose because of mistakes. I have baseball ideas that will help us win out," I explain. They know I am a devious bastard and agree. Oh, and Jack has done his job again, via pay phone. Niiice.

We take the field. Well, we take the field after batting and stranding two runners. The Chief is not amused. He hates us, and he hates me especially. The field nearly takes us later. What a mucky piece of shit. It sucks your cleats when you try to walk in the outfield. The icy crater behind the Chief really is getting larger. Seriously, it is making him look all Navy getting closer behind the catcher. Our catcher keeps hitting him in the nuts with an elbow because of it, driving him into the frozen puddle on occasion. Good times.

It's a sloppy game, but our fans are getting boisterous and tipsy. Yes, there is more than beer involved. And, as if the terrible condition of the field is not enough to want to give up this business, the mist turns to sleet, and the wind picks up. In the fourth inning with the score tied at naught, Able had a runner on first and third. In baseball, this would be a dire situation, but it is bad enough here despite no one being allowed to steal a base or take a lead from their base. I am playing first base when the batter hits a screamer head high right down the first base line. Him being right-handed, I was playing off the bag. The first base runner leaves for second the instant the ball is hit. Luckily, I was quick enough to just barely snag the ball, stepping on the vacated base while doing so. Then, I arrested my momentum toward the fence, spin a bit, and gunned the ball home to Stafford. The runner from third, tagging up, was trying to run over our catcher and knock the ball out of the glove, but Stafford was having none of it, manfully tagging that maggot with both hands on the ball in his glove. Triple play.

The fans in our section of the stands went nuts. Van Halen's "DOA" starts blasting. Multiple female voices call my name in their cheers and then all turn to each other. Bridget is wearing a smile. Rachel is dumbfounded. Stacy is clueless. Bobby Jo at the top of the stands begins to giggle when Happy's wife pats BJ gently on the upper arm and tells her drunkenly, "God, I wanna fuck him." The other ladies turn back to see who said that. Then it really starts as we all take the bench. I wish I was batting instead of having these blithering hoochies yakking behind me in the stands.

"What?" asks Rachel.

Crosse looks at Rachel and asks, "Who are you?"

"I am the one who is fixin' to marry Hal. Who are you?" Rachel retorts.

"A coworker," Crosse responds.

"What's this 'fixing to get married' horseshit?" asks Stacy with no small vehemence. "I'm the one draining his balls around here!"

Bridget starts erupting with giggles over all of this. Rachel asks who the hillbilly is in increased frustration. "Just someone in line, I guess," Bridget answers while still giggling. "Hal saved my life the other day. Literally." The giggles leave, but the smile remains. "I don't believe we have been formally introduced."

"I'm Rachel. I work at the Post Office. A friend who works with me there went to tech school with Hal, so she and her husband were the only people he knew when he first got here. I've known Hal as long as he has been in Japan, so I have known him the longest, I guess," Rachel concludes. The look on her face gives one the impression that she thinks her conclusion gives her first dibs or some damn thing.

"I was at tech school with Hal before all of you ASVAB-waivered fucktards," says Stacy to Rachel. "Not that it matters who was when or whatever." This goes on while we are trying to win a game. Sheesh. Peter Gabriel's "I Go Swimming" is playing, I finally notice.

Zeus is about to bat. I decide to dispense some advice. The man gets on base frequently but is as slow as Dutch Elm Disease. I tell him, "After you get on base, Zeus, I am going to slam the ball to deep right field. I want you to not stop until you are on third, at least. Got it?" The big doofus nods and ambles toward home plate. I remain at the on-deck circle area but can hear the discussion in the stands.

"So wait a minute. Aside from me, who *isn't* fucking Hal?" asks Dinger as she raises her hand. Jack can't hold it in anymore and is red in the face from laughing. Both Bobby Jo and Mrs. Happy raise their hands at the same time and say, "Not yet." Tango has her little hand over her mouth to hide her giggles and has an intake of breath over all of this. Others, like Crosse and Bridget add "not yets," and Rachel says stridently, "Maybe soon, on our honeymoon," looking at Stacy.

Stacy is in high dudgeon and, while looking at Rachel, says, "I guess I am the only one here getting their guts rearranged by Hal." Laughing and applause follow while Stacy stands and takes a bow. This is followed by the pop of a bat. Zeus has hit a dinky little hit over the shortstop's head. More cheers and the focus from the crowd is back on the game.

I confer with Sammy before going to bat. Then I make my way to home plate. Damn the field is in bad shape. I eye Zeus looking at me, and I nod at him deliberately. We need to manufacture a run to end this scoreless game. I am batting right-handed, and the first pitch lands with a splat in front of my left foot. The umpire calls it a strike, and everyone from Charlie Flight in the stands goes nuts. I step outside the batter's box and look up at the sky, letting the sleet land on my cheeks and glasses. At least the wind has died down again. My glasses have, of course, been treated better.

The insults and screaming at the umpire keep mounting. Shouts like, "You're the reason the gene pool needs a lifeguard!" and "You fucking oxygen thief, why don't you go play in traffic!" Others ask things like, "Is your ass jealous of all the shit that comes out of your mouth?" Most of these come from our female fans. The outright booing seems to be coming from the men. The funniest female one is, "I don't know what's wrong with you, but I bet it's hard to pronounce!"

The manager for Able Flight calls time and comes to the plate. "Chief, we want to kick these assholes' asses fair and square. That was a ball. Don't do this." The Chief is about to retort when Chief Bender comes to our rescue again.

"Frenchy, the boy is right. Call a clean game," he says, having clearly drunk many beers and something else. The umpire is not happy about getting called out. I guess douches like him don't like mutiny. Why the bastards tend to have Irish accents, I have no idea.

Someone who had been standing behind and to the far side of our section of the stands came forward. He has a baseball hat down low and his hood up on his Air Force Academy sweatshirt. "Got a spare beer, Bender?"

Chief Bender had not been looking his way when this was said. Someone pointed at the stranger. I couldn't see who it was, but Chief Bender peered through the sleet and then straightened up completely and said, "Yes, sir!" The voice was familiar. The umpire went as white as a ghost and announced the previous pitch was a ball. Cheers abound.

"If you Able Flight faggots want to beat us, put the damn ball over the plate this time," I tell the pitcher with a smile.

"Slipped out of my hand," the pitcher replied sheepishly. My grin widens. I take a practice swing toward the left field foul pole and yell out, "Better move back, maggot!" to their left fielder. The universal replies indicate they think this is a fake and the outfield moves in. Then it happens. Tommy yells, "We need the Matt signal!" and some asshole, must be Mattison, drops his dungarees and under britches and moons everyone. Suddenly, a boom box is cranked to M's "Pop Muzik." Everyone in the stands on our side starts to robot dance. I join all the players on the field in laughing. It takes a minute to settle down.

I come back toward home plate. I lock eyes with Zeus again, turn my back to the catcher, hold up my left hand to block the view the other way, and hold up two fingers from my other hand. After a second or three, he grins and nods. I get into the batter's box and get ready. The pitch is perfect, and I move my right foot toward the plate and step away from first base with my left, slamming the ball intentionally foul and out of play to deep left. The Able Flight fans are outnumbered but simultaneously say, "Whoa..." Charlie Flight fans are going nuts for no apparent reason. The dancing is getting ridiculous. Yup, I got all of that one—nearly a home run, but intentionally foul.

Now the Able team thinks that maybe I was being all Satchel Paige in calling out the left fielder. They begin to shade to left field, and the left fielder steps back. I start to go back to the batter's box when "(I Can't Get Me No) Satisfaction" by Devo comes on. The Charlie Flight area of stands is filled with more exuberance. Beers are being poured into each others' mouths from distant sources while the dancing gets more manic and stupid. Mattison keeps shaking his naked ass. I get the giggles and do not enter the box. It's practically a wet T-shirt contest in the stands due to the poor aim of the "bartenders." The catcher looks at me, and I point to the fracas in the stands. "Damn, you assholes have all the hotties, huh?" I give him a crooked grin and dig in after locking eyes with Zeus and exchanging nods.

The next pitch is more than perfect. It is a beautiful arching pitch toward the outside of the plate. I step back with my right foot, pushing toward the plate with my left and turning my hips late, and crank it as best as I can to the opposite field. It lands five feet fair and dies in the bad, wet soil nearly at the outfield fence. Zeus, to his credit, starts to huff and puff his way around the bases. I go halfway to first, turn, and bow to the fans. I then go to first. Some have no idea why I stopped at first. Zeus was stopped by Happy the third base coach out of breath but with a great smile on his face. The Cars' "Tonight She Comes" is on a radio.

Sammy is up, and he did what I told him to do—try for a home run. He was going to do it anyway. He hit a very deep fly ball to the fence in center field, but it was caught. Zeus tagged up, and even I made it in when the wet ball was poorly thrown by the center fielder. I did not have to slide headfirst but did so for showmanship. The cheers were wonderful. Yes, I ended up sliding so the Chief had to jump and the bastard ended up face down in the icy mud puddle. The next instant, the boom box boy played "She Sells Sanctuary" by the Cult. The Charlie Flight crowd erupts. That is the last of our scoring during this inning, but we are up 2-0.

Bobby Jo asks, "Who wants to clean off Hal?" More than one hand goes up—lots of them, really, with many shouts of "me!" Wow. How did this happen? Damn. Jack is just shaking his head. Husbands are wondering about their wives.

The game ends at the same score. Interestingly, the Charlie fans' DJ with the great boom box plays "Obsession" by Animotion as we leave the field. Hopefully, Mattison has his clothes back on. I call out to Stacy and tell her I hope she has a good time at the Jerry Reed show. She gives a sort of smile of mild disappointment and a weak wave as she turns away. I ask Jack who the hoodie was, and he did not answer as we went to my car. As it was unlocked, we both get in, and I put Penny through its motions. I also turn on the boom box. "Radio Free Europe" by R.E.M. comes on. Nice. When the song ends, I put the car in gear to hit the barracks to change clothes. "Behind the Wall of Sleep" by the Smithereens comes on next. After I park the car, I ask, "Back here in twenty?" Jack nods.

Twenty minutes later, we are back in the car. After we make our way off base, I interrupt the silence. "It's dark. I have no idea where I am going," I say to Jack.

"It was the colonel," answers Jack.

"Huh?"

"It was our new commander in the hoodie."

It is silent for a bit. Neither of us speaks. Jack occasionally points when I have to make a turn. We arrive at Sage's shack soon thereafter.

The shack's lighting is dimmer than normal. The Sage is lounging on a sofa, smoking. "Good, I was wondering if you two were going to make it." He seems a little unsettled. It just occurred to me there is no real art in this place, or at least in this room. Go figure.

"The game before ours went into extra innings," I inform. Jack nods in agreement.

"Did the umpire mess with you much?" he asks with a grin.

"It got squelched very quickly. In fact, I wonder how long the Chief will be with us," Jack adds then explained what happened. A tiny radio is playing "Somebody" by Bryan Adams softly somewhere. I wonder where the cutie-pies are. It occurs to me that I am not perfectly certain what their status is. Bar employees? He is an owner of multiple clubs, after all. Girlfriends? Agents?

"I am having some doubts about your little vacation plans, Hal," the Sage confessed and paused for a few pulls of his smoke. "I don't know what we can get out of it that we can't get from satellite imagery." Inexplicably, "Why" by Bronski Beat started playing.

"That's just gay, sir," I respond with a big grin. We all laugh. The tension in the room starts to ease. The Sage seems to be more relaxed when the cutie-pies are here, I guess.

"The radio or my reasoning? Don't answer that. But you do see what I mean, right?" And I do.

"Yes. So, let's just talk it out and brainstorm what we can do and not do, okay?" He nods in agreement. "Jack, I'd love to hear your thoughts as well," I add, looking at him. He had just been zoning out while smoking. He seems pleased. The Sage stands up and leads us to the bar area, handing me my notebook from previous meetings out of a hidden safe. "Runaway Boys" by the Stray Cats comes on next on the tiny radio. I don't know how to take that considering the preceding song and the proceedings here.

"Are you concerned that Hal will get nabbed for being undertrained and unable to speak the language, or are you worried that, even if he did succeed, he would learn little more than we can gather from satellites?" Jack inquires. Perceptive. There is much setting up drinks, glasses, and ashtrays. "Pump It Up" by Elvis Costello comes on just then. Niiice. I just avoid getting up and dancing.

"Yes. Yes to all of it. And we will have to use a lot of resources if we want to get this done. Hal would have to be escorted by people we are either not completely sure of in terms of loyalty or have little training of their own. Even so, I don't want to burn all of our meager Far East contacts," summarizes the Sage. "Oh, and I am starting to think that those against this because of Hal's SIGINT talents have a good point."

"Hmmm..." Jack lost his eloquence, I guess. He isn't really replying and is instead being a professional smoker.

"Beer?" asks the Sage. After our nods, he pulls out a bucket of ice with a couple of large Sapporo bottles. He is about to come back around the bar when he sets out two Japanese beer glasses. He looks around like he is making sure he isn't missing anything and then puts up a shot glass and a half-empty bottle of Jack Daniel's.

We settle back down and I say, "Okay, let's talk hypothetically about where I would go, what I would discover, and how I would get back," I respond. The Sage is about to interrupt, but I put up my hand and add, "Perhaps if we talk that part out, we can either find out whether or not something can be accomplished at each location or if the lack thereof is further testament to my not going." The Sage grins, nods, and takes a tremendous pull from his bottle of beer. I pour Jack and me a glass of beer; we clink them together and drain them. I pour a shot of JD and drink that. First, I ask for a music change. Soon, Florence Price's "Five Folksongs in Counterpoint" comes on. I look at the Sage as I pick up my pen and say, "Shoot."

Sage confesses that final destinations are still being debated, but I would enter the Soviet Union at Nakhodka since Vladivostok is forbidden to foreigners, it being the home of their Navy. He assures me that I will be dressed Russian-ish and will not stick out. According to the Sage, this village is not exactly teeming with people at the docks or on the streets.

"Cool. Assuming I am arriving there with a Japanese fishing boat," I say, and the Sage nods, "then how do I look Japanese when we arrive and not Japanese a few minutes later?"

"You'll have enough sailor gear on that your face will be covered. All sailors fishing in that part of the world do so to keep warm.

Then you will enter a building where you will change clothes, pick up a modicum of equipment, and be given to someone else who will drive you toward Svobodnyy."

"You're right. This will use up a lot of contacts and assets. What can I find out on the way and at each location? Remember Hokushin-ron? The latest briefings say that the Sovs are concentrating more and more on Europe at the expense of Siberia, where all of their resources are. The idea of a buffer state between Russia and Japan while stealing their future prosperity sounds kinda fun...like how we stole the American West from Mexico just before gold was found in the People's Republic of California," I propose. The Sage and I are jotting down all of these ideas as we go.

"Hokushin-ron?" asks Jack, looking at the Sage.

"Remember how the Japanese created a Greater East Asia Co-Prosperity Sphere during World War II?" Jack nods. The Sage continues, "Well the Jap Navy won that argument wanting to free the Asians from colonialism by white people, Nanshin-ron. The Japanese Army wanted to invade Siberia and conquer land all the way to Lake Baikal, calling it the Northern Road, or Hokushin-ron. They needed raw materials and decided to be Great Britain a few centuries too late. War to conquer and steal, war being theft on a grand scale, had fallen out of favor in the more modern era. No, I don't think a border state created out of Siberia is viable, but it would be interesting to know if their Far East is starting to fade."

I pour Jack and me another dose of beer, which we quickly empty. The Sage takes another pull on his beer straight from the bottle and opens another pack of Lucky Strikes. As he is fiddling with his vices, Sage observes, "So you think you can do more than the original mission, the brief observation of a rocket base or so, and can instead also turn this into a limited fact-finding mission? Interesting. I still wouldn't want you too far west considering how remote it all is, the dangers involved, etcetera. Huh, interesting."

"Why would you change this from a rocket forces observation mission to some sort of economic, cultural, or political mission?" asks Jack.

"Nah, just adding other things that can be done," I admit. "If the mission is only for observing the rocket forces, what if I don't notice anything our satellites would already see? Then the mission is costly and risky for no reason." Jack seems to understand, and the Sage is smiling. "How far west would I be going? Oh yeah, still being debated. Okay, what are some of the options being proposed?" I ask.

"Some asshole wanted you to go all the way to Irkutsk. I told them that Lake Baikal is the absolute limit. People just don't get how big that damn lake is. So you probably wouldn't go past Chita."

"Wait, Drovyanaya is just southwest of there and has a rocket unit there, right?" I ask.

Sage nods in approval. "You've been paying attention. Good man. You are definitely right."

"And you want me to travel by car? I once heard there is little traffic in the area other than the railroad and military traffic. I understand that a motorcycle would stick out, especially since I don't know how to ride one. But that is a long way to travel by car. Are there checkpoints? And how does one get gasoline in that part of the world? Not like there are truck stops every twenty miles, one would think. And will the cars be reliable—the commies are not known for their precision," I observe. As I speak, I continue to make notes for myself in my own shorthand. I notice the Sage does as well.

"Now you are giving reasons not to go," Jack says, looking up at the roof and shaking his head slightly. Sage is grinning, which causes me to have a small, crooked smile.

"Jack, we are just having a conversation. We are not deciding whether or not to go or not. We are just exploring all of the challenges and possibilities, alright?" I remind him gently. He purses his lips and nods in understanding.

The Sage is still writing things down. No doubt his notes contain specifics while mine have only generalities.

"Two ideas. No, you won't like either one, sir," I say to the Sage. "I make frequent stops so I will not be testing the reliability of any one car too often. This would give me more time to take in the local color and get people to gossip. You may not have had the time to notice, but I can get anyone to divulge more than they normally would through humor and more. Second, I would need a backstory to talk to the locals and the authorities. We may have to involve State[33] and have an explanation of sorts, like my being an errant son of a diplomat who is checking out Russia. I could be an estranged college student son who is on a barely authorized trip in an attempt to rejoin father and son or some damn thing. With all of this perestroika and glasnost by splotch-top nonsense, that would cover a lot to include my lack of language skills."

"Yeah, because they are just letting people through the Brandenburg Gate, Hal," Jack says derisively. He is right. That probably won't ever happen. Oh well.

Sage is taking it differently. "That makes quite a bit of sense. Let me work on that. This might work. I hadn't really digested until now the effects of the reforms by Gorbachev might have on this mission. It might be nice to find out how it is affecting this region as well, if this does indeed also become a fact-finding endeavor. Huh."

"It is still a dictatorship, man," observes Jack.

"Yeah, but with the slight opening up of freedoms internally, the economy and the slight opening up of political freedoms seems to be leading to unintentional consequences. This might work," the Sage says with increasing enthusiasm.

"Make sure I am the right man for the job is all. I don't care about dying for my country, but I'd rather the mission be successful than not, okay?" The Sage nods. Jack seems disturbed. Maybe he forgot the possibility of death was involved. I pour the last of the first tall beer into our glasses. Jack reluctantly clinks glasses. Then I pick up the bottle of Jack and drain the dregs. "I think we should end this here and continue the mission another time. Do you have a drop-off where I can update you—a secure one?"

"Not a phone," adds Jack. Chopin's "Ballade in A-Flat Major" comes on next.

"Good man, I hate the phone. All of them," I add.

---

[33] The US Department of State.

"I'll see what I can do. Thanks, Hal," the Sage says holding his hand out. We shake. He takes the time to thank Jack and shakes his hand as well. Good man.

Jack and I are gathering ourselves up when Jack asks where the hoochies are. Sage responds, "I wanted Hal to focus without distractions."

"The big head is in charge of the little head," I respond with a smile and a mild shake of the head.

"From what the cutie-pies say, they are the same size," the Sage says with a chuckle. "Maybe I did not want them to be interrupting us, okay?" Jack's grin is wry and mine is very wide.

"Have a good night, sir," I say to a man who is finally not wearing aviator glasses. He has intelligent, tired brown eyes. The limpid strains of the piano music from inside wearily escorts us out into the night.

Jack and I mount Penny, and I go through the usual routine on the old girl. While we wait for the car to warm up again, I reach into my pocket and unsheathe a Zippo, light a smoke, and put the light toward Jack without looking. He had just put a cigarette in his mouth and was digging around for a light. He saw that I had been checking the perimeter instead of paying attention to him. "How do you do that?" he asks.

"We are creatures of habit. Thank you for your concern about the mission, though."

When it's time, we head out. I have FEN soft on the box. Rockpile's "Play That Fast Thing" comes on. Wow. Apparently, Jesus is still Lord—great song. Jack just looks at me with a droopy look.

"Yeah, it's all about you, huh?" Then he smiles. He knows I love roots rock. Like I said, we are friends. I smile, and we start driving back to base.

"You really want to do this, don't you?" he asks.

"No, but the Cold War mission might be better off if someone goes. If it has to be me, so be it." I have no regrets or doubts about that as a Christian.

"But...but what if you die?" he asks with a little sorrow in his voice.

"The cost of war," I respond. There is no more conversation until we enter the barracks and leave each other's company with "see you at work" and such.

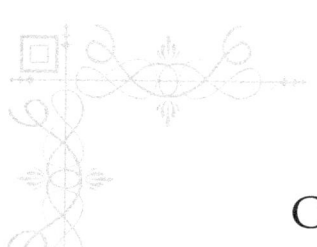

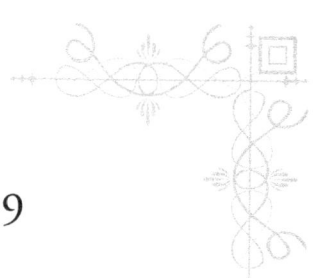

CHAPTER 9

Day One of Swing Shift

Oh goody. The first day of swings. You wake up, go to the gym, and there are usually tourists there, people who won't be there long, and worse. Some enormous asshole left his hoodie on a machine I wanted to use. I politely asked him to move his gear. He stood up and looked a wee bit larger than Mount Rushmore and challenged me. I put a few fingers in his throat and put his gear on his head while he lay on the floor, gagging. Bastard. I have never liked bullies. In the middle of the night at the gym, you can do what you want. Before swings… not so much. Everyone was very surprised this mountain hit the deck. I assured them the bully would live. Not happily, but fuck him.

Then after showering and putting on my utility greens, I visited the chow hall. They wanted to shut down just when the swing shift needed to eat before work. It appears I should get the new commander on this. Mid-shift is worse. I go in, and they treat me like a peasant. They only have things left that others have not eaten. They do not like it when I stand at the counter and light them up verbally. Yup, the commander really does need to see this. Sooner than later. That would be awesome. In this case, I took my tray and threw it over the divider at the bastards and demanded fresh food. It only glanced off of one asshole's head. They seemed a little pissed. Think about it. There are maintainers and flight guys going through the same thing. It isn't just us on Security Hill. The entire base is filled with shift workers. There is a line of them with me now. The chow hall leader asks us to wait just a few minutes and returns in ten minutes with piles of burgers and fries. At least it is something. Someone else with a farmer-strong body and grease under his fingernails had brung me another tray and such. Yup, even us different units can stand together. We shake hands silently. I eat two cheeseburgers with mayonnaise and one order of fries with multiple coffees. The latter are awful.

Afterward, I get into Penny, go through the usual procedures, and turn on the radio while she warms up. "Heavy Metal (Takin' a Ride)" by Don Felder is on FEN. Not bad. I light a Camel and wait. When Buffalo Springfield's "Rock & Roll Woman" comes on, my cigarette is about done so I put the car in gear. It's a nice drive to work. I hope the softball field recovers somehow by the time we hit mid-shift. No games on swings. Cool.

After getting to work, I immediately ask Jack, since I do not see Sammy, on the format to make a memo about the chow hall. He gives it to me, and I give Walker a heads-up that I am taking care of administrative business. I go to the admin room, and the little bitch there starts to stand up. I assure him that I am just there to use the typewriter and sit down. I proceed to formally light those bastards up. I consider adding the third shift problem but decide to take my time on that. One step at a time. Then Sammy shows up just on time with a grimace. "Sorry…that bitch!" Hmmm…the marriage is going as well as I thought.

"Crossfire" by Eric Clapton starts to play. "Sammy, maybe we should get breakfast and let you vent." He looks at me, and I glare back. "Dude, you are acting like a little bitch. Seriously. Let's hand the mission off, get breakfast, and settle this here, okay?" He nods, then sorts out things in Block 3 with a modicum of hand gestures, and we get ready to go. Good. While he does his thing, I continue my attack via memo. At the last minute, I include the third shift shit because the commander needs to know. Done. We let Walker run things for a second. Maybe it will wake him up.

"Addicted to Love" by Robert Palmer comes on a small radio, and I ask Sammy if I need to go alone for breakfast. No, he comes with me. He starts his bitching about his marriage on the way, and I let him vent without interruption. He goes on and on and on. We get to the little itty-bitty diner to the old Japanese women and order, but he insists on paying this time. Old people—go figure. We are quiet on our way back and go into the admin room. The kid is about to leave when I tell him he can stay as long as, like his security clearance says, he can shut the fuck up about what we discuss. He nods and we dig in.

"What do you think, Hal?" he asks. Being the delicate flower petal everyone knows me to be, I am obviously going to treat my new supervisor well. He's a good guy.

"You are a fucking idiot, Sammy. Seriously, every man on planet Earth would want to fuck the snatch off of your hot wife. She is funny, intelligent, and hot. What the fuck is wrong with you?" No, I hold no punches. I absolutely glare at the man.

He has his face full of a walkaway sammich. "Whut, really?" he says through the food.

"Yes, really. What the hell is wrong with you? You treat her like shit, and she is awesome. I am sure you treated her better when you guys were dating and first married. Treat her like that, and fuck the hell out of her, damn it! Show her you love her, and your marriage will become everything it should be. Otherwise, give her to me. I'd love to help those baby-making hips for a while," I say, nodding and downing greasy food. "Or seriously, pull your head out of your ass, and remember why you two got married, okay?"

"You'd fuck my wife if she was single?"

"In a damnyankee second. You married well, Hoss."

He straightens up. "Oh, well. Uh, let me rethink this." Jerk. God help me if I end up like this.

I ask him to read my chow hall memo, and he approves. He had no idea about that either. Married supervisors have no idea about barracks-living problems. Understandable, I guess. He puts the other walkaway in his face and asks with his mouth full, "What about the other thing?"

First, I tell the kid to leave the room, who had returned from a head break, promising we will only be a minute. He smiles, and I thank him as he goes. I give Sammy a broad update. He nods and lifts a finger to let me know he has to swallow. "Look for idle vehicles.

They'll be lining them up and neglecting them from the Afghanistan conflict if they are, indeed, in decline." "The Way It Is" by Bruce Hornsby and the Range comes on the box, softly. Interesting. I had not consciously thought about that. What if they have their own boneyard? And what about their rocket silos? If you don't maintain them, they just become water-filled holes in the ground…but satellites should be able to see a lack of maintenance. Er, right? Maybe.

I thank Sammy, and then we leave, letting the kid back in. Before settling in at Block 3, I visit some of the other sections. Yes, I know I have my own spot to man, but I also have a new mission as well. I ask the kids in Block 8 if anything is different with the enemy. Then I go to the satellite kids. I even ask the kids in DF if there are target areas that seem more important. What everyone tells me is interesting and not illuminating. I leave to go back to Block 3 and John Williams's "The Jedi Steps" comes on as I leave. It should not be inspiring for the mission, but it is.

I get back to Block 3, and Iron Mike reluctantly gives up a contact list. Not a proper continuity list, but it was what he had. Instead of deriding the bastard, I thanked him. He says, "Hail Satan," and then leaves. Sheesh. Then I dug into the list and found fun.

I called out freqs to Tommy and Rocker and then hit the rest on my own. Then I remembered Leanda and gave her an easy target. After that, I caught the rest. Niiice.

The Block 3 analyst, Frogface, was not used to being used in this way. You know, the one who looks like a frog, can't get a date and reeks of tobacco. Poor lil' fella. I would be copying things with my left hand on the keyboard and writing in a notebook on my right at the tiny half-assed table every rack has. I had my cans cockeyed on my head so I was listening to a target network from a small speaker on the right side, while keeping track of different enemy morse conversations on my left. The analyst was flabbergasted but had to enter things into adjacent racks on my right that I heard on the speaker. Lots of fun being able to keep track of which morse code transmitter is who based on sound or the way it is sent. Taking care of two such transmission conversations takes practice. Even Sammy is impressed. One does what one must do. *She Works Hard For The Money* by Donna Summer has been playing, but I just now notice.

After all is captured, I go around and check on everyone. Their spirits are up; they are happy at doing such a good job without the stress of worrying we are about to have WWIII and a nuclear war. I even check on TWT, whatever her name is. I get there at the same time as that pockmarked analyst does. I heard once he is good at his job though. I ask him in front of TWT how she is doing. He says she is coming along nicely, just that she needs to stop missing the beginnings of transmissions and to watch her formatting. I give her a smile larger than she deserves and say, "Good girl." It has the effect I wanted.

Leanda seems impressed with what just transpired, as well. Sammy comes over and asks what he can do to help. I am still near TWT. "Landslide" by Fleetwood Mac has come on. I tell everyone to start writing down targets, their names, the frequencies used, and the time when possible. I tell them we will create a continuity book for each rack and for the entire block. Then I look at Scottie and say, "We need your smoking hot wife to get us a half dozen binders, lined notebook paper, typewriter paper, and lots of laminated pages so spilled coffee doesn't ruin it all." He smiles and gives me a thumbs-up. Then he writes it down on a little "honey do" notebook he keeps in his pocket. Good man. I add, "That is just for our block. If the others follow our lead, they will need their version."[34]

Peter Frampton's "Do You Feel Like We Do" (live) is playing lightly on the corner radio. Niiice. Inspiring. And why couldn't this hippie play this well when he was in Humble Pie? And what the hell is a Sherman (in my hand)?

I catch Sammy's eye, raise a finger, and tilt my head toward Block 2. He nods and keeps writing. I go to Jack and find him at the end of a transmission. Once he passes it to an analyst, he asks, "What's up?" I tell him what I am up to in Block 3 and that, if he did

---

[34] Now, dear reader in the future, why wouldn't we just requisition these items? We need them *now*. If we went through channels, we would find out months later that our request might be denied.

the same in Block 2, it might help his career. Then I tell him the mission items Sammy and I discussed over breakfast and asked him to get that to the Sage. He agrees and tells me that he will let me know when we will next go to the shack. I thank him and head back to Block 3. "I Would Die 4 U" by Prince and the Revolution, Survivor's "Is This Love," and Hall & Oates' "I Can't Go For That" play during our late shift activities. The shift ends with no more excitement. Good, I guess. It feels good to leave on time after only one shift.

I mount Penny and wait. Before lighting a cigarette, I turn on FEN playing "Land of Confusion" by Genesis. The Camel tastes great. I love this car. It makes one reflect. Maybe this is why the Japs are running the world except the fact their cigarettes last only a second or three. The Nips smoke like the French—from birth and seemingly continuously. I relax and empty my mind. "You're All I've Got Tonight" by the Cars comes on. Funny. I wait until my smoke is gone before I put old Penny in gear. She runs better that way. Like foreplay with a frigid hottie.

Even so, I hit the corners a bit too hard and slide occasionally. It is still winter/sleet/rainy season, after all. The early part of the cruise to the barracks included "My Old School" by Steely Dan. I bet Cheryl loves this. I wonder where the hoodie she sent me went. She sent me a lovely hoodie from William & Mary where she is attending university. Hmmm... The last part of the drive had Van Halen's "Cabo Wabo" playing. Everyone loves the original Van Halen, but this version is awesome. I get back to the barracks safely in spite of myself and purposely pursue relaxation with a book and a bottle in the second-floor dayroom. The roommate is already asleep and snoring. I sit down in the dayroom with a couple of beers that I had brought in the back pockets of my jeans, the bottle of JD in my right hand, and a book, *This Kind of War*, by T. R. Fehrenbach, in my left. I was about the only one there when I arrived. When I looked up after a few pages, I realized there was quite the crowd, thankfully quiet, with a radio playing INXS's "Listen Like Thieves." That we do; it's our profession.

Eamons is across the way reading a scientific journal. Once again, I wonder how many people reside in Eamons. Justin is kicking back with a Michelob and a cigarette. I don't see the linguists, Crosse and Corrina, but Tango is sitting by Bingo again. Zeus moves over and lets Balls sit in his place…good man. I hear Jewface but don't see him. Since I was last here, some of the lighting is out. No doubt he is mucking up the quietly intense discussion in the dark corner. I decide to help out poor Balls.

"Good to see you, Balls. How have you been?"

"Better if I had a better nickname," she laments.

"Are you kidding?" I ask, surprised.

O'Phelan's roommate agrees, adding, "I know two kickass maintainer friends on main base named Grease and Vomit." Soft, but universal laughter ensues. Justin had been taking a pull of his beer and begins to choke a little, laughing.

"Yeah, but it isn't like I am named after a god like Zeus here," she says.

Zeus chimes in, "It isn't what you think." She looks confused. "These pricks call me Zeus because I did not show enough dash upon arrival. It means Zero Enthusiasm Unless Supervised. That I am better now has not gotten rid of the nickname. I am not mad. It's a good reminder to pursue the mission every day."

"Really," Balls says, astonished. "No hard feelings?"

Zeus shakes his head. "We are warriors. We are at war. There is no place for sensitivity here. Just honor and duty."

Some nonsense, "I've Found Someone of My Own" by Free Movement is playing on a nearby radio. Yeesh. I find the maggot playing the music and stare him down. Guess Who's "Hand Me Down World" is next. I might let the bastard live. Then I look about again.

I smile and look up to see O'Phelan's roommate also smiling, and then my smile leaves.

"Shit!" I get up very suddenly when I realize Bridget is on the same couch.

"Watch this please?" I gesture toward my beer, booze, and book. Bridget nods. "What is up with Smitty?" I ask the room. Lots of shrugging. "I'll go check with Jack."

Justin puts up a cigarette-holding hand as he drains the rest of his beer. "I'll check with Jack, Hal. It's on the way. Need anything?" I nod and tell something to him in his ear. He nods and leaves.

"What are you reading this time?" Bridget asks. I show her. Then I ask Balls, "Ever read this?"

I swear to God, Jesus, Buddha, Allah, and L. Ron Hubbard, Olivia Newton-John's "If You Could Read My Mind" comes on FEN. Yes, the Soviets may very well win. Son of a…

Balls shakes her head.

"It's one of the greatest history books ever written. It is set in the Korean War, but it really addresses what it takes to fight a war regardless of the foe or the location. For instance, the post-WWII US Army was not trained, not properly equipped, and was being civilianized in the early parts of the Cold War, since we still had the draft but also did not think there was a new war on the horizon. Thus, we were unprepared for war in every way, which is how the Norks and Chinks kicked our ass for so long. Those decisions of being 'nice to our troops' in peacetime cost them their lives in war." I can see in my mind's eye those boys fighting a "police action" with no training, little equipment, and poor leadership. Imagine the terrain, the lack of roads, and the weather. Never fight a land war in Asia indeed.

"Wow. When you are done, may I read that?" Balls asks.

Justin walks in just then and I reply, "No."

"Smitty's okay, Hal," Justin says and throws something underhand to me, which I catch. I face the disappointed face of Balls and say, "But I have a spare copy you may keep as a gift, young lady." I respond with a smile. Her mood jumps along with the rest of her to take the book. "Thanks!"

"Don't mention it," I reply. I look at Bridget and tell her with a grin, "That is my last spare. Sorry."

"I forgive you this time," she responds with a glowing smile. George Benson's "On Broadway" begins on FEN. Between you and I, dear reader from the future, I think we need to call in an air strike against FEN.

I turn my head to Justin and request, "Please give me the straight dope, Hoss," while hearing some funny details between Leanda and

Fern, that short hick girl from the Ozarks, in the opposite corner of the room.

"The VA has lent Smitty all he needs in the way of legal help getting the kids with him as the legal guardian, in addition to the family attorney working pro bono. Local officials, veterans groups and more are trying to ease his taking over his grandparents' house and cars. Local news has put his story in the paper and on the local television station, and he is getting offers for work in both the private sector, like car dealers and such, and both local, state, and federal places, especially the VA are trying to get him working for them. His family's church has given money, as has the local veterans groups. Smitty is good to go, Hal."

Everyone is about to cheer, but I put my finger to my lips. I realize there are tears welling in my eyes, so I try to change the subject. "Have you been listening to this?" I ask, pointing toward Leanda and Fern. Justin shakes his head.

Leanda had mentioned that she and the Rabbit were going to go to an early lunch while on mid-shifts at the 1,000 Yen restaurant. Fern had replied that Leanda was "gonna git summa dat good Injun fuckin'." Leanda assured her they were "only there to dine" and that she wanted to know more about "his people." Sheesh. White people. Leanda is polite enough to ask about Fern and the Ozarks.

Balls looks at me and asks if there is anything else she should know.

"Yes. Aside from your Bible studies on alcohol—not trying to convert you on that, just thought the knowledge would help you expand your reasoning—I thought you might improve if you knew the meaning of what it means to be a good wingman. The Army calls it being a battle buddy. We each need to have each other's six. We are all far away from home on the American Empire's frontier. There will be a time when each of us will be down for whatever reason, work burnout, bad news from home, whatever." I was about to say more when Eamons jumped in.

"But what about dem lazy niggas who just want other people to take care o' dem, making better people dey slaves while dey do nuffin' on welfare?" he says, and his eyes are all lit up again.

Fern adds, "It can be the same with some white folk where I am from in Arkansas."

"In Appalachia, too," adds Bridget.

"Den whut does we do, Hal?" Eamons asks desperately.

"Exactly this, if some people act in such a way, ask them if they believe that all good Christians should be their brothers' keeper. When they agree, ask them how *they* are being *their* brothers' keeper. The Bible does not say that some people are to be served, and the others are to be their hard-working servants. We all should thrive with work as its own reward. And when some of us start to fade or wane, the stronger can lend a small, temporary hand in assistance. Understood?" Eamons nods vigorously. Leanda from the other corner nearly claps her hands.

"Hal, I have never heard that so eloquently put—bravo, sir!" Damn, this De Loughrey broad sticks out, huh? I thank her.

Tango starts to talk to Bingo with great intensity and energy. After nearly two or three seconds, Bingo says, "I have to bingo."

"But where?" Tango practically shrieks.

"To the ER," Bingo answers as he leaves the day room. He probably needs to get a prescription for earplugs as well.

"I'll help!" Tango yelps and dashes to follow him.

I can't help but smile. I look at Bridget, and she can see their future as well. Just then, the B-52s come on the radio. "Love Shack." Funny.

Balls seems lost in thought, but finally asks, "Are there biblical examples of being a good wing buddy or whatever?"

"Sure. How about Adam and Eve? That drunk, Noah, and his Ark. Then there is the story of Shadrach, Meshach, and Abednego as well. Also, Jesus was always helping people, and we were told a story about this in Matthew, uh, 25:31–40, I think. Lastly, there is the story of that hottie, Esther, saving the Jewish nation at the risk of her own life in the Old Testament."

"Thanks, Hal," responds Balls. I nod in reply. Then the discussion in the corner spills over our way. And yes, Jewface is right in the middle of it.

"You see? Eamons reads the same journal," Jewface says proudly. Catcalls and derision are his reply from the madding crowd. I put my finger to my lips and ask, sotto voce, what was going on.

"I was informing these rubes that there will be a communications revolution soon, Hal," Jewface tells me. I raise my eyebrows, and he announces, "Mobile cellular phones."

"Uh-huh," I reply doubtfully. I have no idea what nonsense he is talking about. Maybe it is a joke. "We already have phones, sir, and I hate them."

"These phones are mobile," Jewface states proudly.

"What is their range? Are they like SAT[35] phones or what?" I ask.

"The same range as satellite phones without the use of satellites. The signal would reach from phone to phone by a series of cell towers, making the phones wireless!" His teeth are bright and shiny against his dark skin.

"How would the signal know where in the world to go? There aren't enough people to route them all, if this invention is to be widely used. The infrastructure and computer software to manage all of this would be enormous," I observe. "And these cell structures, er, towers would also be wireless?" He nods. "Regardless of weather and other interference?" Another nod.

"Besides, we already have wireless communications. We call them walkie-talkies," Bubba adds and nearly falls down laughing. Someone else does. Another says through their laughter, "…so stupid!" Jewface is less than amused at the response. I try to keep my composure, but this idea is ridiculous.

"It sounds fascinating. I just don't see the need. We have phone booths wherever they are needed outside of offices and homes, which also have phones. Truckers and policemen have radios aplenty for the communication they need while traveling. When else would you need an extra phone in your pocket or briefcase?" I ask, trying to keep this conversation as rational as possible. Jewface is normally smarter than this.

---

[35] Satellite.

"You could call home from the car and ask your wife if you need to pick something up on the way home. That way she can meet you at the door with a beer and a kiss instead of grabbing your briefcase and sending you back out to get milk while she watches the kids. If you have a kid at college, you can keep in touch more easily than playing phone tag and letter writing. The same with keeping up with older relatives living alone who might need help in a different state. You were the one saying you have a lot of family in Minnesota, but your home is in Virginia," Jewface answers.

"Well, as I said, there are already phones everywhere. I just cannot imagine the expense and the technology needed being invested in a project that might be of some small convenience to some, but not a necessary convenience to most. Oh, and think about wives being able to reach out and nag at all hours of the day! Why else do husbands go to work but for peace and quiet?" Even Bridget laughs at that one, especially because I was quite theatric about the last bit. "Besides, smart husbands call from the office before leaving to see if their Missus needs anything."

Sounding like Frederick Douglass, Eamons intones, "You both make good points. Perhaps we should let this topic rest for now." I had never heard such a sonorous baritone from Eamons. Wow.

Jewface is agreeable. I see that Tommy and Rocker were among a discussion group with Bubba and such. Those two are on their way to me. Bridget looks like she wants to say something. I hear steps coming up behind me. Different people say, at the same time, "Hal, can I ask you something?" Tommy and others, I see. I look behind me and see Jack. I ask him, "Mission-related?" He nods, and I ask the others to excuse me. I motion toward my stuff to Bridget, who nods. Good girl.

We walk into the hallway, and Jack gets right to the point. "I didn't want you to hear this from anyone else. If your girl Stacy says she is pregnant, that kid will probably not look like you." I can tell he is worried about my reaction. I raise an eyebrow and he adds, "She and her friends were out all night and morning drinking and fucking with Jerry Reed's band or whoever they were." I start to grin, and Jack looks surprised.

"Great news! Now I can leave her a polite note saying she is free to date whomever because our different shifts and my extra work duties are keeping us apart. She doesn't have to know I know about this. Whew!" This is good news. As much as I enjoyed getting superimposed and horizontal with her, she is as crazy as a rat in a tin shithouse.

"Glad you are taking this so well, Hal. Still no word on when we'll see our friend again. Oh, and the new girl in Block 2 seems to like me. You were right, some want maturity and stability." I smile and congratulate him. I bet it is the oddly shaped girl. Yuck. Good for Jack, I guess.

"I put everyone else on hold in there." I gesture toward the dayroom. "I had better get back." We say our goodbyes with a side fist bump, and I go back to sit beside Bridget. The Nitty Gritty Band's "Mr. Bojangles" is playing Niiice. I think there is a statue to him in Richmond like all of the other great Southrons. Before sitting down, I decide to throw away my two empty beer bottles. I ask Bridget if she wants anything, and she says a Pepsi. Thus, I buy her a Pepsi from the machine by the trash can. When I sit down, I try to hand the soda to Bridget, but she is in an animated but friendly conversation with Balls. I set the pop beside my leg, take a pull on my bottle of Jack, and see Tommy and Rocker looking at me in anticipation. "Shoot," I tell them.

They are all excited about something musical. Tommy wants to start being a DJ in his spare time like the Stafford twins—one of which is our catcher—and Rocker wants to form a band and asks me to be the singer. I congratulate them both, tell them each of the ideas are great, but I am going to be busy in the near term. I tell them I will be going TDY, but when I return, I will be happy to see what we can get done.

They keep yapping, and I pick up the Pepsi and try to hand it to Bridget. She is ignoring me. I take a pull from my bottle and start gently tossing the soda up and down. People start to look at me oddly. I ask Tommy what his DJ idea is. He wants to introduce new music to this part of the world. Too often, a band that is a huge hit in the US and Europe is still unheard of to us at the tip of the spear for months. Jewface acts like he is going long, and I throw the Pepsi in a perfect spiral to him in stride with a flick of the wrist. His return throw is a bit wobbly, but I *just* keep it from hitting Bridget in the head. Rocker informs me he wants to play heavy metal, and I tell him that I might not be an ideal fit in that I prefer blues-based rock or at least something with a bounce to it like so many of the new hair bands. In contrast, A-Ha's "Take on Me" comes on. Just then, someone else starts talking to me.

"Oh, is that my Pepsi?" asks Bridget. The can is starting to swell, but I say, "Yes!" Apparently, she was the only one in the room not watching what happened to the can while she was chatting because she proceeded to open it. You can imagine what happened next.

Everyone's jaw dropped except for Bridget's. Time seemed to stand still for a second before the can erupted. I dove left with my book and JD, everyone else dodged hither and yon, and Bridget just sat there for another second with the can above her lap erupting on her side of the couch. She then proceeded to chase after me past the soda machines, out of the dayroom, and down the hall. The can was just about spent when she yelled, "Damn it!" and threw the can at me. I picked it up and tossed it in a bin.

"Let's get you to your room," I say with a smile on my face. She nods and then starts laughing.

"Guess I wasn't paying attention," she observes. We walk to her room, and she tells me to come in. "I am going to have to get you back, Viking Talker. Damn, my skin is sticky," she observes while taking off her button-down blouse like it's a football jersey. She still has on an undershirt and bra. Not bad-looking, really. I guess her blouses cover up her figure.

"How may I serve you then, Missy?" I ask like the gentleman I am.

"Get your pranking ass in the shower and help me clean up," she retorts.

"If it will help with the war effort..." I respond. She responds with a surprised smile. The shower is available, so I do my duty as a good wingman. Once again, come in, indeed. It being a work night, I am only there until the mission is completed. Only an hour or so—I bet you, dear reader from the future, will understand.

CHAPTER 10

Day Two of Swings

I get up a little earlier than necessary, so I walk to the dayroom window to check out the weather. The sidewalks don't look too slick, and the sun is trying to come out from behind a few clouds. Good. I put on my running shoes, sweats, and head out. Well, before I head out, I leave a polite note for Stacy telling her that it isn't fair for her to wait for our shifts and my other work to align interfering our chances to date, ending by encouraging her to see other people. That done, I feel great. Besides, it seems like months since I have had a run. I was a runner in high school, too. Quick, but not fast, so I trained for long-distance races back then. Despite a lack of natural talent, I had some success by outworking the competition and by being a sneaky bastard. That thought is interrupted by a car radio stopped at the same four-way intersection I am at. I look down, and it's the same handsome Negress that works in Block 2 at the weather rack. She notices it is me and says, "James Brown's 'Out of Sight.'" I give her a thumbs-up and get back to running. She whistles at me as we both go our own ways. She has been surprisingly flirtatious lately. Good-looking woman, too. I have no idea what she sees in me. She seems too mature to want to be involved in my hijinks. Then again, I have been a pretty good boy the past few months.

Someone passes me slowly, and they are playing "Smokestack Lightning" by Howlin' Wolf, which has to be one of the top 10 songs in history. I don't know what it is about this run, but I am cruising effortlessly. I catch up to the car that was playing the Wolf, and the next song is "Eyesight to the Blind," but it is not Sonny Boy Williamson performing it. I ask them at the stop sign who it is, and I think they say it's Mose Allison. I thank them and change direction so that I will eventually head back to the barracks. I am in a residential district on base now. Mostly retirees. One is cleaning his car and is playing Roy Montrell's "That Mellow Saxophone" along the sidewalk on the other side of the street. I yell out a hello and "Great song!" to him. He responds.

"Have any requests, young man?" he asks with a grin.

"'Elk's Parade' by Bobby Sherwood and His Orchestra," I call out. He points at me and laughs with joy. "Will do!"

That last bit of talking was harder to do, not being in great aerobic shape after the long winter. I am not quite out of breath, but I am glad I turned toward the barracks. Some cars have their windows down since it must be all the way up into the upper 40s. I can hear the music from other cars too because they have their windows cracked to let out their cigarette smoke. I hope this weather holds when Charlie Flight goes on mids and has to play ball again. Otherwise, we might have to be sneaky bastards like when I was a runner in high school.

Just remembering it makes me smile. I was a fair cross-country runner, but only succeeded due to outworking the competition. During spring track season, the races were shorter than suited me as I had no speed. I would run the mile race at a near-dead sprint as part of my warm-up for the two-mile a half hour or so later. It was good for the team since I would usually end up in the top 3. During the two-mile races, I would run just about flat out, nearly as fast as I could run. If the competition tried to keep up, they would die of exhaustion. If they let me get away, they would rarely catch up at the end. I would run that fast through the first six laps and hold on for the last two. Of course, if anyone was within two hundred yards at the start of the last lap, they might catch me. At one hundred yards, they probably would. Like I said, I had no kick. Then again, I won half of these races when I had no business winning any. Whatever it takes.

I get back to my room in the barracks, and the male whore roommate has actually showered. He could use some clothes, but I am nearly impressed. He asks, "May I hit play on your radio?" I smile and nod. He presses play on the left tape player of the boom box, and the end of Rolling Stone's "Think" comes on. "Wow, not bad," he says and pauses. "Wait, is that the Stones?" I smile and nod again.

Then an underrated song comes on. "Ride Me High" by J. J. Cale comes on to end the tape. Graham is floored. "Damn!" He practically starts swaying like a Latina in his tighty whities. Meanwhile, I am setting things out so that I can jump into them after my shower to get ready for the chow hall and work. The tape ends. "May I?" he asks. Not to sound like a robot, but I smile and nod. He plays the tape deck on the right, and Ricky Nelson's "Waitin' in School" is up first. It is a complete Ricky Nelson tape, or so I am told. It was a gift. I hope the songs from the movie, *Rio Bravo*, are on it. I finish straightening up my gear and uniform when the song changes to "Travelin' Man." I hit the showers feeling like I can conquer the Soviet Far East. Traveling man, indeed. Yeah, right.

At work, Sammy has been all over the mission. The binders and such are all there. He is about to pitch the box when I tell him that we'll need storage. I restore the box, grab a marker, and mark it "Charlie Gear" in big letters. My idea that we keep our binders under one of the racks never used is agreed upon. I also stress to everyone that this is not to be better than other shifts but merely to gather knowledge over time to eventually share with every shift. The administrative day shop intelligence nerds are supposed to do things like this, but they don't. I hear that whole section is full of garrison-thinking morons.

After setting the box down, I take a short detour to Block 2 to see Jack. I say hello to Dinger at her post, and she waves to me. I raise my eyebrows and raise a finger. She assents, and I continue to Jack. He pats his little table at his rack, so I get in a catcher's kneeling position so he can tell me something in private.

"Tomorrow night after last swing, Hal. Alone. And he gave me homework to give to you. He does not want this seen in this building, so he wants you to be discreet in your room." I was about to say something, but he stopped me, saying, "He knows, but you should also know field officers do this out in the world every day. Hell, SIGINT guys in wartime give classified information to those not cleared for it because someone has to tell our warriors who is to be killed and where, okay?" I nod. "At shift's end, walk with me, and you will end up walking out with 'personnel papers.'" I give a thumbs-up and head back to Block 3, not forgetting about the Senior.

Dinger smiles when I approach. "Yes, ma'am," I say politely.

"Thanks for what you have done to my Balls," she says with a soft voice and a widening smile.

"Just being a good Christian, Senior. What else may I do for you? Sammy needs me." Admittedly, I was worried that Dinger was attracted to me, so I was thinking of trying to escape. I have enough women problems. Note that I also avoided laughing at how her statement came out.

"One thing. Well, first off, you let me know if you need any help. I hear you are always on the edge of getting in trouble. Here's the other thing," she says as she looks around for anyone listening in. "Is your roommate single?" I get quite a case of the grins.

"No one steady. The ladies find him quite attractive for some reason," I inform.

"I bet…thanks," she says and waves me toward Block 3. Wow. Dinger wants a boy toy.

The workday is rather routine except for my reminding the kids to log their work. I pay extra attention to TWT and Leanda for different reasons: TWT to make certain she is at the go when her targets are ready to start since she is slow to react, and Leanda to see if she wants to be more properly engaged in the mission and what she thinks her level of SIGINT competence is. After she says she could never do what I did the day before, copying two Morse conversations at once, I assure her it is just like getting better at anything (e.g., if you want to be a good golfer, play golf every day). She smiles and says that soon she would be happy to accept more. I leave her with my smile and a tap on her little rack table. When I look back, she is glowing. Good girl.

Then I check on Tommy and Rocker, who sit side by side for good reason.[36] They tell me how they love the importance of their mission. I ask how they're logging the data (e.g., freqs, times, unit names, and so on). They are less than enthusiastic about this. I ask them, "What happens when one or both of you are reassigned. The new kid, maybe fresh out of tech school, misses and messes up everything, and we lose WWIII?" Properly chastened, they try to make it up with what they know. I am just glad they are now on it. This will need constant supervision.

I think about Jack and his proposed homework and, since I am near Dinger, tell her Jack has a great idea about creating continuity books for Block 2. After all, their mission is so diverse and all... besides, he is so shy in pursuing personal recognition and awards. The Senior jumps on it. See? I try to be a good person sometimes.

I get back to my part of Block 3 and light up my rack. Someone's tiny radio is playing "Spirit of the Radio" by Rush. I bet those Canadians had no idea what real men were doing with radios. Still, it's a great song. I remind my comrades to note their notebooks in the same way to make creating and using a continuity binder for each rack and the block a whole easier. Besides, what happens when someone has to cover their rack? Having a uniform format will aid in effectiveness. Work is relatively routine, and after seemingly no time at all, the swing shift ends.

Since Jack had nothing except a promise that he would visit me later, I went "home" to my room in my barracks since I did not see him after work. After changing into my Huck Finn drag and so as to make certain he did not miss me, I sat in the dayroom with my book. Just as the room was filling up, I heard him say, "On your right." Bridget was just sitting down. I go with my book and meet with Jack in my room. He has my stuff in the back of the room where I sleep. He will not leave until I give him leave from his post. Another problem comes from the influx of partyers from the dayroom to my room. I tell them I need them to fuck off for work reasons. Fine

---

[36] Sorry, dear reader of the future; some things are still classified.

Americans like Justin, and Jewface get the rest to leave. All that is left is Bridget and me…and Jack.

"I have homework. Sorry. Jack, do you have to go? Bridget, sorry but I have some work-related need-to-know stuff going on. No offense, but I am about to go on a TDY. You'll understand." Bridget understands and looks worried as she leaves. Jack stands up and goes to the bathroom door. After listening through the door, he comes back toward me and points to the stereo. I nod and play a classical compilation on tape that I like. Jack looks at me curiously, and I reply, "Fuller range of sound. Besides, this is *Romeo and Juliet* by Tchaikovsky."

"No offense, Hal, but you aren't my type." We both come just short of laughing.

"Neither of us is in the Navy. I just thought Peter Ilyich noise would help conceal the discussion."

"Hope so," answers Jack. "Let me show you what this is and how it works." He proceeds to show how the accordion folder contains not personnel paperwork but a smuggler's area hiding small instruction manuals and maps. "Some of this is tradecraft, some maps, some just what we know about the regions you will go through. Don't stay up all night memorizing this, but you need to mentally inhale it all in the next few days. Oh, and the Sage wants to meet after the last swing shift, the evening the day after tomorrow." The song is really starting to accelerate and get interesting as he says this. "Need anything from me?" Jack asks.

"Yes, a piece of shit military messenger satchel for me to take this to and from work every day. Soon everyone will think it is part of what I do and will be looked upon as normal. If it is new, then it will attract attention. This way, you and I can exchange items in this 'personnel folder' whenever we need to at work. Second, small shitty footlockers to hold each block's binders for the new project. I bet the Sage has them in a shed somewhere and would love to get rid of them. I'll pick them up when we meet. Do you need anything from me?" I ask, all business.

"No. You have a place to stow this folder when you aren't here?" I nod in response. "I think that you should go to the day room and do two things. First, calm the kids down since it is a work night. Second, check and see if Bridget is there. I think she likes you. She's kind of cute, you know?" Jack is spot on. We get up, and he goes to do whatever it is he does. I forgot to ask how he and his little JEEP are doing. She reminds me of the John Cougar line, "...you ain't as great as you are young." Not a looker, but I am happy for Jack. I stow the folder.

I do my usual—put a beer in each back pocket, grab my latest bottle of Tennessee's finest and a book, and head toward the dayroom. Glad the roommate was not here when Jack wanted to meet. I wonder which chick the roomie is shacked up with now. I get to the dayroom, and Bridget comes up to me and smothers me in a kiss and whispers in my ear, "I told them you were working on a research project." Smart girl. I forgot there might be questions. I reply to both the kiss and the message with, "Nice to see you too," with a smile. Not a beaming smile in reply. Just one that shows appreciation. This hillbilly-ette might be okay, but I am not exactly swept off my feet.

I turn, and we both sit on the usual couch. "Need a Pepsi?" I ask. I get a glare. "Nooo..." Some laugh. Then I take in what is happening. Some are having quiet conversations over a small drink. Others are only deterred from getting drunk and arrested downtown by the weather. I remind them it is a school night and we are at war, to keep a relatively clear eye. Some point to my beverages. "I said relatively," which is responded to with giggles. I see Justin and the roommate sitting together having a beer. Are they contemplating the new JEEPS? Dunno.

"What are you *really* working on, Hal?" asks Jewface. His eyes are narrowed in accusation. I give a crooked grin in response.

"Unfucking a research project from one of the war colleges. Some nerd came up with this magisterial tome on the weaknesses of some sections of the Soviet Union based on culture, weather, and terrain. He, or she, doesn't know the Far East for beans. I also doubt their idea of a two-pronged invasion in response to WWIII will work since I don't think we have the forces necessary on this side of the world to do much but deter them. Besides, one would hope China, now stronger, would take advantage of the situation and interfere," I respond with less than the truth. However, if you have to lie, be specific. I'll have to pass on the lie to Jack so he can confirm, just in case.

Jewface seems unconvinced. Forrest Graham Hobarth, the male whore roommate, comes to my defense in between long drags from his cigarette. "Duuude..." he says as he shakes his head. "Hal is always doing shit like that. It's horrible to watch. He focuses so hard, he doesn't even recognize the bitches that come asking for him. He has," he says, pausing for another bout with his smoke, "a problem," he ends judgmentally, looking at me with a grin. I respond in kind.

"Hal, if I may," starts Leanda, whom I did not notice at the table diagonal from me in the day room drinking something fancy in a fancier looking glass, "what was that you were listening to earlier? When we were ushered out of your room, you started to play some music, but through the door, I could not make it out. I was at loggerheads as to where to go and ended up here."

"Peter Ilyich Tchaikovsky. *Romeo and Juliet* by the Royal Philharmonic Orchestra in 1977. Just a compilation tape I have. I prefer my classical CDs, though the sound quality is worse. If you need to borrow some, please let me know. The BX is pretty good at providing a selection," I respond to her astonishment. I think she is going to slide out of her chair. Also, I can feel the glare from my right from Bridget as I discuss this to my left across the room.

"Classical music, Hal?" asks Justin, who then tries to pull on this cigarette and Michelob at once.

"There is more to life than just blues, Hoss," I answer without laughing at his physical and mental faux pas. "Sometimes the best classical composers got melody ideas from minstrels in pubs. Good for them. And before you say it; yes, I know we are merely discussing sixteenth, seventeenth, eighteenth, and nineteenth century cover bands," I say which is responded to by a few teeheehees.

Tango stumbles in with a secret smile on her face. Interesting. "How's Bingo, Tango?" I ask.

"Sleeping," she replied with a shy, sly grin. "He is going to be okay."

"Good to hear," I say when I am interrupted.

"What are your favorites, Hal?" asks Leanda. She looks like I made her drink all of whatever fancy drink she brought with her. Someone behind her points to a bottle of Brandy. It's TWT who adds, "That's muh name," with a giggle. Oh goody. I am just noticing that Train Wreck Tits has a Texas accent. Maybe drinking brings it out more. Of course, she sounds a bit less than smart. There is a lot to like about Texians, but they should squeeze Austin like the zit it is.

I answer, "Normally the Krauts. Beethoven is best, especially his piano sonatas. Mozart is fun. The best waltzes are nice. Telemann, ah yes, I know, Baroque, should be better remembered. Franz Josef Haydn, yes, an Austrian, is outstanding. But others can be good. The Italians are fair but obsessed with their damn violins. Prokofiev reflects Russia well. Ravel had one hit for France. Chopin moved to France from Poland, and his piano playing was truly 'talking to God,' as George Sand is reputed to have said. Debussy is underrated to an extent since no one remembers anything but 'Clair de Lune,'" I say educationally. I cannot believe everyone is actually listening.

"Alright, alright, thank you for dazzling us once again," says Jewface. "Who in the hell is George Sand?"

"Amantine Lucile Aurore Dupin was a French novelist in France—bigger than Hugo in her time."

"Her? George is a bitch?" asks an exasperated Jewface. Bridget, on my right, is starting to get the giggles. I pat her knee. Doing so makes me remember the night before and has the usual effect. Damn it.

Leanda helps out. "It was common for women writers to use a male pen name, especially when writing about topics that were considered taboo at the time."

O'Phelan's roommate remarks, "Leanda sounds like Ginger Grant on *Gilligan's Island.*"

There is some laughing, and Leanda blushes. Then she looks at me like I am an island of sophistication in a sea of commoners. Shit.

"You sound like a pearl to me, Leanda," I say, then turn to Bridget. "Didn't you need me to fix your equipment?" Bridget nods enthusiastically. "My apologies to you all, I have to go. Don't stay up too late, it's a workday tomorrow." A few nods and a few "yeah, yeahs" come from them all. I might light these people up tomorrow unless the mission beats me to it.

Bridget insists we go to her room. This time I notice why. She lives alone. Nice. The door barely closes before she starts diving in and making me bare. We have marital PT sessions all over her room. After only a few hours, I ask to leave so as to get ready for work.

"Yes, Viking Talk…" She slipped off to sleep. I make certain her alarm clock is set and leave. Wow. I was not expecting fun from this girl. I could grow to like her, I guess.

I get back to my room, and my roommate must be in the dayroom. My fancy Japanese boom box is playing the other side of the tape, nearly all Chopin. After what I have been through, he sounds like a delicate pansy masturbating when I have been busy fucking. The tape gets fast-forwarded and removed. Freak. Then I bundle myself to bed after only a little bit of reading.

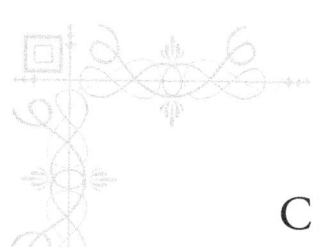

CHAPTER 11

Day Three of Swings

Day three of swings. I would think that swings would be good for teenagers, but I am past that in a few ways. No, not just age, but shift-work experience and such. My legs are a little sore, so I look outside from down the hall. I'd look out of our barrack's room, but the buildings are so close together that you cannot get the whole picture. It looks cold, cloudy, but not too rainy. I man up for another run. I decide on intervals, fast, medium, slow, etc. It's always good to mix things up as you, dear reader from the future, no doubt know. Not that I am trying to lose weight; I just want my physicality at its best, especially considering my TDY location.

After the run and the usual ablutions, I get dressed in yesterday's still crisp green uniform with the tuck-in shirt and go to the chow hall. I am early, but not as early as yesterday. They have no food. Zero. No, I am not kidding. I go behind the counter to the commander's office. I pick up the phone, and the captain smacks my hand like a bitch. "I have my orders!" he shrieks. I put him down and make the call. Dumbass cutie-pie at 6920 ESG/HQ answers the phone. I ask to be put into the commander. She does so, for no apparent reason.

"Colonel, you owe it to yourself to see what and who is feeding your Airmen. You need to see this now before the evidence is removed, sir."

"Hal? Is that you? What is going on?" he asks.

"Sir, there isn't just food poisoning food here. There isn't just rotting French fries. There is no food. Nothing at all. For all of second shift for all of the shifts on the base. Please come now, sir. Soonest." He thanks me and hits the road. With guys from all sorts of shift units from all over base, we hold everyone working there hostage. Luckily, the Man is a prompt person.

He walks in, and I gesture toward the food area. "Second shift meal, sir." He is about to explode. I try to calm him. "Third shift rats[37] are *much* worse, sir."

The colonel, to his credit, loses his damn mind. He uses the chow hall commander's phone to call the base commander. Yes, he notices and discards the fact the chow hall commander is on the floor unconscious and bleeding, but only a bit. The base commander cannot be bothered to care so Givens calls the PACAF[38] commander, who then starts shrieking down the chain. Funny.

My commander looks at me and is trying to calm down. He asks, in a stage whisper, "What else is wrong with this place?" I tell him about everything while stressing the third shift chow situation. He cannot believe it. He says, "If it is as you say, catch a ride, wake me up, and show me." I nod and thank him. This will be good.

I go to work foodless. Once at Security Hill, I grab all sorts of gut grenades from the little old ladies at the Walkaway Café. I use the time to eat in the administrative room and read some of the data the Sage gave me since I am early for my shift. Some of this stuff will need to be practiced. I don't know if I need all of this James Bond training, but maybe learning a few techniques, like the brush pass, might prove useful one day. It sounds like FEN is playing softly in the corner. Bachman Turner Overdrive's "Roll on Down the Highway" is followed up by "I Am Just a Singer in a Rock 'N' Roll Band" by the Moody Blues. Not a fan of the latter at all. "I'm So Anxious" by Southside Johnny comes on next, which is much worse. Damn. How low can these assholes at FEN get? I do not need torture while learning the Sage's documents.

I am nearing the end of my grub when I see something interesting. It is a paper on the weather patterns of the areas I may encounter.

---

[37] Rations.
[38] Pacific Air Forces commander.

Russia is cursed. No wonder Napoleon and the Nazis had such a hard time. Yngwie Malmsteen's "Heaven Tonight" comes on the box. Typical hair band rock, but damn if this hippie isn't a talented guitar shredder. I wonder if he will ever legally change his middle name to "Fucking" since that is how everyone refers to him. Looking at the report again, I decide to reattack the quality of the roads with the Sage. It wouldn't do to be stuck in the middle of nowhere in Commie Land with a road washed out and only military patrols and KGB going through the area.

I dispose of my rubbish, grab my satchel, and go to Block 3. I am there first, so I set my rack up and greet everyone as they come in, asking them to bring their binder and come to me before they get started. I explain to everyone except Brandy that, since they have multiple Racal radios, they can keep some on frequently used enemy frequencies and search for targets using one or two others. I also answer any and all questions. With Brandy, I tell her to sit on her targets but to start learning to search on a spare radio when her mission is not transmitting. If she finds something she cannot figure out, I told her to ask me to listen to it or tell Walker what she has found if I am copying enemy Morse code at the time. Sammy is last. He looks a little tired.

He sits down and slouches a little, which is unlike him. I look at him, and we both smile. His smile made me smile, which made him smile more and so on. "Well, you were right, Hal," he tells me.

"I told you we would win this tournament," I reply, leaving him dumbfounded for a moment. Then he laughs.

"Funny. What I meant was you were right about the Missus. I was the problem. Me and my thinking. Stinkin' thinkin'."

"Mental halitosis."

He gives me a crooked grin in response, "Okay, what gives with the tournament?"

"Before we go to work for our first mid-shift, we play Dawg Flight. If we win, then it is us versus the admin pukes for the championship," I inform. "Want me to pass that along to everyone? Who else knows?"

"Sure. How did you find out?"

"I found out by accident, so yeah, I should go ahead and tell everyone. The other teams have done a good job knocking each other out of the tourney."

"Thanks for getting everyone settled before I got here."

"Nopraw," I say as I get up to leave. "Oh, and I will be telling everyone that this next game is a trap game. We need to pound these assholes like cheap veal." Sammy nods in agreement and turns his chair toward his work. I go to the satellite section first then back through electronics giving the same data and warning. I notice that Happy is missing, and I don't even see Bridget. There is someone there I have never seen before. He sees me and walks up.

"Hi, I'm Norman the Mormon," he says as he shakes hands. I was about to introduce myself when he stopped me, "I have heard all about you, Hal. It looks like the fictional version is pretty close to the truth. Allegedly we are both smart and crazy, but I don't drink or get arrested."

"So I am ebony to your ivory?" I ask, and he laughs.

"Precisely!" he responds with a gay wink. I look and I see a wedding ring. Good. "No, I don't know where Happy and Bridgie are. I'll let them know you were here." I thank him and ask if he has kids. "Seven and a third."

"Yeah, the Mormons back home in Virginia had big families, too. Congratulations. Good for you," I answer and give my leave. Blocks 4, 1, and 2 greet the news well. Jack in Block 2 reminds me of my date with the Sage tomorrow night after work. I nod in agreement and return to Block 3. Sammy is waiting for me.

"Two things. The new commander is thankful for what happened before work. Second, after we beat Dawg, he wants us to play the admin pukes on the evening of our first day off after our last mid. That way all of the Charlie Flight families can come to the game."

"I just want the damn thing to be over with. Well, after we beat those admin maggots, of course. Sorry I did not cover what happened with the commander before you found out from him. Hope it went well," I respond. The other Stafford twin hears FEN play "Crazy Train" by Ozzy Osbourne and cranks it a tad too loud right where Block 2 and Block 3 meet. Sammy walks over to him and turns it off.

"You ever pull some shit like that again, and I will shove this goddamn thing up your ass and rip off a stripe or two, got it?" It appears Sammy is a bit testy, huh? Normally good fucking calms a man for longer. Well, maybe old people fucking is as good as you can get at that age and has an expiration date, like them. Then again, we all have one of those.

The Stafford twin complies immediately with remorse.

"Where were we? Oh yeah. Well, I told him that when an Airman like you puts something through channels, nothing gets done. As to the delay in the final game, it does give us a breather for a rematch if Dawg wins," Sammy tells me.

"That makes sense. Truly sorry I did not give you a heads-up first though." He holds up a hand.

"No harm, no foul. Let's kick these commies' asses today, okay?" he replies with a sly grin. Then he says quietly, "And thanks for helping the kids and improvements and all." I smile and give him a small nod.

Stafford the catcher comes over toward me. I am putting my cans around my neck and getting the Racals sorted when I hear, "This is who I was telling you about." I look and see he is talking to a woman, so I stand.

She puts out a hand and says, "Melody Olson." I reply with a very big grin, which does not go well with Staffy.

"I haven't heard that accent since visiting family all over Minnesota," I respond. "I was raised in Virginia though. You?"

"South Dakota." Stafford has to get back to his workplace but sings Melody's praises and tells me to treat her right. She isn't beautiful but has a friendly face, intelligent blue eyes, red curly hair, and a fair figure. However, I get the impression what I want to do to her to treat her right would catch hell with my catcher.

"Sammy," I say to his back, "we have a new analyst. Would you like me to give her a mission brief and SITREP now or after you give her a more formal introduction to our work area?" He agrees to the latter, for which I am thankful. She isn't hot, but she is on the way there, and her baby-making hips are having an effect on me.

I look around and see everyone is where they are supposed to be. I remind Brandy and her TWT to turn the volume down; I could hear the static from her cans from my rack. Walker seems a bit listless but not quite merely going through the motions. I remind myself that if there is any write-up about the Soviet exercise we covered, he gets plenty of credit. Leanda seems to be a hard worker and asks good questions. Tommy and Rocker are less than focused. I whistle softly, and they turn. I point to my rack and raise my eyebrows. They get the message and do some work.

I open my binder and look at Iron Mike's freqs, setting up some of my radios for them, and interrupt my searching through the bands by checking on the others listed. I am still getting a feel for the Block 3 mission, as many of us are. Using these new radios is a pain in the ass. The older ones had a dial to search through the frequencies. These have something less than real buttons. Many times, to get a real read on a signal, you had to dial it in off a proper number since the Soviet equipment lacks precision. Thus, for example, when a target thinks he is sending from 9596, he is really sending from 9595.223543. The difference, depending on distance and range, strength of signal, weather, and other factors can be great. No, not every change is for the better. Joseph Heller was right when he said change was usually for the worse. So the new radios were more like car radios than proper war radios. No doubt someone with no mission experience made this acquisition decision. Garrison-thinking will lose this war.

Then I get two different conversations on multiple frequencies. Thankfully, I was smart enough to pull out a notebook and pen and set it down beside the little speaker on the little table that should exist for coffee and ashtrays. I look to see if I can pass one to someone, but everyone is busy. Thus, with my left hand, I type on the keyboard, the new kind we got at the same time as the new Racals, and with my right, I write out the conversation from the little speaker. Justin showed me how to get multiple radios to play out of the same speaker. Since they transmit one at a time to each other, it works. I am too busy to call DF to ensure who is saying what to whom. Hopefully the call signs will break and inform who is who after the fact.

I find I am too busy to talk for a time. When I do get a second, I call out for an analyst. Someone comes behind me, and I point toward the seat beside me on my right. That someone who smells lovely sits beside me but does nothing. When I can speak again—I can't speak and listen to two Morse conversations at once for some reason—I tell them that this (I slap the notebook) goes in there (pointing to the rack computer). I continue to type on the left and write on the right. The analyst tries to take the notebook, and I slap their wrist as I keep writing. When I have a second, I tear off the page or three I have so far and pass it to them roughly. It occurs to me that I should number the pages.

I look briefly to my right and see it is indeed Melody. Sammy is helping her read my writing, understand the shorthand, and properly format what goes in. This goes on for a short while when the other analyst, Frog, saunters in. Nothing gets him rankled, so I can never know if he is lazy or has it all under control. He has already become used to me stealing anyone to do the job we should have enough operators to do. Of course, typing what was written down should be easy and only take less than a moment.

All of a sudden, I hear Walker say, "Shitshitshitshitshit..." I tell him I am getting it, too. I turn to the Frog.

"Hey, it might be nice to know why everyone sent at the same time, huh? You have thirty seconds to get your ass in gear. We might be in a shooting war in a few minutes," I tell him.

I think he is surprised I can talk and type at the same time. However, when truly epic messages are sent, they are sent strong, clear, and slow. The other targets shut the hell up to hear it transmitted to them. Sammy and Melody are waiting for me to explain. I raise a finger as I do not want to have any errors. Then the transmission is over.

I look at them and say, "The Sovs have sent the codeword to launch their air forces against us. I do not know if that includes nukes or if this is a simulation. Sammy, would you tell Dinger about this and have her people look for that? This could just be a local exercise, or..." He lightly taps my desk and goes. I look at Melody, who is calm. "Walker and I got these messages. I have no idea if they are the same message. Even if transmitted with different characters on different freqs, they could be the same message encrypted differently. If they are different networks and sent the same characters, they may have sent different messages to different locations based on how the code breaks. Are you good?" She nods, and I thank her for her help.

Sammy comes back and asks what to expect. "Well, this could be a tabletop exercise, and nothing happens. If they want to test their aircraft status and efficiency, then everything they have will be in the air. If so, we might need others to help us since we are still undermanned and there will be a lot of planes. Of course, if they are coming on the attack, then we have just a few minutes to live."

He looks at me suspiciously. "They will not just launch conventional weapons but chemical weapons." I educate. He is less than happy with this.

"Oh, and tell those useless bastards in the Fish Bowl to alert the base commander. Oftentimes no one bothers," I finish. He nods and gets at it.

Melody walks past me. "Done," she says. "Now what?" I tell her the same thing that I told Sammy. This may be a tabletop exercise for their leaders, it could be an exercise for the launching of their weapons systems, or it could be WWIII and we will all die of a chemical attack. She looks at me with a raised eyebrow.

"Some of their first conventional attacks will be on the Elephant Cage and our building, followed up with chemicals. They will want to keep the airfield intact if they want to take Japan. The issue with you is, we may have a ton of Soviet aircraft taking off, and everyone copying their whereabouts will call for an analyst. Not all aircraft will be caught due to the dearth of manning. You will need to keep calm and figure out how close they get. Also, you will have to do your magic analyst bit to see if we need to sortie our aircraft from this base. Personally, I would wait. Wouldn't want them to know how good our SIGINT is, right? If it is an exercise, of course," I tell her.

"Huh, I hadn't thought of that before," I realize to myself after the fact to myself, even though the Sage mentioned it. I see Sammy coming back. "What if this is a test of our SIGINT capabilities? It would behoove us to have everyone ready in their own way, but not give our capabilities away, right?" I tell him. He catches on instantly and goes off.

"You know, most Airmen don't operate this way," observes Melody.

"They should. I hope you will, too." I cannot tell what is behind those blue eyes. Interesting.

Then all of the usual suspects went off, blasting code all over the place, with some being missed by lack of manning. Now we know the planes are actually taking off. I see Frog wandering around, seemingly doing nothing.

"Are Iron Mike and Hesse supplementing?" I ask the bastard. He nods. Good man.

"Are they copying the same bastards we are, you stupid cunt?" He is not happy with this response since he has no idea. I wave Sammy to me and tell him that, as busy as we are, it will reflect poorly on him if we are all copying the same targets. He internalizes that and goes at it.

It all works out. We did not launch our aircraft until they were in radar range, which makes them think we have planes always on the hot pad. Apparently, our new commander has an informant and shows up to watch his people capture a situation. Of course, he is missing much. He is thankful the Sovs did not attack. That does not mean we had an appropriate response. PACAF decisions had to be handled at my level. What happens when I am gone? I communicated to other blocks for temporary manning while not losing significant mission. Also, who communicates with the other blocks, electronics, satellites? There was no preliminary product delivered to anyone who needed to declare war. Our day shop assholes should be doing this every hour of the day but cannot do this during their three martini lunches and nonexistence at serving on the shifts for experience. In my opinion, they are absolutely useless.

The rest of the shift is routine. Even Brandy improved. She is a child, but this is what we have to work with. The others have been doing their jobs, but Leanda seems especially voracious for mission knowledge. I should recommend her for my spot or something.

Tommy and Rocker are okay, and Walker is as well. That reminds me...

Sammy is packing up, and I tell him to write in his Big Chief notebook that Walker was a *big* part of our "this is WWIII" exercise from before. He looks at me like I am crazy, but I remind him of the Z messages and such.

He responds, "I bet you are right. *You* did everything, but Walker was the first focal point. We'll keep your name out of this again. Thanks. I'll see to it." He leaves me with a nod, and we all pack up to leave. The report will not be seen by the common Airman, but still. Jack reminds me of the meeting the next night again as we make the long walk to our cars.

Ahhhh...getting Penny to start after work. I relax with a Camel from the Tar Heel State and wait for her to warm up. I start to feel a little bit like a traitor since, being a Virginian, I am smoking a Camel. Phillip Morris is big in my hometown of Richmond, Virginia, having a regional headquarters and manufacturing there. Their world HQ is in NYC, but one day they will move to America. I guarantee it. Taxes. Smoking regulations. And just leaving that godforsaken hell-hole filled with damnyankees will be worth it. I just prefer Camels to Cowboy Killers. Go figure. I like Marlboro Lights but can't get myself to drink diet beer or smoke diet cigarettes. I reach back to the radio box, and "Who Made Who" by AC/DC comes on. Niiice. When the song is replaced with "Back on the Chain Gang" by the Pretenders, I switch from FEN to tapes and from neutral to drive.

"Crazy Train" by Ozzy Osbourne comes on not long after I reverse out of the parking place and put Penny into forward gear. Good pop song. I guess it is a good hard rock song, but he seems to be walking the line between hard rock and pop, right? Like KISS. They had all of the blood and fireworks and kabuki makeup, but they were usually a hard pop band, right? When you have time alone driving in the dark, you can think these thoughts. Like why isn't fertilizer called grassoline? Jewface mentioned Alaska vehicles have engine warmers or some such. He contends that there will one day be car chair warmers, but laments that the term *rear defrosters* has already been used. How would that even work...deployable electric blankets? I am starting to wonder about his sanity. Queen's "Crazy Little Thing Called Love" comes on. Now this is a rock and roll song. Different than the rock music they normally play. Yes, there is a difference. Compare Chuck Berry to Rush, for instance. You're welcome.

I park and attack the evening. I was going to stop at the chow hall but decided against it. There is talk that you have to be in uniform after swings to get food and, even though I am in uniform, I won't give the bastards the satisfaction. I'll just overload at breakfast in the morning. I get to the room, and it is empty for a moment. I am changing clothes when the roomie hobbles in.

"Damn…" comes from him. He was taking off his uniform when he simply collapsed onto his futon.

"Nice to see you," I remark seeing his disreputable uniform situation.

"Uh, yeah…uh…yeah," he responds.

I keep changing my clothes and get ready for my usual after-swings night. I have not arranged any plans. Swing shift beer or two with a swallow of JD or five while reading a book. Yes, I know my reading will be interrupted. It's the way of my people. Graham is already snoring.

I get to the second-floor dayroom, and there is a conversation going on. Apparently, some young man was going to have a night with a slightly older person. She was into interesting things, which scared him, but there was worse. Not only was there a lot of interesting gear at the location, but also lights and mirrors from floor to ceiling. After she walked in, when he saw through her slip-less clothing walk through the lights, her hoo-hah looked like it was giving the bat signal. The young Airman was terrified. The rest of us damn near died laughing. Says he ran for his life.

"Well," I say while trying not to laugh, "some say the light at the end of the tunnel one sees when you die is just you being shoved through another vagina." Grimaces abound. "How many kids has she had?"

The kid has no idea and is just looking at the lovely carpet on the floor.

"Women don't stay virgins forever, Hoss," Justin informs the kid. "Nothing wrong with being some woman's boy toy either, given the lack of snatch at this base." Nods all around. Just then Balls, Bridget, and Leanda arrive through the two doors from different directions. Tommy and Rocker arrive soon thereafter, then Zeus and Jewface. The usual suspects, I guess. Tommy asks if we mind him playing music on his tiny boom box. I nod and put a finger to my lips. He nods and presses play and adjusts the sound levels. I just now realize Eamons, Casper, Cobra, and Dirk preceded me. They really need to fix the lighting in here.

Leanda and Bridget had been talking. "Look, I am glad you have someone, but yes, I am saving myself for marriage," continues Leanda.

"So you just…" Bridget starts and is interrupted.

"No. That is why I am happy you have someone. Masturbation is evil. Fingers are for diamonds, not for ringing the Devil's doorbell," she assures Bridget. I just realized how short Bridget and how tall Leanda is. The latter's flowing clothing makes it hard to figure out her figure.

Balls seems astonished and turns to her. "Really?" she asks all wide-eyed. Leanda turns to her, determined.

"One should never self-rape one's sin cave," Miss Caviar insists. Wow.

There is the usual talk everywhere else. I read my Fehrenbach book. I look up and see Bridget has stationed herself right beside me. Oh goody. Doesn't she have a hobby? She just sits there. Sometimes she talks to Balls who sometimes talks to Zeus. The gazes come back to me. It really sucks being aware of everything. I hear that is Zen, but I have no idea what that shit is exactly. Tommy is playing "Run to the Hills" by Iron Maiden. That came out a few years ago, I think. Not bad, but not my cup of tea. Not exactly the new music he claims to know all about. I am having a hard time focusing on the book. Tommy must have seen my smirk at his last song. He is playing "Human" by the Human League now. Some of the girls perk up. I was just putting some beer down my throat and start to gag, which leads to some laughter.

"That's just mean, man," I tell Tommy. He points to Rocker. "Whatever, why aren't you two chasing skirts or something?" I notice some of the beer went onto my book. Damn it.

"You sound like something out of a 1940s movie, Hal," Rocker observes.

"Uh-huh. If only I had the clothes. I wonder if it is correlation or causation, now that Americans dress like peasants and bums, manners are leaving," I observe.

"Well, yew dress like yew is a-going to church and yew act better," says O'Phelan's roommate.

"Jaguar and Thunderbird" by Chuck Berry comes on. Rocker and Tommy are looking for my reaction. I give them a shrug to their consternation. Many, myself included, are struck by the Red Man chewing cohort's observation.

Jewface chimes in, "That may be more true than I had imagined possible." Nods all around.

"Out in the Streets" by the Shangri-Las is played next.

"You can just stop it now, motherfuckers," I inform the two idiots. There is general agreement on this.

"Wow. I mean, I drink, too, but is that something 'Merican?" O'Phelan's roommate may have had a beverage or three before showing up. His accent is incredible. Ah, he lifts a bottle of Jim Beam and takes a medicinal sip—the kind one needs if you are about to have your leg cut off. Conversation is at a minimum tonight for some reason. Fatigue probably. I get back to reading when "Real Wild Child" by Jerry Lee Lewis comes on, and the mood lightens.

"I thought 'Wild One' was by Suzi Quatro," opines Bridget.

"Similar, but different song," I respond.

Just then, that chick from Dawg Flight walks in. I forget her name. Since she has chopped off her dark hair, added tattoos and various piercings, I barely recognize her at first. Also, she is not at work with her cohorts. "Get It On" by Power Station comes on. With this chick's ass and attitude, hell yeah. Bridget would probably disapprove. Then again, with that high and tight haircut, Dawg Flight chick may be batting from the other side of the plate. Interesting.

"Enjoying some leave?" I ask, welcoming her to the couch. Bridget moves nearly into my pants so Dawg Girl takes the other end.

"No, I have decided to leave the Air Force and go back to America," she answers. She seems very sure of herself. I am uncertain of her efforts, but her certainty is certainly interesting. There are many jaws dropped at this announcement.

"Shake Me" by Cinderella follows. O'Phelan's roommate is certainly shaken. "Whut? What do you mean you is just up and leaving? You cain't do that. You signed a contract," he says.

"My lawyer tells me otherwise. It's very simple, I am firing the Air Force. Or as Darth Vader said, 'I am altering the deal,'" says the fetching Dawg Flight chick with the crew cut.

"Looka hear, Tacklebox, that ain't how it works. Abandoning your post in wartime is akin to treason," he retorts, followed by a Jim Beam chaser. Tacklebox. The piercings. Funny.

She leans forward and looks at me around Bridget. "What do you think, Hal?"

"I think we are being poor hosts. Do you need a soda or a beer?" She grins slightly. "Which kind, Bud or Miller Lite?" I ask.

Eamons says he will get it from the beer machine in the hallway when he realizes he forgot cash. I give him the high sign and give him a Lincoln, telling him to get one for him and one for our guest. He winks and goes. Seconds later, he is back and softly tosses a beer to Tacklebox, who thanks us.

"Rain" by the Cult comes on. Great song. Everyone is looking at me.

"He's right in naming the argument that will be used against you if you go to a court-martial," I say, gesturing toward Mr. Jim Beam. "I do not know your circumstances or reason you have come to your conclusion, Missy. Personally, even if I was miserable, I would finish out my contract, but..." I am at a loss. "I hope it all works out best for everyone involved, keeping you here against your will may not be the best solution for unit morale or the mission. I also hope your future is not scarred by your actions." My statement is followed by a chorus of answers and questions and who knows what. I put a finger to my lips to remind them of our shift work status; people are sleeping. The music is turned off, temporarily. I go on addressing the room.

"Hey, what happens if you have a small auto repair shop and you have two sisters running the office. One is great at customer service, and the other is absolutely perfect at bookkeeping and so on. Then they both give notice and leave because their husbands, who are coworkers at the local concern, are transferred across the country. Happened to a friend of the family back home. No, the situation is not quite the same, but for whatever reason, this one," I say sticking a thumb toward Tacklebox, "*wants to* or *has to* leave. Some may not like it. Everyone might not like it, but that apparently is just how it is. I do worry about the reaction of leadership." I turn to her and add, "Good luck."

"Thanks. I think I will take my leave from the room since I am distracting y'alls off-duty hours." She stands up and turns to O'Phelan's roommate, asking, "You're the fellow who dated my old roommate, right?" He nods. "I thought so. You made an impression. She referred to you as the Christmas advertisement." He looks dumbfounded and confused. "Something that always comes too early." That is received with roars and shocked sounds and expressions. I just smile. It's then I realize Benny Goodman's "King Porter Stomp" has been playing. She turns to me and says, "Thanks for the beer. And"—she pauses, clearly having some emotions well up—"thank you for your kind words," looking me right in the eyes. I nod slightly and give a small, sad smile. She really does have a cute butt I observe as she leaves. Everyone starts yakking again as "Rollin' Stone" by Muddy Waters begins.

I put my finger to my lips, and everyone calms down. The discussion continues, and I try to tune it out. John Mayall & the Bluesbreakers' "The Stumble" follows, and Rocker is not pleased. I point to Tommy and then give a thumbs-up. "Music," I whisper to Rocker, who should pursue a singer who is not me for his metal nonsense. Others are pissed at me for another reason.

O'Phelan's roommate delivers a good spit in his spit cup, to Leanda's disgust, and tells me, "Yew let that bitch off easy, Hal." He follows this with a generous swig of Jim Beam, which has to circumnavigate around his Lenny Dykstra-esque chew. I am pro tobacco and whiskey, but this is disgusting. Others agree with the interesting Southerner's statement. When it quiets down and Little Richard's "Miss Ann" plays, I retort.

"I don't like anything about this. She *is* abandoning her post," I quietly say with feeling. "But do we know why? What if she has been treated poorly? What if she, God forbid, has been raped? We don't know the circumstances, so we can only stand as disinterested bystanders wishing for the best, right? Since we don't know what we don't know, we should withhold judgment, to the Lord, if need be. Did you see how emotional she got as she left? She left because she was about to cry. Perhaps leaving her post is tugging at her, or perhaps she is leaving a sexual predator, but she wants to stay and none of us know. And we have no business knowing if she was violated. Thus, we should treat her as a fellow Christian who God can judge, alright?"

Debates on the topic fill the room for a bit. Freddy King's "That Will Never Do" plays next. I give another thumbs-up. Rocker is about to kill Tommy. Funny. The black man wants angry white people music. The white man plays jumpy black man music. That this is followed by John Lee Hooker's "It Serves You Right to Suffer" strikes me as funny. I am overjoyed. Rocker is about to destroy the radio. Eamons may be right; these ethnics may be a bit too emotional. Yup. Damn this is good.

Leanda asks, "Hal, you really like this, uh, music?"

"Of course. Remember, most classical music is derived from bar music minstrels."

"You really know this? Who were your favorites again?"

"Telemann is stable. Reliable. You generally know what will happen next with his music. I also prefer other Krauts like Brahms and Handel and Haydn though Wagner is kind of a dick. Beethoven is king, and Mozart is fun. Diet frog Chopin and full frog Debussy and the Italian, Vivaldi, and maybe Corelli are okay—and what is it with the Italians and their violins? Even Mendelsohn's Italian symphony or whatever it is called is all fiddle. Bach is both boring and a genius. Schumann and Schubert are inspiring, but Strauss is hit or miss. I like the polkas. It was Dvorak who had the reputation of putting traditional folk melodies to an orchestra, right? The Slavs not too much, but Tchaikovsky and Prokofiev are lovely. Grieg is okay, and there are others who are good. This is just off the top of my head and with a head full of Tennessee whiskey and bad beer. A favorite? Tough call. Probably the call of Prokofiev's to the Russians:

> Вставайте, люди русские
> На славный бой, на смертный бой!
> Вставайте, люди вольные
> За нашу землю честную!

> Живым бойцам - почёт и честь
> А мёртвым - слава вечная!
> За отчий дом, за Русский Край
> Вставайте, люди русские!

> Вставайте, люди русские
> На славный бой, на смертный бой!
> Вставайте, люди вольные
> За нашу землю честную!

> На Руси родной, на Руси большой
> Не бывать врагу!
> Поднимайся, встань,
> Мать родная, Русь!
> На Руси родной, на Руси большой
> Не бывать врагу!
> Поднимайся, встань,
> Мать родная, Русь!

> Вставайте, люди русские
> На славный бой, на смертный бой!
> Вставайте, люди вольные
> За нашу землю честную!

Врагам на Русь не хаживать,
Полков на Русь не важивать!
Путей на Русь не видывать,
Полей Руси не таптывать!

Вставайте, люди русские
На славный бой, на смертный бой!
Вставайте, люди вольные
За нашу землю честную!

Or

Arise, Russian people,
On a glorious battle, to the death battle!
Arise, free people,
For our honest land!
Honor for alive soldiers
And thank eternal for dead.
For father's house, for the Russian region
Arise, Russian people!
To the native Russia, to the native Russia
Won't come the enemy!
Get up, stand up,
Mother dear, Russia!

Arise to arms, ye Russian folk,
In battle just, in fight to death.
Arise ye people free and brave,
Defend our fair, our native land!
To living warriors' high esteem,
Immortal fame to warriors slain.
For native home, for Russian soil
Arise ye people, Russian folk!
Arise to arms, ye Russian folk,
In battle just, in fight to death.
Arise ye people free and brave,

Defend our fair, our native land!
In our Russia great,
In our native Russia
No foe shall live.
Rise to arms, arise, native motherland.
Arise to arms, ye Russian folk,
In battle just, in fight to death.
Arise ye people free and brave,
Defend our fair, our native land!
No foe shall march 'cross Russian land,
No foreign troops shall Russia raid.
Unseen the ways to Russia are.
No foe shall ravage Russian fields.
Arise to arms, ye Russian folk,
In battle just, in fight to death,
Arise ye people, free and brave,
Defend our fair, our native land!

My comrades seem a bit astonished. Bridget asks, "How do you know this? And the Russian?"

"I sang in high school. Memorizing Russian noises isn't that much more difficult than remembering Latin madrigal music."

"Dude." Jewface shakes his head. "Sometimes you freak me out," he concludes with a smile.

"Alexander Nevsky, I think. Sometimes I will sing in my room when Graham is shacked up somewhere else," I reply. "Oh, and you should reexamine the '1812 Overture' by Tchaikovsky. It actually tells the tale of Napoleon's invasion of Russia and how God answered the Russian prayers and saved them," I educate my comrades.

"Where do you get all of this?" asks Bridget.

"I read it. Did you know that, Leanda?" She nods.

"My parents taught me that. I felt so grown up being able to pick out 'La Marseillaise' and 'God Save the Tsar' and whatnot at a young age within the '1812 Overture.' Good times," she says wistfully.

Tommy puts in a different tape, and something completely new comes on. We all listen for a while. Rocker seems to like it. It's a tight band, and the guitarists, both lead and rhythm, are good. The singer has some pipes and range but sounds like someone is strangling a cat. Tommy looks at us all when the song is over.

"This is the next great rock band, Guns N' Roses," he announces with a smile.

"Who is that on lead guitar?" asks Rocker with enthusiasm.

"Some guy named Slash. He replaced Tracii Guns. What do you think of the singer, Hal?" Tommy asks.

"He has pipes and range but is walking that fine line between Pavarotti and dragging your fingernails across a blackboard."

Leanda laughs at that. "I didn't want to say anything. I think I am going to call it a night. Thanks for the lesson and a good memory, Hal," Leanda says with a smile and leaves wishing us well.

Rocker and Tommy start debating the music. Both are wondering why I called Axl Rose a pasta. Wow.

I wish more of the softball team were here. I look at Zeus, but he is talking to Balls. They seem to have hit it off. Speaking of that, I haven't seen Bingo and Tango in a bit. I hope Cretin is staying out of trouble. He really does become a monster when he drinks. Good center fielder with a gun for an arm and a solid batter. Sammy is coming along nicely. Hope he is still fucking his wife properly. I wonder if I should check in with Jack. Haven't seen Fern or the Injun either. It appears my thinking is unclear and scattered. That and I am a wee bit bored. Too bad it is a worknight or I would go out on the town. I notice Bridget looking at me expectantly.

"What may I do for you, young lady?" I ask in all politeness. I think my soft Virginia accent melts this hillbilly. Hopefully she won't slide off the couch. Damn her hair is jet black—just noticing that. Eyes nearly to match. Cute country freckles. Unusual looks, but she is kinda cute...and short.

She shrugs. "What is there to do?"

"Grab your coat. Let's go for a walk. I'll see you back here in a few, okay?"

She responds a bit too enthusiastically. She is an intelligent, mature woman, but she dashes as if she were a puppy excited about being taken for a walk. I go to my room to saddle up my coat, a beer for one rear pocket and a pint of JD for the other. I end up deciding to meet her at the stairs. When I was going to my room, my neighbors were playing "Sweet Leaf" by Black Sabbath near the end of the song. It was followed by "Kings and Queens" by Aerosmith as I was leaving my room. Damn if that engineer doesn't like to play his music hard and a little bit loud. Not bad taste in music though.

Bridget has come down all geared up, and we head to the first floor. "Just a sec," I say and turn right instead of heading out the door. I knock softly on Jack's door in case he is racked out. He answers the door in very casual clothes with a fag hanging from his mouth. "Anything?" I ask. He shakes his head.

"Tomorrow." My expression must not be too happy, but he follows with, "It'll be alright. Go enjoy yourself." I nod and turn to leave.

Bridget looks at me with a raised eyebrow and an unspoken question. I shake my head slightly as we head toward the building's main exit. That same asshole I slugged to shut up walks out of the barracks dorm chief office just as we are about to walk past. Must be his shift. It takes him half a second to recognize me.

"Hey! Are you the…" and that is all he got out before I put a hand over his mouth and put the bastard against the wall less than gently.

"Ssshhhhhhh. Real Airmen are sleeping," I whisper harshly, then I let him go and walk out with Bridget in tow. Hugh Hefner walks out of the same office in his usual bathrobe to see what the hubbub was.

"I was telling it the same thing," he says, pointing with his thumb. "Tsk tsk," he tells the moron doing the index finger thing that goes with the phrase. I fear the smile I threw at them both was more smirk and sneer than a smile. I nod and continue to the front door. You can feel the cold before you even get outside. So much for the onset of spring. I haven't checked my mail in weeks. I go toward the mailroom with little Bridget in tow.

Since Bridget was having a hard time keeping up, she grabbed my right hand to hold. Probably not just to slow me down. I hadn't realized that I was walking with such purpose. At least the sidewalks aren't too icy.

"Smells like rain, sleet, or snow," I observe. Bridget nods.

She also realizes where we are going. "Why won't you marry that Rachel girl? She seems to like you a lot. Who knows, you'd probably be a good father, too."

"Too young," I reply and realize she doesn't know about whom I am referring. "Me. Besides, I don't want to just marry anyone. I'd rather be a few years older and choose with some circumspection," I answer. We walk a bit in the cold in pleasant silence. Most of the streetlights are in working order, which is nice. We get to a four-way stop, and two cars arrive at the same time, one to our right and the other in the immediate front of us to the left. The one in front of us is playing Blondie's "One Way or Another" a bit too loud. Cretin is in the back seat drinking and acting crazy. The one across the intersection to our right has another drunk. How appropriate. It is driven by Rhonda. There is someone in the passenger seat who looks like a guy, but not her husband. Wasn't her husband, no longer a useless soldier, now a contractor in the Philippines? How did she get preggers? Hmmm… Then a black-haired female head with a dusky arm holding a bottle of wine comes out of the near back window.

"Hal, the clock is ticking, and I need some fucking and a marriage certificate!" Good to see you, too, Rachel. I wave, and Rhonda drives off past us in some embarrassment. Cretin's car left while Rachel was yelling. I look at Bridget.

"Like I said, I might want to be a bit more careful and have a long, successful marriage instead of a typical military marriage," I observe. Bridget seems to understand.

"Now I see," she replies, nodding with clearer mental vision. After a slight pause, she says, "Is there a strict timeline to any of this?" A military truck passes playing "Tush" by ZZ Top at top volume into the night. Nice fucking song.

"No, it could be months, or it could be a decade. I don't care. Until then I will see what happens," I reply with finality. We get to the Post Office, and each of us goes to where our mailbox is. Mine is eye-high in the penultimate section to the right toward the back.

It turns out that hers is in the same section directly below mine near the bottom. She tells me she is fine, so I open my box just as she does hers. I realize that if anyone came up behind us, it would look like I was getting a blow job in the post office. I guess that would be an improvement over how other government operations screw us all, right?

We start our return to the barracks, but slower. I finally realize that Bridget is as after me as Rachel, but in not-so-trashy a manner. I wonder how old she is. It appears she is a year or three older than me, especially considering her rank as an NCO. Then again, with me losing my hair, appearances would not be a problem were we a proper couple. In contrast, I wonder what it would be like to be thirty years old with a twenty-year-old wife. The sex might be good, but what would you talk about?

"Tell me about your family, Bridget," I say.

She smirks back at me and waits a moment before answering. "I have a hillbilly father and a Japanese mother," she states baldly.

"Sounds like the best of both worlds to me," I respond. She eyes me warily.

"I grew up in Flat Gap, Kentucky, near the West Virginia border. The closest town is Paintsville, which nearly has five thousand people. That is where we go to get groceries and supplies. We live without a lot of things most people in America take for granted. Most of my clothes growing up were made at home. The nearly two-hour drive to Huntington, West Virginia, was deemed too long to bother just for store-bought clothes. My mother stayed home and gardened. Dad was a vehicle mechanic in the Air Force. He retired, got a certification to teach, and teaches auto repair at a technical school."

"No brothers or sisters?" Look at me being a nice fellow.

"One crazy sister. A bit overweight and lazy, but she should finish college soon," she says ruefully.

"Sounds like a nice setup. Being out in the country, does that mean your father has lots of land or whatever?"

"A little less than sixty acres, nearly none of it flat. Pops had a coal company do some digging for a couple of years, and they paid him to do it. By contract, they had to fix it up instead of leaving a hole in the ground. That means he can just drive an old pickup to where they were digging and chip off huge chunks of coal and put it in a heating stove in the house. They live pretty well, come to think of it," she ends with a small smile at the memory.

We are approaching the barracks in pleasant silence. As we go through the front doors, I realize I didn't even have a drink during this walk. Go figure. As we get to the second floor, Bridget says, "Got to get ready for work. Thanks for the walk," and she blows me a kiss. I don't know what to think. She seems okay. Well…I don't know what to think. I gain solace reading through more of the files the Sage gave me to learn. At least they make some sense.

CHAPTER 12

Last Day of Swing Shifts

After the usual work preparations and a mediocre meal at the chow hall, I saddle up Penny and let her warm up. I get a Camel lit and turn on the radio to hear "Riders on the Storm" by the Doors. Appropriate since the wind is picking up, the temperature is going down, and the skies are worsening. Damnation if it isn't as dark as a 1600s Halloween story. Matches my liver, I guess. The music calms me down as I worry about the mission ahead. Damn if this won't be a big few hours. Work. Meet the Sage. Calm the comrades. Then play a game before the first evening before night shift. I should check the weather for next week. Third shift mission can be weird. The song changes to "One Thing Leads to Another" by the Fixx. My cigarette is out. I put Penny in gear and go.

Arriving first, or close enough, I check around to make sure all is well, mission-wise, before checking with Jack and the softball team. It wouldn't do to worry about softball if we were about to have WWIII. All seems well when I see Sammy arrive. He seems okay until he sees me. Then he nods away from our block so I go to him.

"The more I think about your upcoming vacation, the more I think it sucks ass," he says point-blank, not pulling any punches.

"The more I think about you fucking that hot wife of yours, I wish I was you," I respond with a sly grin. He is dumbfounded for a moment, then laughs. "How is Bobby Jo anyway?"

"She is good. We are good—thanks. Although, I think she has a mild crush on you."

"I have that effect on married women. It'll be alright. And I have the same misgivings about the mission. I meet the Sage after work tonight," I assure him.

"Can I go?"

"Let me check with Jack. Also, is it good with you if I remind everyone about the game before we start today?" He nods and waves expansively, so I go. Jack comes first on my list of people to meet.

"Hey," I say to his back. He is just lighting yet another cigarette and inhales deeply as he turns his chair toward me. Once he realizes it is me, he breaks into a broad grin.

"Hey, I know what you are going to ask," he says with a wink.

"So, Sammy can go to the meeting tonight?" He is at a loss.

"Whut?"

"What word didn't you understand, Jack?" I ask with a small grin.

"Oh...er, I dunno. I would think not. I'll try to check."

"And you thought I was going to ask..."

"About the little Jap girls. Yes, they will be there, Hal," he responds sheepishly.

"Will you?" He shakes his head.

"Probably not. I don't think I will be needed. Besides, I might have plans." He looks at that young Airman with the strange build. I tell him I understand. Then I proceed around the building to remind the team of the game. It's been a few days without softball in dreadful weather, and I don't want them forgetting. Two bits of news hit hard.

"Hal, Cretin is in the brig," Francis tells me in his Mr. Rogers-esque way on the satellite side of the house. "Apparently, he was very naughty." I thank him before he starts shedding tears or some damn thing and move on.

Nice kid, but we are going to win this war with the likes of him and Brandy? Damn. Hopefully the commies are worse off. At least he comes across as being somewhat classy and well-bred despite everything.

I go from that end of the building to Block 8, with the usual intention of hearing Happy whine like a bitch about his bitch and then catch the rest of the fellows on the way back to work. All goes well until I get to Block 8. First, Bridget seems too happy to see me. Second, Happy is not happy. I think about priorities and realize I am not having sex at work, so I talk to Happy.

"You haven't been fucking her, have you?" I ask in all politeness. He shakes his head. "Put on a cartoon show for the kids, grab that bitch, rip her pants off, and put her to rights." He seems uncertain. "Dude, at the game, I will put her in her place. Let's face it, if she can't treat a great guy like you right, who will she treat right? She thinks she is at a place where guys are desperate. Ain't *no one* that desperate to pick up that kind of trouble no matter how hot she is. Honest," I conclude. He smiles weakly and nods. As I leave, I tell him about Cretin. I get waves all around from the rest of the team. All is a go.

I start setting up in Block 3 when Bridget comes over.

"Interesting advice you gave Happy."

"Was I wrong?" I look into her eyes with what I hope is a severe look.

"No. No, I was thinking that you and me tonight could…"

"I have plans. Mission. Sorry," I admit.

"Wha…"

"TDY planning. Can't talk about it. You have to take life when it is there, Bridget. The problem people have is they think they have time." I wish her well and go back to work.

I wonder about Bridget. I am not hot for her, but she is a good companion. She seems to like me. I think she is okay. Her slightly advanced years makes up for her slightly diminished education and culture. I have heard arranged marriages work better than "love" marriages since love dies. I wonder. And why am I even thinking about this? Maybe Bridget is a witch.

Sammy seems to be in a good mood in Block 3. Not that this is a bad thing.

"Day shop is not only raving about our coverage. They are bitching about the other shifts not being shit!" he exclaims. I just look at him in disgust.

"It is not a competition. It is a war between us versus the commies. Are those useless motherfuckers aiding the other shifts yet with communal information against the Soviets?"

He shakes his head. He was just happy about being praised.

I call the command section and get the boss's answering machine. I tell him he has a day shop doing nothing (e.g., not providing shift and overall continuity binders, mission statements, etc.). It's a golfing club. He had promised to get on it. I get the feeling he likes having an insider tell him things when he is not informed to know anything by his keepers. Like an outsider getting elected to the presidency and everyone on the inside is against him. A Mr. Smith. Then I get to work, starting on the binders and checking on everyone, especially Brandy, but everyone seems to be doing well. I tell them there is a rumor that I might have to go TDY, but I will make a master binder upon my return.

"Hal, it looks like we have a tour of the USSO," Walker says to me with a smile. I return the smile and tell everyone that we have the opportunity to gather some very interesting intelligence over the next day or three.

Leanda seems perplexed. "Whatever do you mean?"

"The USSO is a slang term for their version of our USO. There are a lot of bases, as you know, that are very remote, and there are no women. So every now and again, the Soviet Air Force flies a plane or so full of booze and whores to these bases for them to sow their oats for a few days." Brandy puts a hand over her mouth with an intake of breath, but Leanda, Tommy, and Rocker smile. "Someone has to go to work, but they usually do so intoxicated and discipline becomes very lax. Many times, they send plaintext. For instance, a drunken commie out our way in the Far East gave us the first indication that Brezhnev was dead years ago. We knew before the Soviet public knew, and many behind the wall first heard about it on the Voice of America," I inform. Sammy had walked up in the middle of this.

"Thus, we need to know where the planes are headed, where they are currently, and so on. Then we need to let everyone with a target on that base know who to look for—now you know why I wanted you to know what units are at what bases, right?" Universal nodding. "Sammy, how do we get this out to the blocks, and whomever else needs to know?"

"I got this. Does this merit an informal warning up the chain?" Smart man. Sucks having a drunken and depressed commie on the other side near a big red button. I nod and call over Frog, the analyst, to tell him what to do. Frogface is less than enthusiastic. Sammy goes to talk to his contemporaries, and I tell Frog he will look awfully good for providing situational awareness if something huge happens as a result. He nods reluctantly and leaves. His acne is getting worse. I think heavy metal causes that and a lack of muscle tone. Sad. Oh well. Funny, FEN starts playing "Walk Don't Run" by the Ventures. I guess we had best get our asses in gear, huh?

I get to my rack and saddle up. I look over at Walker and tell him what a great job he has been doing. I remind him I remain new to plane tracking so he should provide inputs as he deems fit. When Sammy returns, I give him the high sign.

"After we get some cool information out of this, make certain to give Walker and yourself the credit for the same reasons as before, okay?" He is incredulous.

"What is it with you and anonymity?" Sammy asks. I shrug and remind him of the TDY mission.

"Okay, what about your career?" he asks with some small passion. I assure him I don't care two fucks about my career and go back to my rack. Fucking careerists.

I start searching for the enemy when someone walks up but does not speak or tap my table. Shit. What fucking nerd wants to interrupt the mission now? I look up to see the new commander. Oh.

"Colonel Givens at your service, Hal," he says with a grin. "What's going on? I thought I would check in before I bend one into the Missus, you see."

"Ah, you were a fighter pilot once, sir?" He grins in response. Then I tell him what is going on with the USSO.

"You're shitting me. That's awesome!" I could grow to like this man.

"What isn't awesome is that there are no continuity books in any block. There is no list of what targets, frequencies, or who is at what bases by our designation or the Soviet's. Day shop is a pleasure club instead of a warfighting division. They are a support organization that operates similarly to the chow hall except that they play more golf and cause fewer health problems—if you don't count stress and blood pressure versus food poisoning."

"Start Me Up" by the Rolling Stones comes on FEN. The little commander is past being started up and is about to burst.

"Sir, it is new to you but old hat to us," I assure him. "You have some work to do changing the culture around here. Usually someone in your position does not bother with the operational side and remains content in the administrative side...leaving that for your chief."

"I see," he sees as he digests the information. "Mind if I hang around for a minute?" I smile and gesture to a chair. He sits and lights a cigar. Someone told me that he was no longer on flight status and was gifted a last assignment to finish his career. He probably wants a little excitement outside of the cockpit. Good for him.

Walker tells me the planes are landing at an island base near the Sakhalin Islands. Rocks. Nothing there but a runway and a few buildings. One of the bases that will attack us when war comes. Good. I ask Colonel Givens who is at that base, and he does not know. I tell him we have no reference library to check, which day shop is tasked to provide. He smirks, then scowls and is less than happy. Then I inform him how and why this event can lead to good or bad things for us.

"Sir, everyone...and I mean *everyone*, will be boozed and, ah, satiated during this visit. But there are still shifts." Then I tell him about the previous OPSEC failure involving Brezhnev. "But what if a drunken pilot who just got a 'Dear Ivan' letter decides to go all kamikaze against an airline plane or his wife's hometown or one of our ships? Also, there is more than one big red button in case Moscow is incapacitated. This is a situation to be monitored...and would be more easily so with day shop support," I conclude. He nods and watches us with widened eyes. New Order's "Bizarre Love Triangle" comes on softly. Not all music in this era is worth a damn.

Sammy shares the destination with the other block leaders so everyone can keep track of their select networks. When the commander asks, I inform him that Soviet bases often have multiple units and multiple missions—just like us. Most of us Airmen have no idea where their contacts come from. Idiots. When Sammy comes back, I have a question for him.

"Hey, does this affect the X2s or the satellite nerds?" I ask. He doesn't know. I then ask who should distribute this information, him or me.

"Why don't you let me do it?" asks the commander. "I seem to be the odd man out."

I ask him if he knows where everything is, and he shakes his head. I give him a quick rundown in block number order. He thanks me and goes on his way. Sammy and I share a look.

"He could turn out alright," Sammy observes. I nod in agreement.

"Glad I didn't get keelhauled when I jacked him up," I respond and head toward my rack. Then a thought hits me. "Hey, are the linguists copying what is said at both ends of the USSO conversations?" Sammy shrugs. "It might be another way to get some inadvertent intelligence." He nods and passes that along to the appropriate block.

We get back to work, knowing the USSO will be in one place for a bit now that they have landed. Work is pretty routine, and the hours roll by. I hear something and realize Brandy has her volume too loud through her cans. I took that moment to check on her. She sees me and starts to glow with a small smile. She turns down the volume, and I give her a thumbs-up. I follow up by going to Leanda, who seems frustrated. She sees me and takes the cans off of her head.

"It's like all of my targets have disappeared," she says in dismay.

"Where are they located?" She looks at me and realizes she doesn't know. "Any chance half or all of your nets are off the air because of the orgy?" She hadn't thought about that.

"That's right. A lot of my nets have bases due north of us. That's where the USSO is, right?" Her lips are pursing. "I need to educate myself better on these bastards. I was worried about code and format before." She nods to herself and then looks up at me. "Thanks." I give her a small smile and see Walker returning to his rack. I guess he had to hit the head.

I tell him, "You are in serious danger of getting some rewards and laurels for your good work, Hoss." He seems astonished. "You deserve it. Keep up the great work." I pause and look at Leanda and Brandy in turn. "And keep a supportive eye out, please." He grins and expresses agreement. Then I check on Tommy and Rocker.

I get to the two brothers in arms, and I see my roommate in a conversation with Dinger in Block 2. It seems very personal. The conversation ends with her grabbing his hand and giving it a squeeze. Oh my. Tommy and Rocker seem to both be at it. I wonder where Frog the analyst is. And where is Melody?

I go back to my rack to see Sammy back at his desk. "Where are our analysts?" He looks up and has no idea. "They may be way behind in their reporting as we speak. What will happen if that is not done and the shit hits the fan?' He rises and goes to look for them. Glad that I have helped the mission again, I get after the mission. The freqs are pretty quiet. Leanda is right. I feel eyes behind me and turn back and to my right. Brandy is looking at me.

"If I am not copying Morse, just say my name, okay?" She nods.

"Remember when you told me that when I am not copying my targets to search for others on my spare Racals?"

"Yes, ma'am. What have you found?"

"I dunno," she responds and tells me the freq. I raise a finger and check it out. I copy for a while and call DF when I can to get an azimuth fix. I copy as it is sent and then get an idea.

"Brandy, get Jack, please."

I keep at it, and Jack arrives behind me. I take a second to point at the screen and then keep copying. Jack stares and stares. Then he yells, "Shit!" and runs off. Just as I thought. When it pauses momentarily, I look at Brandy. She is nearly printer paper white in astonishment. I give her a grin, a wink, and a thumbs-up. Others are curious and start to walk over, but I wave them off and tell them to get at their mission, not wanting to miss anything.

Sammy comes back without Frog but with Melody. I keep typing but caught her eye and nod her my way. She arrives and I raise a finger. While she waits, I keep copying. When there is a pause, I ask her to find the Frog and ask what Jack saw in my message. She gives me a quizzical look but does as I bid. She comes back, looks me in the eye, and gently shakes her head. I keep copying the Morse until there is another pause.

"Mel, it might be nice to know what this is. Is it Block 3 mission? If not, should we transfer or let me keep at it? Are we supposed to report this? If so, at what level? What the hell is this? Maybe Jack will be kind enough to offer a suggestion. Thanks," I finish. She turns to get to Jack in Block 2. The code starts back up as I notice she does have a nice enough bucket. The ditty-bops are being sent by hand, but relatively slow and clear. Obviously, they want the message to be received exactly as intended. Strange that there is no format. Could this be plaintext? That would be very odd, indeed. Curiouser curiouser.

Ah, the commander returns. How nice. He looks defeated. Once he gets close to Block 3, Givens looks up and sees Sammy and me. He gets closer and asks, "Who is that?" and jerks a hand to his left.

"Hail Satan!" the Airman says while muttering ghoulishly all hunched over his rack as he types less than rhythmically. The enemy stops transmitting.

Sammy just shakes his head. I answer, "It's Iron Mike, sir. Good operator. A little out of line with the other ducks."

"New Song" by Howard Jones softly comes on a small radio somewhere nearby. I hear a grunt behind me, and it is Rocker about to waste the radio playing pop music. Leanda and Brandy tease him by pretending to like it, which makes me smile. My coded message is taking a break or is finished; they did not say which it would be.

"Did you see Block 4?" The colonel shakes his head. "They are so into the mission, they have Soviet imagery and posters where they work. What about Block 8?" He doesn't quite remember. "It's straight that way, sir," I point with a knife-hand.

"I was there! Some black-haired NCO was telling a higher-ranking striper to stop being a pansy and fuck his wife's snatch clean off. Then some handsome fellow came over, shook hands with me, and asked me if I was lost. His name was…shit, I forget." I was about to tell him that was Norman the Mormon, but…

"But, Hal, it gets worse," the Boss says. He looks around to see who might be listening in and gets very close to me. Sammy leans in as well. "Th-there is this…Negro…" He pauses, at a loss. "He started shrieking at everyone, saying essentially that they should disengage their social chatter and pay more attention to the mission. He had the craziest look in his eyes…" You can tell the Colonel can't get the vision out of his head. "His voice shrieked as he called the enemy something like 'red mudak Dragos' or something." Sammy and I start laughing. "What?"

"Sir, as you know the Soviet flag was red, as was the Bolshevik one against the Tsarist Whites back in the day, right?" He nods. "Mudak essentially means dumbass. Drago is the main character in *Rocky IV*, when Rambo defeats the huge Soviet robotic boxer in the ring in Siberia or wherever."

"Hey Porter" by Johnny Cash comes on the little radio, and I hear O'Phelan's roommate give a rebel yell. I am having a hard time not grinning and giggling.

"And we are going to win the Cold War with this asylum?" Givens asks. I gesture him to a chair. All three of us are now sitting down.

"Sammy here has a beautiful, hot wife and a nice home. I hear your quarters are not too bad, sir. Think about the lot of these young Airmen. Most wouldn't be here if they were not both naturally intelligent and independent thinkers. Now put them on the other side of the planet away from the only home they have ever known into one of the most stressful environments anywhere. One wrong keystroke may end in their death and the death of modern civilization. After work, they get to live in tiny holes sharing a tiny room with someone else and sharing a bathroom with the next room. Luckily, they get to eat at the chow hall and be told there is no food or get food poisoning. It's the first stress most of them have ever encountered, and it turns out to be about the worst. No wonder they react in interesting ways," I finish.

The Colonel nods in understanding. "I guess I just didn't realize."

"No fault in that, sir. I understand being in a different situation or being repulsed by some of the idiosyncrasies of our people. Try to embrace it organizationally. It is hard to adjust your thinking to another country or a different culture, even merely a different organizational culture. Yes, the intelligence world attracts the crazies, but it is the crazies who figure out things the rest of us wouldn't. And, of course, by that, I mean independent thinkers."

Sammy chimes in, "I hear scientists and inventors can be an odd lot."

"Look at military geniuses. Stonewall Jackson had a strange, simple diet and used to go about with one arm in the air, thinking he had to do so to keep his blood in balance. And never ate sauce," Givens says in disbelief.

"Funny. Sauce is one of the signs of civilization—a want for something enjoyable instead of simple sustenance," I add. The others seem to agree silently.

We just sit there thoughtfully for a second. I want to get to work. I make a polite noise and gesture toward my rack. They nod at the same time, rise, and shake hands. The commander nods my way with a look of approval and walks out with determination. I start to saddle up my rack again when Jack appears from nowhere.

"You'll hear more about this tonight after work with the Sage," he says and darts back to Block 2.

Hmmm...mystery. Luckily, the rest of the night goes without incident.

I have no idea what this meeting will turn into. Maybe the Sage will not be there so I can take advantage of his girls. Bridget seems hit or miss, and I don't think it's like we are dating steady or anything. I skip the chow hall and get all ready. Generic clothing. My roommate, Graham, comes in asking with apologies that he will need the room for a few hours. He looks up, sees me about to leave, and he brightens up.

"I will probably not be back until after 0200 hours or so," I respond. "Are you anticipating an all-nighter?" He shrugs. "Then I will see what I can do, okay?" He claims I am the best roommate.

What an idiot; of course I am. I finish up, give him a fist-up gesture, and leave.

    I saddle up Penny after walking through some increasingly dreadful weather—cold, windy with the promise of rain or sleet. I don't think it will take that much time to warm her up since I just got back from work, but I wait through a cigarette in silence. I hear other cars, but one car in particular. It seems to be making circles behind me. Hmmm... First, I turn on my little boom box. "When the Levee Breaks" by Led Zeppelin comes on. I look behind me and find some useful tools near the radio. Then I wait until the car comes back, crank up the tune, and get out of my car to approach the vehicle. My car door remains open. They seem astonished. More black-suited nerds. I was holding a softball bat behind me, but it was exposed when I took a screwdriver to their passenger-side tires. Yup, I come prepared. The passenger side tires go down quickly, and so does the side window with the softball bat. I change direction and proceed to the driver's side from behind on the driver's right, puncturing the back driver's side tire on my way and losing the handle on the bat and screwdriver while getting up when the car rolls back a little. The driver comes out to face me...with a firearm at his side. He has leaped aside from the vehicle. Good. I have no idea why the other motherfuckers are still in the car.

    "Which agency are you little bitches from, anyway?" I ask as I walk forcefully toward this moron.

    "What do you mean?" he responds contemptuously with perfect diction. He is calm. The wind is messing up this bitch's carefully groomed hair. Also, he has a firearm. I appear to have nothing.

    "Last call," I respond before I get to him. He only grins.

    I arrive looking like I will run right over him. He becomes uncertain and starts to bring his pistol up. I grab his neck collar with my right hand and his firearm with my left as he falls with help. I start to proceed back to the car with the firearm, and the little black-suited bitches still in the car start freaking out. I quickly turned back to my boy. I descend and deliver a few blows with the pistol butt and take some information and other things from his pockets. I also take the keys and go to my appointment. Who are these people?

Welcome to the Cold War!

"Trampled Under Foot" comes on my radio next. Yes indeed.

I take longer than I need to as I go to HQ[39] Sage. It seems extremely dark en route for some reason. Perhaps the streetlights don't stay on all night in Japan away from town. The music is turned down. I park Penny and turn off the music. I can hear "I Don't Care" by Buck Owens playing inside. I think this singer called his band the Buckaroos, a bunch of clean-cut white guys in suits, if memory serves. I knock on the door, and in an instant, one of the cutie-pies is opening the door with a firearm at the ready. All of the cutie-pies are there with the Sage, and they are not alone. The Sage looks up from a conversation and waves me over. "You're late."

"Nice to see you too," I respond. He is sitting on one of the low couches, and some other men are on the other. He gestures for me to sit by him, but instead, I inform, "I have some things for you. I'll put them on the bar for you."

"These guys are okay," the Sage responds.

I shrug. "I don't know if they have a need to know. I also am not perfectly certain what is going on." He has no idea what I am talking about. "I'll stay at the bar and let you guys finish unless I have a need-to-know about what y'all are doing."

"Are you hungry?" he asks. I nod. "Why don't you get something to eat in the kitchen back there while we finish up, okay?" I nod again and go. "Time of the Season" by the Zombies starts up on the radio. I walk down the hall and almost get to the kitchen when simultaneously I am pulled to the right into a small lit bathroom while someone from the other side in a spare bedroom with small hands pushes me from the other side and shuts the bathroom door. One of the cutie-pies is sitting on a Western-style toilet with the seat and cover down. She puts a slender finger to smiling lips and lowers my pants. I guess it is her turn—I don't think it is the same one. Well, might as well let her do what she wants to do if it will help the war effort.

When she is done, I thank her and give her a kiss on the top of the head while she has a hard time swallowing. I pull up my jeans

---

[39] Headquarters. Really? You knew that, right? Please tell me you knew that.

and go to the kitchen before I am missed, knowing I will have to use the powder room in a moment or two. There is a polite plate of California rolls, sauce, and chopsticks waiting for me. I finish the half-dozen rolls and start to walk to the head. The Sage calls to me, and I call back that I will be a moment. I go back up front when I am done, and the other men are gone. New men have arrived.

"Hi, guys," I say. The Sage is not amused. The tall skinny one has a cigarette in his hand, a perplexed, rueful look on his face, and seems to be at a loss.

"There is more going on than you know, man," says Jack, who takes a deep pull on his fag. "Hypnotized" by Fleetwood Mac comes on. Nice song. Underrated and great like Jack.

"There is more going on than *you* know, man," the Sage retorts. "And who the fuck is this? Let me guess—Sammy the Charlie Flight Block 3 leader." To his credit, Sammy smiles only slightly but nods his head a fraction. "I told you not to bring him!" He looks at Sammy. "No offense…simply need-to-know stuff. I am increasingly impressed the more I hear about you." Sammy remains poker-faced but inclines his head solemnly in thanks.

Everyone is just staring at each other. All we need are Mexicans for this standoff. Of course, Japan don't need no stinkin' Mexicans. After a few false starts, I suggest we go to the bar, and we go one by one. At first, the Sage is being the bartender, and he sees me looking at him. I shake my head. "Cutie-pies!" They come running. "If you please, would one of you stay to pour the drinks so we can have our discussion and do our business without interruption, please?" I ask. Being nice seems to make their knees a little weak. Japanese women are not used to such treatment or so I have heard, but right now, they are glowing. The Sage picks one, and we all get settled in with glasses and ashtrays put out, drinks poured, and fags lit. Well, Sammy doesn't smoke for some reason, and the Sage has an unlit Cuban cigar at the ready.

We start looking at each other again, and I realize "25 or 6 to 4" by Chicago has been playing. Damn, Sage *is* a hippie. Yeesh. What a dreadful song. I look at the Sage and raise my eyebrows. He nods and raises his hand slightly, giving me the floor.

"Clearly, everyone thinks whatever is going on with them is extremely important. Until we have all the cards on the table, we won't be able to judge who has the best hand. What if they are all intermingled or are instead mounting, separate issues?" All nod. "Rocky Mountain Way" by Joe Walsh comes on. Niiice. "I say, because this is his HQ, and he is in charge, we let the Sage go first." All are in agreement. The Sage takes a breath and then proceeds.

"Hal, where did you get these?" he asks, gesturing toward the items I laid on the bar earlier.

"From an asshole in a black suit who pulled this gun on me in the barracks parking lot as I got ready to come here," I answer and describe what happened while unloading and safing the weapon. It helps that the weather sounds like it is getting increasingly raw outside, adding to the drama of my tale.

"Do you realize what you've done?" he asks. I shrug. "Ruined his career. You have things an agent, a proper agent, cannot lose." It seems the Sage cannot decide whether to be happy or sad.

"I don't give a shit. Are they on our side or not?" I ask rather vehemently. "Are they really American agents? If so, why are they attacking Americans? Revenge? And why were he and his boys so pathetic? Why didn't the other guys come out? The whole thing stinks," I conclude.

The Sage seems stunned over this, holds up a finger, and makes notes. "Next, Jack, what is so damn"—he stops, being at a loss—"whatever it is."

"Up on Cripple Creek" by The Band comes on next. Finally, some good hippie music. I hope it helps Jack.

"This one," Jack says jerking a thumb at me, "came across a message that has no classification. TS/SCI[40] may not be enough. We are not sure who it is from. We are still decoding it. I don't know if it is from the military breaking from the government. I don't know if it is powerful people desiring to create a secession movement in parts of Eastern Siberia. What if it is the government nationally or locally restoring order? Some of it is encoded, and some of it is plaintext but

---
[40] Top Secret / Secret Compartmentalized Information.

not really making sense. We have a fix and azimuth on this," he says and hands a copy to the Sage, "and we don't know what is going on, but it sounds like a clarion call for something. Maybe it could be a call to restore order from the 'chaos' of glasnost and perestroika. We have never seen anything like it." Weird times indeed.

There is a moment of silence. Everyone is in deep thought. None of this prevents me from having a drink or three. "Peaceful Easy Feeling" by the Eagles comes on. The cutie-pie behind the bar is looking at me and gives me a slight curtsy and a wink. I softly smile in return. The Sage raises his head from his notebook.

"Damn," he says. I guess that sums it up. He has faraway eyes for a moment or two and then looks at me with a questioning look.

"I guess, at first, this could be any one of those many things. A commander or cadre of them is sick and tired of, what looks like to them, the chaos of glasnost and perestroika. It could be a sign of preliminary secession or a version of federalism. It could be a strange regional coup or the prevention of one. Also, I doubt my trip will tell us the whole story, but it may provide indicators of contributing factors," I conclude. Nods all around, but no one has an immediate response for me. "Anyone have anything to add?"

"I guess I never really thought about it. The Soviet Union's Far East is worse than our cowboy West. A lot of people in Wyoming, Montana, and Idaho do not feel good about having their lives dictated by distant Washington, DC. I bet it is worse in Siberia, with the distances, races, and nationalities so different," Sammy observes.

"Could the Soviet Union break up?" I ask.

"Maybe into their former countries," answers the Sage who gets up, goes around the bar, and pulls out a bottle of tequila and the appropriately stemmed glass. The cutie-pie got the hell out of his way awfully quick, and I wonder why.

"What happens to the nukes if the USSR breaks up? A lot of them are in Little Russia,[41] right?" I add, being the Soviet Rocket Forces expert in the group.

"Oh shit!" Jack is alive, apparently.

---

[41] Ukraine.

"So we'd be better with the Soviet Union intact?" I ask with some amusement. The Sage nods for a moment, and the others remain silently ambivalent.

"The Balkans," the Sage adds. Oh shit. The only reason there is not some other European war from some "damn fool thing out of the Balkans"[42] is because the USSR keeps those assholes under their thumb. They have thousands of years of acrimony. Damn. Thank God for alcohol. The cutie-pie is increasingly busy. All of us are at a loss. Finally, the Sage looks up.

"How did Sammy show up again?"

"He came to my room and was very vehement about being included," answers Jack with clear understatement. The Sage nods. I can imagine he is less than enthused.

"Should we delay until we know what we are sending Hal into?" Sammy asks. Good grasp on the obvious. The Sage just shakes his head.

"You are going to give me ulcers," the Sage says looking at me. I grin in reply.

"I say we just play it by ear as we gather information. There are a lot of assets already in place, and we may not be able to wave them off or alter our plans easily. Thus, I am more inclined to either go when I am supposed to or completely wave off," I opine, sounding more confident than I truly feel.

There is agreement all around in various nods and grunts. "I need you to study what I gave you, Hal," says the Sage with unexpected earnestness. "Kick the shit out of Dawg Flight before work. You and I need to meet more often, and that cannot happen on softball days. Oh, and the girls have been loading up your cars. You now have the old footlockers for your binders and an extra for gear like coffee stuff for you, Hal," the Sage says and grins.

"Kick-ass," Sammy states in a loud whisper. "I could grow to like you, Hal. You," he says, looking at the Sage, "I dunno. I am going to go to bed, bend one into the Missus, and sleep on it."

---

[42] Look up Otto von Bismarck.

"Might want to lose a little belly first, Hoss, wouldn't want to crush Bobby Jo," Jack adds with a leer.

"You'd think those rockin' hips would support Sammy if he passed out on Bobs, but I don't know much about her lung situation," I add informationally. Sammy finally gets the joke; he had a dumbfounded visage before.

I shake the Sage's hand and head out the barn door.

"Wait!" orders the Sage. "I have gifts," he says as he tosses a carton of smokes at Jack, a bottle of Jack Daniel's to me, and gestures to a fresh case of Asahi Dry 5.5 for Sammy. We all grin, thank him, and leave with our loot. It must be nice to be a multiple club owner.

I saddle up Penny after walking through some godawful weather. The cold wind is back, and the precipitation is once again sleet. The wind goes right through you. I get Penny started, crank the heater, and fire a fag. A battle buddy from Chicago back in the day said those types of winds are lazy winds; they won't go around you. The heat has started working, and the defrost is on high as I dig out a semi-fresh tape for the boom box. It's dark, so the choice is indiscriminate. Dave Mason's "We Just Disagree" comes on, and I think about Cheryl back home at college. Oh well. Jack is probably right. The first love is the hardest to get over. She is probably having a great time at William and Mary. "Madlinka" by Sinead O'Connor comes on afterward, and I realize I hit the wrong button; this is the Forced Entertainment Network. Damn it. I fix this. Well, sort of.

My cigarette is done, so I put Penny in gear. It takes a second for the tape to play what I hope will be good music. Instead, the tape plays "Bluebird" by the James Gang. Didn't Buffalo Springfield do a song called this? Could it be the same song? I reach back with my left hand switching to a tape playing J. S. Bach's "Concerto for Three Violins in D Major" while keeping my eyes on the road through the weather and dark country roads. I hope this dreck weather is gone before we play ball in a few hours. The weather and this wonderful music do *not* go together.

I get back inside the barracks, change into dry clothes, grab a book and the appropriate beverages, and go to the dayroom. No sign of the roommate back in the hole we live in. I get to the dayroom, and it is very full, surprisingly. Well, not so surprisingly. After a change in shift like swing shift to mids, you have to stay up most of the night so as to sleep all day to go to work NLT 2200 hours refreshed. Rotating shifts are a bitch. I cannot imagine families doing this. The kids must raise themselves, which explains a lot of the children here on base. And the weather is keeping my comrades from the bars…but not from drinking.

All I want to do is read a book, have a sip or three, and go to bed. My companions are not amenable to this. Luckily my spot on my couch is empty. I even have room for my electrolytes on the coffee table and between my legs.

"Hal," says Tango, glowing.

"Hi," I respond with as much vigor as I can assume. She giggles and recedes back into the cushions on the couch across from me. Good, I can ignore her. I think she is drunk. Someone plays Smokey Robinson and the Miracles' "Going to a G-Go." I see Eamons smirk, which makes me smile slightly. He is reading too—some academic journal called *Foreign Affairs* or some such. Cobra is in the far corner having a discussion with Rocker. I wonder where Tommy is. All I know is they all need to find themselves a girl. Maybe I should suggest Rachel from the Post Office. She might have horny, needy friends. I don't see Crosse or Corrina either. Probably for the best; I don't want a raging public hard-on. Brandy is talking to some of Francis's furry faggot friends. She and they, minus the train wreck tits, look like they are ten years old. "Jane" by Jefferson Starship comes on. Niiice. Damn the singer has good range. And the guitar solo is perfect with that tom in the background.

"Hal," says Tango again.

"What may I do for you, young lady?" I ask politely.

"Me and Bingo…we had the sex," she says as if she is two years old and just got a new teddy bear.

"Good for you, Tango," I respond with feigned serious politeness. She nods with a silly smile and leans back into the cushions, just glowing. I return to my book.

Luckily, I get a ways into my book, *A Case of Lone Star* by some nerd named Richard Samet "Kinky" "Big Dick" Friedman. I hear he was a country singer back in the day. Kinky Friedman and the Texas Jewboys. Funny. I didn't know they let Jews into Texas. Then again, a Texan told me that lots of south Texas was filled with German immigrants. Thus, the Shiner Bock, I guess. Well, that and the place names. New Braunfels. Boerne. Fredericksburg. Luckenbach. There used to be lots of Jews in Germany. Germans and Mexicans in one place. Imagine a conversation between the two cultures: "We must do this right now!" says the Kraut. "Si! We will do this mañana or whenever, sir," says the Latino. Sheesh.

"Hal," says Tango. Really?

"Yes, dear?" She teehee-hees over this.

"We did lots of it."

"Good for you, Tango. It's good for you. Healthy," I advise. She nods, smiles, and sinks back into the couch. She seems to be talking to me intermittently like most Americans attend church.

I take a medicinal swallow of Jack Daniel's and go back to my book. As you can imagine, this does not last long. Within seconds, seemingly, Jewface and Bubba are in my business. I try to ignore them to no avail. "Lips Like Sugar" by Echo & the Bunnymen starts playing in the corner. Maybe the radio is talking about Tango. I'll have to ask Bingo. At least it is not "All Lips 'n' Hips" by Electric Boys. Then again, their guitarist is fair enough.

I look up and see the two bastards looking at me like I am a fish in a tank. I wish I could fire a round at these pricks.

"Yes?" I ask less than politely.

"We wuz talkin' 'bout duh Revolution," says the white monkey. I think he nearly has a mullet. Obviously, they have been drinking. Go figure. I hear when a mullet gets to one's shoulders, an angel gets its jean jacket.

"Good for you. How does this help me relax and sleep before the game and work?" I ask politely. That I would have needs seems to have evaded them both. Manners as well. Bridget proceeds to sit down beside me. Good timing.

"Did the Revolution come from the South or the North?" asks Bubba. Oh goody.

I get funny expressions from both. It's like they are waiting for their slot machine to win after they put in their quarter. Luckily, I can disappoint both.

"Yes," is my answer. This is not met well.

"The Revolution was mostly a matter of thought as a result of the Enlightenment." They look at me like I am crazy. "Think. The war was something else," I explain. "The realization that the colonists could not only survive outside the British Empire but thrive while creating an ideal country and society began many events leading to the armed conflict, which was the Revolutionary War," I inform. Bridget is beaming. I think knowledge she doesn't know makes her wet.

Jewface and Bubba look disappointed. Could they look and be any more different?

"So, uh...both?" asks Bubba. "I Just Want to Make Love to You" by Foghat comes on the box. Maybe Bridget should be put to good use tonight, I think.

"Exactly. The American Revolution was a political and ideological revolution between 1765 and 1783, if memory serves on the dates. What amazes me was that such diverse persons in the colonies could unite against England. Remember the immigration patterns, even the English immigrants settled in different areas—the Roundheads to the north and the Cavaliers to the south. They had fought their own civil war on their fair island. Catholics to Maryland. Quakers in Pennsylvania. The desire for an industrial north and protective tariffs that began to be enacted after the war was already in bloom while the desire for an agricultural paradise and free trade was already being praised in the south, but slavery was everywhere. Thus, part of the seeds for disunion nearly a century later were already there."

"And I thought you didn't know nothing about history, Hal," observes Jewface with a leer. I smile in return.

"The American Civil War is a hole in my knowledge, but I have begun to mend that," I assure one of my favorite Negroes.

"Nigga please! You be bodderin' duh Hal," Eamons chimes in. Oh. Now I see the bottle of tequila. Someone should keep an eye on him. Never know what demons will come out of Eamons. Maybe I can get radio nerd to play classical and get a different personality to arrive.

"Baker Street" by Gerry Rafferty starts to play the nanosecond after Justin enters the room. Nice horn. Great production. Justin plays a fair blues guitar but loves this song, which makes me wonder if he has magic powers or connections with what must be FEN.

"It's okay, sir," I say benevolently to Eamons. "Besides, we were almost done. Thanks though."

"Mend that, my ass. Immigration patterns too? You are double-tying that knot, aren't you?" Jewface challenges.

"Half measures are for pansies." Bubba's eyes are a little bit wide, and Jewface leaves grinning with Bubba following. I raise my chin to Justin who returns the gesture.

I was going to start talking to Bridget who was about to talk to me, which would have led to both of us laughing, but we were interrupted. Tango has returned to our planet.

"Bingo says next time we will try doggy-style," she informs as if I should care. She has the seriousness of a small child but is instead inexperienced in drinking and fucking and is far from home. Strange place to grow up, I guess. Tango eases back into the couch. Bridget and I share a bemused look and were about to talk except we hit the "noyoufirstnoyoufirstno*you*first" when Tango reemerged from the couch cushions.

"Does that mean I will get a treat afterward?" Tango asks in all innocence. Bridget is soon laughing so hard she cannot retain her balance while sitting on the couch or make noise. Or breathe. I might have to do something to get her breathing again soon. I retain my equilibrium while tracking Bridget.

"That is between you and Bingo, dear."

Just then I see her eyes light up. I turn to where she is looking, and I see Bingo. He tilts his head toward the hallway, and she leaps up from the couch with very little grace, nearly face-planting. After recovering, she leaves running with "thanksbyebyethanksthanksbye!" I realize "Girls Got Rhythm" by AC/DC has been playing.

Bridget just looks at me, still barely recovered from the laughing fit.

"Would I get a treat afterward?" I nod. She looks at me questioningly.

"An immediate second fucking," I respond. Her mouth opens in astonishment for a second, and it is abruptly shut. "Blitzkrieg Bop" by the Ramones comes on the radio.

"Let's go," she says with some determination and heads toward her room. Well, anything to help the war effort. It is in this fashion that I both went to bed and stayed up nearly all night. Not my bed, but still. Blitzkrieg Bop is a good description of our PT session.

CHAPTER 13

The First Day of Mids... with a Preamble

I woke up in my own bed. I don't quite remember how I got here. Wow. Sore. My head could use some coffee, but one look at the weather outside says I am forgoing a run or the gym. It's not just the sex; I think I am coming down with something. Of course, useless positive mental attitude motherfuckers would say they were coming up with something. Those pricks are like political science majors. Too often the worst of them think all they need is the will to get things done then all will be okay. Uh-huh. Then reality hits those freaks.

 I look out the window again and realize the weather is even worse than last night. Hard to believe. The clock says I have time to get some grub before the game late this afternoon. Personally, I think we should call the game. I wash the detritus and funk from last night off of me, throw on some civvies, and go look for the teammates that are in this barracks, telling all I find to bundle up for the game. When I leave the last one on the first floor, having gone from the fourth floor down one floor at a time, I see someone vaguely familiar at the end of the hallway. I start to walk to him, and, when I am about ten feet away, he turns around surprised to see me.

 "I am the captain of the Dawg Flight softball team. You are the cocaptain of Charlie Flight, right?" he asks in complete seriousness.

He is taller, bigger, and looks like he works out. I could outrun him in a distance race, but I think he could knock me flat with a sneeze.

"Hal. Yes. We should have the game called," I reply.

"Yeah, but they won't. Between us, scuttlebutt has it that this whole clusterfuck is supposed to end as fast as possible and to be forgotten nearly as soon," he says darkly.

"Makes sense. Anything I can do for you?" I am so mannerly, no?

"Let's get this fucking game over as soon as possible. I am going to tell my guys to go for dingers on every pitch to get this game over with. You?" His eyes narrow.

"I agree with one disclaimer, we have fewer sluggers. Even if we try for the fences, a few of us will fail. I agree to get this over and done with regardless of the outcome though," I acknowledge. "At least they are only seven-inning games."

He smiles slightly. "Good." He starts to leave and passes me but stops and turns around. "I hear the Chief has a special place in his black heart for you." I nod. "We should irritate the bastard and make his life even more miserable than ours," he observes. I grin heartily in reply. We side fist and go our own ways. Niiice.

This might turn out great.

*****

"Great! Just fucking great!" Zeus sounds mildly irritable. It's a bit raw here at the softball field.

"Hey, guys," I say, calling everyone to me. I tell them what the Dawg dude told me with special emphasis on the last bit. They all eye me with determined agreement. That rat bastard needs to pay.

I look to the stands that are better inhabited than I had hoped. The bane of our existence, Chief Frenchy von Holstein, yells, "Play ball!" so we get to take the field since we have the best record.

"Who brought some tunes?" I ask the crowd in the stands. Justin raises a hand and hits play. "Night Time" by the Strangeloves comes on in a quarter ton of decibels. Charlie Flight folks on and off the field raise a few rebel yells.

The game proceeds rather quickly, and Dawg Flight performs as promised. The big ice puddle behind home plate has expanded, so the umpire is practically spooning our catcher. It is so cold, the puddle is frozen solid. When the Dawg batters crush one to the fence for an angry out, Stafford, the catcher, jumps straight up into the Chief to see it. The Chief falls on the ice more than once during the game, but his fat ass does not break through. Damn. It is very cold out here.

However, three pitches and three outs. Back to us.

Our leadoff hitters, including me, do not hit home runs. We were trying to do so, but we are not as studly as the Dawgies. For good and for bad in this terrible weather, with the soil wanting to suck our cleats off, we load up the bases. Singles only because the footing is too slow for more. Sammy is up at the cleanup position and should, because of the circumstances, try to advance the runners. No. He cranks one to just right of center, and it is a home run. Four runs in. Nice. Then the outs pile up. While on the benches to get our gloves, Sammy tells me it is his first ever.

Dawg Flight does the same thing they were doing before, swinging for the fences. Our crowd is getting animated. I suspect more than beer is at work. I wonder how some of these people will perform on the Hill, but many in the stands are civilian dependents and friends. The most calm are Bingo and Tango, sitting in the very center of the bleachers under many layers of clothes and blankets holding hands. Cute. Innings pass. Out. Out. Out. Multiple times the Charlie Flight stands got up and yelled like berserkers, but the opposite side is much more reserved. Now the radio is playing the Ozark Mountain Daredevils' "If You Want to Get to Heaven" on the jam box Justin has during the fifth inning, and everyone on our side is dancing. Strong drink may indeed be involved.

We reach the middle of the fifth inning, and Dawg Flight concedes. We thank them and wish them well. There is a dash to get to transportation and out of this dreadful weather. I am glad I was smart enough to put towels on my car seats so my clothes won't wet the cushions. I get Penny started and crank the heater. I was going to reach for a cigarette and decide against it. Instead, I throw a tape in the boom box, and "Radio Free Europe" by R.E.M. comes on. It focuses my mind toward my pending visit with the enemy. My mind is adrift when I realize the radio has been playing "Runaway" by Bon Jovi. No, I am not a fan of Bon Jovi. Not a hater, but it seems like much of their music lacks soul or blues-based rhythm despite their talent. I let it keep playing and get the car in gear. It appears I am nearly the last to leave.

The drive back to the barracks is uneventful; the roads aren't too slick yet. Someone in the day room on the second floor is playing "Rattlesnake Shake" by Skid Row. Not a bad band. Catchy songs. I prefer Cinderella and their turn toward blues-based hard rock to a lot of other hair bands. That singer, Tom Keifer, is apparently the heart and soul of the band while the rest are just necessary extras. That song "Bad Seamstress Blues / Fallin' Apart at the Seams" by them is outrageously good.

I get to the room to find the male whore roommate spread-eagled on his back and snoring. I get ready for work, thankful we can wear our utility uniform instead of blues in this weather. I decide to shower again to get the chill out of my bones and skip the chow hall. Afterward, I dress, adding weather-appropriate gear, wake my roommate, and go to work. Skipping the chow hall will work out; I have a jones for a walkaway anyway. If I get to work early, I can set up the footlocker. Also, I decide if the mid-rats suck, I will let Colonel Givens know at another time. No reason for our commander to be dragged out of his warm quarters in the middle of the night in this weather.

Carrying the footlocker into work in the bad weather is as fun as you would think. Getting through security was a complete pain in the ass. An old footlocker that was as empty as a campaign promise seemed to the ASVAB-waivered retards in the security shack to be a grave threat to national security. Ever notice how they always give the stupid ones the guns? Eventually, I got through and lugged the damn thing all the way back to Block 3. The Baker Flight Block 3 leader asked, "What's that?" Wow.

"A footlocker," I respond after setting it down as I start the walk back to Walkaway Station to get a sack of grub and some coffee. When I had set the footlocker down, I noticed it was stenciled as "CHARLIE FLT BLOCK 3 GEAR." Niiice. At the diner, when asked to order, I ask if they have a box that I can carry a large order in. The little old lady looks at the cook, who begins to throw food on the grill with gusto, then looks at me and says, "Hai," Japanese for yes. I grin and order eighteen walkaways with coffees and nine taters, making half of the sandwiches butter and half mayo while asking them to mark which ones are which. Of course, I insist on lots of napkins, stirring straws, various sweeteners and creamers, and such. Had I been more awake, I would have seen they were already ahead of me in all of this. I pay the bill without checking if the order is right because these are proper Nips.

When I return to Block 3, I see the Baker Flight leader looking through my footlocker. I put down my care package and walk over to the asshole. He is kneeling and facing the opposite direction. I pick him up from beneath the armpits and slam him backward on the floor.

"That was only a warning. Next time you are fucked, asshole," I inform him from above.

"Let him live, Hal," comes a voice from behind me. Sammy looks his counterpart in the eyes with disgust. The nosy prick gets up and starts to bitch, and Sammy takes the footlocker he brought and slammed it into the man's face. "Do you really want us to press charges, Senior?"[43] asks Sammy. "Get the fuck out of here." Baker Flight nerd leaves, wiping his face.

Sammy looks at me with a rueful grin. "This one is for the coffee gear. I will try to have that in tomorrow. Damn if I couldn't use some coffee now and a snack," he observes as the rest of the block arrive in mass, obviously all having ridden on the same bus.

"I made a diner run. Anyone need a walkaway and/or some coffee?" I ask loudly enough for everyone to hear. Excited noises answer me. The first mid-shift is hard. With the long, stressful workdays, the shift work that the new people are not used to, the weather…the

---

[43] A Senior Master Sergeant is often called Senior. Just like a Chief Master Sergeant is called Chief and so on. Pretty sure you should have already figured this out.

being so far away from home for the first time. Nothing like a morale boost, even if it is only a sammich and coffee.

My comrades dig in and go to their racks with their booty. I remind them mission comes first, but eating walkaways and drinking coffee can always be done while searching for the enemy. I am greeted with full-cheeked grins, nods, and various thumbs-up. They are also reminded about the USSO and to look for anomalies, plaintext, and so on. This is responded with steely looks and grins. Our block is G2G.[44]

It appears fewer people are fans of having mayonnaise on their walkaways, leaving more for me. Sammy, seeing the buttered ones are running low, picks up one of the good ones for a second course. "Might as well try one to see why you like them so much," he says, grinning at me. Good man. I start chugging coffee and sammiches while searching for the enemy. Lots of shipping out there tonight, but we don't monitor freighters. Remember how loud those bastards were? Freighter boats practically bigger than Rhode Island blasting away indiscriminately, sometimes half a freq from one of our guys. Nice that the private sector always has better gear than any military. For example, remember the Air Mail Fiasco back home? I think it was 1934 when some moron said companies in the private sector used fraudulent means to get government contracts to deliver the mail. FDR agreed it was a good opportunity to "clean up corruption from the previous administration," so he canceled the contracts and told the Army Air Force to deliver the mail while his administration sorted out the scandal. Socialist jerk.

The Army Air Corps did the best they could. I don't think they lost a bit of mail. I hear a young Major, Clarence Tinker, in charge of the Salt Lake City to San Francisco run, was very critical of the entire venture. If memory serves, a dozen flyers and sixty-six planes were lost. Good timing, too; the whole thing started in February. Good flying weather over the Rockies and elsewhere. Well, at least everyone found out the military had worse planes than the private companies and worked to improve our air fleet before WWII. It also

---

[44] Good to go.

pushed forward better air corps leaders in the years leading to World War II. I think Tinker was an Osage Injun from Okieland,[45] and that is why there is a base near Oklahoma City named after him. Thank God there is a base in former Indian territory in the prairie to defend themselves in case Texas invades after a bender of too much "Fiesta Texas!" or some damn thing. Maybe they do something else nowadays. That reminds me, where have Dusty and Fern from Oz been lately? Not in the dayroom after work, that's for sure. I guess I am only assuming Dusty is from Indian Territory.

All of us are doing our thing, mission first, and for the most part, everything is routine. Then I see Hesse coming toward me with less-than-perfect grace and a small piece of paper in his hand. I also see that he looks scared to death. He hands me the slip, and I thank him. Melody and her cute but slightly dumpy ass is walking away from me, her red hair swaying back and forth in counterpoint to her hips. Wow.

"Melody, a second, if you please," I direct. I get on the frequency and get at it. A network is going fuck all crazy. Immediately, I tell Melody what I think it is and ask her to get a linguist's attention and then to come back. Walker starts "oh shitting," and I tell him that I am on it as well. Sammy looks up, wondering what all of the fuss is. When I think I can, I tell him what is going on in the briefest of statements. He is more astonished than he should be when I tell him the news: "Rogue MiG."[46] My next syllable is "Frog." That useless bastard should be shot, rarely at his station.

Sammy leaves to find the amphibian-faced analyst, and Melody returns. I cock my head toward Walker, and she walks over there. She is keeping her calm, but you can tell this is freaking her out just a little. She should have a more experienced analyst to help her. Maybe he is at the Navy section sucking dicks. When I have a microsecond break in my session, I ask if Walker and I are copying the same conversation. Melody says no. My guys send a transmission indicating

---

[45] Oklahoma.
[46] Mikoyan Gurevich Soviet fighter planes. We faced MiG 23s and 29s (the one with the dorsal hump) mostly, if memory serves.

they are all changing freqs. Damn it. *This* is why we should have a continuity binder filled with likely frequencies. It gives me a minute.

I rip through the freqs on the useless new Racals while setting some to Iron Mike's suggestions from before and tell Melody that one is probably dealing with the idea of a rogue MiG. A linguist may be able to capture the conversation between command and the MiG pilot. The other Morse code op[47] would be copying the other MiGs out to shoot the bastard down or tracking any of our F-16[48] aircraft sent to intercept. I keep at the Racals and tell Melody that we need to notify the base commander if it is really headed our way—and as soon as possible. And then it finally happened. Frogface shows up with what was probably not a self-caused lurch with Sammy behind him. I am betting Frog will be feeling those bruises soon. Good. He comes to me, and I point a thumb to Walker, who is still engaged in his target.

"Please, bring him up to speed and come back," I ask of Miss Melody. I know the world is in danger of an incident leading to WWIII, but I think I could shape up those buttocks with the appropriate PT[49] sessions. Too bad she is dating Stafford. She really is a lovely person and would be perfect with the proper exercises I could give her. Oh well.

Sammy comes over, and I tell him that if the MiG is coming our way, base operations and the base commander need to be told. He looks at me like he does not know the next step, so I prompt him to let radar know to look for this commie flyboy prick. The light comes on, and he leaves in nearly the right direction. He corrects himself just when I get one of the freqs for my target, the subordinate units. Yes!

Then I simultaneously copy rapid code conversations while looking for the command frequency, even though it is probably not sending at the moment. It appears, as is usual, that the lead transmitter is on one freq and the peasants on another. I find the command

---

[47] Operator.
[48] The General Dynamics F-16 Fighting Falcon. Their reliability was such that we referred to them as lawn darts.
[49] Physical training.

frequency by a combination of skill and luck. Understandable, if you think about it, having one freq for the boss and the other for the subordinate units keeps the conversation orderly. The subordinate units only speak when spoken to.

Sammy comes by with the news; the MiG pilot is coming at us. I was trying to say that he should call the base commander, but I was too busy copying code. Sammy tells me the base commander has told us to fuck off after base ops refused to make a decision on their own. I raise a finger, and Sammy waits as I copy.

"Get Givens on the line, now!" He leaves in a big, husky hurry. No wonder Bobby Jo wants to get in my pants. She must be a great cook, or he is just built barrel-chested.

I am back at the mission, and the code is nuts. I have no idea what it is since it is encoded, but these people are going crazy. Decorum barely exists with the senior command transmitter *just* able to keep order. Personally, I think the disorder is because someone less than "senior" decided to have an independent mind, in this example a fighter pilot. In the Soviet state, you cannot do something not dictated by the state. That with glasnost and perestroika going on, these are weird times for these people. After Chernobyl and the failure in Afghanistan, maybe the empire has lost its mojo with their people. I might have a fun trip downrange.

I am back at it when Sammy says the base commander is still "reluctant to answer our messages," and the person answering the phone at our commander's home is reluctant to "wake our commander."

"Jack." Sammy goes to fetch him. When Jack shows up, I am copying furiously, so I glance up at Sammy and then to Jack, when Sammy gives him the dope and our thought that we should call in our commander. Jack spins and gets on it. The commander is woken up, dressed, and in the building in no time. Jack was smart enough to call ahead, have a driver and have the security check-through expedited, etc. Good man.

"Coffee?" Sammy asks when Givens arrives. The commander nods and is led to the big box full of the remaining walkaways and coffee. Givens pulls a cup of coffee and a sammich with a questioning look. I nod, and Sammy adds, "It was Hal's idea to bring a care package for the team when so many are on their first set of night shifts." The boss has a small grin/smirk for me while asking to be filled in.

"Sir, remember when we taught you about the USSO? Well, not much intel has come out of it yet, but a Soviet fighter plane took off unauthorized and is headed our way. We keep reporting it to the base commander, but he isn't having it. I think he thinks we are messing with him. Besides, he says no one could fly in this weather," Jack informs the Boss with Sammy nodding beside him. I see the other ops facing Jack instead of their racks, and I wave at them and gesture toward their workstations. Good kids; they jump to it. I am still copying very fast Morse.

"Sammy, where are our analysts, what is Walker's status, and what is going on with other blocks dealing with this, especially the squirrels who speak commie?" I ask quickly when I have a short break. Then I look at Givens. "Sir, I think you should call the base commander with a tape recorder keeping track of the conversation. Then, while you call PACAF, we send a CRITIC message to DC. Or if you hate the useless bastard, we skip calling him. You have less than a minute, the MiG is coming awfully fast, sir," I conclude. Givens turns on his heel and goes to call the base nerd—I forget his name.

Frogface and Melody show up at the same time. I hadn't noticed before, but the pride of Dakota has a little thigh gap at her divine fulcrum, despite everything. Froggie comes to me, and I point a thumb over my right shoulder to Walker who is still furiously copying. My net is quieting down. It almost sounds like they are giving up to fate. Melody comes over to me, wanting to talk to me.

"I checked in with the linguists. They have the rogue fighter pilot, but he isn't talking much. Another has a net of other pilots trying to cajole him back but really seem to be searching for him to shoot him down," the redhead says to me with lit-up blue eyes. I smile back.

"Good. Good on you," I respond.

She is about to leave when I start both copying intermittently and asking her for something. "Please check that Givens is on the phone with PACAF, then get ready to alert DC via CRITIC or whatever that we are about to be either attacked by a rogue MiG or accept a defector, but the base commander is standing down, got it?" Her eyes a bit wider, she nods and leaves. I copy and stare at her hips working. Stafford needs to work on that butt. I wonder if he would be willing to subcontract that activity out. I am always happy to help the war effort.

Givens comes out of the admin room with emotions ranging from rage to shaking his head in resignation. He sees me seeing him as I keep copying code. He walks up and asks if he can have a chair. I nod, and when I have a second in between enemy transmissions, I say, "Get some more grub and coffee, sir." He smiles sheepishly but dives in only as much as senior officer decorum allows.

Melody shows up. She has a worried look on her face. "How do I say what is going on for the CRITIC?" The boss is at a loss with a full face of sammich.

"One MiG en route to Misawa Air Base close nearby to attack or otherwise. 432 Tactical Fighter Wing commander unwilling to address the threat, disbelieving intelligence provided and has stood down," I respond. Givens grins and nods to Melody. "The formatting is yours, young lady," I call to her diminishing backside. I see the commander looking too but refrain from commenting. I think it is in men's DNA. Besides, we are warriors; maybe we can claim we are checking for weapons. "Ranking Full Stop" by the English Beat comes on the box. Niiice.

"Is she with someone?" Givens asks. How unchaste.

"Yup. Steady and she is unsatisfied, but not willing to give him up for singlehood."

"You should steal her. With your last names, you must have much in common. She is a lovely girl," he observes.

"Sir, I don't cheat, and I do not break up couples," I respond.

"She will end up marrying him, having a kid, and divorcing in the course of three years. Honest," he says with authority.

"Uh-huh," I respond, "so what do you bet she asks me to marry her after she is pregnant before marriage?" I follow down his line of thinking.

"*You* should not bet against it," he responds. I am noncommittal, but I nod as I copy. Then I jump.

"Sammy!" I announce, followed by a sudden cough. He is there in an instant. "Jack," I tell him. He leaves, having no idea what I am up to. Nice to have trust. Jack shows up, and I start copying a bit. I raise an index finger during this. When I get a moment, I ask, "What if this is a distraction? Can you help the nuke kids? I am busy here." Jack dashes back to Block 2. When I get back to the rack, "Hot in the City" by Billy Idol is on a radio somewhere. Really. I think he is talking about Noo Yawk, and I am living in a place with worse weather than Buffalo. At least the mission is hot.

"What now?" asks Givens.

"Now we find out if we are going to accept a defector, receive a strike attack, or something else. I hope it is not something that will lead to WWIII," I educate.

"You seem so calm," the Boss observes.

"God is on our side, sir," I offer. He nods. It takes him a minute, then he realizes that we have a bit of fatalism his former flyboy comrades lacked. Before he was serving with children (i.e., pilots). Now he finally has a serious command. Diner coffee and sammiches have magical properties, apparently. Or the situation helped clarify the way of the world to the man.

We get word that PACAF directs a response as we track the rogue fighter. The commie is nearly here. The order is late, and the fighter buzzes our flight line on the deck, one meter above touchdown. He was playing with us. The commie is going back home with no apparent interest in returning. With a fighter plane's fuel tanks, that makes sense.

I realize a full report is in order. I also realize others should do the work. I gather the evidence and hand it to Melody. She is about to walk away when I softly say, "Hey." She turns my way. "Great work. Thanks," I say, meaning it. Something happens in her eyes, and she gives me a shy smile. With a slight nod, she leaves to send in a report.

"She wants to fuck you." I know, Givens. I know…

The carts carrying in the mid-rats show up just then, which reminds me how much time has passed. I get a thought.

"Walker, does Melody have all of your copy?" He shakes his head. "Your work needs to be seen too, okay?" He grins and goes to the analyst reporting area with his stuff, staying to explain it. Good man. How could I have been so wrong about him? Maybe he just hates physical work.

Givens is looking at the floor, maybe wondering what he has gotten himself into. This is going to be good.

"Sir?" He looks up. "The mid-rats are here." He looks at me questioningly. "The green food I told you about. I will let you check out what we get to eat without me altering the product," I tell him with a grin. I know it will be horrid. If you can trust anything, it's the Lord and the chow hall fucking up. Maybe gravity, but that is a distant third.

I look over to Block 2 and see my roommate having an interesting discussion with Dinger. He looks like he has put on ten pounds since I last saw him. They seem to be really hitting it off when it hits me; he really is her new post-divorce fuck toy. There is fraternization and there is fraternization, but damn. This isn't a complete shock since he'd fuck anyone, and she is good-looking for her age. I bet she is fifteen years older than him. I wonder what kind of stepfather he would be. Yeesh. Yes, I get back to looking for targets on my Racals after I observe this.

"Motherfucker!" Even though that is what I was thinking about in regard to Block 2, I bet Givens is thinking of something else. He looks at me as I turn back toward him with a small grin on my face. He is standing over the mid-rats.

"It would be scandalous if *one* of these looked like this. *They all look like this!*" He needs to calm down. Stress is a killer. I certainly don't think we should send anyone like him on a missionary mission to Africa. What a ruckus that would cause.

He is trying to calm back down to senior officer decorum. I keep grinning to the point of giggling. He starts shaking his head at me, and I respond with, "Sir, we have been dealing with this for some time. We are very happy to have you as our commander." He nods when I add, "It keeps us from having a revolution on this base. Now when you have fixed this, there is more," I add to his unhappiness.

"No." He just looks at me. "Really?" I nod.

"Your Chief is after us because we were attacked by one of his people, Grace Jones." I raise a hand before he can respond. "And the Dorm Chief keeps tormenting and trying to extort us." This makes his jaw open a little in astonishment. "You now know some of what we deal with outside of work," I add.

He responds, "I have a tour later tomorrow…er, today. I may have to reschedule," he follows with a noise of anguish.

"Colonel, none of this will be solved in an instant. That you are here means some of this might be solved soon enough. We are very happy to have you. By the way, as much as we love the mission, we do not want to die by the chow hall. *That* will be a great morale booster, sir," I advise.

He is about to respond when I get a target. I raise a hand and start copying. Then when I can, I point a finger at him and then toward the door with a wink. He responds in kind, adds a thumbs-up, and leaves. Good man. I see Jack giving me a thumbs-up and a wink. Good, the Boss is able to get some sleep because his transportation is up and ready. Nice. I wonder how Jack is doing with his JEEP. I hope she is emotionally stable.

The night is rather normal after that. Well, until we get the news.

"Misawa Air Base Commander removed for lack of confidence," the FEN announcer says.

Yeah. Later, I heard he and his family were told to get on a plane and their belongings would follow…maybe not to where they wished. Wow. *That* is cold. Glad the Givens is gone. I hope he does not hear the news until he has had enough sleep.

The rest of the night is comparatively uneventful. Sammy asks, just before we pack up and leave, "Anything else we need around here, Hal?"

"What Is Love" by Howard Jones is playing softly on the radio.

"No. Wait. Yes, can you ask your pretty Missus for locks for the footlockers when you get the coffee gear?" He nods, coughs, and promises to get on it. I wonder if the godawful weather we played softball in is getting us all sick. Wouldn't that be great? I offer the remaining walkaway and coffee to my replacement and make the long walk to Penny and head "home" to the barracks.

In no time at all, I am sitting in the usual spot on the usual couch wearing jeans cuffed up, no shoes or socks, and T-shirt like a bum. Having finished the Friedman book, I am reading a book called *Co. Aytch* by one Samuel Rush Watkins. It is a firsthand account of the American Civil War from a Confederate enlisted soldier who fought with the Maury Grays in the First Tennessee Regiment. He has a good eye for detail, tells the story well, and has a delightful sense of humor. "Rain" by the Cult is playing on a small radio.

Soon I realize the nearly empty room has become rather full, but not loud. Most have a beer despite the early hour. Nothing wrong with an after-work beer. I am having one too, which pairs well with something else from Tennessee. Balls and Zeus are sitting together, the former reading the book I gave her. Justin and Jack are at a far table smoking. I see Justin has a Michelob that he is nursing. Jewface, Cobra, Rocker, and some people I do not know are having a discussion all the way in the far corner. Fern, Leanda, Crosse, and Corrina are sitting with some other females I do not know discussing chick stuff, I guess. Nice to have such good people in this fight. America is lucky to have them. Of course, the sartorial displays are sometimes even more casual than mine. Jammies abound, but I guess it is a bit like loafing in one's living room.

I realize a small radio had been playing Melissa Etheridge at Cobra's table, but it is followed by Def Leppard, Whitesnake, and others. Bridget and Francis walk in from different directions at the same time through different doors. Bridget sits down so close our thighs touch. She puts a hand on my thigh and asks me how I am doing. I don't answer but nod slightly. I guess the shift just took it out of me. Getting sick helps, too. Francis sits on the couch opposite of me beside Zeus and Balls. He seems quite troubled.

"Is it always like this?" he asks, looking at me.

"Sometimes, but here isn't where we should discuss mission, sir," I respond kindly. "It's going to be okay," I assure him. Jewface was about to speak when some rather tall, well-built mammals walk in. I have no idea who they are.

"You bastards the ones who got our Boss fired?" asks the biggest one.

"It was my doing," I tell them. They don't look very happy and are standing in the middle of the room instead of behind me.

"Yeah, that thar rat bastard commander played pussy and got fucked!" adds Fern. How eloquent. It does give a few of my comrades the giggles. I wonder where Rabbit is.

"Here's hoping your next commander isn't so, ah, French," I tell them.

"Get up," demands another one to me.

"No thanks," I reply. "I already have a date," I say, nodding toward Bridget.

"I got a hundred bucks on Hal," says little Francis while he rifles through his pockets and brings out cash.

"No bet," replies Jewface with a grin. "These guys are fucked!" There are nods all around. I am thankful for the bluff.

Just then another comrade comes strolling in. He takes one look at the situation, and his eyes go wide and white with rage while he pulls out a butterfly knife with a flourish. "Saturday Night's Alright for Fighting" by Elton John begins to play, and Justin turns it up slightly.

"Time for you niggas ta die," he says behind me.

"Stand down, Eamons," I direct. He remains ready to launch. The big bastards were clearly not expecting any of this.

"We're just sick and tired of you motherfuckers constantly screwing us over, like with the Levitow awards and everything else," the one who spoke first says.

"And we don't care two fucks about you or those awards, we are here to defeat the Soviet Union," I say as my voice starts to show my increasing anger. "Time for you peasants to pull up stakes, pull your heads out of your asses, figure out your mission priorities, and get to work. Next time I see you, I will either be buying you a beer or loading you off to the morgue. Now fuck off," I end with a thumb toward the door.

One of the ones who never spoke got the message that they were being childish and petty and leads the others out. The tension in the room starts to slowly ebb. I realize that Bridget had been squeezing my thigh rather hard.

I look up at Eamons. "Thanks. You did great, sir."

His demeanor became different when he replied with, "Anything for a comrade," speaking with perfectly elegant diction and waves shut the knife. "Tie Your Mother Down" by Queen comes on, and it occurs to me that there are a lot of homosexuals on the radio this morning.

I turn to Francis. "You too, sir. You really had them going," I say with a smirk. I raise my bottle and toast, "To Francis!"

Beers are raised everywhere. "Francis!" He seems to be proud, a little embarrassed, and blushing.

"Astonishing," observes Leanda, who is drinking from a fine wine glass and what appears to be something better than the cheap chick juice Bridget seems to be guzzling besides me. Guess the latter is a bit stressed.

"Hal," Leanda continues, "how could you have fought all of them? You seemed so calm."

"Fear nothing but the Lord, Leanda, and everything else takes care of itself. Besides," I continue with a pull from the bottle, "I don't fight fair, and I suspect I wouldn't have had to fight alone." There are nods all around, and a few raised beers in agreement. She seems to be in a conundrum.

Gesturing at me with her glass, she says, "You always seem to be at the center of things, as if our leaders matter not."

"Let me quote from this book," I answer with a rural Southern accent.

"I always shot at privates. It was they that did the shooting and killing, and if I could kill or wound a private why, my chances were so much the better. I always looked upon officers as harmless personages."

I continue. "Leaders get the credit or the blame for the results of any endeavor. It's the common man, or woman, who actually creates the result. Remember, ours is the first country where it did not matter who your father was. Here we, with the Lord's help, can create our own destiny," I tell her. Funny. "Don't Fear the Reaper" by Blue Oyster Cult comes on just then.

"Hmmm," she says, shaking her head. "That is a lot to think about. I cannot decide if it is what you have just said or the wine that is overwhelming me. Either way, I have to go take a nap before we have our luncheon. Fern, dear, do you wish to join Mr. Rabbit and I at the restaurant?" Fern is gleefully enthusiastic. "Good. We'll meet at noon at the front door. I have a taxi scheduled to be waiting for us." Leanda looks back at the rest of us and finishes with, "Good evening," despite the hour.

Corrina and Crosse get up just then, and I am not certain that I do not gasp. Corrina has on a short T-shirt and Lycra tights that look painted on. What a sight. Even better, Crosse has on a white fucking onesie with silly little teddy bears or something all over it and a butt flap like old-fashioned long underwear. Her big, beautiful round ass is giving those two buttons a fight, and I cannot tell if a little ass is peaking out of the edges of the flaps. And you can bet I looked really, really hard to see if that is the case. I doubt I am alone. I guess I am not the only man who appreciates a nice big butt. Too bad they are so rare, especially on white girls.

Francis thanks me and leaves Zeus and Balls alone on the couch across from me. Balls looks up from her book and says, "Thanks, Hal. This might be the best gift I have ever received." Then she looks up at Zeus, smiles a little, and adds, "Well, one of the best gifts." I assure her that I was happy to do so.

Bridget is finishing her chick juice, and her hand is still on my thigh with her thumb going back and forth. This is not helping the raging boner I have from the interestingly dressed linguists. Damn if I wouldn't love to put those two squirrels[50] on my cunniling-list, as the great Ian Gillian once sang. It appears the raven-haired hillbilly has become a little tipsy. I cough a rough bronchial cough. Conversations are going on all over the room once again, and "Two Tickets to Paradise" by Eddie Money comes on the box.

---

[50] Linguists.

"I have a cure for that, big boy," Bridget says, referring to my cough, with a smile. Then she looks at my crotch, and her eyes widen. With less than perfect couth, she hits me lightly where I am engorged with her empty bottle. I am happy the bottle does not shatter. "I can cure all of your problems. Honest," she says breathily in my ear.

We both get up and start to head out. "Thanks again, guys," I tell the room. We are leaving just in time. "She's a Beauty" by the Tubes is coming on as we go toward the stairs. I hate that fucking song. It takes Bridget a while, but after a few sessions, she does indeed solve much of my physical afflictions. I leave her, thankful she cannot get pregnant, after she has passed out with exhaustion, turning on her alarm clock before I go. Any other woman would be knocked up several times over. Guess I was backed up. I go from the fourth floor back down to the second and go straight to my room. The day room is empty. My roommate is still not in our room, and I rack out.

CHAPTER 14

The Second Day of Mids

I wake up feeling like a bucket of ass when the alarm clock goes off. Despite this, I put on gym clothes and have a relatively light workout, followed by some time in the sauna. I return to the room, shower, dress, and hit the chow hall before work. I am surprised they have fresh food. I get my usual tonnage only to find there is no coffee. I give the workers a tongue-lashing, and they promise to get on it. One two-striper, Slaughter, asks why I would want coffee before going to bed. I explain we work shifts and that currently we are going to be up all night and sleep all day. He thanks me and says he will come out to my table with fresh coffee. I thank him and go my way, making certain to bring multiple empty cups.

I see a table with Leanda, Francis, and Jewface and head toward it.

"May I join you?" I ask, and they give dismissive waves. They are not feeling it either.

We all dig into our grub with no discussion. Slaughter shows up with two fresh pots of coffee and no cups, cream, or sugar. He means well.

Leanda, looking worse for wear, directs, "Please, sir, set those down in the middle of the table and return with cups, sugar, cream, and stirring spoons. Thank you much."

"Yes, ma'am." I don't think he realizes she is not an officer or a senior NCO; her manner and mannerisms do the trick.

Slaughter returns with a tray of the items, and I ask, "When did you arrive, sir?"

"This is my first day."

"Welcome to Misawa, sir. Thank you for everything," I respond. He gives a sideways grin and leaves.

I eat like an animal for some time, and then when I am near completion, I look up at my comrades eating desultorily. They look like zombies. I decide to rehumanize them.

"Leanda, how was lunch?"

"The food was lovely. I underestimated how miserable we would be at that hour. We have rescheduled a follow-on during the break." She takes a bite of something, looks at me, and smiles ruefully at whatever the swill is. I grin.

"I can imagine. Hey," I say, looking at everyone. "We got this." They look up at my confident face and seem to improve slightly.

We finish at different times and hit the road toward work. I am beginning to really like Penny. As she warms up, I stupidly fire up a Camel cigarette despite my new cold, turn on the radio, and "Lust for Life" by Iggy Pop comes on. When "Limelight" by Rush follows, I put her in gear. What a delightful song. Written and performed by commoners quoting Shakespeare, another commoner. I should tell this to Leanda. Well, in a way that makes her certain I am not hitting on her. I get the impression she is the queen of her own world, and the rest of us are just peasants she allows to exist. She is good-looking enough, but she wears clothing that does not really display her figure. Hmmm…

The roads are fair, the wind is a bit cold, but the sleet seems to be gone. I am glad I am early, especially glad when I see someone peaking in our footlockers. My foot meets ass. Hard.

An Airman's head hits the corner of a rack. "Ow!" Well put.

"Equal rights, equal fights, you bitch!" I say as I deliver a right cross to her jaw. She goes down like Madonna in her "Material Girl" days.

"Get this cunt to the infirmary. We'll be pressing charges later," I say to the stunned assholes we are relieving. "Now!" I say to one since the block leader is not there.

"You!" I say to another. "Go to the admin room and have an ambulance meet them," I add. One of them insists he can drive her to the infirmary. Inappropriately, "Why Can't This Be Love" by Van Hagar, er, Van Halen comes on. Not a bad song. Roth was an entertainer and a singer, but Hagar is a rocker. One more reason to believe that not all change is bad.

Sammy (not Hagar) walks in as the useless bitch is carried out on a cart. He looks at me with a sour look.

"Really?" he asks accusatorily. I tilt my head toward our footlockers. He rolls his eyes and throws a bag to me. "The coffee machine and such will be a day or two. Oh," he says and gestures for me to come to him. I do. He tells me the combo for all of the footlocker locks he just gave me. They are the same. Oh goody. I pass the locks to the blocks with the combos until I get back to the last one, Block 1. The fucking senior NCO block leader is wearing slippers in uniform. No, I am not kidding.

I grab the bastard and drag him to Sammy. Sammy takes one look and puts a finger up for us to wait a moment. The maggot tries to leave, and I put him up against the wall. He looks up at me from the wall surprised. Sammy and others show up.

Pugly says, "Get your idiot ass home, and put on your boots, you useless piece of shit." Dumbass is flabbergasted.

"But, but, uh, I just thought…" the maggot starts.

"You aren't Joseph John Rochefort, and we are not the Navy! We are warriors! Grow up, and put on clothes, maggot!" I could grow to like Pugly. Slipper boy leaves in shame. I look at Pugly.

"Thanks, Hoss, er, Senior."

"Thanks for the heads-up, Hal."

He leaves while I smile. Good man. "On the Dark Side" by John Cafferty & the Beaver Brown Band came on during that. Not bad. It's played a few times too often, but it ain't bad.

I get back and set up my rack with my comrades. Everything seems to be okay. FEN starts playing old songs. I especially like "Basie Boogie" by Count Basie. Then they play a blues song. No, I am not kidding. "Take Out Some Insurance" by my favorite nonclassical artist, Jimmy Reed. No shit. "Honest I Do" will change your life, but it is not in the queue this time. Oh well. The next song is a good one anyway, Santo & Johnny's "Sleep Walk." Maybe not the theme we want on third shift, but it fits.

The night is pretty routine in the beginning. Not much flying going on despite the weather clearing up a bit. Maybe last night's excursion has the commies standing down. Brandy picks up someone sending plaintext when her normal targets went quiet. I ask Walker to help her get a DF fix and Frog to figure out who it is. Sammy is curious as to the importance, so I suggest he get one of the squirrels to look at it if they are not busy. Sammy grins and goes to Block 1. I wonder who will come back with him. With so few flights in the air to track, they are probably bored.

It looks like Sammy is coming back alone when he steps aside for Corrina. I can tell she is trying to look at me without being seen doing so. Her uniform fits like a glove, and she looks like she has put on a lovely pound or two. "What You Need" by INXS is on, and I agree. To her credit, she does really well with Brandy. Corrina reassures her she is doing a great job without being too patronizing. I force myself to stop sending laser beams at Corrina's hot ass as she bends forward to read Russian and get back to my job.

As I search the quiet freqs, with visions of the business end of Corrina in my head, Melody visits. "Any guesses about what is happening with Brandy?" she asks me. I nod with a slight grin.

"How much do you know?" I ask her beautiful blue eyes and red hair.

"As much as Corrina has translated," she replied.

"Bottom line up front, I bet it is a transmission from Chita by a drunken or frustrated senior commander—the 23 Army or Air Army or whatever—telling his units to be vigilant during the transition during perestroika.[51] He is telling them the process will make them as prosperous as the West, and the shortfalls in funding and the supply chain are temporary. I am betting a call for vigilance and correcting the false idea that the Soviet Union is breaking up or losing the Cold War," I tell Melody.

---

[51] "Restructuring."

"How do you know all of this?" she asks incredulously.

"I've been keeping track of events, dear," I assure her. She shakes her head and goes to file her reports. I have been searching the radio waves this whole time, but part of me was distracted by Melody's conversation. Now I keep my eyes on her generous hips and plump, slightly unfit buttocks until they leave my sight. Damn if I couldn't help her fix that issue. Stupid Stafford. It takes me a second to realize Jack has been in our block and is standing off to my right about a dozen feet away.

Shaking his head, he says, "You ought to be careful with letting people know how on top of the mission you are, Hal."

"Ah, I should hide my light under a bushel?"

"No, it just makes some people suspicious—you being a junior enlisted guy and all. No one else, well mostly, knows where the Siberian HQ is and who is stationed there. It makes you stick out," he says with a slightly worried voice.

"Point taken, sir," I say and lean back a bit. "It's good to see you. How have you been?"

"I am thinking about getting married. What do you think?" Seriously? Damn.

"I think you should do it, if it is for the right reasons. Make certain she is mentally stable and you two are compatible. Any woman can be an ejaculate receptacle, but a mate for life is something else. And don't tell me about love. Love comes and goes. Oh, and every woman thinks she can improve her man, and every man hopes his girl will never change. Neither gets what they want. However, if she is the one then good luck and God bless," I finish with a small grin. He returns my grin, shakes my hand, and thanks me. He starts to leave when he turns back around.

"There will be another meeting soon, okay?"

"Let me know as soon as you can, okay?" I request with a bad cough. Something came up, but I have no nearby receptacle, so I have to swallow it down. Yuck.

I switch hands on the searching Racal because that arm and shoulder are getting tired.

"Hal," someone says softly.

I turn and see Corrina and Leanda staring at me.

"How can you be so damn smart, and…and…" Corrina begins.

"…and such an irreverent asshole the next?" asks Leanda with mighty frustration. I just sit there with a grin that keeps getting bigger and bigger. I know exactly what they mean. Great advice peppered with phrases like "ejaculate receptacle."

"There's no kill switch on awesome, guys," I say, deliberately baiting them as "Wild Wild Life" by the Talking Heads comes on the tiny radio in the back of the block to my right. I get back to work and hope they do, too.

Sammy has been taking this all in and is grinning from ear to ear on my back left. I see him and try not to bust out laughing. I wink at him and keep working. When Walker gets up to hit the head, I tilt my head after meeting his eyes asking him to come by.

I tilt my head toward not-so-little Train Wreck Tits and ask, "How's she doing?"

"Just fine. It is building her confidence up like you wouldn't believe. I have never heard such easy code, but she thinks she is saving the world so she is very attentive," Walker says with a paternal smile for poor Brandy to me. He starts to leave when I have a thought.

"Easy code. Like someone being slow or slow keyboard code?" I ask him.

"I dunno. It's like keyboard code, but, uh, in the moment—ya know what I mean? Not previously recorded and sent later," he responds.

I nod grinning. "Thanks."

I see Sammy. "Melody, please." He goes to see the Swedish Chef speaking dish. She shows up in no time.

"Would you please include in your report that the rookie Morse op, confirmed by more experienced comrades, is copying a message and that the code seems keyboard made but impulse sent. This is not hand-operated," I assure her. She looks at me like my nose is on crooked.

"What the hell are you talking about, and why should anyone care?" she responds with her hands on her hips. It's a good look.

"You know how the weather messages are at a given time and sent perfectly? Well, they preprogram the message and then press the recorded message on send. A bit fast, but perfect code is sent. Weather data is important to flight operations, right?" I finish.

"Uh-huh."

"This message seems to be sent live via keyboard transmission to avoid anyone not getting an *exact* copy of what Mr. Chita is sending. However, this is not a recorded transmission. It may not be an approved transmission. There may be more turmoil in Siberia than we think. The sender thinks he has to send this message *now*. This being a Russian operation, I bet alcohol was involved. I bet those in charge in Moscow don't know how bad things are in the hinterlands," I finish.

She is still processing what I have told her, not being an operator. "There is worry in the Siberian Command structure that order and production is dissolving in the Russian Far East," I educate. The light in her already bright eyes comes on, and she leaves me. Yes, I look. Maybe I am checking for weapons. Back off, dear reader from the future.

After Brandy's interesting moment, the night is quiet. Before anyone falls asleep on their racks, I ask about my comrades' background. "Tube Snake Boogie" by ZZ Topp comes on, and Brandy jumps right in since her sender is done.

"We has got almost no black fellas back home—sorry, Walker. Lots of Messicans in my hometown, though," she says as if that is an accomplishment.

"Your hometown is a taco truck?" She looks at me with confusion. "How about telling us the name of the town and state you're from, Brandy," I add.

"Oh, I'm from Mertzon, Texas!"

"Really. Some of us hail from outside the Republic of Texas. What is Mertzon near?" asks Leanda with a hint of sarcasm or worse. Just a hint though. She came to work tired, remember.

"Nearest real city is San Angelo, where Goodfellow Air Force Base is. I guess it influenced me to join up," she says, nodding in self-realization. "Seein' all them planes and them thar hot guys when we went inta town."

"Luckenbach, Texas" by Waylon Jennings comes on the FEN radio. Interesting.

Leanda is smiling now. "What is there to do in Mertsville, Brandy?"

"Uh, you mean Mertzon?" Leanda's grin gets bigger, and she nods. "Well, there's caverns nearby. The San Angelo Riverwalk. Pecan farms—pecans is big in Texas. Oh, and Miss Hattie's Bordello!" This makes us all laugh. Poor Brandy is confused again. "Whut?"

"Ah, most American youth get their first job at a fast-food joint, ya dig?" states Walker. It takes Brandy a few seconds, and then she blushes to the clavicle, to her credit.

"Uh, it's a tourist site. Like the 'Chicken Ranch' used to be. That's what ZZ Topp was talking about in 'La Grange,'" she informs. Wow. Who knew?

Everyone keeps searching for targets while we talk. "Leanda?" I ask.

"My past has very few interesting bits. Maybe only one," she replies.

Sammy barges in. "Hal, this is a good idea, but we should keep it in small doses and keep track of the mission with the weird stuff and the USSO going on and all." Good man.

"Righty-ho. The Senior is right. Leanda, would you please share the one bit of your family's interesting past if it is a short tale? Then we had better put our full attention to the mission," I say.

She gets a devious little grin and says, "It was one Peter De Loughry, the spelling having been changed slightly upon arrival to America, who made the key that sprung De Valera from the Lincoln jail."

"Eamon De Valera?" I ask. She nods slyly.

"We need to talk sometime," I say, looking back at her. I widen my gaze and say, "Back to work, fellow workers of the world!" This gets some giggles, but they seem slightly rejuvenated.

After that, all was routine. Even the mid-rats. The bologna sandwiches were moldy and rotten. I guess Givens can only deal with one thing at a time.

However, I get an idea when I see Jack walking by. I catch his eye and silently ask him to come to me. He gets close, and I tell him my idea sotto voce. He giggles and agrees. It's a slow night, so this can be done. He is about to leave when I give him an add-on to make this really work. He winks and leaves me. When he comes back from whatever he was doing before I waylaid him, I ask him about messaging. He shrugs. I tell him that I am on it, and he should just do the latter bit.

I tell Sammy that I have to give a message to the softball team. That is true. However, I am going to kill two birds and get stoned with this message. Before I venture off, I tell him to look in the non-mission footlocker. During my odyssey outside Block 3, I find some who have access to small Japanese utility trucks to help us. It's going to work. I get labor from NCOs who think they have some underemployed kids. This is really going to work. Wow.

Work ends, and every single Airman carries their mid-rats "home." The married folks have theirs loaded onto small Jap trucks and take them to a building right near the barracks. The Inspector General team is there when we all arrive. What we do is not what they expect.

I nod to a companion, and he says, into a military walkie-talkie appropriated from somewhere, "*Go!*" We all head in, Leanda holding the front door. I ensured the crazies would come in the back. No one thought to lock the loading dock area of the chow hall. All of us go behind the counter and shower the people there with the pathetic boxes of pathetic "food." "Kick Out the Jams" by the MC5 is on the radio. In the fracas, I save young Slaughter from the worst of it, so good for him. IG is impressed, not positively, but they are shown the uniformity of the food. And we did one better.

Stars and Stripes cameras and reporters are everywhere. Ev-er-y-where. They take pictures of everything and enjoy having a scoop. I had heard they were in to report the removal of the other base commander. No doubt they will write this off to his incompetence. However, other bits come out:

- "Sometimes they open late, and even then, there is no food. If we did that on the Hill, we'd be Article 15'd."
- "How could anyone send this poison to another Airman without protesting?"
- "Their hours don't match the mission."
- "If you come here before third shift, you have come here to die before working another third shift. So there's that."

Yes, so there's that. Funny, "How Much I Feel" by Ambrosia comes on next on the little box in the chow hall. Then some assholes from *Stars and Stripes* come to me with a million questions. Apparently, they think I did all of this. Uh, er, uh…nah…pshaw.

After being asked about it, I answer, "How many years can you stand this?" I say this, pointing to the pile of mid-rats. "It was a spontaneous revolt among good Airmen talking to one another and the word spreading around. We have great hope in our new commander on the Hill, but this has to stop now from main base with the new main base commander," I tell some asshole reporter. I grab the geek by the collar and make certain he will include my whole statement rather than slander the new Hill commander, and he agreed. I don't trust POGs.[52]

Someone else asked how to phrase the story, and I told them. I also told them they could paint the recently removed commander and the chow hall boss to this. Any wrongful order should be resisted. He did this to us…for what? To save a few dollars? Over the safety and health of our warfighters? Personally, I think they should all be executed.

"Mission is over! It's Miller Time," I announce and most leave, though some, to their credit, stay to help clean up. I bet they are hungry or something since breakfast is the best meal of the day. Most of us walk back to the barracks for the usual after work activities. The

---

[52] People other than Grunts, aka nonwarriors.

newsmen have a story, and the IG team gets to inflate their evals.[53] Maybe this will lead to good food one day. Good thing Givens is not in Nippon, being TDY some damn where. Before I get to the barracks building, I have a coughing fit and end up spitting out a couple of golf ball–sized phlegm balls that are nearly the same color as our uniforms. Yuck. I make a mental note to tell everyone on the softball team who is sick to go to the doctor soonest.

I had just finished spitting out the dregs when Jack comes up to me.

"Guess who wants to see you?" he asks with tired eyes.

"I thought they broke up in the mid-70s," I reply and then start to walk to the door to our barracks.

"What?" He is not keeping up in any way, nearly tripping on the cracked pavement of the sidewalk.

"Bet you that I can't tell him I have no time, huh?" Now he should get the joke.

"Are you crazy?" he asks, narrowing his eyes.

"That has nothing to do with it." I decide to let him get the joke on his own. He doesn't. "Yeah, I'll go. First, I will change clothes, but I will hit the road soonest," I tell my tall, scrawny friend. "Oh, anything I should know or bring to the date? Are you going?"

"No and no," he answers politely. "I just think he wants to go over more of the details."

"Copy. Thanks. And have fun with your beau while I drink over yonder," I tell him. Since he blushes, it confirms his plan of action. About damn time this man got his ashes hauled.

I did as I promised and changed into generic clothing alone since my roomie is probably somewhere he shouldn't be with someone he shouldn't be with. As I was walking down the second-floor hallway toward the main stairs, I see the usual suspects in the dayroom, including Bridget.

"Hey!" she calls out. I wait. "Why don't you come on in…" she starts and pauses. I am dressed for the weather and more. She takes

---

[53] Evaluations.

all of me in with her eyes. Perhaps she is smarter than I thought. "Don't be too long. I'll try to wait, okay?" I smile warmly and leave.

You, dear reader, might be wondering what she saw. I'll tell you, nothing. No team name on the hat. Generic blue jeans, white oxford button-down shirt, boring belt compared to the country folk and Westerners among us, and even my ball cap was plain, matching my coat. Just some boring geek off to run an errand, right? Well, this was a boring geek not wanting anyone to have any identifying features to include my hairstyle, which can't be seen under the hat anyway. Trying to get lost in a crowd of two, if need be. It appears Bridget is perceptive, smart, but just not all that well-educated due to where she was raised.

In the barracks, when hanging with everyone, I will often have on something identifiable (e.g., my father's University of Minnesota T-shirt that no longer fits him or some such). Walking out on the town, one will see me in a ball cap with a team on it, or I could be dressed in nice slacks, shirt, and bolo tie with a sport coat depending on the weather. Oh well. I am nearing Penny. Yes, my thoughts are a wandering a bit.

Penny starts right up, but I wait a minute to make sure she is warmed up despite being run not long ago. Since I have a bronchial cough, I skip the fag but find a tape and put it in the slot. Manfred Mann's "Come Tomorrow" starts playing. I press the shut the hell up button and replace it with something else, all left-handed no less. Well, the Japs do drive on the Brit side of the road for no apparent reason after all, so that is how that must be done. The next tape begins with "A Natural Woman" by Aretha Franklin. Not bad. Not what I was expecting, but so cool I don't have the heart to change it. Funny driving with the windows down, the song cranked and singing with it at top volume. I got some looks, I tell you. Of course, I took a detour on the way off base to check for bogies.[54] After the weird shit I have seen lately, can't be too careful. Just as I was driving through the gate the tape turns to "Bad Girl" by the New York Dolls. Sounds like early punk rock to me personally, but I know better.

---

[54] Enemies.

Nowhere near their best, but it matches the spirit of the day—revolution. It ends as I drive up.

Just as I knock, one of the cutie-pies opens the door. I notice, for the first time, that it looks like an old, heavy, and disreputable door but is instead rather formidable. The Sage has got a pretty good place. I was just about to ask where he was when I have another disgusting coughing fit. The cuties start running about like ants when you lift a log. One puts a trash can below my head, and I gratefully spit into it. They see the color, and this apparently impresses them even more.

One, after I stopped coughing and was hardly expecting it as I was just getting my breath back, hit me hard in the upper center of my back. This made me gag, and I spit up an enormous ball of goop. I look into trash can girl's eyes with deadpan eyes, and she waved off another blow from behind-me bitch. Another brings fresh fried dumplings or some damn thing, and another brings a carafe of hot sake. A really nice blanket is wrapped around my shoulders, probably by back whacker. They must think that I am going to die. I thank them in Japanese, which makes the ones I can see smile.

I wolf down the dumplings and start taking shots of the sake. Damn it's warm. Not as easy to drink as Korean soju. The girls encourage me to finish the little carafe of sake, pouring the clear liquid into the tiny Nip shot glass that matches the carafe. It looks like fine China…so to speak. When I finish, I ask where the Sage is.

"Bidzee," one says. Okay. When I ask when he will be at his own house, most of them shrug. One says, "Zoon." Perfect.

I don't idle well, so I wish I had brought a book. I am looking about the place when I realize the little minions are conspiring together.

"Hal-san," one says, beckoning me with a finger. Uh-huh.

I go back and there is a bed. "You must rest with cold," she says. Good girl. There are all sorts of blankets and pillows and whatnot.

"Please wake me when he arrives," I request.

"Uh-huh," they all say at various times when, as I got comfortable laying on my right side, they went to work.

One is taking off my boots, another my pants, and the next my underpants. I get a blow job from someone with another kneading my buttocks and another giving me a shoulder rub. All we need is a foot rub specialist, and all will be perfect.

I reach my moment when a radio transmitter goes off with something I cannot make out.

One shrieks a command, and the rest get at it after the most important one finishes draining me. One leads me to the bathroom, which I use. When I come out, everything is perfect. No blanket or sake set and the bed is all set up. These girls are good.

I dress and wait at the bar for him to arrive. He does in just a minute and asks if I want coffee. I ask for the usual. He grins and nods to the girl behind the bar who already has a fresh pot of coffee for him and is getting my beverages and glasses of choice.

"I worked all night. Needs muh sleep, suh," I say like a zombie slave. "Big Bad John" by Jimmy Dean comes on the radio.

He just looks at me. I have one of my coughing fits, and the cutie-pie behind the bar talks to him in Japanese. After listening to her, he looks back at me. "Good timing. Probably that damn softball game. I'll have someone fix that for you. And your work coffee situation." He goes away, and I have a drink or three of beer and JD, not always in that order. Yes, I have issues. I try not to look at the cutie-pie behind the bar too much, but she is funny without words while flirting. I feel awful, but her actions make me smile. And horny. I seem to have a surplus of that.

When the Sage comes back, the cutie-pie loses the smile in a damn hurry. What the hell? Anyway, he tells me to hang out, and we will discuss the mission while waiting for two care packages. Okay. So we discuss the mission. Maps. It turns out there are not a lot of real roads in that part of the world. Oh, goody. We discuss what I will bring, how I will dress, and more than one likely cover/identity I will presume to be. We discuss local cultures. Some were new to me since they had no military value (e.g., the Jewish Autonomous Region). Cultures, contacts, equipment, rations, what to note, and how I am going to get back are all discussed. I may never see the mystery nuke location, based on circumstances.

Two things were unsettling. "It doesn't matter about the end result. Do what you can, and then get out. You seem sick. I am getting you meds. Second, I hear your Block 3 guy's wife is having a hard time with the coffee mission. I think I have that covered as well," the Sage says with a grin.

"Alright. I feel like a bucket of ass. Are those nerds of yours delivering this stuff here or to my room?" I ask.

"Here. Just a minute," he says, and he looks out and sees what he wants to see. The medicines are loaded. "Get in Penny, get some rest, and kick ass at work. I will contact you again."

I nod and wave as I lurch to my car. There are things in my limited hatchback. Okay. I get back into Penny, and it looks like there is a sizable bag full of drugs for my sniffle.

I drop off the coffee crap at Sammy's house and then, once at the barracks, bring up the drugs and pass out in my room. No, I do not even bother looking into the dayroom for Bridget. She'll understand, or she won't.

CHAPTER 15

Day Three of Mids

I sleep until my alarm goes off. Damn. I guess that Japanese illegal-for-Americans cough syrup really works. No time for the gym, but that is for the best, considering. My health is, uh, not great. Not too bad, but it could be better. I shower, dress, and leave my room. No sign of my roommate. I think he may have moved in with Dinger in the high-rise apartment on the other side of base. Just a guess.

The drive to work is routine. The weather is not as cold, and the skies are clearing. I play a classical tape on the way; it's Pachelbel's "Canon in D" playing through the ethereal night on the way to work. I take in some meds and pick up some grub at the Walkaway Diner on the way toward Block 3. The drug instructions are in Kanji,[55] but I am betting one should take them with food. One of the cutie-pies had explained to me the instructions while walking to my car, and I wrote little abbreviations as to whether it was a morning or evening drug only or both. Of course, morning and evening are relative in shift work.

My rack is empty when I arrive, so I use the little table to set down my bags of drugs and food and stand there, eating and drinking coffee…and taking medicine. Nice to be early. As I eat, I turn around toward the Fish Bowl and see some good and some pathetic SNCOs.[56] We have too many of them, in my opinion, but if we cut

---

[55] Japanese lettering.
[56] Senior Non-Commissioned Officers.

down the number, we would probably end up with an insufficient number of the good ones. This is as deep as I can think while feeling like a bucket of ass, barely able to finish a single sammich. Someone softly clears their throat behind me.

I turn around and see that chick I decked yesterday. I say nothing but slightly raise an eyebrow.

"Hal...thanks. I want you to press charges. I had a 'come to Jesus' meeting with people I respect and my supervisor yesterday. You taught me a lesson I probably would not have learned any other way. I am sorry personally and as an Airman. Please forgive me and no hard feelings on my end on whatever you do," she says, keeping tears down and maintaining her military bearing. Good girl.

Since I feel like shit, my response is not delicate-sounding with a raspier-than-usual voice. "Good. We aren't here to investigate each other, but the enemy. Why don't we dedicate our time against the commies instead of each other and forgo charges, okay?"

"As you wish, Hal. I was serious in what I said," she says with genuine sincerity.

"Me too. Now, make us all proud by becoming the best person, American and Airman you can be, okay?" She nearly comes to tears but contains them. Then she puts out a hand. I wave it off to avoid getting her sick, and we side fist, then I let her leave. She stops and then turns to look at what I brought to work.

"Look at that pile of drugs. I am as sick and disgusting as a politician in Washington, DC. Hard to be the best you can be while coughing up furballs, right?" I appease with a grin.

She responds with a small grin of her own. The kid is about to say something...and stops. Looks me in the eyes and nods with strengthening authority. Stout fellow. No, I don't check her out while she leaves. I am in no condition to be thinking about such things. Yes, I must be very sick...

My Block 3 comrades start coming in just then. Sammy is acting like a puppy after a successful pee in the backyard. "Woohoo!" he yells. I guess his Missus put out again.

He comes over to me and informs me that he brought the new equipment from home out and sees what was needed for our operations. He says he has everything we need. He starts handing out plain white coffee cups when I show him that I have a cute coffee cup sent many months before by my mother—it says Twin Cities with a nice drawing of such, from her home. The darling lady sent me a piece of her. I may not deserve my parents. Great people.

Sammy is explaining the different roasts he brought and asks what we want. I raise a hand. "Is everyone as brain dead as me?" Everyone nods. "Mild blend, Sammy."

"Whut?" Yes, he is at loggerheads.

"Dark roasted beans and grounds have most of the caffeine roasted out of them. Superstrong mild is what we want. If you can't figure out how to make it not too strong-tasting, I have a solution to that as well," I inform. He shrugs and gets at it.

I mention needing to make a quick trip to the softball team, and he gives a small papal wave. I make my lap backward so as to get to Bridget sooner rather than later, feeling a little guilty. When I get to her block, I ask Happy if all is well, and he is noncommittal. "I mean health-wise, the rest of us are sick." He nods. What a dumbass. Bridget walks in just then. I nod to the side, and we walk a few steps away.

"Sorry I did not check on you. Still sick. Er, when I came back, I was sick. Sick and exhausted. I didn't even take off my clothes. Sorry," I admit.

"I know," Bridget responds. I narrow my eyes and raise my eyebrows. "You didn't lock your door. I checked in on you. I figured you were sick or drunk. I forgive you, Viking Talker," she says with a grin. I respond with a pathetic grin of my own.

"I'd kiss you here and now if A, we were not at work, and B, I was not sick with the bubonic plague. Thanks," I say, meaning it. I raise my chin slightly to her and turn on my heel to another block. There's always more to do. Like tell the other softball morons to get to the health clinic and buy drugs from the BX. I assure them that, if need be, I will drive them to the BX for the purpose. Then I get an idea.

Just before I get to Block 3, I turn right into the Fish Bowl instead of left into Block 3.

"Pugly!" He looks at me as if he would throttle me. I look at him as if he was a munchkin singing about his union in the *Wizard of Oz*. "I need your help, sir," I put forward, chastely. I tell him, and he is ready to respond immediately. Good man.

I get back to my rack, and everything everywhere is rather routine. In fact, it is all dead quiet. I wonder if there is a sort of standdown or if the enemy is really running out of funds for flying hours. Checking with my comrades, they report the same. I ask Sammy to check with the other blocks, but he is busy finishing our first pot of gourmet coffee. The apparatus seems to be finished, and Sammy is acting like little girl who just got a Barbie house.

"I have sugars, nonsugar sweeteners, powdered creamers, and everything!" he announces.

"Sammy." He looks at me.

"I have real creamers if anyone wants some," I say as I gesture with my head toward my walkaway plastic bag. Yes, there is ice in the bottom. There is no kill switch on awesome. To their credit, some don't care, including Leanda. I think she is building up her "I lived with military peasants" thing. You can bet your ass I used my creamers. A few others did as well. The coffee is not bad. Rocker and Leanda ask for it to be stronger next time. I ask Sammy how much grounds he used, and clearly that is not enough for mid-shift. I tell him what to do for the next brew since the pot is empty and give him what he needs from the walkaway bag.

A great song, "Bringin' on the Heartbreak" by Def Leppard comes on the small box. All the males start singing along, but before a few seconds of it go on, Sammy corrects them. I tell them to hold the line and address the mission. I know. Hard to do. Harder to do when the enemy is not transmitting. What the hell? I look around, and everyone is searching the empty freqs for a target. Through the fog of a drug-filled mind, I think of something. Sammy is fooling with the coffee maker, so I go over there to ask him something.

"Any word on the USSO or the plaintext messages we have been copying?" He looks at me like I am crazy. I know the cold is making my voice sound like a bad horror movie villain.

"Who would I get that from?" he asks in bewilderment.

"Day shop support folks, if they knew their fucking jobs. Scuttlebutt from the other shift leaders. Wherever," I sum up, slurring my words a bit. He just shakes his head. Then, out of the corner of my eye, some nerds in civvies come walking up to us.

"This is the one I was talking about," says Colonel Givens to some younger female, referring to me. Really?

Just as the colonel began to speak, she puts out a hand and introduces herself. "Captain Wythe," she lets me know with an accent that sounds like it is from the Tidewater section of Virginia. "I am the new Charlie Flight commander." I raise a hand up to the side of my head, to her disappointment.

"I'm sick. No use in you being greeted to your new assignment with the bubonic plague or whatever," I tell her with a weak smile. She seems very sure of herself. She also looks like she is one of those people who has trouble keeping their weight in check. Ever met someone who could just balloon up in a weekend? Yeah, like that.

"You should see a doctor and rest. Would you like me to order you back to the dorms?" she asks in all puffed-up seriousness.

"I was properly beaten as a child, but no. Today and tomorrow—then we are off for a few days. Besides, I have already received medical attention," I say, gesturing to my bag of drugs.

She looks like she is going to get bitchy for being stood up to, so I add, "You have the look of a competent commander, ma'am. That would be a nice change. May I inform the group commander about something troubling us in regards to the mission?" Mollified, she nods. Givens grins.

"What is it, Hal?"

I remind him of the USSO and discuss the oddity of the plaintext messages. Then I talk about the dearth of support from the admin day shop dorks, who are supposed to be sharing information with all of the operators lessons and data that are learned on all shifts. Sammy joins just then and tells them about our binders and footlockers. We also add the emptiness of the freqs.

"Captain Wythe," she says with a hand extended to Sammy. While she has his hand, she adds, "I hope your leadership knows what great ideas you came up with and have rewarded you for it."

He grins sheepishly. "Blame Hal, but he doesn't care about his career…just the mission." She seems astonished.

"Told you," Givens says with a smile at Wythe. "Let me show you around to the other sections, Captain." We welcome her again and wish her well. Sammy watches them leave and has a faraway look about him. He catches me looking at him, and I raise my eyebrows slightly in question.

"Can't be worse than the last one," he admits. I nod as there can be no disagreement about that. I am betting she just got off the plane to her new assignment.

"I worry that she might be uptight. Garrison thinker. Like Fatty," I observe loudly as Fatty walks past. He is startled to see me when he hears his other name and instantly walks faster in fear. Peasant.

"What do you think, Hal?" Sammy asks with some reticence. Funny. "Hot and Nasty" by Humble Pie comes on.

"You didn't feel it?" He shakes his head. "That bitch is giving it off. She'll be fucking everyone in the enlisted ranks soon and should, if my thinking is right, be changing her thoughts on collecting INTEL however it can be had as well," I say. "Really, go back to the barracks with a sniffle?"

"How did you pick up on that, Hal?" Sammy wonders.

My eyes meet his and my lips close. He nods. It's just one of those things that you pick up on. Asshole intuition or something.

Leanda had apparently been waiting for us to finish our conversation. "Hal, Sammy, whatever did you do to the coffee?" Rocker, Walker, Leanda, and Brandy all nod in agreement. Sammy looks at me, so I speak.

"You put the tiniest amount of salt grounds in the filter, no more than five, then pack it with as much coffee grounds as it will hold. It turns out mild and strong instead of bitter and chewy."

"The only thing stronger than this is cocaine, if the stories are to be believed," added Rocker. Walker smirks. Hmmm…

"Brandy, ever hear of cowboy coffee?" She nods and smiles at me. "Know how they made it?" Brandy shakes her head, and her train wreck tits shake slightly in the opposite direction as her chin.

"Really, there's more?" asks Leanda. I grin.

"Take out the used grounds and do the same thing as if to make another pot of coffee. Run the coffee you have been drinking through the new coffee grounds. Cowboy coffee. Allegedly, the coffee ain't done if you can't throw in a horseshoe, and it stays standing up instead of leaning to the side," I teach. "It must be tough on the trail to need coffee that strong, but there it is. Oh, I once heard a Latino gentleman say that Third World shift-working laborers would mix very strong iced coffee with Coca-Cola, or perhaps one as a chaser. Apparently, it had a symbiotic effect and was quite the stimulant." They believe me, but they are also sickened by the idea. Oh well. Maybe they really did drink one and use the other as a chaser, which would make some sort of sense.

The mission, aside from the transfer of the USSO from one godforsaken hellhole to another, is boring. One would think they'd fumigate the bitches somewhere in between one site and another, but that is not my concern, I guess. Yeesh. Perhaps they do it on the plane. Imagine having that job.

I ask Sammy about that, and he gets all cattywampus. Good name for what happens to their special lady parts, I guess. Or maybe catty-swamp-puss. Yuck. I guess if you have to, you have to. Then again, these Jap drugs are really strong; my mind is wandering. Jimi Hendrix and his Experience is on the box, "I Don't Live Today." The sounds are really trippy right now on this medicine. "The Loner" by Neil Young follows, and his annoying voice doesn't seem so bad through the fog of medicine.

The freqs seem to be freaks by not being used. This is a universal situation. Then FEN saves us all by announcing some classic American song show. Both Frog and Rocker groan. "Jump Back, Honey, Jump Back" by Gene Vincent & the Blue Caps starts it off. Dad seemed to not be a fan of Vincent or Presley. I heard once that, after Elvis got his inoculations for the Army live on television, polio vaccinations went up from nearly nothing to nearly universal. Another example of awesome from a good Southern boy. But the freqs remain mostly empty. Well, except for FEN.

One sender from one of my old targets from Block 2 had a habit of tapping out a rhythm on the side of his transmitter. Thus,

I could find him—even when he was not sending Morse. It resembled my old high school marching band's drum beat. A nervous tic, I guess. Cute. Anyway, I heard it again, and I asked DF to find him. He was somewhere else than his usual station. I posted that but went to Block 2 and told Jack the news. He gave it to some new girl. Oh, his fiancé. Whatever. I just want to make certain that everyone knows their PCS[57] patterns. Maybe NSA is as retarded as our setup but should like to know it. Pretty sure, based on the evidence given about those DC bastards, those pricks are that damn useless like the fucking morons here in day shop on Misawa's Security Hill. They would not understand a horse's head in their bed. Dumbasses. I'd say freaks, but it would sound like freqs. No, I have no idea how we will win the Cold War. I am in a fog of stress, no restful sleep and medicines.

The rest of the shift goes on relatively smoothly. Of course, with good coffee, everyone is all over the mission and a bit chatty. I advise Sammy to stop the coffee a few hours before shift change. It just wouldn't do to have our people unable to sleep after work. I catch Leanda checking me out a few times though. Thankfully, Francis comes by to visit her on occasion to interrupt this. What he has to tell her, I have no idea. Good for them both. I am thankful they both are serving God and country, but I am also glad they can talk to each other rather than me. Funny, "The Ballad of John and Yoko" by The Beatles comes on the box. I guess I had not been listening—unlike me. I heard that half the time Paul and John showed up alone for many of their tracks, with Paul playing bass and drums and so on. Hopefully the CMSGT is not still trying to crucify me. These drugs are something when listening to this song.

When the shift ends, I go home, take more Jap drugs, and crash. I don't even have a proper drink. No, there is no roommate.

---

[57] Permanent change of station.

CHAPTER 16

The Last Day of Mids

I wake up to phlegm on my pillow. At least it is not as green as before. I have just enough time to pretty up myself, throw on the same uniform I wore yesterday, and go to work. After the usual procedures, I find the drive to work nearly pleasant. The box wanted to play a rock song, but I turned it off. The silence is nice. Then I play a different tape. "Fair Phylliss" by John Farmer goes through Penny. Great song. Better than "Paint It Black" by the Rolling Stones before coffee. I buy grub from the Walkaway Café on my way to Block 3. I am not the first one there, but that is okay. I am tired. I don't know if it is the shift work or the cold. My stomach feels a bit worn out, so I may have been coughing while I slept. It might be nice to have Stallone abs as a result of the plague.

As everyone arrives and I sit down, the radio in the back of the block is playing Beethoven's "Symphony No. 9 in D Minor." That is a surprise. Well, FEN tries to satisfy everyone. And they can say they did this while also doing so when few are listening. I once heard that CDs are of a certain length to accommodate this recording. Good. Also, good that the others are arriving. They seem to be in better spirits and mood than I am. Leanda comes to me instead of going to her rack.

"We've missed you in the day room, Hal," she says. Oh goody.

"I have been ill, Leanda. Will you be at the championship game today?"

"I wouldn't miss it, sir," she says. Oh shit. Like I need another one.

I go to Jack and tell him what we will need to compete for the championship. He grins and insists he will be on it. Good man. When Sammy comes in, I tell him I have to brief the softball team. He nods and I go. I tell everyone that beer, water, and that new Gatorade drink is allowed, but no whiskey since we are all sick. After the game, they can drink all the whiskey on the island. This is agreed to. Cretin is back, and he agrees…even when I tell him that he can only have beer after the game since the Russians are right about beer not being alcohol.

"Holstein is trying to kick me out of the Air Force. I want to stay in. *No* problem, Hal," he says. "Oh, and thanks." I raise an eyebrow. "You were right," he replies with some comely shyness. "I am allergic to alcohol. I am giving it up…with some difficulty, but I am giving it up."

I was going to reach for his hand and instead give him a bear hug. He does the same.

"If only I were as strong as you, Hoss," I answer.

"Well, my girl helps," he answers sheepishly. "The, uh, girl you met that one night at 007s."

I smile, smack him on the arm, and go to the rest. Thank God he might be okay!

When I return, all seems set in order except for me. I eat a walkaway and take the requisite drugs. As I slug my walkaway coffee, Leanda pours me coffee into my mug. Oh shit.

I look up and say my thanks. This could go really wrong.

I ask about the block if the nets are still quiet, and everyone says yes, even Brandy. I see Melody and ask her to visit.

She looks like she has lost a pound or two since I last saw her. Or I am just now really seeing the gap between those wonderful Dakota thighs. Damn.

"Is there a way to send a message saying there is nothing to send?" She looks at me in confusion. I don't blame her.

"A message saying there is a strange lack of traffic?" She says she will find a way. I think I have shown her that the rules are just guidelines. Good girl. Even better watching her go off to do that. No, I did not call her over for that reason, but I am not upset having done so. Wow. That lovely, dimply ass needs professional help, and I would be happy to do so.

Back to the mission. The mission is picking up a wee bit. Brandy is slightly busier than the rest of us. I notice that Beethoven's Ninth is still on. Maybe that is why Leanda was after me. I should send a letter to those bastards to let them know that good music interrupts the mission. Or maybe she is drunk. I don't know. I need another Rachel like I need a hole in the head. I already have a Bridget and worse. They seem to accumulate like rain gutter debris.

I'd love to tell you about cool SIGINT collections, but on this night, there was none. Sorry. No Givens visit either. Good.

Also the 16th Chapter—the game…

I got to the barracks and collapsed. When the alarm went off, I took some drugs on an empty stomach and went to the field, feeling like a bucket of ass. When I arrived, the team was there and so were vendors and tons of our fans. I got a bad hotdog from a vendor, an illicit slug of JD from Bridget, God bless her, and a beer from some stranger. Yes, a bit of the pint, and yes, the whole damn beer. For the first time in my life, I littered. Of course, I littered the beer can into the stands who were cheering my arrival, but still. People were grabbing at my detritus as if I was a Beatle. How I merited cheers, I have no idea. I was staggering in illness. I saw Bridget, asking her to procure more JD. Good girl. Good people. Yes, I realize I am a complete hypocrite. A radio plays Queen's "I Am In Love With My Car." No whiskey, indeed.

When I got to the dugout, the others looked at me, worried. I had my reply.

"When I am on the field, I will be at my best. My very best. By that I mean my goddamn cowboy up best. These motherfuckers are going *down*! Now who is with me?" I end with some volume.

Cheers all around. "We are not only going to win. We are going to make them know that we have won, okay?" (More cheers all around.)

Luckily, the umpire remains Chief Holstein. Remember, these are his troops we are playing. Wonderful. Well, wonderful if my comrades have done their jobs. I don't bother checking to see if they did; I have faith.

Happy decides just then to turn in our lineup at home plate and check to see if there are any updates. I decide to join him, knowing we are the only undefeated team. The admin pukes' manager arrives at the same time when Frenchy gives us the news; Charlie Flight is the visiting team.

"Okay," says Happy. Dumbass.

I get nose to nose with the Chief and loudly growl, "Fuck that shit! We have the better record. We are the home team, you cheating maggot motherfucking piece of shit!" I have been told that my singer's voice tends to carry. It must have happened this time because our stands erupted in noise before I was even finished. Our foreheads may have connected. Yet, the excitement died down oddly behind us at home plate.

"Chief," someone says behind us. Holstein turns around before he starts screaming back at me and looks like he has been struck across the face. "Don't fuck this up so close to retirement, Frenchy," says Colonel Givens, looking crisp in upper-class casual civilian clothes. The Chief is close to retirement? Oh. Funny. News to him, I guess. The Chief turns back to us quickly.

"My mistake, Charlie is the home team. Be careful as the footing is still less than perfect."

I look at the bastard through narrow, mean eyes and say, "Thank you, Chief," in a polite voice, which belies my expression. "We will pass on your information about the field and send the boys out."

As we walk back to the dugout, I catch Jack's eye and mouth "thank you" and tilt my head toward our commander. He acknowledges me and goes to sit in the stands. I see he is sitting with that future wife of his. She seems happy. Happiness makes her prettier. I hope they both are good for each other.

I hear Happy muttering something about how he doesn't know how I get away with everything, which makes me smirk. We arrive at the dugout, and I stop the boys from hitting the field.

"Guys, the field remains in treacherous condition. Let's play mistake-free ball. By that, I mean no big plays. Don't try to do too much. Outfielders hit your cutoff man instead of trying to sling it to home plate; the ball will no doubt be slick at the wrong moment. When we hit, try to level out your swings unless we ask for a sacrifice fly to advance a runner. Classic ball, okay?" They all take in my words with nods and grins all around. "Oh, and no dirty play. Hard, but nothing dirty. Remember, let's keep God on our side." I look at them all with a hard expression. *"We will remember this game for the rest of our lives,"* I finish with a gravel-voiced finality. There are shouts, and everyone turns to hit the field.

"Cretin," I say rather softly. Surprisingly, he heard me over the cheers from our stands and turns about. He has sad eyes, clearly upset at having missed part of the series. With a small smile, I tell him, "Nice to have you back, sir." He replies with a warm smile and, after we clap gloves, goes to center field. I go to first base and check to see if we are all in position. I nod to Happy, and the game starts with a bang.

They have changed their strategy since last time. One of their sluggers is leading off. He is one big muscular kid who swings at the first pitch and nails it to the right of our shortstop. How Spaz got a glove on it, I have no idea, but he was able to knock it down. He gets up, picks up the ball, and tries to make up for not having caught it by throwing it sidearm to me too hard. The ball is sailing to the home plate side of first base, and I have to leave base to catch it. Just as I do the admin puke barrels right into me, sending me sailing with me landing hard on my back with less air in my lungs than is optimal.

For no reason, the big bastard stops at my bag. I cannot get up for a minute. The crowd is practically Middle Eastern in their frenzied fury…or worse, Irish. The umpire is in the odd position of having to worry if I am okay. Nearby teammates help me up. Before Holstein arrives, I wave him back, saying, "No harm, no foul. I was in the basepath by accident." I turn to the dumb kid on first, while still being raised from the ground, and show my glove to the crowd and inform him, "You're out." I had held onto the ball. The Charlie fans go absolutely nuts. The baserunner is incredulous but moseys back to his dugout on the third base side.

I look over at the shortstop. "Spaz, you were not listening," I tell him dryly. His roommate, Townie, on third base tells him how he fucked up by trying to do too much. The dumb bastard seems to understand. Happy walks up to me, wanting to talk.

"Tell me plain, do you need to be subbed out?" I grin in response.

"I think the bastard knocked the fog from my brain from being sick. I am better because of it," I answer with fake enthusiastic joy. He smiles wryly, shakes his head, and heads back to the mound. Happy takes a deep breath, lets it out, and lobs his second pitch.

The second batter is smaller and is batting left-handed. He hits it to the second baseman's left, but Gunn makes a good diving catch, not quite having to lay all the way out. Even though he caught it the air, he tosses it while on the ground from his knees, backhanded, to me anyway, and I step on first just in case the ump did not see the play clearly. Gunn brushes his britches and looks up at me. Noticing my half-grin, he gives me a thumbs-up and a wink in return. No need for words; he knew it was a great play.

Happy takes the pill to the hill for his third pitch of the game. The batter is a little taller than the previous one—sort of in between the first two hitters in size and build. He is batting right-handed and swings at the first pitch like the others. Spaz at shortstop lunges up in the air at the line drive, quick as a cat, to his right, and nearly snow-cones the ball. Instead, he knocks it into the air, and Townie catches it like they practice that play every day. Wow.

The crowd absolutely loses it in the Charlie stands. It was an amazing play. All the boys get into the dugout, when Stafford tells us all, "Watch out for the icy lake behind the ump. When he stepped into it just now, it was almost up to his knee in depth."

Zeus asks, "Did he sodomize you, Staffy?" There is a bit of giggling, but also an answer.

"Nah, I think they altered the field by a foot to keep that sort of thing at a minimum." Happy looks at me, and I shake my head.

"Not enough to bitch about, let's pick our battles." He nods his agreement. I see Bridget coming toward me through the teeming crowds while I get ready to bat.

"Are you okay?" she asks with genuine worry. I answer with a slight, confident smile.

"Thanks for before. A sip or three on occasion from the pint will help. If no one has one, check my car in the back for more. Also, a beer or so in between innings will help me keep my electrolytes up. This cold is killing me in that regard." She glares and gives me a pursed-lipped look but gets on it. Hmmm…she is wearing flattering jeans. Not a supermodel, but it makes for a nice enough vision. Voices sound behind me. Oh yeah. Game.

I take my time getting to the batting circle. The big bastard who knocked me on my ass is still playing catcher. The ump is up his ass to avoid the semi-frozen lake behind him. He couldn't requisition dirt to fill that up? Maybe the dirt rejected Frenchy. I grin at the thought.

"Recovered from our collision, little fella?" I ask the self-important, well-muscled prick behind the plate.

"Fuck you, man," he replies with some strange accent. Damn. Nothing good about this kid.

"If you need me to, I can get a Midol for you, you little bitch," I reply as I bait him, bland as grits with no butter.

He immediately stands up and squares off with me. Both sides of the stands stand up at this. Frenchy tells his boy to return to the game. I give the Chief a glint-eyed sideways glance and get ready for the first pitch. The fat bastard they have on the rubber delivers. He has an odd fat back, like a bad stack of tires.

"Strike one!" announces the umpire. The ball landed just in front of the plate and stuck in the cold mud. I leave the box and walk away from the plate toward the other dugout. The Charlie Flight stands are throwing bottles and invective at the fence in between them and the field. The opposing side seems embarrassed by the all-around display and the events in front of them.

I just stand there in front of the other dugout, twisting my batting gloves on my bat as if I am going to do something interesting with it—maybe not softball-worthy. I look them all in the eye one by one and then say, "Really?" Their manager gets up and goes to home plate. He and the Chief go to the back fence behind the icy puddle. I guess the other manager is begging not to be embarrassed by cheating. There is a discussion. Then it happens.

"Save face and your career, Laddy," says Chief Bender behind the fence. "You are only embarrassing yourself and will be sent home like that dumb bastard base commander. This tourney is your idea. It was the dumbest of many a damn dumb idea you have had. Get out of this without being sent home in disgrace, son."

It was delivered sotto voce, but I have great ears. Holstein nods, and Bender looks at me. My lips purse with a slight nod in thanks, and I walk back to the plate. I am still down a strike, but maybe we will have a semi-fair game.

The second pitch hits me. It not being baseball, I do not take a base. The catcher is less than useful.

"The ball is always wet or muddy!" their pitcher complains. I wave to my stands, and a towel quickly arrives.

"Chief, here is a towel you can use to fix a bad ball. Or you can change into a new ball during every pitch," I educate. He is not amused but puts the towel through his belt.

Fatback's next pitch also hits me. "My bad," he tells me. Somehow, I recover from being hit by a slow-pitched softball. The next pitch is better.

Fat Bastard throws a ball on the outside corner. Niiice. I, being right-handed, bring my right foot back and step with my left toward the right of the second baseman. I then turn my hips late, bring my shoulders and arms around, letting the barrel trail a bit, and hit the shit out of the ball. The other team had been playing to pull, so when it goes to the far-right corner, I can go through the bases cleanly. The right fielder finally fields the ball in his corner and delivers it in time to keep me on third base. I could have had an in-the-park homer but decided against it. My being on third base puts them on "prevent mode" despite the wet, muddy conditions and will allow our following batters to do more damage.

Cretin is up next. Surprising. I guess Happy is playing with the lineup. Good for him. Cretin hits a rocket that the other team's second baseman tries to catch and immediately starts being upset about having only knocked it aside. The ball ends on the ground in short center, so Cretin slowly takes second. He looks at me in wonderment, and I raise my hand and grin on third. Apparently, he does not know baseball strategy. I make certain that Cretin sees me and point to my eyes with a grin. He nods, but he does not understand. I wave to Cretin to watch me.

Sammy comes up and fails to hit a dinger. I do not tag up when it is caught. Zeus comes up and hits a pathetic ball past the pitcher. Both the shortstop and the second baseman race toward it, wanting to fire it home. I remain near third. Once the pitcher squares himself to throw Zeus's slow ass out at first, I break for home. Cretin breaks for third. The catcher is out of place. Their first baseman sees this and is diverted from catching the ball from the pitcher. The ball goes to right field just outside the foul line, having bounced off the fence. Zeus lumbers toward second because of the diversion, and Cretin had already gone home after me. Niiice.

We end the inning with two runs after Happy hits to right field after pulling two left-field fouls, being right-handed. I think he hit the ball off the end of his bat by accident. Two runs to none. First fucking inning. Niiice. Admin is up next. I get a swallow of Tennessee's finest and of beer from Bridget before I go back onto the field. Our stands are definitely in a good mood and quite loud. I tell her thanks, but she can't hear me. Uh oh...she looks like she is getting the feelings as she is glowing in response. I wink and hit the field.

Everyone on the team seems pretty well chuffed. Happy looks at me before he tosses the first pitch. I call out to the team, "Remember what we learned during the first inning. Townie, remind your roommate." I say to third base, "Eyes open!" I nod to Happy and look at the batter. Ah, a big sonofabitch[58] batting left is up. "Wait." Happy steps back. Sammy and Cretin are yacking in the outfield instead of

---

[58] Remember, it is pronounced "sumbetch."

watching the game. "*Hey!*" They shut up and look. I point to my eyes and then the batter. They adjust. "Get 'em, Happy."

Happy's fourth pitch of the game is swung at and struck—hard. It is an absolute rocket, pulled by a southpaw, above my head. I am not a great athlete, but I have quick reflexes and jump to catch it. When I stab my glove up the ball smashes into the palm of the glove and careens off it behind me over the foul line in short right field in foul territory. I have trouble with my footing after landing, the ground being so screwed, but I race as best as I can toward the ball. I dive into one of the fence poles and catch it. It takes me a moment before I try to get up. Damn, that's twice I've been knocked hard, and this time I can't blame anyone.

I start to get up when my head clears, and the air returns to my lungs after some ugly coughing when I realize I have Sammy, Gunn, and Cretin picking me up, multiple bitches worried about me, and Happy looking unhappy. "Hal?" he starts again...

"Tis but a scratch!" I declare.

"But your arm's off!" answers Cretin. Good man.

"C'mon, you pansy!" We pretend-joust with our gloves. Happy just shakes his head at this display. The guys shake their collective heads and grin.

I walk unsteadily back toward my position to see the dumb bastard on first base. "Uh ain't called out, Hal," he says through imperfect orthodontia. I have a reply.

"Justin! Rocker! Music!" A quarter ton of decibels of "Hair of the Dog" by Nazareth comes on. I toss Lefty the ball. "Yer out, Scooter." Then the fun begins.

The big, lumbering hick comes at me with haymaker after haymaker. I duck each one, slug his jaw with a jab (he being taller than me and outweighing me by at least 50 lbs), bull him down on his back while he is woozy from a default uppercut, and proceed to Rochambeau him with my fists a bit. Not sure I was successful since I was still a bit off my pins from the severe kiss with the fence. Thankfully, I was pulled off the asshole; I was getting tired.

Frenchy was less than happy. I am only a little wobbly as he comes up. "Might want to call your dogs off, Hoss, before this becomes criminal," says Sammy behind me toward the Chief. Nice. Frenchy looks apoplectic, ready to explode like Mount Saint Helens or Three Mile Island. Not an inappropriate look, I guess; both were pathetic disasters.

"Laddy, be glad it isn't worse. Your boys should be in the brig," says Chief Bender from the fence near where I had caught the last out. "Get on with this—this isn't our only drinking date tonight."

Instead of smirking, I make my way to first base. It is just then I notice the bitches. Bridget, Bobby Jo, Rachel, Mrs. Happy, Brandy, Leanda, and more were there at the fence where I hit it. Oh goody. The moron on first and what is left of his balls goes back to his dugout.

I wave dismissively to Happy as we take our positions. A big right-hander cranks one to the fence, only to be caught by Cretin. Every pitch an out. Well, so far. The next fellow must be a civilian as he is too old and soft to be in military service. The bald prick hits a beautiful loping line drive over Spaz's head, dropping it onto left centerfield with it dying in a divot. The bald bastard wheezes as he runs past me to second where he stops. I think he stopped from fatigue. Some clean-cut black fellow is next. He, like all of them, swings at the first pitch. Spaz is able to knock it down behind second base but cannot get up with it in time to throw the batter out at first. Fast kid. Baldy stayed at second.

The next guy looks like a baseball player. Fit, slim, long-legged, and absolutely loose and sure of himself. He tees off on the first pitch and pulls it foul over the left outfield fence into the next zip code. The next pitch is greeted by a mighty swing, but the wet ball is knocked straight up high toward the other team's dugout. Townie is playing deep at hotbox, so I look to Stafford to try and catch it. He is blatantly interfered with by Frenchy when he tried to get up. I don't think Staff could have gotten to it, but this is just wrong. What happens next is not something you will read in any other military story. It seems that quite a few people lost their military bearing.

Stafford is in the Chief's face chewing him out, differences in rank be damned. Everyone in both sets of stands is loud, but ours is as nuts as Nuremberg in their roar. The batter is pushing my catcher and Frenchy away from each other while cussing the Chief. Townie and Spaz fly in from the other side of the infield to administer some frontier justice. Those two roommates are met by admin kids, not in attack mode, but to prevent a brawl. The manager for the admin side is really lighting up the Chief as well, telling him they can win without his shenanigans. Bender and Givens come onto the field and order all to stand down. The second there is relative quiet, I yell, "Charlie!" My guys look at me, and I point a thumb out toward their positions. I was still recovering from my two collisions but able to help restore order.

After a brief discussion between Chief Bender, Colonel Givens, and Frenchy, the former two come to me. They take their time, adding to the drama of it all. I wave Happy over to me since he is nominally the captain. Bender and Givens look at each other, and Givens signals with a slight dip of the head that Bender can speak first.

"Boy,[59] what would you have us do to Frenchy?"

"What do you think are my choices?" I answer, hoping my smirk isn't too bad.

Givens responds to that. "Either finish this with him or get him out of here before there is a riot."

"I am for the latter, me-self," says Bender.

Just as I am about to answer, Rush comes on the box with "In the Mood." The fence bitches go nuts, calling my name and promising all sorts of post-game entertainments. I look at Givens with a snort and grin, shaking my head slightly. The latter activity hurts a little, which reminds me that my emotions are being affected by my illness and injuries.

"When did you join the Beatles?" asks Givens, which makes me chuckle. "Oh, there she is, Hal. Staring at you instead of her boyfriend." Ah, Melody is in the stands.

"Chief Bender, good idea, but I disagree. I say we let Frenchy finish." I look at Happy, who nods slight assent. "It's his clusterfuck. Inform the gentleman that I say he can be a decent human being, or

---

[59] It sounds like "bye." I guess when he drinks, he sounds like a Mick or a Scot. Of course, I have never heard him speak any other way...

'lose faith by his superiors in his ability to lead' and be sent home in disgrace for being a vindictive, petty, and toxic leader. Remember, we aren't asking him to cure cancer, we are asking him to be as honorable as the common one-stripe Airman."

"Agreed. Bender, see if you can tell him this via your Chief's mafia talk or whatever, okay?" Givens requests with a grin. The summit ends, and we split up. "Rainbow in the Dark" by Dio is on the radio. Our stands erupt. Happy looks at me. I look about and give everyone a "two" signal, noting we have two outs. I turn back to Happy and nod. He lofts a beautiful pitch. Too beautiful.

Slim hits the shit out of that poor softball. It goes out of sight in no time at all. I wonder if it will hit somewhere on the island or in the sea. Damn. He dutifully makes his way around the bases, and I give him a high-five while congratulating him. He does not linger and thus does not show up our pitcher—not as big a deal in slow-pitch softball as it is in baseball, but still. I call out to the field, "Still two outs!"

The next asshole goes yard as well. Cretin yells at me, "Stop saying that!" I grin and nod to him.

The next pitch is hit right at Happy, who catches the supersonic liner as if he is playing catch. He drops the ball on the rubber and makes his way to the dugout like he didn't just make an amazing catch. I put my arm around his shoulder and tell him how awesome that play was. The guys are less than happy, in more ways than one. One did get the idea the boys thought the game was over after what we did in the first inning. I knew they were wrong. Now they know they were wrong. We all crowd into the dugout. I see Mrs. Happy and say, "Hey, good catch!" pointing at her husband. She looks at me like I am a retard. She saw him catch the ball as well. I shake my head and admonish, "No, *good* catch." Now she gets it. She has a good husband. She is lucky. She has been a useless, hot cunt. You can see she finally understands this. It makes me smile a little.

"Hal!" Oh shit. Which one is this? I look around a little. Ah, Bridget. I was afraid Rachel was going to try to abscond with me and duct-tape me to her. I walk over to the end of the dugout, get a swig of JD and a swallow or three of beer. "Thanks," I say, showing a little gratitude, turning to leave.

"Hey," she responds. I turn back to her slowly. "Are you going to be alright?" She seems very sincere and a little too caring. I guess the horde of bitches has us both freaked out.

"Yes. Thanks. My mind was elsewhere. Maybe after," I reply. She smiles and goes back to her seat. I am just well enough to check out what she will be sitting on. Not epic, but not bad. Hmmm...

The boys are trying to get outs as fast as they can. I sit next to Happy. "You're welcome." He looks at me in askance. I grin and get up.

"What the fuck, guys? Level out your swings." Never mind. Back to the field.

The innings go on. Three up and three down all around. Sammy finally hits a dinger in the sixth, tying it up. The top of the final inning goes with the other team getting quick outs. I am going lead off at the bottom of the final inning. I go to Cretin.

"I am getting a double. I need you to slam the ball to the right side, if you can, to hit me in from there."

"The other guys can hit, Hal."

I have a sideways grin. "Not like you, Hoss. Do your best."

He nods, and I remind him at close quarters, "We will remember this game for the rest of our lives." He grimaces and slightly nods...then gulps.

I take my time going to the batter's box. Once I get there, I act like the delicate flower petal that I am. "How's your snatch, you little bitch?" The catcher is held down by Frenchy. This is the bottom of the seventh inning. The end of the series. Good versus evil...let's go.

"Sunshine of Your Love" by Cream comes on from the Charlie stands. Funny. Fatback seems to like it. I look back to Cretin and back to the pitcher, waiting.

The pitch arrives, and I launch it to center-left field by accident, but still get to second base despite my condition. I look at Cretin, and he knows what I want. The field is terrible. The pitcher tells everyone to play in a bit. He then turns around and pitches the ball too low and off the plate away from Cretin, who is batting right.

"Strike!" calls Frenchy.

"Time out!" I reply to the rat bastard motherfucker behind home plate. As the other team's manager pleads with the umpire for a fair game, and the Charlie Flight stands go from tense silence to a muttering rage, I call to the pitcher. "Yo, pitch! I saw the ball was filthy. Just demand the ball be cleaned each time, and it'll be a square game by default."

He looks at me with some gratitude and respect. "Will do." He starts to turn toward home when he twists back to me. "Thanks, man." I nod back with a small grin.

When he gets the same filthy ball, he walks up and asks for a clean one. The ump refuses, but Fatback informs him, sotto voce, that they need a clean ball to throw us out without error. My hearing still works, and I really dig his subterfuge. He returns to the hill with a clean ball and a sideways grin on his face. He winks at me, holsters the smile, and turns toward the batter. His next pitch is much better, arching beautifully and just a bit outside of the center of the plate. Cretin gets all of it near the end of his bat, but it slices just foul on the right field side.

I look at the stands and see for whom I am looking. "Jack!" Surprised, he looks at me. I point to him and then to Cretin. Then I use gestures that Cretin just needs to hit it to the right of second base and not down the right field line. Jack nods and goes to get out of the stands and toward Cretin, who is looking at me. I point to Jack. Cretin calls time and gets three seconds' worth of instruction. He comes back to the batter's box looking like he could defeat all of the communist hordes alone. I look to the stands.

"Music!" I yell. Tension mounts. What would it be? Can't win a war listening to Burt Bacharach, for Pete's sake. Clearly, my drugged and crushed mind is wandering. "Run Runaway" by Slade comes on with some force. Our crowd comes alive, and Fatback the pitcher pauses, seeing the humor in it all. He looks back at me and shakes his head slightly at the nature of the likes of us Charlie Flight folks. I tell him, "Good luck, sir." He winks again and turns back to pitch. The music is so loud, it practically shakes the ground. The pitcher steps forth and lofts one.

Cretin, to his credit, as eager as he was, waited on the ball and hits the round ball with his round bat squarely. It is a laser to the second baseman's right that normally would have rolled to the fence without great fielding. The nanosecond the ball left the bat, I left second base. Spaz is the third base coach. For no apparent reason, he is jumping up and down like a toddler who got a righteous Winnie the Pooh bear. Both sets of stands are roaring. Spaz wants me to hold up at third base. Maybe he should stop being such a little bitch who can't get a real girl. Then again, that semi-retarded girl he is shagging is cute when she cleans up. That isn't often enough though. Maybe they should fuck more often in the shower. Yes, time is moving slow, and my mind is wandering. The music fills me up, and I turn the corner toward home. Have you ever heard this song?

I see what Spaz was spazzing about after I make the turn. Cretin's ball, instead of rolling or scooting to the fence, hit a big water-filled divot and died. The short fielder has dashed to it and was about to throw it to the catcher. Since I am the curious combination of scrawny and invincible, I keep going. The short fielder has a pretty good arm and throws the ball toward home plate as I make my way through the mucky mud toward home. The ball sails toward the third base side of home plate by a few feet, but the catcher adjusts and snags it when he and I are about ten feet apart. Frenchy is behind him, also blocking the base path on the third base side of home plate. Good.

My cleats are starting to catch the dirt more cleanly. My attitude is becoming more and more mean. I aim to bury these evil motherfuckers, and they are standing in my way. The catcher has the ball and begins to grin. He is rather big, and I am not. He thinks God is on the side of the big battalions[60]...if the prick thinks at all. All I know is that he thinks he is going to win this engagement. Wrong-o fuck-o. The idiot is standing straight up. I meet him with increasing speed. I guess he has never had anyone smaller get into a conflict with him. Leverage is a wonderful thing. I lower my shoulder and hips, driving that gym-enhanced bitch backward, pushing hard with

---

[60] Check your Voltaire.

my bent legs. This meant he was raised just a little from the ground so that he nearly had his ass driving Frenchy's face back toward the puddle. The catcher lost track of the ball while he and the umpire fall back into Lake Loser. Soon, Frenchy was *in* the puddle...and being crushed by his boy into the ice water.

I should have stayed above them and drowned Frenchy, but I had a bigger fight. After putting those two bastards into the water behind home plate, I touch home plate with my hand and looked for the ball. I knew the catcher had no idea he no longer had the ball while slithering like a lizard, trying to get out of the puddle, but von Holstein was completely submerged and going crazy so Midol-boy was having a hard time rolling off.

I crawl toward the ball at the back fence, but Givens picks it up before me. "I got this," he says, nearly in my face. Niiice. Cretin follows.

Everyone in both stands is on their feet, both sides waiting to be disappointed. I slowly stand and nearly drop before my comrades catch me. I left everything on the field. Embarrassing. I try once more to stand on my own, and that does not work well. Damn it.

The umpire is screaming, "They cheated!" He looks like a mucky hog now that he is out of the icy mud.

Givens and Bender are there. Givens shows von Holstein the ball to his face.

"No." He looks at the Chief in disgust, without—maybe—the ability to fire the bastard. "In more than one way, you and your people *dropped the ball.*"

Colonel Givens raises the softball with one hand and my hand with the other. "Charlie Flight wins!" The other bleachers stand and politely clap. Frenchy sounds and looks like a bucket of ass. Givens is grinning at me. My guys are jumping up and down all around me. The Charlie Flight stands are going absolutely bonkers, so much so I have a hard time picking out individuals. Then again, I am not at my best after being sick, drugged, and knocked around. The world is a blur. Some radio is playing "Words," by Missing Persons. Yes, Charlie Flight is robot dancing.

I know you are supposed to say certain events are the best moments of your life: a marriage, the birth of a child, etc. I was young, debt-free, and fighting the good fight for God and country. To tell you the truth, that moment might be the greatest I have ever felt—maybe even now so many years later.

So how soon until I take a little trip?

ABOUT THE AUTHOR

Henry Edmund has lived all over the world in and out of uniform. Mr. Edmund served in the United States Air Force after high school and the United States Army National Guard after gaining a World History / International Relations degree at Virginia Commonwealth University. During both stints in military uniform, Mr. Edmund was a signals intelligence operator and a Class VI inventory reduction specialist. He currently resides in flyover country west of the Mississippi River and east of the Rocky Mountains with a loving family, a gutless guard dog, and a fat worthless cat surrounded by a half dozen guitars, hundreds of albums, and thousands of books. Mr. Edmund, whose Hollywood friends think is the greatest method drinker of all time, is currently a professional historian and business owner.